Ella's Choice

Spirited Hearts Series

Book 1

Ruby Merritt

Acknowledgements

Who knew it would take a village to bring a book to life? So here's to my village.

First and foremost, thank you, Jessa Slade of Red Circle Ink for making me think about what type of story I wanted to write and then helping me develop Ella's Choice into the story it is today.

Next, thank you, Linda Carroll-Bradd of Lustre Editing, for educating me about expletive constructions, dangling participle phrases and a host of other craft issues I had nary a clue.

And, of course, thank you, Jen Andrews, for proofreading Ella's Choice. It truly is the job no one wants and I am eternally grateful you applied your eyes and ears to this story.

Thank you, Gabrielle Prendergast, of Cover Your Dreams, for tackling the task of catching the reader's eye by not only creating an awesome cover but designing the branding too. Special thanks for insuring the print cover rendered perfectly at CreateSpace.

I can't forget my critique group. Thank you, Lori Ryan, Kate Baray, Kay Manis and Jessie Winter for all your feedback on the smallest details like 'A hero never clucks' to the big picture items like 'Where do I buy my ISBN?'

Special thanks to Kay Manis for being there whenever and for whatever: a final read-through of Ella's Choice, advice on how to build a following on Facebook, keeping me company in editing hell and most of all for always making me laugh. Always!

Historical Note:

The Powder River Country, which covers parts of Montana, Wyoming and South Dakota, was the hunting grounds of the Plains Indians. The Laramie Treaty of 1868 protected this area for the Plains Indians by closing it off to the settlement of white men. With the discovery of gold in the Black Hills of South Dakota in 1875, the area became more valuable and the white men entered the protected territory virtually unchecked by the United States Government. In 1876 President Grant ordered all Plains Indians moved to the reservations by whatever means necessary. This essentially nullified the Laramie Treaty and officially opened the Powder River Country to white settlement. These events triggered The Great Sioux War of 1876-77.

Miscellaneous Note:

In *Ella's Choice* I have chosen to refer to the Plains Indians as the Plains People because the more appropriate term, Native Americans, was an unknown term at that time.

.

Prologue

The Powder River Country, Wyoming Territory, 1866

Standing outside the stationhouse, Thomas Hastings viewed the land stretching before him, wide and open, treeless, unmarked by man. He filled his lungs with the fresh, crisp air, reveling in the opportunities awaiting him in this uncluttered place. Awaiting him and his daughter, he amended, as nine-year-old Ella Hastings screeched to a halt next him, her eyes alive with the excitement of being on the adventure of a lifetime.

"Papa, Papa," she cried. "Buffalo, everywhere. Millions of them." She grabbed his hand, tugging him in the direction from which she'd come.

Together, they crested a rise and saw the massive creatures filling the landscape to the distant line of buttes ahead.

1

"Have you ever seen buffalo before, Papa?"

"Can't say that I have," he said, taking in the lively indigo of his daughter's eyes and the russet wave of her hair tied hastily back this morning with a ribbon. The coloring of her eyes and hair were Lillian's, to be sure, but everything else about Ella was his.

Suddenly, a worried pucker appeared between her delicately winged eyebrows. "Are we going to see any Indians?"

"I doubt it." *I pray not.* There was a risk of Indian raiding parties on any of the trails in the western territories, but the Bozeman Trail was the most direct and well-watered route to the Montana gold fields. Opportunities for a new and different life awaited him and Ella. Not that he was looking to find gold, just opportunity. And a little adventure along the way. Besides, the reestablishment of Forts Reno, Kearny and Smith along the trail assured him travelers were now well protected. What's more, the fast-moving stagecoach didn't put them at the same risk as turtle-paced wagon trains. With an armed guard riding shotgun atop the stagecoach and his sharpshooter skills, he had every confidence any encounter with hostiles could be managed handily.

He gave the tail end of his daughter's hair a playful tug, but the pucker between her eyebrows didn't vanish, it only deepened.

"Do you think Mama can see us from heaven, Papa?"

He ran a hand through his hair. She'd steered the conversation in a direction for which he was totally unprepared. He gave the question some thought before he answered. "I don't know for sure, but I'd like to think she can."

"Do you miss her, Papa?"

The serious look on Ella's face gave him another moment's pause. Wondering about her mama was more than likely normal for a nine-year-old girl. He hadn't talked much about Lillian since she'd passed on just after Ella turned five, but what little girl wouldn't wonder if there was no one to tell her about her mama?

Thomas sighed. Did he miss his late wife? Absently, he stroked Ella's hair. Not only the color but also the texture was the same as her mother's. He'd told Lillian it was like spun silk the first time she'd allowed him to touch it. That was a heady moment for the seventeen-year-old newly turned-out soldier. But Lillian had been his commander's daughter.

No good could have come of their tryst.

The ex-soldier stared at the serious look still on his daughter's sweetly questioning face. He took Ella's face in his hands. No, that's not true. Something good *had* come of his and Lillian's union, and he'd do anything to protect the gift he had been given.

"I do miss her." For your sake, he added silently, to keep from speaking a lie. He dropped his hands to her shoulders, giving them a playful shake. "But there was nothing your mama disliked more than sadness." He put the best spin he could on Lillian's obsession for the gaiety of parties and balls. "So I'm sure she'd want us to enjoy our adventure to its fullest."

"But she wouldn't have wanted to come with us." A flush crept up Ella's neck then flooded her cheeks as she added quickly, "I mean she never liked to take walks in the woods with us, because she was afraid we'd get lost and attacked by wild animals, no matter that you said otherwise."

Inwardly, he cringed, hoping Ella was merely recalling only Lillian's words and not her disdain for any activity that had to do with the outdoors. "Your mama didn't share our love for adventure and the outdoors, Ella, but she would have joined us once we'd gotten settled."

Ella swiped at a tear that slid down her cheek.

He wondered if she was feeling more than just sadness.

"Grandfather Russell said you're going to ruin my life like you ruined hers."

Thomas released his daughter's shoulders to keep from hurting her as he fisted his hands. "Even if such a thing were true–which it isn't–your grandfather was wrong to speak of it to you."

"He didn't." Ella gripped the locket her grandfather had given her for her ninth birthday as she stared at the ground, her voice a quavering whisper. "I overheard him."

Small consolation, Thomas thought as he lifted his daughter's chin with a press of his knuckles. The overwhelming pain in her eyes set up an ache in his heart he hadn't felt since Lillian had spurned him. "Honey, your grandfather is letting grief rule his life."

"But why does he think you ruined Mama's life?"

He gave a hefty sigh. How to answer that one without damning all involved? Particularly his innocent daughter with her whole life ahead. "Ella, honey, sometimes people get angry when life doesn't go as they imagine it should."

"And Grandfather's angry?"

"Mostly he's sad, but yes, he's a little angry." Thomas didn't dare say anymore than that for fear of tarnishing Captain John Russell in his only grandchild's eyes.

"But didn't Mama choose to marry you?"

"Yes, she chose to marry me." Not completely the truth as theirs was a shotgun wedding. But what they'd done prior, to land them in the marriage, had been her choice, as well as his.

"But I don't understand." That characteristic pucker appeared between her brows.

4

"Sometimes, people don't think about the consequences of their choices before they make them, and then afterwards, they choose not to make the best of them."

"Is that what happened between you and Mama?"

Did she know how miserable he and Lillian had been together? Maybe if he'd insisted they move out West after they were married where they would have had only each other, they might have settled into a life together. But it was too late for "what ifs." "Whatever happened between me and your mama is in the past. No one can change that. All we can do is make the most of today and all the tomorrows to follow." He ended with an encouraging smile, hoping his words would return Ella's spirits to what they'd been before talk turned to Lillian.

She tried to return his smile but failed miserably and her gaze slid away. "What if I made the wrong choice in coming with you?" she choked out, one hand clutching the locket at her neck.

"Ella, honey, look at me," he said, waiting until her gaze met his before continuing. "If at any moment you change your mind about going on our adventure, you give the word and we'll turn back."

"But this is your dream, Papa." She gave him a childish scowl when he shook his head. "But that's what you—"

He put a shushing finger to his daughter's lips. "Coming West is one of my dreams, but not the most important one."

"What's..." She scrubbed at her eyes now filling with tears. "What's the most important one?"

"To give you a happy and secure childhood, to watch you grow up into a young woman, to see you have a family of your own some day."

The tears spilling over, she turned and threw her arms around his waist. "Oh, Papa, I love you so much."

Thomas lifted his sobbing child into his arms. For the first time since this adventure had commenced, he doubted if he was qualified to guide a young girl successfully into womanhood, particularly out here in the western territories where adventure abounded but civility was almost nonexistent. Maybe folks had been right. Maybe the best thing would be to wait here at the stagecoach stop for the return coach.

He shifted his daughter's weight so he could retrieve his pocket watch. How long did they have before the departure of their coach? He flipped it open, and the engraving caught his eye.

Thomas James Hastings
Welcome home forever
Your loving daughter,
Ella

Ella had presented the watch with shy anticipation, and it'd been the icebreaker they'd needed to become reacquainted with one another after his long sojourns in the war.

He clamped the lid shut and put it away. He trudged back to the stationhouse, and his daughter, solely his responsibility and the last of his family, weighed heavily in his arms.

Hours later, the stagecoach creaked as it rocked, the dust swirling through the open windows into the cramped and stifling interior. Most of the passengers held heavily soiled hankies or bandanas over their mouths and noses to block the choking dust. Many held pacifying hands over churning stomachs while others clamped the edge of the seat to minimize the effects of the lurching coach.

Suddenly the vehicle swerved, throwing the occupants to one side, then righted itself.

Thomas shifted Ella from her place next to the window to his other side. He lifted the leather curtain, but with dust roiling, the coach creaking and horses hooves pounding, he could discern very little out of the ordinary.

Then he heard it, as he knew Ella heard it, because she clutched at his arm. The war cry outrivaled any rebel yell he'd witnessed on the battlefield.

In an instant, Thomas retrieved the rifle lying on the floor behind his feet. "Arm yourselves," he shouted to the other men within the cramped interior. The first gunshot rang out, but with the lurching of the coach and the blinding dust, he was having a hard time setting his sights on a target.

A body pitched to the ground from atop the stage, and he prayed it wasn't the guard. With war cries louder now, he had a better idea where to aim. A form materialized out of the dust. He squeezed the trigger, the crack resounding sharply in his ears, and a shadowy form dropped away but a split second later, frantic screaming filled the coach.

His heart stopped at Ella's terror-laden cries and he whirled to locate her. He ripped off his coat and threw it on the flames licking the hem of her skirt. In seconds, they were out, but the coach skidded to a sickening halt that threw all the occupants into one corner.

The coach now at a standstill, maniacal yells filled Thomas with an all-encompassing dread. He scrambled to the window, dragging Ella with him then pushed her to the floor. "Stay there, Ella."

-*-*-

Ella crouched on the floor of the coach, hands over her ears, blocking the sounds of the attack, the war cries, the gunshots, the frantic neighing of the stage horses, the pounding hooves of the Indians' wild mustangs circling closer. Her lips moved in silent prayer as salty tears squeezed from the corners of her eyes and burned across her wind-chapped cheeks.

An object swished through the air, followed by something heavy thudding on the seat above her. An arm swung down into her line of view, limp and lifeless. Her mouth opened but no sound came out.

The door of the coach was wrenched open. The stench of sweaty and unwashed bodies caused her to curl deeper into herself. She was dragged from the coach. An unfamiliar and harsh-sounding language filled her ears, and she kept her eyes tightly closed until a stinging yank to her hair forced her eyes open.

Staring into a face as brown as a chestnut, the red and yellow lines striping from cheek to hairline and across the broad forehead, forced her into action. Held only by her hair, she twisted away from her terrifying captor, intent on making her way back to the stagecoach and her papa.

Her papa lay across the seat of the stagecoach, a swath of blood across his shirt where an arrow had pierced his chest. Her knees buckled and darkness swirled around her.

Chapter 1

The Powder River Country, Wyoming Territory, 1876

Beech Richoux had been following the day-old trail for several hours, but now it split, imprints of shoeless horses peppering the soft earth in both directions. As he studied the diverging paths, soldiers muttered behind him. Someone tunelessly whistled. A snippet of lyrics '...of his terrible swift sword' followed. A gun chamber clicked open, spun then clicked closed, the tension torquing within him. Although this mission was one of peacekeeping, the men would welcome an excuse to skirmish just to break the monotonous task of tracking.

For his part, tracking was something Beech enjoyed. It was a peaceful but all-absorbing activity that pushed his senses to their limit. And the job paid well.

Ignoring both trails for the moment, Beech rode to the crest of the ridge to get a better feel for which trail to follow. There, he held up a hand, halting the military unit. He'd seen no further signs of the trail in this direction, but the breeze stirred, carrying the faintest neigh, a whiff of smoke. Something was just over the next ridge.

Captain Baldwin crowded Beech's mount with his own. "What is it?"

I feel something on the wind.

That's what Beech wanted to say, but that would be the Lakota Indian in him talking and not something a white cavalry officer would take as a reason to approach the crest of the next ridge with caution. "Wait here while I ride to the next ridge then I'll report back."

The captain's hard, measuring gaze never left Beech as he motioned to his second in command. "Lieutenant Cummings, accompany Richoux to the next ridge."

Beech didn't question the necessity of the order in the captain's mind, just urged his horse down the ridge while Cummings fell in line behind him. His half-breed status always put a question mark in the honesty and reliability column with whites and Indians alike. There was a time when gestures such as the captain's would have stirred the fires of anger and resentment inside him, but now he accepted it as a part of his world.

A world in which he straddled two languages, two cultures, two lifestyles.

Several yards from the top of the ridge, Beech halted his horse, August, and dismounted. The lieutenant did likewise. Digging a spyglass out of his saddlebag, Beech crouched and advanced toward the ridge. Within feet of the crest, he dropped to his belly and crawled the rest of the way. Beech sensed Cummings beside him. *At least someone has enough common sense to follow my lead.*

Beech parted the prairie grass and peered into the ravine below then heard Cummings mutter an oath. A Lakota village sprawled across the plain below them. Beech counted twenty-five tepees. He put the spyglass to his eye, studying the inhabitants below.

Women worked at the campfires or scraping skins, young children ran around playfully, a dog here and there lazed about, but he could see no men of warrior age or status. The mustangs, hobbled at the far side of the encampment, numbered thirty-one. With the number of mounts almost matching the number of tepees, Beech figured these horses were for transporting the tepees and the braves of the village were out hunting.

Or raiding.

Beech didn't condone the raiding by his mother's people, but they had been dealt a harsh blow with the confiscation of their hunting grounds and increased pressure to remain on the reservations.

Beech collapsed his spyglass and inched his way back to his horse. He swung onto his horse then trotted back to the cavalry unit.

"Well, what did you find out?" demanded Captain Baldwin.

"A Lakota village. Twenty-five tepees. Thirty-one horses. Mostly women and children. The braves must be out hunting."

Captain Baldwin gave Cummings a squinted-eye look.

Cummings jerked his chin towards Beech. "It's as he says, sir."

The captain turned to his unit. "Lieutenant Cummings and Richoux will come with me to the camp to make contact with the tribal leader. The rest of you will fan out around the perimeter of the encampment—"

Beech leaned a forearm on the saddle horn. "Better to position your men behind the ridge with a couple of lookouts hidden at the top."

The captain spun his gelding to face Beech. "You have military training?"

Beech legged his big black horse square with Baldwin's mount. "No, but I know these people. To surround their village with armed men is a sign of aggression."

11

"It's for our own protection."

"Since their warriors are out hunting, it's unnecessary."

"What's unnecessary is to put officers of the United States Army at risk when faced with savages that have no regard for human life."

Old feelings flared to life on behalf of the peaceful people just beyond the next ridge. "I refuse to enter the camp under such hostile conditions."

"You are under my command."

"No, I am in the *employment* of the United States Army."

"And therefore under my command." Captain Baldwin's chest rose and swelled at the deliverance of the statement.

Beech stoked the fires of his anger, gathering the head of steam to launch his tirade against the arrogant officer, but the breeze, rippling the prairie grass like waves upon the water, stiffened. It cooled his heated skin, calmed his raging emotions and carried his mother's words to him.

When the words will not be heard, let the silence speak for you.

Dwelling on the wisdom of the words, Beech allowed the fight to recede but not the fire. He held his tongue and his stance, letting the knowledge sit silently between them. Captain Baldwin, commander of the detached unit of the 7th Cavalry Regiment of the United States Army, had no hope of peacefully communicating with the people beyond the next ridge without him.

Him.

Beech Richoux, a half-breed tracker.

The tense moment lengthened. A horse at the rear of the unit pawed the ground. Lieutenant Cummings cleared his throat less than delicately.

Suddenly, Captain Baldwin wheeled his mount to face his men. "Attention, men." Speaking no less decisively than before, he outlined the plan Beech had recommended. "We ride to the next ridge. Argyle and Neely will be the lookouts at the top. The remainder of the unit will wait below out of sight while the lieutenant and Richoux ride with me into the village to make contact."

"At any sign of trouble..." The captain tossed a glare in Beech's direction as he reeled off his final instructions. "You have orders to enter the village, weapons drawn."

Beech spurred his horse forward, leaving the captain to spend his bluster on those he had authority over.

-*-*-

Little Brave lifted her gaze from the task of scraping the deer hide stretched before her. Her senses heightened from calm alertness to wary expectation. Ten winters, two with the Blackfeet who had captured her then eight with the Lakota who'd adopted her, had taught her heeding her senses could mean the difference between life in this world or death in another.

She glanced to Grey Owl sitting cross-legged in the sun in front of the tepee, his eyes closed, his face raised in morning tribute to the day. Although the revered chief of the tribe gave no indication of what she had felt on the breeze, arching the prairie grass their direction, she knew he'd felt it, too. Others in the tribe, those younger and stronger, those hungering to prove their prowess against the white man who crossed into their hunting grounds in larger and larger numbers each summer, would say Grey Owl had lost touch with his senses. That he was not fit to lead their people against the onslaught of the white man. That peaceful negotiations with the white man would only lead to their demise. But Little Brave did not doubt Grey Owl. She did not doubt his senses or his wisdom. She did not doubt that his path of peace was preferable to that of violence and bloodshed. Little Brave had seen enough violence and bloodshed to last her life—this one and the next.

She scanned the peaceful outlay of the village from her position beyond the shade line of the tepee. From the campfire where the deer meat boiled, a faint curl of smoke wisped across her eyes, momentarily blurring the image of the three men on horseback riding toward her and Grey Owl. Once it cleared and the image firmed, she noted the two men dressed in dark coats with gleaming buttons were soldiers of the white man's army. There was a rigidity to their bodies as they rode through the village that was not present in the third rider who was dressed in buckskin and moccasins. Although his horse wore a saddle, he rode with the ease and grace of the warriors of this village.

Peace had reigned in the eight winters since Grey Owl's esteemed cousin, Red Cloud, signed the treaty with the white men. The agreement had given the Plains People the land drained by the Powder River for their hunting ground. Still, Little Brave hunched back on her heels, warily watching the riders. She fingered the handle of the knife hidden within the legging of her moccasin, ready to launch to Grey Owl's defense at the first sign of aggression. She'd been powerless the day she'd lost her white father, but she was not powerless now.

The men halted in front of Grey Owl. Only the buckskin-clad man dismounted. He was very tall, like the Crow, and unlike the soldiers, he wore no hat. His straight hair, touching the collar of his buckskin tunic, held the blue-black sheen of the Plains People. When he greeted the old man in the language of the Lakota, his voice was deep and richly timbered.

Little Brave glanced at the soldiers. The one with the most glittering objects upon his dark coat, Gleaming Chest, intently watched the exchange. The other one, whose

14

hair rivaled the sun for brightness, Sun Hair, glanced curiously about him.

Grey Owl rose, and the man guiding the soldiers motioned for them to dismount. "Daughter," said Grey Owl with a glance in her direction, and the tall man with the raven hair locked his gaze on her.

If he observed any differences between her and the regal chief, he gave no indication as she rose to join her adopted father.

Grey Owl ducked into the tepee. The soldiers followed.

Why had the man who resembled the Plains People more than the white man led these soldiers to Grey Owl's village? Butterflies flitted around in her belly as she considered the reasons. She waited for the scout to follow the soldiers, but he made no move to enter. She looked up at him. That's when the similarity between them registered.

His eyes were as blue as hers.

Departing from Lakota tradition, he motioned her into the tepee ahead of him. Something struggled for recognition deep in the shadowy memories from the first nine winters of her life. A notion she couldn't quite recall but which made her feel respected by this simple gesture.

As a woman, Little Brave was very much aware of the man entering the tepee behind her. Aware as she'd never been with Running Bear or any other warrior of the tribe. She knelt beside Grey Owl while, across from them, the soldiers struggled to contort their legs into the traditional cross-legged style. The man, who she now realized was of mixed heritage, dropped into the configuration with an ease and grace befitting anyone in the village.

Once all were seated, Grey Owl invited the men to speak with a motion of his hand. Gleaming Chest spoke white man's words that Little Brave struggled to understand.

Eight winters immersed in the Lakota language had faded the English language she'd known as a child.

Little Brave listened as the raven-haired man across from her interpreted in that voice which vibrated the air between them.

"Greetings and good news from the Great White Father of the East."

"Greetings from the Lakota who remain trusted and loyal friends of the Great White Father of the East," returned Grey Owl.

Still only understanding a few words here and there, Little Brave listened intently as Gleaming Chest launched into a lengthy explanation of their presence, his arms waving to emphasize his words, his voice taking on a stern note as she recognized the English words 'reservation', 'buffalo' and 'hunt'.

The scout's attention was focused on Grey Owl, which allowed Little Brave to study the movement of his well-defined lips as he translated, the stretch of his buckskin breeches across his tautly muscled thighs, the ample length of his fingers as they rested quietly upon his knees. But most of all, she was fascinated by the light in his eyes. She could have attributed it to the indigo hue versus the almost flinty black color of her adopted people, if she'd not seen a similar light in Grey Owl's eyes when he looked across the prairie at the sunset, or in the eyes of the older squaws as they gazed upon their grandchildren. Regardless, she'd never seen such a light in Running Bear's eyes or the braves who followed him.

"The Great White Father of the East wants to honor his friends the Lakota by giving them great gifts."

"The Lakota are honored the Great White Father remembers us so kindly."

"The Great White Father wants to give you a land for all your people, plenty of food to fill your bellies, and special help to adjust to living in the white man's world."

"The Great White Father is very kind and generous, but we live in our own world. Here, the land and the buffalo take care of us."

Little Brave noted the officer's posture stiffen, his mouth opened for countering when the report of a rifle sounded somewhere west of the tepee.

Everyone leapt to their feet. The white men moved swiftly, flanking the entrance of the tepee before peering outside.

The scout glanced at Grey Owl but with a shift of his gaze included Little Brave in his instructions. "Stay here until we find out what's going on."

Watching the three visitors exit the tepee, Little Brave heard a sudden melee of rifle shots from several directions but no lusty battle cries. The warriors must still be out hunting, for if they had returned early to find white soldiers in the village, they would have attacked.

With rifle shots still sounding, Little Brave withdrew the knife from the legging of her moccasin and scurried across the skin-draped floor to the opening in the tepee. The dust rising in the wake of nervously prancing horses clouded her vision. She could see little beyond the officers and the scout plastered against the side of the tepee. They were using their horses as shields as they withdrew their rifles from the scabbards on the saddles. She tried to see if the villagers had taken cover.

As suddenly and inexplicably as it started, the rifle fire stopped.

Little Brave remained crouched in the entranceway of the tepee, the knife gripped tightly by her thigh. Grey Owl had joined her. The dust settled as the horses quieted. As the soldiers and the scout relaxed, so did Little Brave. But that didn't answer her questions as to why the rifles had been fired. But finding out those answers would fall to Grey Owl. Her first concern was for the people of her village.

She and Grey Owl stepped outside the tepee.

Instantly, Gleaming Chest shouted. His face contorted in rage, he gestured at her knife.

She understood he wanted her to sheath it, but as long as he continued to rage at her, she would not.

He started toward her, but the tall, broad-shouldered scout stepped between them. Words spewed between the two. The scent of her protector assailed her: trail dust, male sweat, worn leather, and another very faint scent, a scent vaguely familiar. Another memory stirred, but she couldn't quite place it.

Her protector turned to her. "Sheath your knife."

Little Brave shook her head. "I do not trust these men."

The man held up his hands. "We are here in peace."

She noticed the calluses on his hands. He was no stranger to hard work. Honest work.

"Trust me."

Little Brave looked at the men standing beyond him. Gleaming Chest stared at her, still full of rage. Sun Hair looked neutral but wary. He had very few glittering objects on his coat, which meant he had very little power against the raging man. She looked back to the raven-hair stranger, who spoke the words of the Plains People and seemed to know their ways.

This man didn't seem to be under the power of Gleaming Chest. She looked into the blue of his eyes that matched hers, at the light shining there. It spoke, as words could not. It told of his quiet strength. It implored her to trust in him. Something deep within her grasped for that strength and that trust although her life experiences warned her away. But at the moment, he was the buffer between her people and the white men's soldiers. Reluctantly, she replaced her blade in the legging of her moccasin. "I need to check on my people."

18

The scout said something over his shoulder to Gleaming Chest.

The man's curt "no" did not need to be translated.

_*_*_

Beech whirled to face the officer who denied the reasonable request of the woman called Little Brave. She was a mystery, from her presence in the Lakota camp and Grey Owl's reference to her as daughter, to her warm, russet-colored hair and deep-blue eyes that matched his own. "If there are any wounded, they will need tending."

"The wounded can tend to themselves unless it's one of our own. Tell the villagers to break camp. We move out in one hour."

"Move out? To where?"

"The nearest reservation."

"You have no right to move these people to the reservation."

Captain Baldwin replaced his rifle in its scabbard then released two gleaming buttons of his dark military jacket and withdrew a folded piece of paper. "That's where you're wrong, half-breed. I, as Commander of this detachment of the 7th Cavalry Regiment of the United States Army under orders from President Ulysses S. Grant, have the right to move any and all hostiles my unit comes in contact with to the nearest reservation." He opened the paper and held it out to Lieutenant Cummings. "Lieutenant, kindly read the orders to this uneducat—"

Enraged at the condescending presumption, Beech snatched the paper from the captain and scanned it for himself.

With the passing of the January 31ˢᵗ deadline for
all non-treaty bands of the Lakota Sioux and
Northern Cheyenne to return to the reservation,
all regimental units stationed within the western
territories of Dakota, Montana and Wyoming are
ordered to seek out noncompliant bands and
individuals, and escort them to the nearest
reservation. Military action, as deemed proper
under the circumstances, may be taken against
uncooperative bands or individuals.

President of the United States and Commander
in Chief of the United States Armed Forces,

Ulysses S. Grant

"So you had no intention of peaceful negotiations."
Beech flung the paper at the captain. It caught in the breeze
and fluttered toward Lieutenant Cummings who grabbed it
out of the air and refolded it.

Captain Baldwin took the orders from Cummings,
replaced the paper inside his jacket then refastened it. "Not
in the least, Richoux. I like peace as much as the next person
but when peaceful means fail—"

"You haven't given peace a chance." He stabbed a
finger in the captain's direction.

"They're savages, Richoux. They know nothing
of—" The captain's breath caught sharply. He pressed a
hand to his side as his eyes glazed over. Instinctively, Beech
reached out to steady him as did Lieutenant Cummings, but
as suddenly as it had come, the episode passed. The
captain's eyes cleared, his hand dropped away. He shook his
head a couple of times, cleared his throat then continued as
if nothing had happened although his tone held considerably
less bluster. "Now either you speak to these people so they

can *peacefully* break camp, or I will have my men forcefully round them up."

Beech blew out a long, hard breath as he stared at the two military officers before him. There was no doubt in his mind now this job would only bring him trouble. Trouble he didn't need. He turned, gathering the reins of his horse, and met the expectant look on Little Brave's face. Damn, he didn't want to be caught between the Army and his mother's people. He just wanted to earn the money to buy that stud stallion for his breeding operation.

He looked beyond the mysterious woman and scanned the tepees populating the village, reminiscent of those he'd visited in his youth. Those who'd housed his grandparents, his aunts and uncles, and numerous cousins. These weren't just his mother's people; they were his people, too. He couldn't in good conscience let them be mistreated. He turned back to the captain. Before he could speak, a scuffling beyond the nearest tepee caught their attention.

Two soldiers emerged with a boy of eight or nine years writhing fiercely between them, Blood oozed from his nose, a raw scrape marred his shoulder.

"What happened to you, Bird Hopper?" asked Grey Owl.

Eyeing Beech, the boy shrewdly declared with a shrug, "They shot my pony while I was out riding."

No doubt, the boy had been riding for help.

"Why did you shoot the boy's horse?" demanded Grey Owl of the captain.

"We found this boy, trying to escape," said one of the soldiers still struggling to maintain his hold on the rebellious youth.

"Is that what all the shooting was about?" asked Captain Baldwin.

21

"Yes sir," answered the other soldier then he threw out his chest. "I was the one who finally shot his pony out from under him."

"Good work, Argyle, but it shouldn't have taken that many shots to drop a pony," scoffed the captain.

The first soldier's face reddened. "The boy rode into the trees along the creek so our sight was limited, sir."

"Very well." Captain Baldwin waved a dismissive hand. "Bind his hands and feet so he can't attempt another escape, but keep him in your sights at all times."

"I do not understand." Grey Owl held out a restraining arm as the soldiers moved to leave. "Why do you hold the boy?"

Beech interpreted Grey Owl's question then the captain's response. "He does not want the boy to leave the village."

"The white man has no right to say who comes and goes in my village," Grey Owl countered, his regal bearing, underscoring his authority to speak on such matters.

Beech began to interpret Grey Owl's declaration.

The captain cut him off, his words issued through clenched teeth. "Tell these people we move out in an hour, Richoux."

Beech supplied the words of deference the captain had omitted. "The Great White Father has honorably requested his friends, the Lakota, relocate to the new land he has set aside especially for you. He has sent his warriors to escort you safely there."

"The Great White Father speaks of another land, but my people do not want to leave this land. *I* do not want to leave this land." Grey Owl's arm swept wide. "If this new land is such a good land, let the white man live there."

Beech did not bother to relay Grey Owl's refusal to the captain and instead spoke earnestly to the old chief. "Grey Owl, if your people are not ready to move in one hour, the soldiers will force your people to go with their rifles. I know you do not want your people harmed."

The old chief looked around at the villagers who were now gathered loosely about them then beyond them to the soldiers positioned around the perimeter of the camp, their rifles held at the ready. He closed his eyes as if in communion with some inner wisdom. When he opened them, he said, "Let me speak with my people."

"He needs to talk to his people," Beech informed the captain.

Captain Baldwin stepped closer.

Beech fought the urge to step back from the stench of sweat mingling with wool as it filled the small space between them. Instead, he took perverse pleasure in the fact that the captain's chin had to lift in order to look him in the eyes.

"One hour, Richoux, or my men take over."

Chapter 2

Grey Owl lifted his arms and widened them as he beckoned his people to gather around him. As the circle tightened, Little Brave's gaze traveled the faces of the people who had become *her people*. Smaller children who raced playfully around the camp just moments ago now clung to their mothers' skirts. Older children mimicked the proud stance and impassive features of the adults. The group shifted to allow the old men and women to take their places at the front of the group.

With his arms still outstretched, Grey Owl said, "The Great White Father has given us a land apart from this one. These men have come to take us there."

"Without our warriors?" asked Nimble Fingers, whose hands, so well named for her beaded work, crushed the intricate renderings of buffalo ranging across her deerskin skirt.

"Our warriors will follow."

"This is our home. Running Bear will not be happy that we leave without fighting for it," said Stone Skipper, her dark eyes fiery, her words sharp. She shared Running Bear's thirst for vengeance against the white man.

"If we resist without our warriors present, many of us could fall to the white man's guns." Grey Owl's hands swept low in emphasis of his point.

"There is honor in death at the hands of an enemy," rasped Black Feather. His fingers, bent and twisted with age, grasped the hilt of his knife tucked into the sashing at his waist.

There were many things Little Brave appreciated and treasured about her adopted people, but their readiness to do battle always awakened her anxiety over the senseless loss of life, and the pain and suffering to be endured afterwards. But she could understand their fear of losing their home and their willingness to fight to keep it.

"You have lived long, Black Feather, and you speak wisely, but for now we go peacefully with the white man's soldiers," countered Grey Owl.

"There can be no peace with the white man," spat Stone Skipper. Her glittering gaze sought Little Brave's. She held darkness in her heart toward Little Brave since Running Bear had asked for Little Brave over Stone Skipper last summer.

Little Brave lifted her chin and squared her shoulders in the face of such animosity. It was not her fault Running Bear had not sought Stone Skipper as his wife when Little Brave turned down his offer of marriage.

Moon Howler, a sinewy youth anxious for his first foray with the braves, held aloft his knife and yipped in agreement with Stone Skipper's declaration. Several others raised their knives or their fists, uttering their high-pitched agreement.

The cocking of rifles rent the air. Little Brave spun.

The scout shouted words in the white man's tongue, his arms outstretched as if to keep the distance between the soldiers and her people.

Gleaming Chest returned his shouts.

The scout whirled to face her people. "Drop your weapons." He stepped toward them as one approaches a wounded but still dangerous buffalo. "The soldiers have been ordered to shoot if you don't drop your weapons."

Weapons and fists held their position. Fire burned in narrowed eyes, lips curled back, baring teeth. Words from the white man's scout did not sway them, and any movement by the soldiers would only engage them.

Little Brave looked to Grey Owl, as did all their people. Her heart thumped in apprehension, not for what he would say, but for how they would heed it. She knew those old eyes. They did not see the forms of the people before him as clearly as they had in years past, but they saw distinctly the vision of their survival today.

"There is honor in death well spent, but not in death spent foolishly," Grey Owl said. "Here, against these soldiers, without our warriors, there would be lives wasted. I know not when or where we will reunite with our warriors, but we must wait for them. Wait to be whole once again."

Little Brave was well pleased with Grey Owl's words. His wisdom, of waiting for the return of their warriors, spoke to her people. Slowly, their arms dropped, their expressions eased into guarded wariness. She breathed a sigh of relief when she did not hear the scout translating Grey Owl's words for she knew they would have not have set well with the belligerent leader of the soldiers.

Gleaming Chest spoke stridently and the scout returned an equally strident response. Gleaming Chest glared at the scout, repeating himself.

The scout, positioned to keep both Gleaming Chest and her people in his sights, said with a slight shift of his eyes toward them, "Come forward one at a time and hand over your weapons."

There was no movement among her people.

Gleaming Chest shouted more words, and the soldiers moved as one from the perimeter of their encampment toward its center. Their circle tightened steadily around her, around Grey Owl and her people.

Inevitably as a noose tightening. If her people did not heed Gleaming Chest's orders, this day would end in senseless bloodshed—much like that long-ago day on the stagecoach. Back then, she hadn't the power to save her white father, but the circumstances were different this day. She would make a choice to save her people.

"Wait," Little Brave held up a hand to signal her peaceful intentions.

In response, Gleaming Chest held up his hand, giving an order which stopped his men.

Little Brave slowly bent to retrieve her knife from the legging of her moccasin. She eased upward and turned the knife, hilt out. She heard the murmurings of her people, couldn't mistake the disgust in Stone Skipper's "traitor," but assurance filled her as she heard her adopted father's words, "Well done, daughter."

Little Brave made the few steps to Gleaming Chest a tribute to her adopted people. Her chin lifted, her posture erect, she allowed her gaze to travel the ring of soldiers before her. In turn, she dared each one to look her in the eyes, to deny they were the same—people who breathed, lived, loved, laughed and died. Most looked beyond her or through her, a couple stared at her with narrowed looks or sneering lips. Sun Hair actually held her gaze for a moment, something flashing in it, before it finally dropped away from hers.

At the end of her perusal, her gaze collided with the scout's. She read sorrow and a hint of admiration there. She hurried her gaze past him. She did not need the pity of a man who so resembled her people, but worked against them. And she certainly did not want his approval.

She stepped within Gleaming Chest's reach, the hilt of her knife held out. She held the cold, gray eyes in defiance and challenge. He gave an order. Its meaning was clear, but she ignored it. Refusing to be treated as less than she was, she waited for him to take the knife from her hand.

While she waited, she studied the pouches beneath the man's eyes, the sag in his jowls, the wrinkles creasing his face attesting to the many years he had already lived. But she could see no peace there. Not like the peace Grey Owl held for a life well lived. For a moment, Little Brave felt a pang of sorrow for the soldier's lack of peace then squelched it with another lift of her chin. Still, she waited. She heard the tweeting of birds joyous in their spring tasks, the wind rustling a loose flap on one of the tepees, the bubbling from the contents of a simmering pot. Would she still hear these sounds in the new land?

Gleaming Chest's nostrils flared, his eyes narrowed. He spoke some words.

She heard the question in them but she did not understand the words, therefore she did not answer. Instead, she opened her hand. The sun's rays caught the metal of the blade, its glimmer warring with the gleam of the white soldier's chest.

Finally, Gleaming Chest took the knife. Both the notching of its grip and the weight of its blade, crafted for her hand, made it rest awkwardly in his much-larger one.

"You will take care of it for me until we reach our new land," Little Brave said then she stepped aside and looked to her people.

Sings For The Moon came forth next, her hobbling gait causing her to move with effort, but she held out her knife to Gleaming Chest just as Little Brave had done. Now Gleaming Chest had two knives in his hand, and Nimble Fingers was waiting with her knife as Sings For The Moon stepped aside to stand beside Little Brave.

Gleaming Chest shouted, "Argyle," and gestured to the soldier who had bragged about shooting Bird Hopper's horse. He hurried to do as Gleaming Chest directed, disappearing between the horses and returning with a bag.

One by one, Little Brave watched the handing over of her people's defenses. The clink of each knife as it was dropped into the bag chipped away at their independence and their hopes, but she took great pride in their dignity. After each one turned away from Gleaming Chest, she gave him or her a look of fierce promise that they would prevail when their warriors returned.

Soon only the sinewy youth Moon Howler, Stone Skipper and Grey Owl remained. None of the three made a move to come forward. As was his right as chief, Grey Owl would be the last to hand over his weapons so he waited on the youth and the young woman.

Moments passed. Anxiety fisted in her stomach. Knowing she held little sway with Stone Skipper, Little Brave looked to the youth, willing him forward.

Fists clenched at his sides, he remained as defiant as Stone Skipper.

Gleaming Chest issued an order. The three soldiers closest to the holdouts closed in. There was no movement from either Moon Howler or Stone Skipper, but Little Brave knew they were tracking the movement of the soldiers with their senses.

Grey Owl knew too for he turned toward the pair. "You will be of no help to us when our warriors come if you are dead."

The barrels of the soldier's rifles were within inches now—a rifle trained on each holdout. Instinctively, Little Brave bent, reaching for the knife in her legging then growled her frustration when she remembered it was no longer there.

The next moment, Moon Howler and Stone Skipper spun away from the rifles.

Little Brave launched herself in their direction, shouting, "Father."

Rifles cracked as a pair of strong arms banded about her. Moon Howler jerked and fell to the ground. Stone Skipper stumbled and the butt of a rifle landed hard against her skull, dropping her flat.

But it was Grey Owl whose form she sought through the curling wisps of smoke.

"Are you crazy?" The scout's voice grated harshly against her ear. "You could have been shot."

"Let me go." She twisted in his hold, her heels kicking at his shins. "I must see to my father."

"He is fine."

"I must go to him." Her heel landed a particular heavy hit, and the scout grunted, but he didn't loosen his hold. Against her will, memories of a bloody past welled up inside, her struggle intensifying, more against those memories than the embrace of the white man's scout. She had lost one father; she could not lose another.

"See him there?"

His tone was gentler now. She ceased her struggles, relief rushing through her when she saw Grey Owl standing alive and well. She sagged against the scout, an odd feeling of security invading her within the solid strength of his hold. The warmth of his body seeped through her dress, reigniting her awareness of him as a man.

Gleaming Chest marched by, tossing harsh words to the scout as he passed.

The scout released her and her legs gave way. He grasped her arm to keep her upright. "I will walk with you to your father." When she resisted, he added, "For your safety."

She wanted to deny her need for his help or his protection, but the blood spreading from beneath Moon Howler's chest, the stillness of Stone Skipper's body and the three armed soldiers hovering around them held her tongue.

Grey Owl's gaze did not lift to hers but remained on his fallen children. "We need Speaks With Spirits, our holy man, to pass Moon Howler to the next life."

"I will get him," replied the scout then headed back to the quivering knot of her people who waited to hear the fate of Moon Howler and Stone Skipper.

Gleaming Chest spoke with the three soldiers then motioned the one with the bag of weapons over. Upon orders, the soldier retrieved the weapons from the inert forms.

A wailing erupted from Moon Howler's mother, Two Baskets. She stumbled her way over to the fallen youth, and the holy man soon joined the grieving mother.

Little Brave's heart ached in sorrow for the senseless loss, but she refused to show it here in front of these men who had taken Moon Howler's life.

Stone Skipper stirred and Little Brave pushed between the soldiers, her fear of them forgotten in her relief the young woman yet lived. She knelt beside the dazed woman who struggled to sit up. Little Brave lent her a helping hand then touched where the soldier's gun had struck Stone Skipper's temple. Only a slight twist of the wounded woman's lips indicated her intense pain. Anger and disappointment at Stone Skipper's rash actions fueled Little Brave's admonishment. "That was a foolish action. Be glad that you yet live."

After a moment, Stone Skipper blinked and her gaze found its focus, her fire weakened but not snuffed. "I welcome death if it means I acted bravely, instead of cowardly, in the presence of my enemies." She jerked away from Little Brave's gently palpitating fingers, and her eyes glittered contemptuously when Little Brave attempted to help her move closer to Moon Howler.

Two Baskets now knelt beside her fallen son. Together, she and Stone Skipper wailed his passing. Sings

For The Moon dropped to her knees beside them, mingling her keening with theirs as was her special duty as the oldest woman of their band. Speaks With Spirits chanted of a life honorably led, a death comparable to that of a warrior in battle and implored the *Wakan Tanka*, The Great Mystery, to guide the youth on safe passage from this life to the next. Soon, all their people were gathered close in mourning, and the soldiers retreated from the sacred ceremony.

-*-*-

Beech stood apart from the mourning people. Their sad, eerie wails invoked his sorrow and pain over the passing of his own Lakota mother, Swaying Willow. As Beech watched the group, his attention fell upon the chief's daughter. She was standing beside her father and was unusually quiet in her sorrowing.

He couldn't help but wonder what her answer to Captain Baldwin's question, "Are you a white woman?" would have been if she had answered. Had she not answered the question because she'd forgotten the white man's tongue? Or perhaps she'd never known it. If she was of mixed heritage, her features and coloring marked her more white than Lakota. But his younger sister who was half Lakota easily passed for a white woman. Whatever her heritage, there was no doubt she held true love for the man she called father, and sincere affection and caring for the people of Grey Owl's band.

"They can do little harm now." Captain Baldwin weighed into the conversation of the soldiers reliving the violent turn of events. "Be sure to put that bag of weapons some place where the hostiles cannot filch them, Argyle."

Beech heard the clinking of the weapons receding and knew it would not be long before the captain would be ordering him to get the bereaved people moving.

"Richoux," came the summons.

Reluctantly, Beech turned toward Captain Baldwin.

"Let these people know that we leave in one hour, with or without their possessions."

Beech nodded and moved toward the cluster of mourners. He stood silently at their edge beside Grey Owl until the old chief acknowledged him. "The captain wants to leave in one—" Beech wondered how best to convey the span of one hour. He looked to the sun hovering behind the branches of a budding cottonwood tree. "We leave when the sun frees itself from the branches of that tree." He pointed.

The old chief nodded his understanding.

Little Brave looked around Grey Owl, her eyes red-rimmed and moist in her sorrow. "There is much grief among our people," she hissed beneath her breath. "The boy's mother is so full of sadness and grief over the death of her son she cannot possibly be ready then. And there is still the task of finding a resting place for Moon Howler." She huffed in frustration. "You have no heart."

"It is Captain Baldwin who has no heart." Beech replied, startled at the fiery woman's pronouncement. Had he not helped her and her people at every turn?

She recoiled, resuming her position on Grey Owl's far side.

An abrupt move that took away his ability to refute her unjust declaration, he fisted his hands and looked skyward.

"We will be ready," Grey Owl stated.

Thankful for at least the old chief's cooperation, Beech exhaled then dropped his gaze to the soldiers as he stepped away from the mourners. Captain Baldwin had posted several sentries on the ridge to watch for the returning braves. The remaining soldiers took up posts around the perimeter of the camp. Bird Hopper, trussed at his hands and feet, sat on the ground next to one of the soldiers on the ridge. From the alertness in the boy's body, Beech knew he watched for the returning braves, too.

Soon, the mourners broke apart and scattered to their various tepees, except for the three women who worked at wrapping the youth in preparation for his burial.

Beech roamed the camp, mainly to insure confrontations did not ensue between Grey Owl's people and the soldiers. Occasionally, he stalked up the ridge to look for signs of Grey Owl's warriors.

Beech knew the Plains People's emotions ran as deeply and as passionately as any other people, but they were experts at their nomadic lifestyle. Despite their grief, by the time the sun had disentangled itself from the tree branches, they had completely dismantled the camp. The wrapped youth along with his meager possessions rested on a scaffold in the upper branches of the cottonwood. The barren campsite bore twenty-five tepee-sized circles of trodden grass with just as many fire-sized ashen circles. Well-worn footpaths curved among the circles, a web of ties that bound the people of Grey Owl's band to one another.

Half of the soldiers flanked the rear of the Lakota procession—a herd of resilient prairie ponies carrying at least one, sometimes two passengers and more often than not pulling a travois loaded with all of a family's belongings.

Captain Baldwin, with the other half of the soldiers, stood at its head. When the captain gave the signal to pull out, many moments passed before the rear of the column moved forward.

Once the entire cavalcade was in motion, Beech urged August forward, heading for his position far beyond the front of the procession. His duty would be to scout for the best route, possible campsites for the night, and trouble. He had no idea when Grey Owl's braves would return, but return they would. And he had no doubt they would view the movement of their village as a hostile act, retaliating with an attack to regain what belonged to them.

When the sun dropped low in the sky, Beech found a bluff overlooking a bend in the Belle Fourche River. The river bottom was heavily populated with cottonwoods whose budding branches provided little shade, but there was an abundance of firewood to be gathered. Most importantly, the bluff provided a wall of protection. One couldn't ask for a better campsite for the night. Beech rode back to the procession.

"What is it, Richoux?" asked the captain. "Trouble ahead?"

"No sign of trouble, but there's a place to make camp about twenty minutes ahead."

Captain Baldwin acknowledged Beech's suggestion with an order to Lieutenant Cummings to alert the soldiers at the rear.

Behind the soldiers, Grey Owl regally rode astride a black-and-white paint pony. To his right rode Little Brave on a palomino mustang.

Beech hauled August in beside them. "We'll be stopping soon to make camp."

Grey Owl nodded in acknowledgment.

Beech's gelding pranced sideways in protest at moving at such a slow pace, and he pushed him forward a step so that he could look directly at the woman whose mysterious circumstances he'd been pondering all day. If a Lakota mother hadn't raised him, he wouldn't have registered her notice of him by the merest resetting of her shoulders.

While she didn't share the high cheekbones, cinnamon coloring or ebony hair of others in the band, she looked no less regal and at ease astride her horse than Grey Owl. The sun caught the russet-gold highlights of her hair, turning them to flames, and her delicately chiseled features glowed a honeyed brown. His thoughts strayed to how soft and womanly she'd felt in his arms today when he kept her from rushing in to save Grey Owl. While there was no doubt he admired her courage and dedication to her people, he was attracted by her ethereal femininity. With her Lakota ways and her white woman features, she was unlike any woman he'd ever met before.

"Richoux," Captain Baldwin shouted.

Reluctantly, Beech left off his musings to return to the head of the procession.

Once the camp was erected, the horses untacked and seen to for the night, Beech squatted beyond the ring of light from the campfire in front of Little Brave's tepee. Although Grey Owl was seated by the fire with a blanket wrapped around his shoulders, the tepee belonged to Little Brave. This he knew from his mother. The tepees belonged to the women of the tribe. Typically, when a brave asked for a maiden to be his wife and she accepted, he gave a horse to her parents and buffalo hides to his chosen. She would then spend many hours preparing the skins to be their first home together. She alone was responsible for maintaining the tepee, erecting it, taking it down and hauling it from site to site. If ever her husband left her by choice or death, the tepee would remain with her.

Beech wondered to which of the braves Little Brave was married. No doubt she would have had her pick, with her unusual features and coloring—not to mention her status as daughter of the chief. He would have offered three horses to Grey Owl for her. At the startling thought, Beech bolted upright. What kind of foolish notion was that? He had plans for both of his broodmares and his trusty gelding, but none of them included acquiring a woman.

Beech's sudden movement must have alerted Grey Owl to his presence for the chief motioned to join them within the ring of light cast by the fire. Little Brave did not acknowledge his presence.

"How many sleeps to the new land?" inquired Grey Owl.

"Three sleeps."

"My band has never lived on a..."

"Reservation," said Little Brave, using the English word but not looking up from her work.

Beech knew the Lakota didn't have a word for the concept of a reservation. Their culture had no notion of the ownership of the land or confinement to any particular location. Land was a resource to be shared and used wisely among everyone who partook of its bounty.

"I've never lived on a reservation, either," Beech said. Although he knew that was of little comfort to the old chief.

"We have survived off the bounty of the land, going where it pleased us, when it pleased us. I hear this new land does not provide for us. In it, we cannot go where and when it pleases us."

Beech had no response that would give Grey Owl comfort so he made no further comment.

Grey Owl fell into silence, but beyond the cast of the firelight, the sounds of life that thrived during the night hours overwrote his contemplative silence—tiny scurries of mice, the larger, slower movements of rabbits and hares, the sudden flapping of a myriad of bats, soaring from deep within their cavern in search of hordes of the tiniest insects.

Finally, Grey Owl stood. "Long ride tomorrow." Then he disappeared into the tepee.

The fire popped and crackled, a log broke, a shower of sparks shot toward the sky. Beech looked at Little Brave who remained bent over her work. Her hair reflected the glow of the light, her hands worked steadily and quickly at her beading.

Beech surmised the tunic must be for Grey Owl as the pattern she worked was of an owl, but its choice of coloring was puzzling. One half was worked in white, the other half in red. He would have liked to ask her about it, but recalling her sharpness toward him earlier during the passing ceremony of Moon Howler, he did not.

Instead, he shifted until his back rested on the tree trunk behind him. Uncrossing from the traditional Indian posture, he pulled his knees to his chest, resting his forearms on them. The rusty gold highlights of Little Brave's hair shimmering in the light of the fire stilled his thoughts while the rhythmic movement of her needle in and out of the deerskin caused his eyelids to drift downwards.

-*-*-

Only moments after the man they called Richoux reclined against the tree, Little Brave detected his even breathing. Her hands stilled and she watched him uninhibited. Her people had experienced much sorrow and anguish at the hands of the white man's soldiers and this scout today. And yet, the scout slept here before her tepee, within the heat and light cast by her fire. How did he do this?

The scout stirred, his legs stretching out in front of him. He looked like her people. He had the power and stealth of their mighty warriors. She set aside her work and approached the slumbering man. He spoke the white man's tongue fluently, knew their ways as well as those of the Plains People. Yet, he was not under the spell of the blustering military man. How did he live in two worlds?

She crouched beside him and watched the steady rise and fall of his muscled chest. More than once today, he'd stood between her people and the soldiers. He'd kept her from rushing into gunfire when Moon Howler had been killed. Yet, he'd carried out Gleaming Chest's orders to move them from their village. In which world did his heart beat?

For long moments, she scrutinized the strong angles of his face sharpened by the cast of the firelight and found no answers. She shifted, intending to return to her work when suddenly, a hand clamped around her wrist. She gasped and would have tumbled backward if he hadn't steadied her with his other arm about her waist.

He muttered something she did not understand. She shook her head and he switched to the language that was more familiar to her now. His voice gentled. "I'm sorry, I grabbed you. A reaction from too many nights being on guard."

Staring into eyes as blue as her own was disconcerting. There was kindness there, but it was accompanied by something more primitive. Similar to that she saw in the braves' eyes when they looked at her. Unlike the braves, the primitive gleam in Richoux's eyes did not annoy or unnerve her. It gave her an airy feeling that stole her breath.

He released her wrist and shifted his arm lower on her waist.

Her stomach fluttered strangely when his hand moved to her hair. He stroked the errant strands framing her cheek. She was no stranger to what went on between men and women, their tender looks and loving caresses, their passionate kisses, but the intense heat left in the wake of this man's caress surprised...and excited her.

A shiver ran up her spine and she licked her lips, wanting to feel more of these heady sensations. His fingers traced the line of her jaw. Her gaze flickered to his full lips. As if he sensed her desire, he cocked his head and her breath caught in anticipation, but he did not lean in to kiss her. His fingers stilled beneath her chin and she waited, her heart beating faster than hummingbird's wings. And when his fingers curled ever so slightly beneath her chin, inviting her forward, she touched her lips to his.

His lips were full and firm beneath hers, slightly moist. They shifted against hers and took over, gentle but sure, tasting and teasing hers. A sizzling feeling moved through her, intensifying like the fires that often swept the prairies after a storm.

Soon, she responded in kind. Her hands moved to the hair brushing his shoulders, her fingers twining into the silky strands—their softness another sensation to revel in. One of his large hands cupped her cheek, while the other caressed her from waist to hip. Every stroke tightened a coil of need deep within. Suddenly, that womanly place between her legs moistened and throbbed for something more. Every kiss, every touch and every breath she shared with him edged her toward that something more, a fulfillment of a yearning within them both.

A twig snapped. His lips froze against hers, his hand stilled its caressing. Another snap...closer. Whoever was coming was not concerned about being heard. He released her, and Little Brave scrambled to her feet. Richoux did likewise, but she noticed he did it more slowly than she had.

The soldier Sun Hair appeared.

At the sight of those gleaming buttons and the stale smell of the dark clothing that all the soldiers wore, Little Brave regained her senses.

Words issued from the soldier's mouth, and just as easily, the white man's words fell from the scout's mouth in response.

The telltale huskiness of his voice suddenly filled her with shame at what she'd been doing. This man had led the soldiers to their camp and was helping to rip her people from their home. They'd been forced to relinquish their weapons. Stone Skipper had been wounded. Moon Howler had been killed. She did not know what would be forced upon them next, but she knew she could not involve herself with such a man. Her people would not accept him. She would become an outcast.

And she would lose another father.

Sun Hair left, making his way back through the trees.

The scout turned. "I am on watch now but—"

She glanced his way, fear and shame evident on her face.

"What is wrong?"

"It is dishonorable of me to betray my people like this."

The scout regarded her for a few moments without blinking then he exhaled slowly. "My intention was not to cause you dishonor."

Little Brave, resenting her flare of admiration for his careful manner, retorted, "What was your intent?"

The scout shifted, settling deeper into his stance. "Since you approached me, perhaps you tell me yours first."

She was angry that he gave an answer as wily as one Running Bear would have given her. "Do not come back here," she said in a low, hoarse voice. She wiped the back of her hand across her mouth and spat out the taste of him on the ground at his feet then turned and marched back to her tepee.

Chapter 3

After a long day on the trail, Beech's skin itched beneath the heavy buckskin and his stomach growled rambunctiously. That coupled with a serious lack of sleep had him craving a cold dip in the river, a hank of fresh meat and a night free from guard duty. He sighted along the barrel of his rifle. He could do nothing about the cold dip and a guard-free night, but there might be something...his finger squeezed the trigger...something he could do about that fresh meat. His shoulder absorbed the kick of the rifle, the acrid scent of ignited gunpowder filled his nostrils and the whiff of smoke from the barrel blurred his view of the target, but there was no mistaking its drop.

Beech sent August forward, circling the prone deer to approach opposite of its antlers in the event some life yet remained. A few feet away, Beech dismounted, dropping the reins to ground tie his gelding, then cautiously approached the young buck. Its antlers contained only four points, but its body was fresh meat. The eyes were glazed. As his mother had taught him, he took a moment to thank Mother Earth for sharing her bounty.

Setting his rifle on the ground within reach, just in case the gunshot had attracted the attention of some unwelcome visitor, Beech withdrew a long, sharp blade from its sheath at his waist.

The sun was resting on the horizon as Beech rode into the camp that had been pitched for the night, the field-dressed deer flung across the haunches of his horse.

Captain Baldwin rose from his place at the fire as Beech approached, his hands rubbing together. "Fresh meat. It's about time you earned your keep, tracker."

Beech rode past the captain without a glance. Stopping at a low-hanging branch of the cottonwood tree next to Little Brave's tepee, he threw the end of the rope attached to the hind legs of the buck over the branch. Dismounting, he pulled the rope until the buck was suspended from the tree. He removed his long knife and deftly sliced the skin from the deer.

As the hide slipped free, he glanced to Little Brave moving around the fire.

Another woman sat nearby, talking to her as she worked—the pretty maiden with a gentle way about her who'd been one of the first to hand over her knife after Little Brave.

Other than the lowering of their voices, neither gave any indication they were aware of his presence. He did not fault Little Brave for ignoring him. Regardless of his efforts to make this move as peaceful as possible for her people, he was still aiding the soldiers to tear them from their homes and relocate them to a place they did not want to be.

It is dishonorable of me to betray my people like this.

Her words from last night still rang in his ears and beat in his heart. They were no easier to forget than the kisses they shared, the passion that rose between them. He admired her courage and determination. He'd never met a more beautiful or sensual woman. Her Lakota ways were home to him, but he would do well to forget her for his plans did not include a woman in his life.

43

His horse ranch was his life now. Hard fought and won, the ranch gave him a path to existing as a Lakota man in the white man's world. Having a white woman as his woman, regardless of how Lakota her behavior, could only bring trouble down on him.

He gripped his knife a little firmer, tilted its blade to negotiate the inward sweep of the haunch. As for the dishonor and betrayal Little Brave had spoken of—twigs cracked and popped beneath a heavy tread of feet.

Captain Baldwin appeared, followed by Argyle. Wherever the captain went, the younger soldier was sure to follow. The admiration Argyle had for the older man was plain for all to see, but Beech could not understand what he saw in the hardened captain.

"What do you think you're doing, Richoux?" Captain Baldwin asked.

"Skinning." He did not cease his sure, swift slices nor did he look at the captain.

"Why is this deer here? It should be in the soldiers' camp."

"The soldiers have weapons. They can shoot their own game."

"Your priority is the men of this detachment, not...not...these savages."

Beech clenched the handle of his knife more securely as he continued separating the hide from the flesh. "No, Captain Baldwin, that's where you're wrong. My priority is women and children whose men are not here to provide for them."

The captain sputtered, his customary bluster rising, "The moment we reach the reservation, your services will be terminated."

Beech stilled his knife then and looked at the captain, wondering if that near fainting episode, two days ago in the Lakota camp, accounted for such hardness and belligerence in the military leader. Would the captain's ill health make his behavior more tolerable? Could Beech endure an entire summer of such behavior? Being terminated would put him far short of the amount he needed to buy the stud stallion that would make his horse breeding operation a fulltime job. Once that happened, he could immerse himself in work he loved and be free from the likes of Captain Baldwin.

Beech shook his head. Even if the captain relented, there was a reason why Little Brave's declaration of dishonor continued to dog him. The words were as true for him as they were for her. For him to help move any more of his mother's people to the reservation was a betrayal.

With a slash, Beech severed the final hold between hide and meat and watched the skin fall away and land in a heap on the ground. He speared the captain with a look. "I stay on until the reservation only to insure these people arrive safely."

"I should have known better than to trust a half-breed," Captain Baldwin scoffed then wheeled, twigs snapping at his retreat.

Argyle gave him a look echoing the disdain of the captain's words before he turned to follow the captain.

"You two butt heads often?"

Beech turned to see Grey Owl standing a few feet away.

"There's not much we agree on." Beech wiped his knife clean.

"There is no honor in agreeing with one who is wrong."

Honor. Beech looked at the certainty in Grey Owl's face. Unfortunately, honor would not get him his stallion. He sighed as he picked up one of the sticks from the nearby pile and whittled it to a sharp point.

"You are the son of the Lakota woman, Swaying Willow?"

45

Beech nodded, wondering how the chief knew his mother. Were they related? He glanced over to Little Brave who stood as one of the old men of the tribe approached. He said something to her then she looked over at them.

"Father, Black Feather has something he wishes to discuss," she said to Grey Owl.

Grey Owl left to speak with the old man.

Beech sharpened the ends of several sticks. He carved hunks of meat from the carcass, skewered them and carried an armful over to Little Brave's fire. Both women stood, impassivity ruling their faces in typical Lakota fashion, but Beech well knew Little Brave's feelings by the wariness in her eyes. Being the white man's scout meant she did not trust him.

He held out the meat.

Neither woman moved.

Apparently, the gentle maiden took her cue from Little Brave. "Take the meat and roast it over the fire," he said.

Still, they did not move.

"You do not want your people to go hungry," he prodded further.

"Our people are not hungry," Little Brave said with a lift of her chin.

What could he say to convince this stubborn woman to take the nourishment he was offering? "Fresh meat will give them much energy for when your warriors come."

-*-*-

The hairs on the back of Little Brave's neck rose while her stomach tightened at the scout's declaration. Why was the white man's scout helping her people? Had he told Gleaming Chest their warriors would return? Was he here to learn more to aid the soldiers? As it was, Grey Owl circulated among their people, shoring up their spirits, stirring their fires to be free from the soldiers, readying them to flee, and fight if necessary when their warriors found them.

Her pondering paralyzed her so it was Nimble Fingers who finally stepped forward to take the meat from the scout. When still she did not move, she watched him kneel and enlarge the reach of the fire, tempering the flames to roast the venison, rather than burn it.

He arranged and stacked rocks around the fire then took the skewers from Nimble Fingers and balanced them on the rocks, meat end over the fire. His preparations were no less and no different than what she would have done. Although it was women's work, someone had taught him well.

The scout stood and nodded to Nimble Fingers then left without another word.

Little Brave stared at his back.

"Why do you not want our people to have the meat?" Nimble Fingers asked.

"I do not trust the white man's scout."

"Letting our people fill their bellies so they can be ready when our warriors return does not mean you trust the scout."

Little Brave looked sharply at her friend. What Nimble Fingers said was true. Little Brave was not reacting to the situation, as her friend understood it. She sat, pulling her beadwork into her lap to avoid Nimble Finger's detection of the heat surging beneath her skin. Unlike her dusky-skinned brothers and sisters, she had no natural defense against such a telltale sign of guilt—guilt over having been drawn in by her dangerous fascination with the scout and her yearning to fulfill her desire last night. She did not trust herself around him with such need for him burning within her.

47

If Nimble Fingers became aware Little Brave had acted on such desire, she would consider that a betrayal. A betrayal that would, at the very least, bring shame to her adopted father and, at the worst, relegate her to the fringes of her people's society. Little Brave stabbed the needle into the deerskin. She could not go back to the limbo she'd experienced with the Blackfeet after her white father had been killed and before she'd come to Grey Owl's band.

Nimble Fingers turned the meat. Fat sizzled across the flesh, dropping into the flames, feeding its blaze. "Do you think our warriors will come tomorrow?"

At the thread of concern she heard in Nimble Finger's voice, Little Brave looked up from her work. She knew her friend well enough to know the worry was not for *when* their warriors would come, but *if* Stands Tall would survive the battle with the white soldiers when they did. Although warfare was a way of life for the Plains People, and their warriors preferred to die in battle rather than grow old and feeble, Nimble Fingers held home and family life close to her heart. "Our warriors are powerful and cunning. Stands Tall is the most powerful and cunning among them."

"Except for Running Bear." Nimble Fingers' eyes, glowing in the firelight, said what her mouth did not.

That Little Brave, if she tried hard enough, could find room in her heart for the mightiest of the warriors in their band.

"My heart does not and never will lie with Running Bear," Little Brave said, shaking her head. She did not want to have this conversation with Nimble Fingers when she'd been stirred by the white man's scout—stirred the way she'd always imagined she should be by a man. The stroke of his fingertips had set her skin on fire, and the touch of his lips had sent a jolt of lightning through her and melted her insides. He had put her under a spell she'd been powerless to escape on her own. Little Brave shuddered at the thought of what might have happened if it had not been for the soldier coming to gather *Richoux* for guard duty. The needle slipped, piercing her finger. She put her wounded finger into her mouth to keep the blood from dripping onto the hours of work she'd put into the beaded tunic.

Nimble Fingers tsk'ed at Little Brave's misfortune then gave her full attention to her beading. Silently and steadily, the two women worked while the venison cooked. Each time Nimble Fingers rose to turn the meat, the aroma filled the air, making Little Brave's belly growl and her mouth water.

Grey Owl returned. He sniffed appreciatively as he took his place near the fire. "The scout brings meat to all our people's fires."

Once more, Little Brave bent over her work to hide the flash of shame at her realization of the scout's generosity. When he'd left with more skewers of meat, she'd assumed they had been for the soldiers. Now she understood the anger in Gleaming Chest's tone when he had spoken to the scout while he worked at skinning the deer. All was meant to feed her people, not just the sizable portion that popped and sizzled over her fire.

To avoid more conversation about the scout and her contradictory feelings towards him, she asked, "How do you find our people?"

"Being held under the eye of the white man's soldiers has made them eager for the coming of our—"

The hairs on the back of Little Brave's neck rose in warning as she knew Grey Owl's did when he halted his words. Nimble Fingers' needle stilled, as well.

The firelight lessened the inky darkness enough to reveal a hulking form like that of a buffalo, but bent and awkwardly perched on two human legs. The faintest clink sounded as the image sharpened into a man carefully settling a bag on the ground beside him.

Realizing that the figure was the white man's scout, Little Brave's wariness eased. He stepped into the light cast by the fire, leaving his bundle behind. Little Brave stood, sighing in relief not because it was the man, Richoux, she told herself, but because he was not one of the white man's soldiers.

Grey Owl and Nimble Fingers stood, as well.

"I have brought your weapons," Richoux said quietly. "The soldiers shouldn't miss it as I've replaced it with a similar bag full of sticks and stones."

"Why do you bring our weapons?" Little Brave squared her shoulders.

"It is not right that your people travel unarmed," Richoux said matter-of-factly.

Little Brave ignored the warning look Nimble Fingers gave her. "It is not right that my people are forced from their homes."

"No it isn't," he agreed.

The easiness of his agreement irritated Little Brave. "And yet, you help the white man's soldiers."

"I will no longer help them once we reach the reservation."

"Why wait until then?"

"You wish there to be no one to speak on your people's behalf?"

His sound logic was maddening in the face of her unreasonable ire. "You do not speak for my people."

"Daughter," Grey Owl said firmly but not unkindly.

Little Brave stilled her tongue, but she did not lower her gaze before the scout, as she would have done before another with whom her father had counseled to curb her tongue.

Grey Owl gestured to the bags. "Put them in the tepee then you will eat in thanks for your help and kindness toward my people."

Once the bags were stashed, Grey Owl nodded toward the women and the two men sat before the fire.

Neither woman moved—Nimble Fingers because it was not her place, and Little Brave because she did not wish to serve the man who had such a dangerous hold over her.

"Daughter," Grey Owl prodded.

"The meat is not fully cooked."

"Slice off the parts that are."

"I do not have a knife," Little Brave said, her chin lifting in her defiance.

"Use mine," said Richoux, catching her gaze. He closed the distance between them with easy strides. Halting before her, he pulled the knife from the sheath at his waist and presented it, hilt out.

From this position she could easily thrust the knife into his belly, rendering a fatal wound, but his confident gaze told her he knew she would not. He had been kind to her people and hurting him would only bring on the wrath of the soldiers.

Maintaining the defiance in her eyes, Little Brave closed her fingers around the hilt of his knife, the lingering warmth of his touch seeping into her fingers as they adjusted to the grip meant for his larger hand.

"Sit," Grey Owl said.

Richoux resumed his seat next to Grey Owl.

Little Brave crouched before the fire, and sliced meat from one of the smaller pieces. Her ears remained tuned to the two men behind her, but they sat in silence while they waited for their meal. Laying aside the knife, she stabbed the meat with sharpened sticks then pivoted and handed the first skewer to Grey Owl.

When she held out the stick to the scout, he cupped her hand. "Thank you," he said, his richly timbered voice vibrating the air between them, that kind light once again glowing in his eyes.

Little Brave pulled her hand free, her skin tingling from the scout's touch. Turning from the man who set her desire leaping to life with such ease, she retrieved his knife, its too-large hilt reminding her of those large, calloused hands, cupping her smaller, now trembling, one. She adjusted her hold, tightening her fingers to steady their shaking as she carved meat for herself and Nimble Fingers.

After Little Brave handed Nimble Fingers a skewer of meat, she settled beside her friend who murmured, "The scout's gaze follows you wherever you go."

"Stands Tall would not be pleased to know that your gaze follows another," Little Brave said to divert Nimble Finger's attention from speculation about the scout's interest in her.

"Little Brave, you would not say such a thing to Stands Tall," her friend hissed.

Little Brave blew on her meat to cool it, grateful the younger woman's worry over displeasing her future mate was so easily invoked. "I will if you talk more of the white man's scout."

Nimble Fingers huffed her irritation at being denied such titillating talk on women's matters but fell into silence as they ate.

Twice more, Little Brave returned to the fire to carve more meat until the men licked their fingers in final tribute to the roasted venison's tastiness.

Then Richoux rose. "It is time for my watch." He nodded to Grey Owl, but did not look her direction before he disappeared as silently as any of their warriors.

Little Brave leapt to her feet, struggling to ignore the unreasonable sting from the scout's slight. Quickly, she gathered the skewers and tossed them into the fire, but the raucous sizzling and popping as the fire greedily devoured the grease-laden wood did little to soothe her.

"Daughter."

Grey Owl's summons broke through her churlish mood and she looked at him.

"Help me sort through our weapons."

"I must go," Nimble Fingers said. She gathered her work and stood, her mischievous smile revealed by the flickering firelight. "Perhaps your scout will bring a buffalo for our dinner tomorrow night."

"He is not my scout," Little Brave huffed, but Nimble Fingers had already disappeared into the inky darkness.

When she entered the tepee, she saw Grey Owl sorting the defenses of their people more by touch than by sight.

"Go quietly among our people. Tell each family to send one member to fetch their weapons," he said.

"Yes, Father." Little Brave turned to exit the tepee.

"Daughter," Grey Owl said once more.

Little Brave held her position, crouched in the tepee's low entrance, dreading her father's reprimand.

"You disappointed me tonight with your behavior toward the man who has been so generous in helping our people on this journey."

Little Brave gripped the edges of her tepee, the tepee she'd inherited when her adopted mother, Prairie Fire, had passed from this world to the next three winters ago. Little Brave hung her head in shame at how she'd disappointed Grey Owl tonight. But it was the memory of Prairie Fire and the generosity and hospitality her tepee had represented during her days in this world that brought her greater shame. She'd dishonored her adopted mother.

"I am sorry, I disappointed you, but—" Little Brave turned in the doorway and dropped to her knees, her hands slapping against her thighs. "The scout works for the white man. How can you be sure that he will not trick us?"

Grey Owl stilled, his hands pausing above the weapons. "I knew his mother, Swaying Willow, when she was a girl. Her father, Old Oak, was a cousin of mine. He was a fierce warrior and a wise leader for the Lone Tree clan of our people."

"I have never heard of her," Little Brave said, as if that alone could render the scout's connection to her people invalid.

"She left with the French trapper, Jean Luc Richoux, many years before you came to us."

"Just because your blood beats in his heart does not make him honorable." Little Brave fisted her hands against her thighs.

"Just as the absence of my blood in yours makes you dishonorable?"

Little Brave's face burned at her embarrassment over the way she'd fallen into Grey Owl's trap. Of course, her wise, old father did not judge the scout by the blood beating in his heart but by his actions.

Grey Owl held out her knife, serenely looking at her until she took it from him.

The clinking resumed, telling her she'd been dismissed. Little Brave returned to the fire, contemplating Grey Owl's regard for the scout's helpfulness. He was kind and giving now, but when their warriors came, would he fight for their people, or against them? The man called Richoux appeared as powerful as any of the warriors of Grey Owl's band. She shuddered at the thought of a clash between him and Running Bear if the scout chose to fight against her people.

By now, the warriors would have returned from their hunting foray and surmised what had happened. They would follow the blatant trail left by such a large number of horses pulling travois and attempt to regain what belonged to them. She knew their pride and their hunger for retaliation would allow nothing less. Only one more sleep remained before they arrived at the reservation, so tomorrow would be the day for the braves to attack.

Little Brave sighed as she slipped her knife into her legging. Disturbingly, its cool weight against her bare leg did not give her the sense of safety and comfort she usually felt with it there. Slowly, she turned toward the darkness that ringed the perimeter of her camp, worried and anxious for the fate of her people as she set out to give them the news of their recovered weapons.

Chapter 4

The morning ride was proceeding smoothly, but Beech wasn't convinced it would continue that way. Although the skies were a clear, cloudless blue, the air held a tension he couldn't pinpoint. Horses, notorious for sensing danger, had been jigging and tossing their heads all morning. He couldn't say for certain what the threat was, only that he needed to heed it. In the last hour, he'd gained the captain's grudging permission to bring along Lieutenant Cummings for an extra pair of eyes. Cummings was a quick study, and Beech had to admit he liked the quiet, unassuming man's company. So far, they'd seen nothing suspicious.

A few hours into their ride, the captain caught up to their position. "What are those rock formations up ahead?"

"Canyons." Heat waves shimmered off the barren stone faces. "We'll skirt to the north of them."

"The reservation lies directly beyond the canyons?" Captain Baldwin asked without looking at Richoux.

"Yes."

"How many hours to skirt them?"

"Several, but avoiding them will still put us on the reservation sometime tomorrow as originally planned."

"How much time do we save if we ride through the canyons?"

"I don't recommend that."

Captain Baldwin glared at him. "I didn't ask for your recommendation, Richoux. I asked how much time we save if we ride through the canyons."

"Almost as much as we'd lose by skirting them. If we could move quickly enough. But with so many horses pulling travois —"

"We'll ride through the canyons." Captain Baldwin waved a hand in dismissal.

"Captain, there is more." Beech was determined to have his say whether the military officer wanted to hear it or not. "Some of the passes through the canyon are very tight, only allowing the horses to move in single file." Beech gestured to the procession, laboriously making their way toward them. "Almost sixty horses strung out single file along the trail will greatly reduce our defenses."

"Are you saying we're being followed?"

Beech hesitated. "I haven't seen evidence, but I have a feeling...and being caught deep in those canyons with little maneuverability and an enemy behind us or even above us—"

"The possibility that we're being followed is based on a feeling?" The captain looked at him with eyebrows pressing low over his eyes.

Beech felt his hackles rise. Not only did the man not have a heart, he didn't have gut feelings. Or if he did, he didn't heed them. "Rarely have my feelings led me astray."

"You may have all the time in the world to devote to these hostiles, Richoux, but I—" The captain couldn't hide his pain as his hand pressed to his side. He clenched his jaw and his eyes bulged at the effort not to cry out.

"Captain, these episodes are only becoming worse," said the lieutenant, kneeing his mount closer.

"Is the captain fit to lead this expedition?" Beech asked, his gaze moving between the two men.

"I am fit as a fiddle, Richoux," the captain huffed between gritted teeth.

"Sir, I think—" the lieutenant said.

The captain gave his second in command a quelling look as he dropped his hand from his side and straightened to his military posture once more. The pain had passed. "We'll ride through the canyons up ahead." The captain reeled off the orders. "It'll put us at the reservation today instead of tomorrow. Inform the rest of the men, Lieutenant."

"Yes sir." The grimace on the lieutenant's face was hidden from his superior officer as he turned to head back to the procession.

"Now," the captain said, addressing Beech once more, "if the only evidence you have is a feeling then we ride through the canyons. The sooner we arrive at the reservation to offload these people to the Indian agent, the sooner my men can get relief from their saddles."

Relief for his men? Beech figured that reaching the reservation sooner rather than later had more to do with the captain's episodes of pain than with relief for his men. Like most white men, the captain was taking the path that worked best for himself and his own interests.

What if he refused to lead the group through the canyons? Chances were they would become lost. With very few water sources, they could die of thirst before they ever found their way out.

Then there was the danger from attack—whether from Grey Owl's warriors or warriors belonging to another band. The villagers were at risk for getting caught in the crossfire or worse, retaliation by the soldiers if the battle went badly. Either way, once they were in the canyons, they were all vulnerable, strung out in a long line, rather than in the open where they could gather together for protection.

Beech eyed the landscape that had been steadily changing from rolling grassland to barren and rocky

58

wasteland. A wind gusted about them, full of stifling dust and dry heat. A fit greeting from the wasteland, he conceded, and his ominous feeling strengthened as they rode toward the canyons.

Suddenly, the gust died and the faintest breeze stirred. Cool and crisp, it shifted the hair from his forehead as loving fingers had in his youth.

Do not abandon my people.

Beech closed his eyes, willing the breeze to stay and his mother's voice to continue to guide him. But as quickly as they came, they left. With reluctance, Beech opened his eyes.

Captain Baldwin stared at him, dust already gathering on the brim of his hat. "Are you leading us through the canyons, or am I?"

Beech urged August forward, adding more dust to the captain's hat as he kept his eyes peeled for the pass into the canyons.

Once they entered the stone maze, its walls rose quickly to hem the trail. Within a few miles, the trail split and Beech chose the fork that ascended steeply onto a ledge hugging the northern wall. "The lower trail becomes too narrow for the travois to pass," Beech said in answer to Captain's question of why he'd abandoned the path below.

The narrowness of the ledge strung the procession out single file. Per the captain's orders, half the unit rode up front behind Beech and the captain while the other half brought up the rear. The horses picked their way over the rocky trail, and an occasional stone skittered beneath the weight of the travois, ricocheting between the walls of the abyss below. Heat pooled in the yawn of the sheer rock faces.

Beech ignored the trickle of sweat that slipped into the corner of his eye. Instead, he concentrated on detecting any sign of movement from the opposite rim of the canyon.

59

Close enough for the reach of arrows, this would be the place most likely for attack.

The ledge widened and Beech dropped back next to Captain Baldwin but kept his gaze vigilant on the surroundings. "Just ahead, there is a trail out of the canyon. Steep but doable."

"How many more miles through the canyon?"

The words were issued with some effort, and Beech chanced a glance at the military leader whose hand was once again pressed to his side. He returned his gaze to the opposite rim. "Several. But the trail narrows again after this with no way out until we reach the end."

"But once we're out, we'll be close to the reservation?"

"Just a few miles away."

"Then we'll continue through the canyons."

Beech scoffed silently at the captain's decision to stay the course and rode past the hunched-over man to find the entrance to the escape route. The trail was barely discernable even to one who knew what to look for, and he didn't spy it until he was almost upon it. Suddenly, the air stilled. No cry of a hawk sounded overhead or the scurry of a lizard rustled on the rocky walls that surrounded them. Only an echo, very faint, but distinct to him.

Now. My people must get out now.

He paused at the well-hidden entrance and waved on the captain and the soldiers. "The trail narrows again just beyond that bend." He held his breath, wondering if the captain would question his reason for staying behind, but Baldwin held that telling hand to his side and Beech breathed easier once they rode ahead.

He looked behind him, catching Grey Owl and Little Brave's attention as they rode side-by-side leading their people. Beech made a running motion with two fingers in the direction of the hidden path.

Little Brave and Grey Owl slowed their horses, waiting for the last soldier to round the bend. Then they parted, wheeling their mustangs, quietly urging their people between them, signing there was a way out of the canyon.

Beech craned his neck to see as far up the escape route as he could. Within a few feet, the path turned sharply between two massive rocks. In no way could a travois make that turn. As the first rider approached, he pointed to the travois and shook his head. The woman nodded. He withdrew his knife and slashed the ties that lay across the horse's back. With freedom from the soldiers within her sight, the woman didn't blink an eye as Beech shoved her family's home and most of their worldly belongings over the canyon ledge.

Riders began freeing their own travois, but still the procession slowed considerably. Once the soldiers at the rear rounded the bend, they would realize the band was fleeing beneath their very noses. And they had to be on borrowed time with the soldiers ahead of them. As if his thoughts had conjured their discovery, he heard a soldier shout.

Lieutenant Cummings appeared.

The sun caught the glint of metal as both Grey Owl and Little Brave drew their blades.

The lieutenant reached for his pistol as Beech reached for his rifle. Before either of them could take aim, a volley of war cries erupted, pitching high in their bloodlust.

The lieutenant shouted a rallying command to the soldiers. Lethal swishes rent the air as arrows launched from the opposing rim. Soldiers pulled rifles and scrambled from their horses, using the animals as shields as they returned fire. The cracks ricocheted off the rock walls.

Beech returned to freeing the travois. His heart raced at the pace of his slashing. If the attacking warriors were not Grey Owl's then the people huddled around him were in as much danger as the soldiers.

_*-*-

Exhilaration filled Little Brave when she recognized the fletching on the arrow as it lodged into Sun Hair's shoulder.

Grey Owl raised his fist in tribal elation. "Our warriors have come."

Little Brave whirled her mare. "Father," she cried, urging Grey Owl to follow her. They reached the scout as the last of their people disappeared between the rocks that flanked the escape route.

"Go," he shouted to her and Grey Owl above the din of rifle fire and squealing horses.

An arrow whistled past, coming from the trail that held their freedom. The weapon entered Grey Owl's chest and he pitched forward, the arrow's bloody tip peeking through his back.

"Father!" she cried. When she saw Running Bear exit the escape route, she let loose an anguished growl. She kicked her mare as she raised her knife in rage. Another arrow left Running Bear's bow as the scout grabbed her reins, keeping her from reaching the traitorous warrior.

Running Bear thundered past them with a triumphant cry, several of his top warriors following in his wake.

"Grab Grey Owl's reins." The scout wound her reins several times around his hand then started for the steep path. He left her little choice—pursue Running Bear on foot, or leave the canyon and tend to her father. Rage gave way to fear as she grabbed the reins but a breath of hope rose in her as Grey Owl's arms tightened around his horse's neck.

At the rim of the canyon, several of her people waited, no doubt guarding the head of the trail. Stone

Skipper rushed the scout, her knife gleaming in deadly intent.

The scout swerved his gelding so that her blade only glanced off his shoulder then swayed in his saddle.

With a gasp, Little Brave realized Running Bear's second arrow had found its home in the scout's chest just below the jut of the collarbone. She rode forward, putting herself between Stone Skipper and the scout. "What are you doing?"

Dark eyes darting between her and the scout, Stone Skipper shifted her fingers for a better hold on her knife. "Running Bear told us to finish off any of the white man's soldiers who tried to escape."

Little Brave glanced around at the confused and fearful faces of the young boys and some of the young women of her band who kept one eye on the trail and the other eye on their chief's daughter. "The scout is not a white man's soldier." She issued that declaration in a voice she hoped sounded as commanding and decisive as Grey Owl's.

"He works for the white man's soldiers," spat Stone Skipper.

"Only to help us." Little Brave gestured to the canyon's rim. "He is the one who showed us this trail so we could escape."

There was a murmuring agreement among her people. Little Brave seized her chance. "Now we must take care of those who took care of us." She searched among her people. "Where is our healer, Soothing Hands?"

Stone Skipper waved her knife. "Now is not the time for healing when our warriors fight down in the canyon."

Little Brave straightened her posture. Lifting her chin, she eyed the belligerent woman with all the authority that was her right as daughter of the chief. "Then why are you still here? Did not Running Bear tell you to guard the trail?" Little Brave gestured toward the canyon. "What will he think when he returns to find you minding the affairs of old women and children?"

Stone Skipper blinked and ruddiness, the likes of which Little Brave hadn't thought possible with such dusky skin, stained the woman's face and neck.

The irate woman spun her horse and headed back to the canyon's rim. The faces of the others charged with guard duty eased at her return.

Little Brave eyed the remainder of her people— mostly old women and mothers with very young children. "While our warriors fight down in the canyons, we must remain ready." Her voice was strong and steady. She did not need to say why they must stay ready. The knowledge they would have to flee if their warriors were not successful was written into the tense faces, in the way the children clung to their mothers. "Stay mounted and watch the canyon while Soothing Hands and I tend to Grey Owl and the scout."

Soothing Hands joined her as she headed toward a rocky outcropping that cast a small amount of shade.

"I will help," Strong Back called then trotted her pony to catch up.

"You do not have to put yourself at risk," Little Brave said.

"My husband fights in the canyon and my son waits at the canyon rim," said Strong Back.

Little Brave nodded. She knew Strong Back's husband, Two Hawks, was a powerful and brave warrior, and their son was already following in his father's footsteps.

"This is very little risk compared to what they do."

They dismounted then gently pulled the old chief from his horse and laid him in the shade. With worry creasing her brow, Soothing Hands knelt beside him. She placed her fingers in the groove next to Grey Owl's throat then laid her hands on his heart where the arrow protruded. "The beat of his heart is very weak."

Little Brave's anger reignited as she recalled the triumphant cry Running Bear uttered after he shot Grey Owl. Her face burned and she clenched her fists. If Running Bear survived the battle with the soldiers, then she would make sure all her people knew what evil he had done.

"There is nothing more I can do," the healer said. "I will check the scout."

Inwardly, Little Brave wailed her grief for Grey Owl and let her anger at Running Bear rage as she watched the two women turn their attention to the scout who'd managed to dismount and now sat beside Grey Owl.

He leaned back against the rock, his eyes closed, a fist-sized seeping of blood around the shaft of the arrow.

Soothing Hands slipped her hands behind his back, searching for its tip. "It did not come through." She pulled her hands from the wounded man's back and prodded around the shaft protruding from his chest. "The arrow must come out or he will die."

A raspy breath issued from Grey Owl.

Little Brave clutched his hand to her chest. "Father?" she said hopefully.

"Daughter?" The word was guttural and said with great effort.

"Don't talk," she soothed as she stroked his brow.

He struggled for another breath.

Little Brave held hers, until he gained his.

"My sun… is setting." His eyes remained closed.

Little Brave selfishly wished they would open. She wished to see, just once more, their kindness, the kindness that had given her hope where there had been none, after her white father had been murdered. "Shhh…" she murmured, but her shushing him was a lie, for she wanted him to go on speaking, to talk of anything and everything, in that steady voice that never failed to utter words of wisdom and peace, to her and to her people.

"Your life…" His fingers tightened around hers but only momentarily.

Desperately, she returned his too-fleeting squeeze. "Father?"

Where his other hand rested on his chest, his fingers lifted slightly, beckoning her closer.

She leaned in, her ear next to his mouth. A breath rattled alarmingly in his chest before the words spilled forth. "You have already lived two lives. One you were born into, the other you were adopted into. Now, you have a third."

"No, I don't want another life," Little Brave said around the aching knot in her throat. "Not without you."

Now it was Grey Owl's turn to shush her, the air wheezing in his throat as he did so. "The third will be yours to choose."

Little Brave held her ear suspended above his mouth, waiting for more. Another exhalation warmed her ear, peaceful and resigned. Her scalp prickled as that warmth receded. Her grief welled up inside her when the warmth came no more. "Why do I have to lose another father, *Wakan Tanka*?" she wailed, her fists winding into the soft folds of his tunic.

Her face dropped to the now-immobile chest. Her father had left her. Somewhere behind her, she heard the grunts of the scout and the murmuring of the women as they removed the arrow from his chest. Even more faintly, she heard war cries and gunshots echoing from the canyon, but she heard no more the breath of her father.

Little Brave knew not how much time had passed when finally she heard victorious sounds of the warriors as they ascended from the canyons. Her people's joyous shouts joined their elated cries. She lifted her face from Grey Owl's inert form, long shadows telling her the sun was nearing its sleep.

Running Bear broke from the jubilant crowd and approached, his coppery muscles rippling and sheened in sweat from fierce battle.

Rage cut through her anguish and grief as a white-hot knife slices through a festering wound.

He stopped short of the shade harboring the body of Grey Owl and turned in a circle, his arms rising high as he addressed their people who gathered round him. "Little Brave yet grieves for our esteemed leader, but when her grief is spent, she will take her place among us as my wife." Running Bear completed his circle, his gaze falling upon Little Brave as she knelt beside Grey Owl.

Their people nodded their heads, murmuring their agreement with Running Bear, grateful their chief's daughter would be so well placed.

But all Little Brave saw in the warrior's eyes was the gleam of devious plotting. She wrapped her fingers around the hilt of her knife housed in her legging. As she rose, she freed it, but held it close to her body, behind the fold of her skirt, tempering her rage, knowing that to attack the warrior physically would only hand her defeat. "I will not become the wife of a murderer," she said loudly enough for those who stood at the fringes to hear.

"I do no murder, Little Brave. The soldiers deserved to die for stealing our old ones, our women and children."

"Your arrow now lives in the chest of Chief Grey Owl."

"An arrow meant for one of our enemies."

"Running Bear says his aim is not true," Little Brave declared extending an arm to their people.

His nostrils flared and his eyes narrowed as his hand gripped the hilt of the knife sheathed at his waist, but he did not draw it.

Little Brave stood taller in the knowledge that her barb had found its mark.

"That my arrow found its resting place in Grey Owl's heart says only that it was his time to pass." Running Bear again turned in place, spreading his arms wide, hawking for their people's agreement.

Little Brave glanced around the group of nodding heads, the looks of relief that dwelt in their faces, for they did not want the fact to be true that their revered chief had died dishonorably. If so, as was the custom of the Lakota, Grey Owl would then be buried face down, a piece of fat stuffed into his mouth to keep his spirit from driving away the buffalo that supplied their every need.

Seeing her people swaying in favor Running Bear's argument lent a desperation to her rage. "Grey Owl knows the truth. He will stalk Running Bear, bring him defeat in battle, deny him sons to follow in his footsteps, turn his words to gibberish when he speaks around the council fires."

Little Brave searched the group and found the faces of those most familiar to her, looking to gain their support, but the warriors remained stalwart after following Running Bear into battle. Their women stood next to them in pride and relief while their children clung happily to their father's mighty legs. At the end of her scrutiny, her gaze snagged on Stone Skipper who stood at the front of the group. The gleeful triumph, beaming in the woman's face, unleashed Little Brave's tenuous hold on her emotions.

Little Brave brandished her knife and leapt at Running Bear. He deflected her with a raised arm but not before her blade grazed his shoulder. She bared her teeth in satisfaction as blood oozed from the slice. She lunged at him again, both hands gripping her knife, holding it high, above her head in determination to send such conniving evilness into the next life.

There, Grey Owl could wreak his vengeance, too.

Running Bear caught her wrists with one hand, holding them suspended above her head.

Deep in her throat, she growled her frustration.

He hauled her closer. "I will take great pleasure in breaking you, Little Brave," he said for her ears alone. "Then I will take even greater pleasure in casting you aside. And no one will have you after that."

The stench of death on his hands gagged her. At the prospect of living with abuse and starvation, as she had among the Blackfeet, Little Brave wished only to pass into the next life with Grey Owl and dwell forever more in peace. With that desire set firmly in her mind, Little Brave took careful aim and spit squarely between Running Bear's eyes.

Reflexively, his eyes crossed to track the offending glob, his jaw going momentarily slack in surprise.

A hate and a vengeance filled his face that did not disappoint Little Brave. She yet held her knife. To release it would bring dishonor on her death, but inside, she readied herself for the fatal piercing of Running Bear's blade.

"She is crazed with grief," said Strong Back.

Little Brave cared little that someone now spoke in her defense; she only willed her own death.

Running Bear unsheathed his knife, his obsidian eyes glittering coldly in the warrior's anticipation of dealing death to one who'd wronged him.

Little Brave closed her eyes, murmuring under her breath, "I am coming, Father."

The moment the blade should have rent her skin, a wild murmuring went around the crowd then unholy shrieking emanated from some of the women.

Little Brave opened her eyes to see Running Bear staring beyond her, a deathly pallor dulling the coppery color of his skin. She craned her neck around to see behind her.

Grey Owl sat fully upright, his eyes glazed and unseeing, but his gaze aimed directly at Running Bear.

Chapter 5

For a moment, terror held Little Brave in its clutches until a memory tugged at the darkest recesses of her mind, it pulled a little harder then broke free. Long, long ago, she had overheard her white father speak about how the muscles of dead people seize up, sometimes causing their bodies to do strange things. Her horror changed to cunning as she looked at Running Bear. "Grey Owl knows and already he watches you," she said slyly.

Slowly, Running Bear turned his stare from Grey Owl to Little Brave. The disbelief and fear on his face was no surprise, for the Plains People had their superstitions and being followed by the eyes of one who had been murdered was a dire one. But Running Bear's skin regained its coppery hue and he returned her sly look.

A shiver skittered along her spine.

He spun them so they faced their people.

The terrified crowd had backed up many steps to put distance between their dead chief and his abnormal posture. The shrieks had ceased, but the wild murmuring continued, their looks downcast to avoid the dead man's glazed stare.

Keeping her arms aloft, Running Bear cried out, "A dead man does not sit up, unless he is under the power of some evil spell." Agreement swept through the crowd, swift and sure. "Here I hold the source of the evil."

No. Little Brave gasped along with her people.

"See how her skin betrays her." Running Bear gave her arms a shake and her sleeves dropped from her wrists to her elbows.

Little Brave followed the gazes of those before her as they lifted and stared at the pale skin exposed by the fall of her sleeves. Her rage rose once again, desire for her death forgotten. She would not let Running Bear defile her in their people's eyes without a fight. "For eight winters, I have lived among you with my pale skin. My heart and my actions have always been honorable and true to you, my people."

Immediately, he countered, "The coming of the white man's soldiers to our village has unleashed the evil of her pale skin."

"I have done no evil." She jerked her arms, but he did not loosen his hold.

"Squaws, where are your travois?" Commiseration flew from woman to woman as they considered the loss of all their earthly possessions. "They lie at the bottom of the canyons." Running Bear yanked down her arms, his grip tightening to force her to release her knife.

But she held fast. The pain he inflicted strengthened her resolve to beat him in this battle of words. "Grey Owl only wanted his people out of harm's way before our warriors arrived."

"And now our warriors will have to hunt twice as many buffalo, and our women will have to work twice as hard to replace their tepees."

"There are many of us. Together, the work will be light," Little Brave scanned the crowd, looking for agreement.

"Hiyee!" cried a woman from the back of the crowd. "Grey Owl's daughter inherited her tepee. What does she know of hard work?"

71

Stands Tall added, "The return of the white man to the Powder River Country has already reduced the number of buffalo."

"Our brother speaks the truth," said Running Bear, "and now we have even less time for hunting, because we must battle the white man as he comes to drive us from our hunting grounds."

Stone Skipper ululated in agreement, raising her knife high in the air. Her people caught the cry and carried it, their weapons ascending to the sky.

"We have much to do," declared Running Bear. "Ready yourselves to return to our home."

Little Brave watched with a sinking heart as her people moved away to do Running Bear's bidding. She yearned to call out to Nimble Fingers, Strong Back, and Sings For The Moon, but she held herself back for not one of them looked her way. Soon, only Stone Skipper stood before her and Running Bear.

"What of her?" Stone Skipper asked, gesturing her knife threateningly at Little Brave.

"She is not your concern. Leave us."

Although it was slight, Little Brave detected Stone Skipper's flinch at Running Bear's sharp tone and his dismissive wave. Little Brave almost felt sorrow for the woman who pined for the affection and approval of such a callous man.

"Your people do not look back as they leave you, Little Brave," Running Bear said, triumph gleaming in his eyes.

"You have twisted their thoughts." Sorrow, darker than a moonless night, enveloped her.

"They know I am a powerful warrior who can lead them in driving away the white man."

"You will never win against the white man. His weapons are much too powerful, his numbers too great." As soon as the words left her mouth, Little Brave gasped. How did she come to have such an opinion?

"You would rather see us herded onto reservations?"

"We could learn other ways of living." Little Brave knew the notion was foreign and repugnant to the warrior, but, above all, she wanted to see the survival of her people.

"You turned Grey Owl into a foolish old man. I was right to kill him."

Little Brave's rage reignited. She struggled against his hold.

His amusement at her efforts rumbled deep in his chest.

She looked at the wound she'd inflicted on his shoulder. It no longer oozed, and in a few days, it would be nothing more than a scratch. Her rage deteriorated to powerless frustration, and she bit her lip until it bled.

Smugness filled Running Bear's face. He bent her arms until the blade of her knife lay against her throat. "I will tell *my* people that grief stole your life."

Little Brave locked onto the flintiness of her executioner's eyes. "Like it stole your father's life," she said.

The smugness fled. "My father died in battle," Running Bear hissed.

"Grey Owl told me your father fell on his spear because he could not live without your mother."

Running Bear notched the blade between the ridges of her throat.

Little Brave's satisfaction blossomed. But it was not yet complete. Not until she'd destroyed the very foundation of his life as he'd destroyed hers. "The mother who fell to her death when she tried to rescue her wandering son." She welcomed the vengeance and hate filling the warrior's face, for it promised to send her to her father. Her eyes drifted closed in peaceful anticipation. But the blade fell away from her neck as an anguished cry erupted from Running Bear. Little Brave stumbled backward as the warrior released her.

He whirled in rage, looking for his attacker as he pulled free the knife lodged in his shoulder.

Immediately, she recognized it as Grey Owl's knife. Only one person could have gained her father's knife. She glanced back to the overhang, but although Grey Owl sat upright and rigid as before, the scout and his horse were nowhere to be seen.

Playing on her hunch that the furious man was unaware of the scout's presence, Little Brave approached Running Bear who clutched his shoulder to stem the flow of blood. "Grey Owl has spoken," she said with a jerk of her chin toward the knife in the warrior's hand.

Running Bear flinched, eyes widening in disbelief as he recognized the hilt of the murdered chief's knife. His fingers dropped it like a hot coal. He threw a furtive look at the upright chief and backed away, but his lip curled with his parting comment. "You were never one of us, white girl. And now you will be alone forever."

Once he reached his people, he mounted his horse and urged their departure. Within moments the entire band was in motion. Her heart wailed at the staggering loss of another family. She watched their familiar figures recede until their dust consumed them.

-*-*-

Beech remained flat on his stomach atop the rocky outcropping until the band rode away, then he slowly eased his way back down. Gathering August's reins, he returned to the overhang, the pain and weariness of each step threatening to overwhelm him now that the rush of emotions from the encounter between Little Brave and the warrior was receding.

Ella's Choice

Little Brave retrieved her father's knife and wiped it against her skirt. Her steps dragged as she turned and approached him, but the shock on her face told the story. She had never expected to be abandoned by her people. "You did me no favor, Scout," she said lifelessly as she joined him in the shadow.

Beech wasn't surprised at her ungratefulness. Although it was unusual for a body to seize up so soon after death, the unnerving occurrence had held the vengeance of the warrior called Running Bear at bay the first time. His timely launching of Grey Owl's knife had halted the second attempt. But both times, he had read Little Brave's longing for death in the peaceful way she'd closed her eyes, the offering manner in which she'd held her body.

He sagged back against the rock wall as Little Brave dropped to her knees beside Grey Owl. She slipped her father's knife into its sheath then rested back onto her heels, and bowed her head. Although he'd heard her wails of grief earlier, she seemed inclined to sorrow silently now. The climb taking its toll, he slipped down the wall into a sitting position and closed his eyes. Moments later he heard a faint swishing sound and opened his eyes to see both of Little Brave's braids lying in the dust behind her. Although a typical act of bereavement for the Lakota people, Beech wondered if he hadn't been here to hear her, would she have chosen to wail her grief aloud instead of shearing her hair? Fighting his own pain, he pushed aside the question, closed his eyes and palmed his wound. Hopefully, the pressure would ease its ache, for the effects of the herbs the healer had applied were fading fast.

When he heard the soft whisper of buckskin against buckskin, he opened his eyes to see Little Brave raising her arms, the mourning slices she'd made across the pale skin of her inner arms dripping blood. Her hands clutched the hilt of her knife, its lethal tip aimed at her chest.

In a split second, he launched himself, fisting a hand around both of hers. His grasp halted the motion of her knife. She howled her frustration and tried to twist away.

He clamped an arm around her waist. She jammed an elbow into his chest, hitting his wound. He grunted at the searing pain just managing to hold onto her as he lost his balance. They tumbled backward.

She landed heavily on him. Her legs flailed, and her heels struck at his shins. With the back of her head, she landed a blow to his face.

He was losing his grip on her wrists. With a deep inhale, Beech concentrated his ebbing strength. He thrust her arms upward as he rolled them. She bellowed her rage at the advantage his size gave him as he held her pinned beneath him. He pried the knife from her fingers.

"You have no right to deny me death," she yelled. Her words reverberated off the rock wall and dissipated into the aridness surrounding them.

With some effort, Beech tucked her knife into the legging of his moccasin for safekeeping. "Your desire for death will fade once your grief is spent."

She slapped her hands against the ground, the dust puffing up between her fingers. "There is nothing left for me in this world."

"There is still much for you in this world."

Her fingers closed around the fine powder, nails scraping against the hardened earth as she fisted her hands. She pounded furiously on the ground, wailing, "I have no people."

The anguish in Little Brave's words tore at Beech's heart, driving him to provide the only comfort he could think of in the moment. "You have me."

"You!" Spittle sprayed the parched earth, as she spewed the word. "And who are you?"

"A man with no people," he said, the spoken truth striking at his soul.

She stilled then, going so limp beneath him he thought she might have fainted. But slowly, her fingers inched open. She flattened her hands against the dust, pressing hard, then crossed her arms and buried her face into them.

He eased off her, sensing that she'd turned a corner, but instinct told him there were more corners to turn.

The first sob heaved through her body, erupting from the depths of her soul.

Gently, he scooped her into his arms, cradling her against him. Her fingers twisted into his tunic, her tears muddying the dust caking her cheeks and neck. He'd never held a grieving woman before, but holding Little Brave, comforting her as she spilled her grief, seemed natural and right. Twilight stole across the sky as she sobbed. Beech caressed the back of her head, his fingers lingering at the softness of her neck bared by the loss of her braids. Hair would grow back to cover that tender skin, but what life would grow out of her loss of Grey Owl and her people?

Finally, she quieted in his arms, but her hands remained twisted into his tunic, her face buried into his neck. When her even breathing told him she slept, he let sleep overtake him, too.

Beech awoke to a chill settling around them. The moon had risen, full and bright. It cast a silvery light over the barren landscape and over the woman sleeping in his arms. The dirt clinging to her skin couldn't hide her elegant beauty, and her shorn hair only highlighted the delicacy of her features. His fingers seemed too large and clumsy as he tucked a strand of hair behind her ear.

She awoke with a startled look and bolted upright.

"You are safe," he assured.

She searched her surroundings until she spied Grey Owl's body. Relief filled her features, but then she shivered. She pushed to her feet, went to the horses and returned with

77

three blankets. She dropped one beside him then draped another one over Grey Owl's shoulders. "That he still sits tells me he is not yet ready to leave this world," Little Brave said as she wound the last blanket around herself. She knelt beside the old chief. "I will sit with him until he is ready."

In spite of his stiffness from the pain and cold, Beech managed to get the blanket spread over his long form. It would be a poor substitute for the warmth of Little Brave's body, but he understood her need to sit with her father. His father had done the same after his mother had died giving birth to his sister. Keeping vigil would be no less than what he would do for someone he loved.

When Beech awoke again, he saw the sky was tinged pink from the approaching dawn.

Little Brave sat cross-legged next to the old chief.

The night's chill and hard ground being no friend to him, Beech struggled to his feet. "I must check for survivors in the canyons then we will need to find water for the horses before the sun is too high in the sky."

Little Brave stood easily, folding the blanket. "I will go into the canyons with you."

He shook his head while she gathered and folded his blanket. "There will be much death down there."

"I care not since they are not my people," Little Brave said as she followed him to the horses.

Beech did not remind her of her declaration yesterday that she had no people. Instead, he strapped the blankets to the back of his saddle. "Death is death, regardless of who it takes."

She led Grey Owl's horse over to the still-sitting chief. "I will not leave my father behind," she said, her voice strong in her determination.

Beech noted the light swiftly filling the sky. In a few hours, the heat of the day would be upon them. They could be back at the river well before then if they retraced their steps back through the canyons. Beech grabbed the rope hanging off his saddle and strode over to Little Brave. He stared down at her. The mutinous thrust of her chin and the firm set of her lips were at odds with the golden glow the strengthening rays cast across her skin, her delicately winged eyebrows and finely chiseled nose, but when her gaze did not waver from his, he said, "Once we enter the canyons, we do not leave until we are through them." There was the slightest easing of her lips as she nodded her agreement.

Once they'd secured the old chief to his mount, Little Brave led the paint pony over to her mare, gathered a handful of mane and mounted in one fluid motion.

Beech marveled that she seemed to suffer no ill effects from the cold and the scabbed slashes on her arms.

"I will gather whatever we can use for our journey." She nudged the horse with her heels and with Grey Owl in tow took off trotting toward the canyon's rim.

The glimpse of the milky white skin of Little Brave's thigh took Beech's mind off the aching of his wound as he hoisted himself into the saddle, but it didn't ease his concerns over what she might see in the canyons. He caught up with her at the canyon's rim. "What if some of your people lie dead in the canyons?"

Her eyes glittering, she said, "Like you, I have no people." What he'd said in comfort, she threw back at him in bitterness. And the way she sent her horse plunging headlong down the trail told him she would still welcome death to end her suffering.

Beech sent August forward at a more cautious pace. As he knew first-hand, grief was not spent in hours or even days. Sometimes months or even years were needed.

When he exited the trail onto the ledge, he spotted Little Brave peering over its edge into the deep ravine that held all of the travois. No doubt she was mourning the loss of all her earthly possessions, but she nudged the palomino forward when she sensed his presence. He fell in line behind her, taking note of the soldiers' bodies as he went. When he reached a body that was lying face down, he dismounted to turn it over.

Little Brave dismounted when they came upon the first dead horse, searching through its saddlebags for supplies.

Beech noticed, whether out of superstition or respect, she did not search the bodies. Most of the soldiers lay where they'd fought, but a few, scattered further along the ledge, had been taken down while fleeing. There been no counting coup—a warrior gaining honor by striking a fleeing enemy rather than killing him—in this battle. Beech found Captain Baldwin, slain where he'd fought, a hand held to his troublesome side even in death.

There were a few soldiers whose identity Beech could not determine for their bodies lay at the bottom of the ravine, but the body count told him three soldiers remained unaccounted for. Beech grimaced at the fate of those soldiers. While the odds for survival on foot and without supplies in this harsh land were next to nil, being captured meant a long, torturous death.

Little Brave stowed the gathered supplies into packs she'd fashioned from two blankets she'd taken from the soldiers' saddles. She draped the bundles over her horse's back.

Resourceful though it was, Beech wondered at the extra effort this cost her. "Why do you not use a saddlebag?"

"Blankets serve many more purposes than a white man's saddlebag," said Little Brave as she wrapped a blanket around her shoulders for warmth, for the sun had yet to shine on this side of the canyon.

Beech nodded in understanding. Living a nomadic lifestyle demanded sparseness and practicality.

Once they'd traversed the entire battle scene, Little Brave remounted and set a steady pace.

Beech followed. Since the ground was too hard and rocky to dig proper graves, he would notify the commander at Fort Fetterman and let him deal with the soldiers' bodies.

Chapter 6

The sky and land opened up as they emerged from the canyons. The earth yet remained barren and rocky, but Little Brave filled her lungs with air that now moved freely about them. She spread her arms, letting the wind move where it willed, cooling the perspiration on her brow, but it did little to soothe the pain in heart.

"Where will Grey Owl begin his journey to the next life?"

The scout asked the question as if he knew where her thoughts were leading. "Far from the place of his betrayal." She jerked her head toward the canyons behind them.

"Why did Running Bear kill Grey Owl?"

The caution in the scout's voice told her he did not want to upset her, but still she couldn't help the rage which returned. She desired nothing more than to push her pony, Sundance, into a breakneck gallop in spite of the horse's thirst. She wanted to leave the scout in her dust as her people had left her in theirs, to track down Running Bear and put an arrow through his heart as intentional as the one he'd put through her father's. But she remained riding beside the scout. She soothed her rage with the fact he knew Running Bear's aim had been true to its target.

Unbidden, the time she'd spent in the scout's arms last night leapt into her mind, the peace and safety she'd felt there. Could there be peace for her in this life while Running Bear yet lived? Little Brave grabbed at that ebbing rage, allowing it to fill her words with righteous conviction. "Many times, Running Bear tried to persuade our people to follow him, instead of Grey Owl. Each time, my father showed our people what foolishness it would be to follow him. There was no other way for Running Bear to become chief but to kill my father."

"Grey Owl was a wise leader, but his time as a warrior was many winters past."

Little Brave understood what the scout was suggesting. With the aggression of the soldiers, the tribe needed to accept Running Bear and the warriors who followed him to ensure their survival. But, regardless of how right the scout might be, that knowledge did not lessen the sting of her people's rejection. *Her people!* Pain cut so quickly and sharply through her that the slices across her arms would be no match if she continued to speak on the matter. "Hiyee," she hissed. "I will share no more words with you, Scout."

She nudged Sundance a few paces ahead of the scout's big black gelding although she knew not where they rode. Several strides later, his horse pulled even with hers. He slowed its pace to match Sundance's. There they rode as silent as the land was parched and dry.

Mile by mile, the rocks gave way to tufts of grass, the dust to dirt, flatness to rises and dips. The horses' ears pricked, their steps livened and their heads stretched downward, cropping at the occasional nourishment which lay in their path. When they came to a small stream, they dismounted. All three horses widened their stance, dropped their heads and greedily siphoned the water between their lips.

Little Brave sank to her knees, hurriedly rinsing her hands in the cold, clear liquid before cupping them and bringing the water to her mouth. Rarely had water tasted sweeter. Once her thirst had been slaked, she splashed her face and neck, freeing the trail dust to wend its way downstream, wishing she could as easily free the troublesome thoughts tangling together in her mind. She rested back onto her heels then rolled her shoulders. She stretched her arms to the sky until she felt the pull of her cuts. The motions worked the kinks from her body, but did not ease her mind. She closed her eyes, hoping to find relief from her questions, but they still cried for her attention. What was to become of her now? Without a father, a home, a people?

Around her, birds twittered happily as they went about their spring tasks. What she wouldn't give to have her energies exhausted and her thoughts absorbed by routine tasks. But she had no such luxury, for the course of this day was no more known to her than the next.

The breeze lifted, lapping the water gently against the opposite shore. It brought a strange scent. Little Brave sniffed again. Not exactly strange. More like strangely familiar. She dropped her arms. The scent, as invigorating as the smell of the prairie after a spring rain, became overwhelming as the scout knelt beside her. The aroma was the one she'd smelled on him when he'd allowed her to enter the tepee before him. Now she understood.

In his hands, he held a whitish bar, its corners rounded, like a rock tumbled for many moons along a riverbed.

Little Brave watched the scout dip the bar in the water, rub it along his arms and face, releasing more of its refreshing scent, covering his skin in frothing bubbles. Its scent was not unlike that of the cleansing aroma of cedar and the comforting balm of sage, yet its fragrance was neither. With a wave, Little Brave gestured to the item in the scout's hand.

The scout nodded his understanding, but did not place the bar into her outstretched hand. Instead he scooped up a handful of water, dribbling some of it along her fingers and into her palm. He moved his fingers so that the last drop fell onto her wrist.

A shiver raced up her spine. Not of fear, but of anticipation. With gentle nudges, his fingers pushed her sleeve back to her elbow, awareness skittering along her skin wherever he touched. The mourning cuts glared red and angry from beneath the dirt and dried blood, caking the pale skin of her inner arm. She jerked away her arm, dismayed at having him view such personal marks of grief.

"Your cuts need to be washed," he said.

His deep, rumbling voice drowned out the twittering birds, the lapping water, and weakened her inhibitions. Those blue eyes, mirrors of her own, caught and held her gaze as he reached for the bare arm she held protectively against her body. His fingers were strong but gentle as they wrapped around her wrist, but it was that kind light glowing in his eyes that was her undoing. She let him pull her arm toward the water.

He pressed her other hand to her elbow to hold her sleeve in place. He cradled her arm with one hand while the other scooped handfuls of clear, cold water over it.

The dirt loosened and began to trickle away, but the blood remained firmly attached to her skin. He rubbed his fingers on the bar that he'd laid aside, creating a great number of those foaming bubbles. Although careful of her cuts as he spread the bubbles on her skin, she inhaled sharply at the sting as they entered her wounds. The scent filling her nostrils was not as pungent as cedar or as light as sage, but it filled her with the same sense of purification and renewal. When he reached for the other arm, she rucked up her sleeve without question and held it out.

When the scout had finished cleaning her cuts, Little Brave closed her eyes to revel in the tingling of her skin, much like that of daily bathing in cold, sparkling streams.

"The white man's word for it is soap," he said, shifting into a sitting position beside her.

"Soap," Little Brave repeated a word she had not spoken in ten winters. With it came long-buried memories of an immense tub filled with water as warm as the summer's air. Splashing, giggling, a woman's outrage at water sloshed onto a wooden floor.

"This soap has a special herb which will help your cuts heal."

She believed the scout, for already the pain of her cuts had receded and they looked less angry and raw. Little Brave pushed the hair off her face and tucked it behind her ears then she looked at the scout. "I will trade you for this soap."

The scout shook his head.

But Little Brave was not deterred for she knew that clever bartering always began with the reluctance to part with an item. She pulled a small pouch strung around her neck from beneath her tunic. She retrieved a narrow strip of shiny cloth a trader had given her in exchange for a brow band she'd beaded. The white man's name for the cloth escaped her, but she held it up, letting the breeze flutter its length as the trader had done with her. "See, it matches your eyes," she said, mimicking the trader's words and enticing tone.

The scout's amusement rumbled deep in his chest before it exited his mouth. "It is a pretty color, but men do not wear such fripperies."

"Fripperies?" Little Brave furrowed her brow as she repeated the white man's word.

The scout's brow furrowed in turn, before he said, "Like the prairie chicken who puffs his feathers and stomps his feet but there is no mate to woo." His hands mimed the expanse of the bird's ruff then the rapid movement of the feet performed in the bird's mating ritual.

Little Brave smiled at the picture that drew in her head. "Running Bear," she said.

The scout's face clouded as he muttered some words Little Brave did not understand, but that did not lessen her craving for the medicine which could tingle her skin with its touch. With her travois lost, she hadn't much left to trade. She clutched at her pouch, considering the other items within. There was one item she would never trade—her father's pocket watch, but there was another item the scout might want. The locket her white grandfather had given her.

Many, many handfuls of times she could have traded the heart-shaped locket. Many more times she had held on to it as a symbol of hope that her grandfather would come for her, but he hadn't. The memories of the earliest days of her captivity flashed across her mind, all the feelings welling up inside her—the fear of her captors, the bewilderment at their ways, the struggle just to survive. Anger retaliated. Righteous and indignant, the anger shoved aside those crippling emotions. She would rid herself of the useless item and the painful reminders it caused by trading it for the scout's cleansing soap.

Keeping the relic fisted in her hand, she withdrew it from the bag. Slowly, she opened her palm to his curious gaze. "I will trade this for your soap."

The scout gave her a questioning look as he picked up the chain and held the locket suspended between them. "This belongs to you?"

"No, it belongs to you." She wiggled her fingers for the soap. She did not want to answer anymore questions; she only wanted the scout's strong medicine.

The scout ignored her outstretched hand, making the sounds of the symbols etched on the front of the locket. "E, L, H." Sounds Little Brave hadn't heard from another mouth for the past ten winters, sounds associated with a terrified little girl who'd been lost long ago.

"Do these marks stand for your name in the white man's tongue?"

"My name is Little Brave." She did not want to think about what those letters represented. Remembering a person she'd ceased to be ten winters ago and a life which was no longer hers was too painful. Her goal was to possess the soap for its healing powers and its cleansing scent.

She snatched at the coveted item lying on the ground beside the scout. She was quick, but not quick enough, for he caught her wrist as she withdrew with the soap. "A trade is a trade," she said, shaking the hair from her eyes. Without her braids to hold it, the strands danced impertinently in the breeze.

"I will not trade for this." The scout jiggled the chain between them.

"I can see by your eyes that your desire for it is great." There was no mistaking the need to possess burning in his eyes, but as Little Brave said those words, she became aware of the warmth of his fingers around her wrist, his scent of trail dust, male sweat and worn leather mingling with her own scent. And now that of their shared scent—the soap she held in her hand. It hung in the air between them, intimately binding them together. And suddenly that yawning yearning was awakening within her, the one his touch had promised it could satisfy on the night they'd kissed.

"My desire is great, but not for this," he said as he swung the locket before her eyes.

Within her, his words echoed in time with the sway of the heart-shaped trinket. He desired her as she desired him.

She inched forward on her knees. A heavy breath eased from his chest. Her gaze slid to his lips for their touch held a special power over her. Power that could block the pain pulsing through her body—pain over the death of her fathers, the betrayal of her people, the abandonment by her grandfather, the loss of her childhood.

Passion had caused her to forget herself the night he'd kissed her. It could make her forget again.

Her gaze went back to his, watching as his eyes darkened when her lips parted to take a quivering breath. She tilted her head and touched her lips to his. The sizzling sensations swept through her even stronger than before, but they fizzled when his lips did not move beneath hers. She slid her hand around the back of his neck, spiking her fingers into the silky strands of his hair which were warm from the glare of the sun.

She angled her mouth differently, but still, he did not respond. Desperation mounted. She could not forget if he did not respond. Touching the tip of her tongue to the seam between his lips caused a groan to growl deep in his throat.

His hands gripped her waist, his lips parting to take her tongue into his mouth.

And then it was as she remembered. Heated desire swept through her, rising to meet his passion. She was surer of herself this time and when she wasn't, her body followed his lead.

Her tongue danced with his. Need coiled in the pit of her stomach and her fingers burned to feel his skin. Between her legs, she throbbed for release. She found the edge of his tunic, tunneled her hand beneath it, stroking the taut skin of his stomach.

He groaned again.

She tugged up on its edge, frustrated by the limitations of the buckskin hugging his torso.

His hands left off the caressing of her back to lift the garment chest-high where he grunted as he worked around his injury. Then he tossed the buckskin aside.

Little Brave's hands began mapping the contours of his upper body, every touch weakening her pain. Lean at his waist, ridged along his ribs, strongly muscled on his chest and arms.

His hands dropped to his knees, his eyes drifted shut, but his breath quickened as her fingers caressed every inch of him.

When she came to the wound from Running Bear's arrow, she palmed his heart beneath it. "I am glad you did not die, Scout."

His eyes opened at that, one hand held her hand over his heart as the fingers of his other hand tunneled into her hair. "Beech."

"Beech?" she repeated.

"That is my name."

"Your name is Richoux."

"My full name is Beech Richoux. My friends call me Beech."

Friends? Pain sliced through her. She had no friends. She had no family and she had no home. All she had was this moment, this moment to forget the pain now threatening to overwhelm her. She dropped her gaze squeezing them shut against the gathering tears, and fumbled with her skirt. She would not lose this chance.

His hands covered hers, their warmth refocusing her on the relief he could bring her. She shifted her weight, allowing him to nudge her skirt upwards. As her gaze met his, the raw desire burning there sent a scorching heat up her neck and into her face. She'd never lain with a man before. But in the next second, those long fingers cradled her cheeks

90

and his lips touched hers, moving enticingly against hers until all she could think of was the fire burning between her thighs. Then he drew her closer and her legs wrapped instinctively around him as she settled into his lap.

She caught her breath at the hard ridge beneath his buckskin that told her he desired her in the way she desired him and she followed her body's urge to angle her hips. Exquisite pleasure shot through her, causing a throaty moan to escape her lips.

Satisfaction spread across his face as he propped back on his elbows and met her next movement with a thrust of his hips. She fell forward, her hands clenching at his shoulders as the resulting sensation rocked her entire body. As she caught her breath, he gripped her hips and eased back onto the tender, spring grass. Slowly, she straightened, fascinated by the way his eyes hooded as he watched her trail her fingers over the strong swell of his chest. A shy smile curled her lips at his shiver when she stroked the taut skin below the span of his ribs.

She reached for the beaded belt at her waist, craving the coupling, which would put her far beyond any remnants of pain. Her fingers fumbled at its ties though, and a moment of self-doubt gripped her. He settled that doubt with a grinding of his hips, which sent another wave of pleasure sweeping through her. Loosening her belt and dropping it beside them, she then worked her dress up her body and pulled it free.

-*-*-

Beech nearly choked on his tongue at the sight of Little Brave tossing aside her dress. Full breasts, pert and rosy tipped, gave way to a trim waist flaring to a pair of luscious hips. Between them nestled a thatch of russet curls, which were a shade darker than the hair dancing merrily

91

around her face. While her arms dropped a little self-consciously to her sides, the slight tightening of her thighs promised a heady pleasure that sharing intimacies with her would bring. But it was her skin, not her nervousness or inexperience, that drew him up short. The expanse of its pale luminosity reminded him who she really was.

Then he knew he must be caught in one of Trickster Coyote's schemes.

He'd never encountered a woman like Little Brave before, so beautiful, spirited and determined. And like him, she had embraced another culture to survive. He burned from the inside out with desire for her, a craving to make her his own, but she was a white woman and he was a Lakota half-breed.

Beech caught Little Brave's hands as they dropped to his chest, her husky laugh dying in her throat at the somber look on his face. In keeping with his Lakota upbringing, he spoke the truth as he knew it. "I cannot lay with you."

Shock and pain chased across Little Brave's face in the few fleeting seconds before she closed her features, and his heart squeezed in anguish for her and himself.

Jerkily, she grabbed for her dress. Holding it against her front, she scrambled off him. The curve in her spine snapped straight as she walked farther up the stream.

He reached for his tunic, struggling to pull it over his head as he followed her, cursing his black-and-white tongue. "Little Brave, my words were harsh but—"

"But you do not want to lay with a woman whose people have shunned her."

She was jumping to conclusions to protect her raw emotions. "Your people have nothing to do with this." Actually, that was only partially true. He took a deep breath, gathering his thoughts to avoid the cut of his earlier words. "Little Brave, you are a white woman."

How he wished she weren't!

She whirled then, her eyes like snapping blue flames. "I am no more a white woman than you are a white man, Beech Richoux."

"The white man won't see you that way."

"I care not what the white man sees."

"You won't have a choice."

"Grey Owl told me before he died that my life was now mine to live as I wanted." Little Brave beat against her chest in emphasis of her points. "My life. My choice."

Beech did not doubt the conviction of her beliefs, but she did not understand the way things were in white society. She'd been away too long to remember. Or too young to know before she'd left. She did not understand the depth of the white man's shunning that could occur if she laid with him. He wanted her as much as anything he'd ever wanted before in his life, but not at the cost of her establishing her place in the white man's world.

"Tell me you do not desire me as a man desires a woman, Beech Richoux." She let her dress drop, her arms hanging loosely at her sides, her chin tilting upward, challenging him to deny it.

His blood sang in his veins and his body smoldered at the sight of such feminine lushness standing mere inches away. "I desire you as I've desired no other woman, Little Brave," he managed to choke past the dryness coating his tongue. He allowed his fingers to trace the ridge of her cheekbones and push those silken strands of fire behind her ears. "But you are a white woman, and I am an Indian. I could be hanged merely for touching you as I'm touching you now."

She dropped her gaze at the seriousness in his voice.

"And you would be cast out to live at the edge of society."

She raised her eyes in defiance. "My white grandfather left me to live far beyond the edge of the white man's world when he did not come for me after I was captured. I lost my childhood. And now Running Bear has stolen my people from me." Little Brave shrugged. "So, I care not for living in society."

But Beech was not fooled. He had been there when Running Bear derided her in front of her people. She had stood tall and spoke eloquently to defend herself, but she had not been immune to the pain their abandonment caused. Add that to the pain of her white grandfather's failure to rescue her, the trauma of a terrified little girl as she adjusted to a completely different way of life. Little wonder, she attempted to drown it out by lying with him. But he knew, first hand, the devastating effects of blocking pain instead of facing it.

His father had buried his sorrow over his mother's death by leaving him and his sister to be raised by an aunt and uncle. His sister, only a baby at the time, had no recollection of their parents, but he'd been twelve years old. Abandoned to a world he did not know or understand, he'd spent almost as many years, literally fighting his way through the resentment and the anger. Only the *Wakan Tanka* knew for sure why he still lived to this day. Perhaps the reason was to keep Little Brave from following a destructive course and ruining any chance she had at a decent life.

Beech retrieved her dress and draped the sleeves over her shoulders so it covered her then turned away. It was better this way. Deny her now while little attachment existed. He trudged back to where he'd lain. The tender shoots still held his imprint as, he was realizing, his heart held the imprint of Little Brave.

He squatted to retrieve the locket glinting its link to Little Brave's past. A small locket, it was most likely a gift to a very young girl. Now it belonged to a young woman with very little comprehension of the ways of the white man's world.

He picked up the beaded belt. The pattern of the two buffalo facing one another had not escaped his earlier notice, but holding Little Brave's handiwork now, he realized that only one buffalo stood whole and healthy although with flecks of gray in his fur. Its mirror image, in form at least, held no flecks of gray in its fur, but blood dripped from many wounds in its body. Skillfully, the arrows and spears piercing its tough hide had been creatively rendered with porcupine quills. The art form was not often seen these days with the influx of the white man's glass beads. Beech compared the weight of the two items. Regardless of which world Little Brave chose to return to, neither held a place for him.

He reached for the bar of soap before he stood. Little Brave had so craved this exotic piece of eucalyptus soap that she'd been willing to trade a cherished link to her past. Suddenly, Beech felt more ashamed than he had for many years. When he'd spoken of his desire for something other than her locket, he'd been referring to his desire to know everything about her, in every way a man could know a woman. He had been wrong to encourage her own desire for him. Nothing could come of being intimate except for heartbreak and ruin.

Beech approached Little Brave and stood behind her as she adjusted the packs on her mare's back.

"What do you want, Scout?" Her hands retraced the adjustments she'd just made.

She was avoiding him. Not wanting to make things more difficult for her, he held her belt and locket over her shoulder. "Here are your things," he said rather unnecessarily.

She took the belt, tilting it so the locket dumped back into his hand. "I have no use for such fripperies."

He took little pleasure in the easy way the white man's word rolled off her tongue. That she tried to hide the pain behind the flatness of her words chipped away at his heart. He closed his fingers around the necklace and withdrew his hand. Spontaneously, he extended the hand that held the soap over her other shoulder. "And this?"

There was not the slightest movement of her head, but he knew her eyes would slide to their corners to gaze upon the coveted item, her nose would twitch at its scent, her skin tingle in recall of its magical qualities.

Slowly, her fingers closed around the bar. But instead of stashing it in her pack or the pouch around her neck, she moved to the water's edge.

Beech followed, thinking she meant to wash.

But she was searching for something. Finally, she crouched before a good-sized rock with a relatively flat surface and set the bar of soap on it. Then she withdrew a knife from the legging of her moccasin.

Since he still had her knife, she must have found this one in one of the soldier's saddlebags.

Methodically, she sawed the dull knife across the center of the soap, flaking away more of it in waste than she accomplished in cleanly splitting it.

Beech retrieved her knife and held it over her shoulder.

She turned, looking at him for the first time since he'd walked away.

The look in her eyes told him the return of her knife meant more than any words he could have uttered. He gestured to the bar.

She returned to it and with one lethal whack, split the bar in two. She sheathed her knife then stood, each palm holding a half, encouraging him to choose.

Of course, he chose the smaller half. He could easily pick up another bar from his uncle's mercantile once he returned home.

Little Brave dropped her half in the pouch around her neck and hid it once more beneath her tunic. "It is a fair trade," she said, gesturing to his hand that still held her necklace.

"It is no trade," he said.

A worried pucker appeared between her delicately winged brows. "I will search my packs for something more worthy."

Beech caught her hand as she turned to go. "No, that's not what I meant."

Now those brows peaked in question.

Although she'd paused to wait for his explanation, he couldn't let go of her hand. He placed it over his heart to show her his words were true. "It is a gift. A gift from your friend, Beech."

Chapter 7

Friend!

Little Brave did not want to be Beech's friend. Nimble Fingers was—had been—her friend, as had Sings For The Moon and Strong Back. But men were not friends. They were leaders, protectors, providers, and in some cases, lovers and husbands. But friends?

As she rode astride Sundance, Little Brave tore at the dried venison she'd found in one of the packs. Pain and sorrow tumbled relentlessly within her, tangling dangerously with frustration. Jaws aching, she gnashed the tough meat between her back teeth. The skill of stoicism she'd learned from the Plains People seemed to have deteriorated in one handful of days.

The exact same handful she'd known the white man's scout. Now she did not know how to deal with all this pain, which she could no longer contain behind that stoicism. She could not forget it through the scout for he'd rejected her. Rejected her for the same reason her people had shunned her. Because she had white skin. Her paleness must be the evilness Running Bear had declared it to be.

"There are trees ahead. I will ride on to see if any are fit to use for Grey Owl's burial platform," said Beech.

Little Brave answered him as she'd answered him since he'd declared himself to be her friend—in as few words as possible. This comment only required a nod. He looked at her, but she did not look at him. It was easier to keep her features blank if she did not gaze upon his face, did not see those eyes which spoke to her without movement from his mouth, the eyes which saw what she did not want him to see. Within her, however, the emotions continued to bubble and brew.

When Little Brave rode into the grove of trees, she saw Beech point to a tree which stood apart from the others. It had a wide V in its trunk. She nodded at his choice, knowing with their wounds they could not fell trees and dig holes in which to set foundation poles for a self-supporting burial scaffold.

Beech dismounted and began dragging downed limbs to the base of the chosen tree.

As with the deer he'd skinned to feed Grey Owl's people, someone had taught him well. The limbs were sturdy and relatively straight. As he walked further into the grove, searching for more limbs, Little Brave dismounted and stomped on the smaller branches to strip them from the main limb. This would give a snugger fit once they began lashing the boughs together.

He returned with several limbs secured between his arm and the good side of his body. They bumped and bounced haphazardly along the ground as they trailed behind him. Perspiration beaded his forehead, his breathing was labored and tiredness shadowed his eyes.

"Rest," she said then ran to fetch the skin she'd filled with water before they'd left the stream. She could not afford to have him fall ill. She had limited healing skills and if his injury did not heal, then what would she do? She had no one.

When she returned, he was hacking away the larger offshoots with an ax. Now the sweat dripped from his forehead as he bent to his task and ran in rivulets down the sides of his face.

"You must sit and rest," she said more firmly as she placed herself between him and the bough. She thrust the skin at him. "Drink," she urged.

He straightened and gave her a look she could not interpret. Finally, he wedged the ax into one of the tree trunks, the dramatic whack it made as metal collided with wood only churned her already turbulent feelings. He tipped the skin and swallowed a large gulp. He left the skin uncorked as he handed it back, his meaning clear.

She was not thirsty and preferred to ration the water they had, but she said, "I will drink if you will sit and rest." He could become ill if he did not pace himself.

He nodded but waited until she took a sip of water before he eased to the ground and propped himself against a tree.

She corked the skin and sat beside him, hoping her presence would keep him resting until his breathing evened and some of his tiredness eased. She let out a sigh of relief when he leaned his head against the tree and closed his eyes, but it was short lived.

"What does the 'E' stand for?"

She should have known he would not let the symbols etched on the front of the locket be the end of his curiosity. In this way, he was too much like the white man. "Only the 'E'?"

"Only the 'E'," he said, drowsiness coloring his voice.

Perhaps as she spoke, he would drift off. Little Brave inhaled, closing her eyes, willing her mouth to form the word she hadn't said aloud or even thought in many, many winters. "E is for El—la—" Her tongue hit the back of her front teeth on the first syllable then dropped away on the last syllable of her white name. It was the name of a terrified little girl. The only person in this world who knew her by that name was her grandfather. That is, if he still walked in this world.

Startling sadness washed over her and her eyes flew open, anxious to distance herself from such an unexpected reaction. She no longer held any affection in her heart for her grandfather. It had died long ago when he did not come to rescue that terrified little girl. Now she was Little Brave, daughter of revered Lakota chief, Grey Owl.

A sudden movement startled her, and Little Brave put a hand to her thumping heart until she realized it was Beech, twitching as he fell deeper into sleep. She remained still, concentrating on his raw beauty so much like the Lakota with his high cheekbones, and raven hair. His skin was more of a honeyed brown than the deep copper hue of the Lakota. The slope of his nose, the set of his jaw and the color of his deep blue eyes, now shuttered in sleep, reminded her of the white man. Oddly enough, she found she did not prefer one look over the other, only the man in whole.

But which of his worlds did she prefer? The Lakota one which had been denied her? Or the white man's which she no longer knew? Being of both worlds, could he help her answer these questions? Help find the world in which she should exist now?

Suddenly, it was too overwhelming to think upon any longer. She sprang to her feet to squelch her musings, but stilled, holding her breath until she knew his sleep had not been disturbed. Now she would occupy herself with gathering items to send with Grey Owl on his journey into his next life.

Once Beech awoke, they finished constructing the platform. With a rope fastened to the gelding's saddle, they hoisted the platform into the fork of the tree. Beech balanced on Sundance's back to secure it with ropes.

Little Brave was pleased with this spot, for Grey Owl would enjoy almost full sun for his journey. Carefully, she wrapped her father with two blankets she'd taken from the white soldiers. Their dull, dark colors were not a fitting color for a revered chief. She longed for sweet grass to burn to drive away the white man's scent, but most of all, she mourned for the tunic she'd been beading for her father. It would have proclaimed him a wise leader, even before words slipped free from his mouth to declare it so. But now they had his burial platform ready, she knew it was time to send him on his journey into the next world. It would be selfish to hold him here any longer.

In the same manner as they'd hoisted the platform, they lifted Grey Owl's body. This time, Little Brave balanced on Sundance's back and guided her father's wrapped form to the platform. Once he was settled, she caressed the blanket covering his face, imagining his features as she mapped them through the blanket. She let her fingers find his crossed hands beneath the layers, squeezing them one last time. "I will stay here until your journey is complete, Father," she whispered then she could say no more as the rock in her stomach rose to lodge in her throat, and tears stung her eyes. Blindly, she scrambled off Sundance's back to keep her vigil.

As the sun dropped toward its sleep, Little Brave knelt for the man who had taken her in and called her daughter, although she'd not been born of his blood. He was a man she proudly and lovingly called father.

As much as she tried, she couldn't keep her thoughts residing completely with Grey Owl and the events of his life. They tormented her with questions about her future. What would become of her now that Grey Owl had left for the next world? Now that her people had shunned her? She had lost herself as a white girl. Her white grandfather had marked her as ruined when she had come to this land with her white father, and his refusal to rescue her only confirmed it. A sense of worthlessness fell upon her.

Sometime after darkness cloaked the sky, Beech set food beside her.

She balanced on the little mare's back once again to place it on the platform next to Grey Owl and resumed her vigil.

When the moon rose high in the sky and a chill invaded the air, Beech settled his blanket around her shoulders.

She had not heard him coming, but the hairs on the back of her neck, prickling like the quills on porcupine, had told her he approached. His blanket warmed her, but not like his body had during the last sleep.

When the sun peeked over the horizon, Little Brave knew it rose to tell her Grey Owl's journey was complete. Slowly, she eased herself into a standing position, working to loosen the stiffness in her joints, to massage the aches in her muscles. When she returned to where Beech had made camp, he was brewing the drink that all white men drank over the fire. Its odor was pungently refreshing, but its taste was bitter and she did not care for it. "I will find Running Bear now," she said.

The scout rose from his squat, those never-ending questions in his eyes. "You want to return to your people?"

"I want to avenge my father's death." The question of her worth had plagued her the entire night. Warriors gained merit by going to battle, stealing horses, bringing back scalps, counting coup, even killing their enemies to prove their worth. Why could it not be that way for her?

Beech grimaced and said something she did not understand. It was obvious he was not pleased with her decision but she stood taller, remembering Grey Owl's words. It was her choice.

"You wish for more death?" he asked.

"Only Running Bear's."

"And if someone wishes to avenge Running Bear's death?"

"I am not afraid of death." She lifted her chin and squared her shoulders.

"I do not doubt your bravery, only your wisdom."

"I have lost not one, but two fathers to warriors' arrows." At her vehement disclosure, one question receded in his eyes, but another one quickly took its place.

"Would either father desire your death as payment for theirs?"

Little Brave shrugged the scout's blanket from her shoulders and tossed it to him to hide her frustration that her answer would have to be *no*. "Both of my fathers were warriors. They would understand my reasons."

He caught the blanket with one hand, slung it over his shoulder as he stepped around the fire. "Warriors fight to protect those they love, not to send them to their death." He stopped within a hair's breath of her. "Wives, mothers, sisters…daughters."

That last word stirred the wisps of hair at her temple, salted the wounds of her loss. She turned away, lest he see the tears gathering in her eyes, but his words did not cease.

"If I had someone…"

His voice softened, low and husky; it held a thread of wistfulness. Little Brave strained her ears.

"If I had someone I loved, and I died protecting them, I would not want my death to be wasted."

Longing filled his words—a longing to love and be loved in return. So loved, that one would give their life for the other. Little Brave bit her lip to keep from offering to soothe that longing. As he'd made clear by the stream, Beech did not want her solace.

Ella's Choice

-*-*-

To speak of things he could never have was a momentary weakness. What woman would want to share his lot in life? With a frustration he hadn't felt in years, Beech snatched up his saddle.

He approached his horse and saw the big black gelding nose the little palomino mare out of Beech's reach then toss his head at Grey Owl's paint pony, warning the smaller horse to keep his distance, too. Beech hoisted the pad and saddle onto his gelding's back, smiling in spite of his frustrations. "Taken a shine to the mare, haven't you?" He tightened the girth, talking to his horse, which, aside from his cousin, had been his closest companion for more years than he cared to count. "I can protect her well enough, but it is not simply a matter of protection," Beech muttered, looking across the camp at Little Brave who knelt before her pack, no doubt searching for something to eat.

He should have hunted for fresh meat yesterday, but he hadn't dared leave Little Brave in case she decided to pull her knife and join Grey Owl in the next life. But sometime between the wastelands and where they stood now, she'd changed her mind about leaving this world. Beech hoped her choice to live wasn't solely based on her desire to avenge Grey Owl's death.

He squatted to undo August's hobbles. Hopefully, their conversation had her rethinking following her path of revenge. If he could convince her to accompany him to the fort, he hoped the commander and his staff would locate her white family.

"Where do you go now?" Little Brave sat astride her mare with the paint in tow.

Beech wasn't sure how to answer her. Instinct told him that telling her about his plans at the fort would not be the best tact. "To Fort Fetterman." He watched for her reaction from the corners of his eyes. Either she'd let down her guard around him in the past few days, or he had become better at reading her for the grim set of her mouth told him what she thought of that idea.

"You have not seen enough of soldiers?" she asked.

"I must let them know about the bodies in the canyons." He set August in motion, hoping she would follow. The gelding jigged beneath him until he knew the mare followed.

"They should not have moved us from our lands," she said. "I will tell the commander at this fort of the wrong his soldiers did to my people."

Beech doubted that a woman, who for all intents and purposes was a Lakota woman, would hold any sway with the commander, but he did not say so. He covered the twinge of guilt over his deceit to get her to the fort by asking, "Your white father was a soldier?"

"Yes, but it was not enough to save us when the Blackfeet attacked our stagecoach," she said, her tone edged in bitterness.

More pieces to fit into the puzzle. "And what of the rest of your family?"

"When I had seen five winters, my mother journeyed to the next life."

"I am sorry. During my twelfth winter, my mother made that journey," he said, feeling her pain keenly.

"It is not easy to lose a mother," Little Brave agreed then fell silent.

The need to know more about the resilient, shorthaired woman riding beside him gnawed at him. Of course, the task of locating her family would be easier with more information. Nonchalantly as he could manage, he asked, "What about your grandfather?"

"Grandfather?" Little Brave echoed, blankness inhabiting her features.

"You mentioned him earlier," Beech reminded gently.

Beech was not surprised when impassivity slipped over her face and she urged her mare into a canter. He'd gambled in asking about the man who'd failed to rescue her. Beech cantered his horse until he caught up, leaving off his questioning for now, knowing Little Brave was not the only source of information. Forts always kept records of search-and-rescue attempts.

As they approached the fort from the north, he spied the flood plain of the North Platte River teeming with unexpected military activity. The fort, perched on a bluff well beyond this white-tented encampment, appeared abnormally quiet and peaceful in comparison. Beech wondered if the staging of these extra troops had anything to do with President Grant's orders to move all Indians to the reservations.

On the outskirts of the camp, Little Brave lifted her chin and squared her shoulders, but the soldiers paid them little attention as they wove their way through the many campfires, tents and horses.

Tents gave way to the more permanent wooded structures of Hog Ranch. Even still the settlement was little more than a shantytown. These towns sprung up near every fort to take advantage of the boredom and monotony of a soldier's day-to-day existence. These rough and tumble towns provided for the indulgences of drinking, gambling and womanizing when the soldiers were not engaged in battle or military exercises. Ever vigilant when Beech passed through this squalid area, he watched every hint of movement. Sometimes, drunken soldiers broke that monotony by picking a fight. Long, hard experience had taught him he was a prime target and would be even more so now a woman rode beside him.

They gained the bank of the river without incident, and Beech heaved a sigh of relief. He dismounted and led August onto the makeshift log raft that served as a ferry between Hog Ranch and the fort.

Little Brave tried to lead her mare onto the raft, but the palomino dug her hooves into the soft sand lining the river's edge and balked, her eyes rolling back to show their whites. Little Brave eased her pressure on the reins and clucked to the frightened horse. Patiently, she let the mare approach the raft at her own pace. The mare lowered her head in exploration and snorted her distrust of the bobbing craft. That's when August gave a low nicker of encouragement.

Beech patted the gelding's neck. "Well said, boy."

"See, Sundance, Big Black has no fear of this boat." Little Brave backed slowly toward the raft, keeping a steady pressure on the reins. Sundance tentatively put a hoof onto the raft then another. Behind the mare, the paint gave an impatient toss of his head, August nickered again, and Little Brave cooed her encouragement.

With a tuck of her haunches, the little mare launched herself onto the raft as if its edge were the bared teeth of a mountain lion. The raft bobbed wildly at the impact, the mare squealing her fright.

But Little Brave kept up an even, low-voiced monologue of reassurance while she tugged at the reins of the paint to get him aboard, too. With August's continued nickers and Little Brave's murmured coos, the mare settled as they pushed off.

Beech felt a surge of pride at Little Brave's handling of the situation. Her actions were no different than he would have done.

Disembarking from the raft on the opposite shore, they snaked their way through the bluffs, along a path that led up to Fort Fetterman. Atop the plateau, a quadrangle of mostly low, dirt-roofed log cabins enclosed the parade ground. The officers' quarters, while also constructed of logs, were shingled and much grander with a porch that ran their length.

Beech headed for the largest of these quarters, which was situated at the far end of the parade ground. Built of the straightest logs and boasting two entry doors flanked with side panels inset with glass, the building housed the commanding officer.

Leaving the horses tethered to a hitching post in front of the quarters, Beech and Little Brave entered through the door that put them into the anteroom to the commander's office.

Little Brave's eyes roamed the room, but as usual she did not comment.

"Sit here while I speak to the commander," Beech instructed, leading her to a chair against the wall.

"Then I will speak to the commander." It was not a question but a reminder that she had complaints to lodge against the United States military.

"Yes, you will speak to the commander next," Beech said, struggling to ignore another twinge of guilt at the fact the commander would most likely not want to hear about her Lakota family. Her white family, yes, but not the people who had been her family on the high plains.

Reassured, she perched on the edge of the chair, her back taking on the customary erectness of the Plains People when they sat cross-legged on the floor.

As Beech approached the commander's office, he couldn't help but overhear the imperious words coming from its interior. "Commander, General Crook wants any and all information you have gathered about hostiles in this area, immediately."

Two men approached the half-open door; Beech recognized the commander of the fort, but not the other man whose insignias on his uniform marked him as lower in rank than Commander Heisenberg. That explained the disgruntled look on the commander's face. Military men were rigid in receiving the respect that rank brought them. Either the lower-ranking soldier cared little for the future of his military career, or something—or someone—had given him the audacity to speak above his rank. Beech steeled himself for a dressing down of the junior officer, looking over to Little Brave who waited patiently, but watched avidly from her perch upon the hard, wooden chair.

Through gritted teeth the commander said, "I will have the information to General Crook as quickly as possible."

The commander's strained tone told Beech General Crook was the 'someone' behind the soldier's impertinence with his superior.

Commander Heisenberg turned his ire on Beech as the soldier swaggered away. "What do you want?"

"I am Beech Richoux...the scout who went out with Captain Baldwin and his men."

Relief broke across the man's face. "Hell's bells, that's just the sort of news I need right about now." Then the disgruntlement returned in tenfold. "Where is that rotten, disobeying scoundrel? When I get done debriefing him, I'll slap him in the stockade for that low-down dirty trick he pulled."

Beech wondered at the trick the commander of the ill-fated expedition had pulled, but he pushed aside his curiosity, gesturing to the privacy of the office beyond them. "They did not return with me."

Commander Heisenberg paused, ignoring the subtle request to retire to his office. He suspiciously eyed the arrow hole in Beech's tunic. "What happened to you, Richoux?"

"Lakota arrow."

"You're back because you're wounded?" the commander said, a little disbelievingly. "You left my men without a guide?"

Obviously it wasn't occurring to the commander that his men were no more. "I will speak of the matter in your office."

The commander glanced around the anteroom, his gaze alighting on Little Brave.

No doubt, she was a contradiction. Clad in a buckskin dress with indecently short hair, the rich russet hue of her hair and the delicate features of her face clearly marked her as a white woman.

Commander Heisenberg grunted something unintelligible then turned on his heel and strode into his office.

Beech followed, closing the door behind himself, unconcerned with impropriety of his status as civilian, let alone a half-breed, at taking such a liberty. His main concern was the woman unwittingly caught in the no-man's-land of straddling two worlds be shielded for as long as possible from the slighting, the name-calling, the disdain, but most of all, from the gazes that passed right through one as if they didn't exist.

-*-*-

Once the door closed behind Beech, Little Brave took stock of the items which held such startling familiarity, but whose names she struggled to recall. A flat surface, held up by four legs, at which one sat for eating or, in this case, for inscribing words upon those impossibly thin white skins. Once upon a time, she had known how to make the symbols, which formed the white man's words. She still knew some of the shapes and sounds of those symbols, like 'E' and 'L' and 'H'. But many more she'd forgotten.

Saying the white man's words came easier. Already, she knew the name for the bitter drink the white man was so fond of: 'coffee'. Others were returning because she heard them constantly like 'horse' and 'water' and 'man'. Still, they were not enough for her to understand the conversation between the commander of the fort and Beech when his door had been open. However, she understood the thoughts and feelings one spoke with one's body. That was a skill she'd been taught well, living among the Plains People. And the look that the commander had given her from across the room had been obvious in its message.

Although the feeling in his look was all but absent among the Plains People, she recalled it from people who were around her when her white mother had left for the next world, and when her father had told them she would travel with him to this land. Suddenly, Little Brave's heart thumped like sparrow's heart when cunning coyote has snared her. People looked in that sorrowing way at you because deep down they are relieved it is you and not they who are destined to become coyote's meal. With new eyes, Little Brave looked at the four walls surrounding her, at the door between her and the wide, open plains. She leapt to her feet. She did not intend to become a meal for coyote.

Halfway to her freedom, the door, through which Beech and the commander had disappeared, opened. The scout came through it, startled at seeing her fleeing. He held up a hand, saying, "You have to speak to the commander."

The commander followed and Little Brave banished all emotion from her face, mimicking the regal posture of Grey Owl when he addressed their people. Beech was right. She must speak for her people.

She waited for the military man to come to her, to hear her words, but he did not come.

Instead, he picked up a stack of those skins, which were bound on top and bottom, and at one long edge with a material as straight and stiff as planked wood. He parted it and thumbed through the skins, each one crinkling like that of stepping upon dry, brittle grass, except sharper, crisper. Locating a particular skin, he traced his finger along it, murmuring white man's words as it went.

The first word she heard that she recognized was 'Ella.' But it was the next, 'Russell,' which stole her breath and stopped her heart in its tracks.

Coyote had indeed snared her.

Chapter 8

With some terse words, the commander thrust the bound stack into Beech's hands and hurried out the door without a glance at Little Brave.

She stared at the item in the scout's hands. Its words held not only her name, but the name of her grandfather too. Why would their names be inscribed on a white man's skin? Perhaps, it was like her people's winter count robe where an event for each year was drawn so one year could be distinguished from another.

Beech scanned the skin himself then closed the stack, his thumb holding the place, where her name dwelt. "Do you know a Captain Colonel Jonathan Russell?"

At the name she hadn't heard from another's lips in ten winters, Little Brave jerked up her gaze. Coldness like that of first winter's storm enveloped her. "He is … he is my grandfather." She did not understand the happiness that shone in Beech's face.

Then he said, "Your grandfather has been looking for you."

Now, bitterness battled with the coldness. "And yet in ten winters, he did not manage to find me."

His face shifted from happiness to surprise. "Finding you was difficult. Soon after you were captured, the Powder River Country was closed to the white man and all forts were abandoned."

"White traders came to our village."

"A white man traveling alone, with goods to offer, is different from a white man traveling with many soldiers, seeking to take what the Plains People consider their own."

"You have seen first-hand why it is dangerous to allow such white men to find our villages."

"Then maybe that is the reason your grandfather could not find you."

The coldness shafted deep into her heart. She knew the reason her grandfather had not found her. It had plagued her throughout the night as she'd kept vigil over Grey Owl. Now she would speak the truth to Beech, and he would know. Then he would cease his questions about a grandfather who did not want her. She grasped at the indifference that would mask the hurt. Cloaking it about her, she straightened her spine and lifted her chin. "The reason my grandfather could not find me is he did not want to find me."

Beech flipped open the skins to the place where his thumb was lodged. "That is not what these words say." He angled them so she could see the symbols etched there, his finger tracking along the words as if they spoke to her as they spoke to him. "He has made inquiries every year since your capture, and twice, he came to participate in the search party."

"Hiyee," she said with a flip of her hand. "White men say one thing, but then they do another." But her heart jumped as sparrow's would if she saw an opening in coyote's teeth through which she might escape.

Slowly, the scout closed the skins and regarded her with a puzzled look.

Boots thudded on the porch outside, and they both looked to the harried commander who came through the door with one of the Plains People behind him. The commander spoke, making hurried introductions between Beech and the man whose tunic caught Little Brave's attention.

The tunic's intricate beadwork with its heavy use of blues and pinks marked it as the work of the Crow. Its beauty made her ache for her own beadwork lying at the bottom of the canyons. Grateful for the distraction, she ignored the conversation among the men as she studied the workmanship of a sun resting upon the horizon. The accents of yellow, rather than red, told her it was a rising, not a setting sun—a scene fit for a man who had no more lines in his face than did Beech. Suddenly, Little Brave realized the room was silent, the commander was gone and the man with the beautiful tunic looked at her expectantly.

"He says his sister beaded his tunic." Beech informed her.

Little Brave gathered her thoughts, which had scattered like Prairie Hen's chicks. "Tell him, I would like to bead as skillfully and beautifully as his sister,"

The man did not hide his surprise that she replied in a tongue of the Plains People, instead of the white man's tongue. "I am Speaks To Many," he continued in the white man's tongue while Beech continued to translate. "My people live far from here, near the beginning of the Elk River."

"Ah." She nodded in understanding. Elk River country was the homeland of the Crow. "You are far from your home."

"I've come to aid the white man's mighty General Crook in his search for our enemies. Many more winters than I have seen, many more than my father and my grandfather have seen, they have raided our villages, capturing and killing my people, stealing our horses. My brother was killed during the last raid."

116

Little Brave could not help but speak to the pain and sorrow in the eyes of Speaks To Many. "My father was killed by a warrior's arrow."

"Perhaps, I will meet this warrior in battle then I can avenge your father's death, too," he said, with a mighty thump of a fist to his chest.

Little Brave did not doubt that Speaks to Many might meet Running Bear or the warrior who had killed her white father, for both the Lakota and the Blackfeet were enemies of the Crow.

As a woman living in Grey Owl's band, she had been shielded from the raiding behavior of the braves, and she'd distanced herself from the enthusiastic celebrating that had occurred when the warriors returned with captives and horses. With extreme distaste, she recalled Running Bear tended to return with scalps, rather than captives. A shiver shuddered down her spine at his reasoning for taking scalps over captives. "They require no food," he'd said. Yet another point over which the bloodthirsty warrior and Grey Owl had disagreed. If raiding must be done, Grey Owl favored counting coup over taking captives and certainly over taking scalps.

The desire to avenge both her fathers' deaths battled with her fear for the safety of Grey Owl's people if the mighty general found them. She found it tied her tongue and she could not encourage or discourage Speaks To Many either way. Instead, all she could offer was, "I hope your journey gives you peace and you return safely to your home."

An admiring light chased the vengeance from Speaks To Many's face as Beech conveyed her sentiments. Speaks To Many stood taller, not as a man going into battle, but as a man presenting himself to a woman who has caught his eye. His next words were sincere and true, but Beech did not translate them. Instead, he positioned himself between

Little Brave and the Crow, speaking firmly to the warrior who was a little shorter than he, but certainly no less built for battle.

Little Brave sidestepped the broad shoulders blocking her view, in time to see Speaks To Many hold up three fingers. She recognized the words 'horses' and 'woman'. The man's intent was clear. He was offering for her. Braves did not offer for her. They had not wanted to go up against Running Bear. Warmth at the unfamiliar but flattering attention spread up her neck and across her cheeks. That warmth turned to heated irritation when Beech stepped toe to toe with her would-be suitor, staring him down, and growled a response that included, much to her surprise, the words 'my' and 'woman'.

The Crow retreated a step then another. He looked at Little Brave, his face as void as the wastelands in which her people had abandoned her. He gestured to the belt she wore, the one with the two buffalos and said some parting words whose sincerity she did not doubt. Then he turned and left.

"What did Speaks To Many say to me before you sent him away?" Little Brave demanded.

"He said you would have much to teach his sister about quill work," said Beech, his fierce stare not wavering from the Crow as the man cleared the steps and worked his way across the parade ground.

Disappointment washed over her at the lost opportunity of working with one so skilled in such an intricate craft. Then pangs of sadness followed as many memories of she and Nimble Fingers working together on their beading overwhelmed her. The sense of loss was staggering, and she grabbed at her anger to chase it away. "You had no right to speak for me with Speaks To Many."

"He would not have made you a good husband."

His authority, brandished with such ease, fed her anger until it rivaled that of buffalo whose hide had been pierced with many arrows. "You do not choose for me. I choose for me. Grey Owl made it so before he died."

"The choice would not have been wise."

"You do know what is wise for me." Her voice shook in her fury, she stamped her moccasin-clad foot, which thudded disappointingly soft against the wooden floor.

Beech grabbed her arm, anger sharpening his features. A determined light leapt to life in his eyes as he marched her out the door and across the parade grounds.

She struggled against his vise-like hold, but her struggles were fruitless.

He stopped at the edge of the bluff which overlooked the river and the plain that stretched beyond it. "How many handfuls of men do you see?" her captor asked, the fury rumbling like thunder from deep within his chest.

Its sound both surprised and awed her as she stared at him.

"Look there, not at me." He gave her arm a shake to focus her attention on the scene below them.

Reluctantly, Little Brave forced her attention from the harsh, angry angles of the scout's profile, and his gleaming dark hair whipping in the breeze, to survey the plain, littered with tents no larger than dots, and teeming with ant-sized soldiers. "I see many more handfuls than moons in a winter."

"Over a thousand soldiers are down there."

"A thousand," Little Brave repeated the word, which was quickly making itself known to her again.

-*-*-

Beech's emotions were like mighty thunderheads rolling across the prairie, dark and unstoppable. Nothing in this visit to the fort had worked out as he'd planned. From

119

Little Brave balking at the news her grandfather had been looking for her, to the ill-timed offer of Speaks To Many to make her his wife, to the thousand soldiers camped on the plains before them. He had to make Little Brave understand that Captain Baldwin's effort to move Grey Owl's people to the reservation was only one blade of grass in a whole prairie of efforts. "Do you know why these soldiers are here?" He thundered on without giving her a chance to answer. "They are here to move all the Plains People in the Powder River Country to the reservation."

"They will not be able to move them if they cannot find them," Little Brave said defiantly.

"Speaks To Many and others like him will track them down. And two more armies are marching to help this army. One comes from where the sun rises, and the other from where the sun sets."

A movement far below them at the base of the bluffs caught Beech's eye. It was the Crow scout who'd asked for Little Brave. Small and insignificant now, Speaks To Many hopped aboard the ferry. Beech silently cursed himself for the overbearing way he'd acted toward the man, who'd only been sincere and true in his regard toward Little Brave.

"It is told around our campfires how my people came to this land long ago. They drove away the Crow, forced them to make new homes upon the Elk River." She looked at him, her eyes full of sorrowful understanding. "It will be that way between the white man and my people."

"It will be, when the white man wins this war." The agony in her eyes over the heartwrenching outcome for her people mirrored that raging in his soul. She was the one person in his two worlds who could understand and share this with him, help fill the emptiness and frustration, but the time had come for him to leave and time for her to focus on rediscovering Ella Hastings and reuniting with her grandfather. Now he would concentrate on putting her out of

120

his mind, this woman, who stirred emotions better left untouched, out of his heart. Wearily, he turned and headed back to the officer's quarters.

Little Brave walked sedately beside him. When they arrived, she said, "Who will you fight for?"

"I will fight for no one."

Her hand caught at the russet strands lashing her face and pushed them aside as that pucker appeared between her brows. "You will fight for no one because you cannot decide between your mother's people and your father's people?"

"I fight for no one because no one fights for me." The admission was discharged even before Beech thought it. He gritted his teeth to keep from revealing more. Damn the emotions that were determined to have their say.

Little Brave clutched at his wrist. "I will fight for you, Beech Richoux."

He shook his head, forcing himself to ignore the warmth of her fingers against his skin. She *would* fight for him, if that's the path she chose. She would fight the way she'd fought for Grey Owl and her people. With intelligence, tenacity and spirit.

"You think I will not fight for you," she said.

He looked to the sky to hide the longing in his gaze. He would give anything to have her by his side, everyday, fighting for him, for them. The battle would be a losing one in the white man's world—one he could not allow her to choose. With a concentrated effort, he blanked his features and faced the determination in her gaze. "I know you would, but it is not your path."

She opened her mouth to say something.

But the commander appeared in the doorway. "In my office, Richoux!"

A flash of pain crossed her face as she dropped his wrist so he could go meet with the commander. Beech entered the office, leaving the door open this time to keep an eye on Little Brave who stood outside on the porch.

"I need you to accompany the convoy to the canyons," the commander rapped out.

"I have told Speaks To Many how to get there."

"But he does not speak Lakota."

"He has returned to the soldiers' camp to find someone who does."

"Dammit, Richoux, with the loss of Baldwin and his detachment, I'm short of men."

"I am not an undertaker." Beech glanced through the open doors. There was no sign of Little Brave, but Sundance was still tethered to the hitching post.

The commander huffed at the blunt comment. "You feel no remorse for guiding those soldiers into the canyon, do you?"

"As I have said, Captain Baldwin chose to ride through the canyons against my advice."

Knuckling his fists on the desk, the commander leaned across it. "And as I have said, if I find the slightest shred of evidence otherwise, you'll pay."

The commander's soured breath blew heated and heavy across Beech's skin. He widened his stance, folding his arms over his chest. "I am a civilian. The military has no authority over civilians."

"Not directly, but the military can file charges in a civilian court." The commander's eyes gleamed as he added. "Against a civilian."

Beech held his ground and his silence. He would not put it past the military man to do such a thing, but with the three armies marching against the Lakota and the Cheyenne, his bets were that this particular incident would soon become the least of the commander's concerns.

Muttering an oath, the commander dropped into his chair, wrenched open a drawer and clinked some coins down onto the desk. "Here's what's owed you."

Beech did not reach across the desk to take the money. "You are still paying me?"

"I'm no cheat, Richoux." The commander slid the coins across the desk.

"I have your word that Lit—Ella Hastings will be looked after until her grandfather comes for her?"

"My wife is looking forward to the female companionship, and just as soon as my aide returns, I'll dictate a telegram to the woman's grandfather."

Beech reached for the coins but he paused, his fingers flat against the money as the commander leaned back in his chair, his head tilted in speculation.

"A trapper, named Richoux, helped out some of my men caught in a snowstorm this past winter. Any relation to you?"

Beech's gut tightened. "Why?"

The commander shifted, and the chair squealed alarmingly. "Something about you reminds me of him."

Beech slid the money off the desk, grappling with the memory of the last time he'd seen Jean Luc Richoux—a shell of the strong and capable man he'd loved and admired. Averse to hearing anything about that man, Beech shrugged. "Doubt it."

"Reckon you're right. Those French trappers were as plentiful as the Injuns until we shut down their fur trade. Once we get the last of the Injuns moved onto the reservations, then this land will be fit for decent folks."

The anger sparked to life at the slur against both of his lineages. He held it in check by concentrating on stowing the coins in the pouch at his waist. He turned to see Little Brave standing in the doorway, her eyebrows raised.

The commander looked to Beech. "What does she want?"

Of course, Little Brave would not forget her resolution to speak of the mistreatment of Grey Owl's band.

"She wants to speak to you about the band of Lakota that she lived with."

The commander held up five fingers saying, "I have five minutes."

Little Brave nodded her understanding then entered the office. She halted before the commander's desk, standing as regally as befitted a chief's daughter.

First she spoke then Beech mimicked her eloquent cadence as he translated.

"I am Little Brave, adopted daughter of Chief Grey Owl of the Lakota." She held up four fingers on each hand. "For eight winters Grey Owl's people gave me a home. They became my people. They are a good people."

Beech wondered about where she'd spent the first two winters after she'd been captured, but he did not interrupt her. She dropped her hands and held them against the beaded buffalo on her belt. She fixed her gaze resolutely on the commander. "Your soldiers did not treat my people well."

"Richoux told me these people were not going peacefully with the soldiers."

Beech clenched his jaw at the conspiratorial glance the commander gave him, but he was proud when Little Brave did not allow the innuendo of whose side he'd been on distract her from her objective.

"Peace cannot exist when one is forced from their home," she said.

With the loftiness that all military men gained when they spoke of the former General Grant, the commander said, "The Great White Father has set aside another land for your people."

"My people do not wish to leave the land the white man gave them through their treaty with Red Cloud."

Commander Heisenberg gave an annoyed snort at the mention of the broken treaty. "Richoux, didn't you explain President Grant's reasons to—?" He gestured impatiently at the woman whose Anglo features were at odds with her Lakota dress and mannerisms.

"Her name is Little Brave," Beech said.

"She is a white woman, Richoux," Commander Heisenberg said, slapping his palms against the desk. "The sooner she starts thinking like one again, the better off she'll be." He pointed a finger at Little Brave. "Your name is Ella Hastings."

Little Brave shook her head, her hair swinging vigorously across her face. She clapped a hand over her heart, carefully forming the English words, "I am Little Brave."

"It doesn't matter what they called you. Soon, we'll have all of them confined on the reservation where they'll be tamed out of their savage ways, or they'll go the way of the buffalo."

Beech floundered a moment at how to take the sting out of the commander's words. Finally, he said, "Change will be necessary in order to survive."

"The white man must change, too," she countered.

"I don't have time—" The commander abruptly switched his tenor from combative to welcoming as he stood. "Ah, Mrs. Heisenberg, you've arrived at the perfect moment."

The commander's wife came through the door with an authoritative rustle of skirts.

"This is the woman I was telling you about." Commander Heisenberg swept an arm magnanimously toward Little Brave. "Her grandfather will be coming for her soon and will be wanting to see a presentable young lady, not a savage fresh off the prairie."

Beech did not translate the savage portion of the statement, but Little Brave set her shoulders and pressed her lips together. Whether she objected to being rendered presentable or she understood the savage comment he hadn't translated or both, he didn't know.

Mrs. Heisenberg sniffed in agreement with her husband's assessments and approached Little Brave, gingerly putting an arm about her shoulders. "Come now, Ella," she said. "We'll have you presentable in no time." She turned Little Brave away.

Little Brave glanced wildly back at Beech.

The realization hit with a jolt that, through all the danger and heartbreak she'd endured since the soldiers had arrived in her village, this was the first sign of panic he'd seen from her. "She will help you, Little Brave," he murmured as way of encouragement, but his heart was not true when he said it.

His lack of heart must have given her conviction for Little Brave planted her feet and spun. "No. I go...with Beech," she said in halting English.

"Now, now, that man is an Indian. You can't go with him," Mrs. Heisenberg said, reaching for Little Brave again.

Little Brave ducked the corralling arm to stand next to Beech. "I am woman of Beech Richoux."

Mrs. Heisenberg fluttered her fingers to her throat as she gave an affronted gasp. "Is this true, Mr. Heisenberg?"

"Is this true, Richoux?" the commander asked, conveniently dodging blame for his wife's offended sensibilities.

"Lit—Ella Hastings is not my woman." Beech coughed to dislodge the words that stuck in his throat. The statement was true. She was not his. And she could never be his. Regardless of how much he might wish it so. However much she might wish it so now, once she returned to the white man's world, her desires would change. Then she would be relieved she had not become a half-breed's woman.

126

Little Brave continued in her slow English. "Not true." She gestured to the Crow scout who now stood in the doorway. "Speaks To Many knows."

And Trickster Coyote yipped his delight at the trap Beech's arrogant tongue had set.

Chapter 9

"What do you know?" demanded Commander Heisenberg of Speaks To Many.

Speaks To Many glanced neither right nor left as he said, "I only came to say I have found someone who speaks Lakota."

"Yes, yes, good, good." The commander waved impatiently. "But what do you know about the relationship between this woman and Richoux?"

Speaks to Many glanced to Little Brave then his eyes narrowed as they settled on the man standing beside her. "Richoux told me earlier today that Little Brave is his woman."

"It was a slip of the tongue," Beech said, willing his features to blandness lest they reveal his true feelings for Little Brave.

"Among the Plains People, saying it makes it so," Speaks To Many said, challenge burning in his eyes. "You dishonor Little Brave by not being true to your word."

Beech cursed the predicament in which his dual heritage had placed him.

Mrs. Heisenberg backed away from Little Brave. "Mr. Heisenberg, you did not tell me I would be taking in a woman who had been intimate with an Indian."

"For pity sake's, Myra, what did you expect after ten years with these people?" the commander snapped. "She's probably been intimate with ten Indians."

Mrs. Heisenberg gave a strangled cry, her eyes widening.

Beech fisted his hands but held them at bay by his thighs. For Little Brave's sake, he willed his tongue, not his fists, to repair the quagmire of misunderstandings. "Little Brave has taken no husband among the Lakota," he gritted through clenched teeth. His chest constricted in pain as he looked at the woman, who now stared resolutely ahead as if she had not been all but called a whore by the commander, disdained by the commander's wife and dishonored by his own rejection.

"No matter," Mrs. Heisenberg huffed. "I would be ignoring my Christian duty if I did not attempt to reform one who's been led astray."

Led astray? Beech could no longer hold his ire in check. "Little Brave adapted to ways that were not her own in order to survive. She does not need to be reformed; she needs time to find her way again in the white man's world." How long had he taken to find his way in the white man's world? Much, much longer than these people would ever give her. He gazed at her proud profile. How long before they wiped that pride from her face, made her ashamed for who she had become in order to survive? With his gut twisting in pain at the memories of his own struggles flashing across his mind, he rasped, "I will take her with me to give her the time she needs."

Little Brave's gaze darted worriedly between himself and the commander as the military man pointed at her, sputtering, "You cannot take this woman. She is a white woman, and I have an obligation to see that she's appropriately chaperoned until her grandfather comes for her."

"Tell her grandfather that she will be living with my aunt and uncle in Cheyenne."

"She must reside with respectable white people," said Mrs. Heisenberg, moving behind the desk to join ranks with her husband.

"Mrs. Heisenberg is entirely correct."

Beech palmed the desk, leaning towards the woman whose prettily trimmed, well-tailored dress and glittering ear bobs expressed her penchant for finer things not readily available at the fort's trading post. "Have you ever shopped at Chapman's Mercantile in Cheyenne, Mrs. Heisenberg?"

Mrs. Heisenberg blinked in surprise.

The commander stepped in front of his wife. "How dare you address my wife directly?"

Understanding clicked in Mrs. Heisenberg's eyes as she stepped around her husband. She laid a soothing hand on his arm. "Mr. Heisenberg, I think it would behoove us to find out more about these relations of Mr. Richoux." She returned her attention to Beech. "As a matter of fact I have, when Mr. Heisenberg was stationed at Fort Laramie. It's the largest, best-stocked store in the territory."

"The proprietor is my uncle."

"Henry Chapman is your uncle?" asked the commander.

"His wife is my father's sister." Beech had never before used his aunt and uncle's status as respectable citizens or his uncle's prominence as a leading businessman to his advantage. Doing so now was alien and it rankled, being beholden to anyone, let alone a white man, but using their status was to help Little Brave, not himself.

"With the railroad going through Cheyenne, traveling there instead of here will be easier for Captain Colonel Russell," Commander Heisenberg conceded. He patted his wife's hand indulgently. "And Mrs. Heisenberg and I can make arrangements to be there when he arrives."

Ella's Choice

Little Brave knew the argument had been decided by the small but self-satisfied smile that lurked on the lips of the commander's woman. Her heart beat like sparrow's. Would she stay with the white, military man and his wife, or would she go with Beech? Her breath caught and held until Beech's hand settled at her back.

"We need to leave now if we are to make the Laramie Mountains before dark."

His deep voice rumbled, but her feet remained rooted in shock. After his denial that she was his woman, she had not expected she would be going with him. His hand pressed more firmly at her back, his expression unreadable, his head tilting in the direction of the door. She did not pause to question his change of heart, eager as she was to escape this place where a thousand white men gathered to impose their will and ways on the Plains People.

Swiftly, she moved through the officer's quarters, her feet making little sound against the wooden floor. Outside, she mounted Sundance and gathered the reins of the paint.

Speaks To Many followed them. Straight and tall, he stood on the porch watching her, his gleaming, dark eyes reminiscent of the people lost to her.

She raised a hand in farewell then followed Beech and his black gelding beyond the wooden structure that marked the edge of the fort. Now, she could no longer contain her curiosity over the change in his decision. "Why do you take me with you now when you would not before?"

"The commander and his woman were not willing to give you time to find your way in the white man's world."

"How much time will it take?"

131

"I do not know how it will be for you, but—" His fingers fisted around the reins as he expelled a harsh sigh. "But for me, the time was very long."

Little Brave was surprised at this. "But Grey Owl said your mother left the Plains People with your father many, many winters ago." With his mastery of both of his worlds, she'd assumed he'd always lived in the white man's world.

"That is true."

The creaking of leather and the plodding of hoof beats filled the air between them. The lazy rhythm did nothing to ease her curiosity. "Where did you live if not among the white man?"

"In the mountains."

He settled deeper into the saddle, his gaze locking onto the wide, open plains that stretched to the horizon and beyond—stretched to the mountains.

"These mountains that we ride to are your home?"

"Yes—no." He took a deep breath then closed his eyes.

She wondered what it was he was seeing inside his mind.

Suddenly, he opened his eyes, and his jaw muscle flexed. "They were my home a very long time ago."

"But it is a home that you have not forgotten."

He looked at her then, his eyes blazing, his lips twisting in pain. "Have you forgotten the home you had before you came to live among the Plains People?"

"Homes," she said.

"Homes?"

"My mother and I followed my father from fort to fort. It made her very unhappy." She had not meant to speak of her past, but perhaps it would help him speak of his. "Was your home unhappy?"

His eyes softened, the twist eased from his mouth. "Not while my mother lived."

132

"And now your father lives there all alone?"

He returned his gaze to the horizon. "I do not know where my father lives."

"He left and did not tell you where he was going?"

With a disdainful snort, he said something in the white man's tongue she did not understand, but she understood the emotion, even shared it. Had not her grandfather left her?

She legged Sundance closer to Big Black, her knee brushing Beech's calf.

He glanced sharply at her, the harsh line of his mouth echoing the intense pain in his eyes.

Her chest tightened in pain for him and she put a hand on his thigh. The muscles bunched beneath her fingers then were gone. Her hand fell back to her side as he kneed Big Black away.

"It was a very long time ago," he scoffed.

"Still, my heart is grateful that you take me there so I can have time to find my way," she said softly, hoping he would accept her sympathy through her thanks.

"It is but a stop on our journey to Cheyenne."

"Cheyenne?" She'd heard this word during the argument and knew it as a nation of the Plains People, but not as a destination.

"The town is where my aunt and uncle live. You will find your way while you stay with them."

She would not stay with Beech? Sweat slicked her palms, making the reins slippery in her grasp. She tightened her hold. He brought her with him just to pass her off? Her stomach churned. What type of people were his aunt and uncle? Were they like him, or like the military man and his woman? She struggled against the knot of anxiety filling her throat. "I do not know your aunt and uncle."

"You would rather stay with the commander and his woman at the fort?" He twisted in his saddle, pointing back to the dirt and wood structures that had yet to disappear from the horizon. "We have not gone so far that we cannot turn around."

Hiyee! The scout would not return her to the fort, would he? She was not so sure as his features tightened, his eyebrows flattening as his mouth slashed angrily across his face.

"I do not want to return to the fort." she said then urged Sundance into a canter.

The big black gelding snorted his dismay at being left behind, but she did not concern herself with him or his master as she bent over the little mare's neck. She inhaled deeply, reveling in the freeness she felt. The freedom was only momentary though as her mind returned to the questions that plagued her about the future.

In coming with Beech, had she merely traded one captivity for another? Would his aunt and uncle be any less determined than the commander and his woman for her to become Ella Hastings again? And what of her grandfather? The white men's skins said he had tried to find her. Memories of her grandfather were only shadowy fragments, but they were laced with a strong sense of a man who believed his way right in all things. If he had not approved of her coming West with her father, he would certainly not approve of who she was now. Could she find her way in the white man's world enough to please him? Could she be happy in the white man's world? She certainly did not remember women riding astride as she did now. In an instant, the sensation of freedom evaporated replaced by an all-consuming desire to flee.

She bent closer to Sundance's neck, urging the little mare to go faster. The ground blurred to a river of green and brown rushing beneath them, the grass lashing angrily against the mustang's legs, the pounding of the hooves echoing the drumming of her heart.

Her fleeing was short-lived as the little mare's head jerked to the right and she slowed considerably.

Beech's hand fisted around the reins. His face had not lost its angry cast and only continued to darken as the horses slowed to a walk. "Are you crazy?" His words rumbled out like thunder rolling across the prairie.

"You dare to call *me* crazy?" She jerked to regain control of her reins, but he held fast.

"Damn right, I will call you crazy, heading toward that gully at the speed you were."

She glanced ahead at the jagged line of earth that had been eaten away by wind and water. He was right. She'd been too lost in her own worries to notice the danger only a few strides away. A plunge down a bank that steep, bent over Sundance's neck like she had been, would have sent them careening head over heels, possibly injuring if not killing them.

Her breath came weak and wobbly, her heart striking against her chest in disbelief of what could have happened. But it was true. One did not last long out here in this wild, untamed land acting rashly and emotionally. If there was anything she'd learned during her time with the Plains People, it was that. Her shoulders slumped. "If I had not been following my emotions, I would have seen the danger." She let her hands go slack against the reins as they came to a stop.

"It is to be expected."

"Expected?" she asked, confusion filling her at what he was talking about.

"To react rashly when one's life is not only turned upside down but inside out."

She squeezed her eyes shut against the tears that threatened. He did understand, and suddenly, she realized how he understood. "You learned the white man's way with

135

your aunt and uncle." She drew a shaky breath and met his eyes. "After your father left."

Pain flashed across his face then was replaced by the unreadability of the Plains People. "Yes, but the time was not easy or happy for me." He handed her reins back.

"But why did you not go with him? You had seen twelve winters." She assumed this had been after his mother had journeyed to the next life. Twelve winters was more than old enough to be a help to a father and not a hindrance.

"I promised him I would stay."

"But why?"

"Because…" He inhaled sharply, his thumb grinding against the weave of the reins. "The reason why no longer matters."

But the roughness of his tone told her it did. Before she could think of what to say to encourage him to speak more, he turned to look at her.

"We need to cover some ground if we are to reach the mountains before dark." Then he urged Big Black over the edge of the bank.

They rode hard until the mountains became a presence looming before them. He gestured to the stream ahead as they slowed. "This will be the last place to water the horses before we ride into the mountains."

After they'd drunk their fill of cold, mountain water, they remounted and crossed the stream. Their climb began, gradual at first, but their pace slowed, their horses reaching for every step as the steepness increased.

It was then she heard his question, "How did you get your name, Little Brave?"

He rode ahead of her on the narrow trail but a bend brought his profile into view. His gaze was intent on their surroundings, but otherwise, his features were at ease. Still, he did not seem the type to pass the time in idle conversation.

"Why do you want to know?"

"I am curious. The Plains People only choose names that mean something. I want to know why the name Little Brave was chosen for you."

It was true. The day Grey Owl had given her name had been a very significant one, the turning point in her sojourn among the Plains People. But the scout had used the white man's name for her to find her grandfather. Her stomach churned at the thought of facing a man who thought her worthless. Suddenly, she realized the scout could use something she told him in her name-giving tale for a similar reason. "How do I know you will not use what I tell you against me?"

"Against you?" His eyebrows rose high above his eyes.

"You found my grandfather because I told you the white man's name for me."

He grunted something unintelligible but then nodded. "You are right; I did. Next time, I will ask you before I use knowledge in such a way."

She felt better that he did not deny it, but even with his assurance, she had her doubts. It must have shown in her face.

When he looked back at her, he said, "I give you my word."

She did not like that he could read her thoughts so easily. "I do not trust your word. One minute you say I am your woman, the next you say I am not. Which words are true?"

He grimaced, leaning forward to ease his weight off Big Black as the gelding navigated a particularly steep portion of the trail. "Both times, I spoke only to protect you."

Her womanly spirits sagged at his explanation, for the emotions behind his "my woman" had seemed sincere. She remembered all the times he had spoken against

Gleaming Chest in defense of Grey Owl's people, and had come to her rescue from the commander and his wife. She had not comprehended all the words during these arguments, but each time, she could see the white man was not happy Beech knew their ways and tongue so well they could not dismiss his arguments. Only in the case of Speaks To Many had his words been unnecessary. Perhaps, he did not realize that. "I did not desire to become Speaks To Many's woman."

His jaw clenched. "You showed interest."

A smile lurked at the corners of her lips. "I wanted to learn more about his sister who beads with such skill."

He released his jaw, a long breath hissing through his lips. "Then I misunderstood." He eased back in the saddle as they reached a level place in the trail, his gaze tracking along the trail once more. "I will understand if you do not wish to share the story of your name."

It had been a proud moment when Grey Owl bestowed her with the name of Little Brave, and she wanted to remember that moment with someone who would understand, but even more, she wanted to hear the rest of his story. The story of the promise he made to his father to live a life he did not want. "If you finish your story of why you stayed in the white man's world, then I will tell you the tale of how I received my name."

"A trade?"

"Yes, a trade."

"Then the trade will be unsatisfactory for you, for there is little happiness in my story."

"There are other reasons to hear stories besides happiness. Like struggle and honor. Are there not such things in your story? A boy keeping a promise to his father even though it puts him into a world he does not wish to be in?"

Ella's Choice

Many moments passed where the only sounds were small stones crunching beneath the horses' hooves. Finally, he spoke. "The story is not easy to tell."

"Often stories that are worth hearing are hard to tell."

He nodded then with a cleansing breath, he said, "These mountains were my home. Amid a very harsh winter, my mother journeyed to the next life when my sister arrived in this one."

He paused, but Little Brave did not prod, for she well knew that tales containing such sorrow and heartbreak must be revealed in bits and pieces. But oh, a sister! How she'd longed for a sister, particularly after her mother died.

"My father was lost and full of sadness without my mother. When the snows melted, he took us to his sister and her husband. I was torn. I did not want to live in a town among people I did not know, whose ways I did not understand, but he said I must stay to watch over Grace."

Grace. She could not remember exactly what the word for his sister's name meant, but it drew pictures in her head of hawk as she swoops and sails upon the breeze.

"After I had been there a year, I went to look for my father. I could find no trace of him. And that's how my life went for many years. To honor my promise to my father, I would live with my aunt and uncle in the winter. The rest of the time, I honored the promise I made to myself to find him."

Here the trees thickened and the trail narrowed considerably. The horses strained in earnest at the steepness of the incline. Little Brave silenced the questions she longed to ask, hoping Beech had not finished his tale. The steep climb leveled out at a break in the trees.

He halted Big Black there, looking to the view that expanded before them. "When Grace had seen four winters,

139

he came. He was not the man I had known. He stayed only a few days. I have not seen him since."

She followed his gaze, over the land stretching almost endlessly before them—land full of hope and promise in its spring greenery, held in check only by the depth of the clear blue sky arched over it from horizon to horizon. How many times had he left his sister as the snow melted—full of that hope and promise that he would find their father? And returned, as the snow flurried—defeated and disappointed? She did not have an adequate word for such determination amid so many defeats. But she had a face for it—in the man beside her.

There was an arresting depth to him beyond the guide who had brought the white man's soldiers to Grey Owl's village, the interpreter who had given meaning to the white man's words, the scout who had led Grey Owl's people out of the canyon to safety and the warrior who had bested Running Bear for her life.

She wanted to crawl beneath his skin and know these depths from inside out, to learn how he balanced all these parts of himself, how he had found his place between his two worlds. But each time she chose to be with him in some way, he turned her away. The ache his rejections put into her heart joined all the other aches that dwelt there. Soon, he would leave her in Cheyenne and return to his work at the fort then she would add yet another ache to her heart.

Her eyes narrowed on the view before them, extending her gaze farther, beyond the horizon where the white man's fort lay then even further to where the buttes jutted and the hills rolled. The aches in her heart could not compare to what lie ahead for her people. The land which had been her home for the past ten winters was a vast territory with bounty for all its inhabitants, but the white man was intent on driving the Plains People from it.

Ella's Choice

What would happen to the proud, resourceful people who had been her family when the three armies of the white man met? Beech said they would be defeated. Could they find a new way of living on the reservation? She clutched at the fabric over her heart, fisting it, tugging at it. But she could no more loosen the pain and worry that dwelt in her heart for the Plains People than she could change the fact her grandfather would come for her. That she too must forget the ways of the Lakota and become Ella Hastings once more.

They resumed their ride and Little Brave dropped her gaze from the view. The trail continued to rise, the trees cutting away to magnificent panoramas along the way, but she no longer looked back to the north.

Chapter 10

Beech had never spoken of the loss of his family to anyone. Not even to Grace. Even she, like his aunt and uncle, and his cousins knew of *his* loss, but not because he'd told them. He'd only spoken of it to Little Brave to reassure her, to regain her trust, not to appease his loss, he argued—a loss which only grew in him as they traveled deeper into the mountains.

The intensity of that long-ago loss rivaled what he'd felt when the Crow had offered for Little Brave. The feeling had caused him to utter the words, "my woman". Those words continued to echo within his mind and hum beneath his skin. They settled decisively into his loins as he turned August off the main trail and onto a smaller path that would eventually take them to the meadow that had been his home for the first dozen years of his life.

He leaned back in the saddle, giving August his head, fighting the notion of making Little Brave his woman. They would stay overnight in the log cabin his father had built because doing so was practical. To skirt the mountains would only have added days to their journey. Days he did not need to spend in her company. To prevent any further rumination on the topic, he said, "Now, you must tell me how you came by your name." He glanced behind him as he spoke.

She shivered, staring off into the trees that lined the narrow path.

"If it's too painful—"

Her gaze darted back to his. "No. You have told me your tale, and now I shall tell you mine." She inhaled sharply, her eyes closing, her voice a steady monotone. "The Blackfeet killed my father. For two winters, I lived with them. It was not an easy life."

Trusting August to safely navigate the trail, Beech half turned in the saddle to keep an eye on Little Brave.

Her eyes opened, but her gaze drifted beyond him, sightless and glazed. "One day, they took me on a long journey to another village to trade. During the haggling, the warrior who had killed my father dragged me from the horse I was on and flung me to the ground."

Her fingers twisted into the palomino's mane, agitation slipping into her voice. "It was no worse than the treatment I received every day in their village, but on that day, my anger would not be caged. I leapt to my feet, intending to harm that warrior, but he was dangling a...the...the..." Struggling for the word she could not reach, Little Brave released Sundance's mane, grabbed the pouch around her neck and withdrew something.

He halted August to let the mare draw up beside him. As Little Brave opened her hand, Beech said, "A watch." He held out his hand.

"A watch," Little Brave repeated, relief evident in her tone. She placed it into his palm.

He ran a thumb over its tarnished surface as she continued.

"I had not seen it since the day my father was killed. The sight of it, in the hand of the man who killed my father, fed my anger. In turn, the anger gobbled up my fear and I—" Little Brave's hand cut through the air in a snatching motion. "'That is mine', I said." She held her clenched fist against her heart, as she must have done that day.

"If it had not been for Grey Owl's braves outnumbering the Blackfeet that day, I surely would have been killed." She lifted her chin in pride, her eyes glinting at the emotion the memory had revived. "That is when Grey Owl gave me the name Little Brave and adopted me as his daughter."

"It is a fitting name for you," Beech said.

Little Brave leaned toward him, her new scent—woman mingled with eucalyptus—filling the air around him. She pressed the release for the cover on the watch. It flipped open and Beech read the engraving aloud.

Little Brave closed her eyes and murmured the words along with him.

> *Thomas James Hastings*
> *Welcome home forever*
> *Your loving daughter,*
> *Ella*

"Your father had been away?" Beech asked.

"He fought in the war between the states."

"Did your grandfather fight in the war, too?"

"Yes," she said evenly, almost carelessly, but her face blanked, her eyes growing cold as she took the watch from his hand. Carefully, she closed its lid and restored the cherished item to its safe haven.

As if talk of her grandfather tainted the memories of her father. "Why do you not want to speak of your grandfather?"

She did not answer. Instead, she sent Sundance on her way along the path, the paint following close behind.

This was the same resistance he'd encountered when he'd showed her the evidence her grandfather had been searching for her.

Beech allowed August to bypass the paint and crowd the little mare on the narrow path. "Is your grandfather a cruel person? Did he beat you?" The blood roared through his veins, his fists clenching at the thought Little Brave might have suffered at the hands of a family member. Maybe that's why her father had brought her out West—to keep her away from such abuse.

"My grandfather did not beat me. He was not cruel in that way."

Beech released his fists, but his blood still raged, recalling all the ways adults had been cruel to him without ever laying a finger on him.

"He—" Her fingers fisted into her mare's mane again. "I am worthless in his eyes."

Worthless? "Did he tell you that?"

"I overheard him the night before I came West with my father."

"Perhaps you misunderstood."

"My ears do not lie."

The mutinous look on Little Brave's face told him she believed there could be no reasonable explanation for her grandfather's words, but Beech encouraged her to think otherwise. "You must speak of this to your grandfather when he comes."

"You believe that speaking of this cruelty will change things? You said I should speak to the commander at the fort about the mistreatment of Grey Owl's people by his soldiers, but it did no good then." She caught her breath then held it a beat before letting it out slowly. She tried to shrug but it came out as a wince as she said, "And it will do no good with my grandfather."

Beech expelled a weary breath at her determination to believe the worst of her grandfather. Like finding her way in the white man's world and becoming Ella Hastings again, renewing the bond with her grandfather would also take time. But the many lonely years spent tracking his father without a glimpse warned him otherwise. Time had not healed his father.

The cabin came into view. Beech dismounted at the porch. "We will stay here for one sleep."

Little Brave looked around the mountain meadow with its soft, green carpet of grass, and wildflowers throwing splashes of color throughout. The breeze stirred, whispering through the ever-present needles of the pine trees, fluttering the newly leafed hardwood trees.

A pleasing softness eased across her face. Beech wondered what was going through her mind as her gaze came to rest upon the place, which at one point had been the center of his world.

"This is your home," she said, her gaze holding reverently to the one-room cabin as she slid from her horse.

"It was my home," he said brusquely to clamp down on memories of what home meant. He set his bedroll and saddlebags on the worn wood of the porch then gathered the reins of all the horses, intending to lead them to the corral next to the logged barn.

"May I enter?" she asked.

Standing beside the porch with the pack slung over her shoulder, the buckskin-clad waif of a woman with the rust-gold hair held a curious anticipation that restarted that tattoo of "my woman" within him. Abruptly, his memories of home shifted from the past into visions of the present and beyond.

"Make yourself at home." He shrugged as carelessly as he could manage then abruptly turned with the horses, fighting the realization that three nights on the open prairie might have been a safer choice than one night surrounded by the walls that held memories of a life that could never be his again.

-*-*-

Standing before the door, Little Brave pulled at the leather strip hanging from a small hole, and the heavy latch released. Pushing it open cautiously, she stepped inside, letting her eyes adjust to the dimness of the interior. Although the building at the fort was the first time in ten winters she'd been inside any structure built by a white man, this entrance held a fascination that the other had not. This place was—had been Beech's home.

She pushed open wooden wings covering the rectangular opening cut into the thick log wall to allow in more light. Although only one room, it was definitely larger than the circle of her tepee. She settled her bundle on the floor and treaded its perimeter, imagining the happiness Beech's family had enjoyed in this small, snug home. The pain in his voice when he had spoken of them told her he missed his mother and father still.

To her left, in the direction from which the warming winds came, was a gaping, stone mouth with a black pot sitting upon a grate within it. The word pot she remembered from the trader who had come to Grey Owl's village occasionally, but she could not remember the name of the long tunnel above the mouth, which, like the hole in the top of her tepee, carried smoke up and away. She continued her circuit, her frustration rising at being unable to recall the names for all the things holding such startling familiarity.

She arrived at the wall blocking the harsh winds of winter, and Beech entered the cabin, saddlebags on his shoulder and a bundle of wood in his arms.

He tumbled the wood into a box beside the mouth meant to hold fire and set aside his saddlebags.

She intended to question him about the long-lost names, but as soon as she saw him lean against the stone mouth and palm his wound, she hurried over.

147

"You should not have carried the wood." She pulled his hand away, searching for signs of blood. "It is not bleeding, but it will be if you try to do more," she admonished as she looked up into his face. The dimness shadowed his features but it did not hide the wary light in his eyes.

Suddenly, she became aware of the warmth of his fingers still wrapped in hers, the lift of his chest as he took a deep breath, the tensing of his whole body as he held it. Wishing to avoid the sting of more rejection, she released his hand, and dropped to her knees before the stone mouth. "I will build a fire."

She reached into a basket containing kindling then arranged the twigs and dried leaves around a piece of rich fatwood. She looked around for the striking stones. Long, dark fingers appeared over her shoulder. She took the stones from him, careful to avoid the brush of their fingers. Her hands shook slightly as she struck the stones to spark the dry tinder. She hoped he had not noticed their tremor.

With strategic puffs of air, she coaxed a tiny flame to life then sat back on her heels to watch it build.

He squatted beside her.

From the corner of her eyes, she could not help but follow the bulge of his thigh muscle until he shifted and she forced her eyes back to the flickering flame. It would not be wise to stoke her hunger for this man.

The flamed faltered and their hands collided as they reached into the basket between them for more kindling.

She gasped at the tingle that zipped up her arm.

His hand retreated, dropping to his thigh, his fingers gripping the taut muscle.

Quickly, she gathered a handful of twigs and busied herself with placing them onto the flame, one by one. Greedily, it licked at the new fodder.

In silence, they watched it grow. At the moment she would have chosen, he pulled some smaller logs from the

148

box and placed them around the flame. She fanned it with her breath, multiplying it until many red and orange tongues lapped hungrily in the yawning mouth of stone. Heat from the blaze warmed her face, but it was the heat from the man beside her that caused her to stand. Her head felt as light as cottonwood silk floating in the breeze, and she swayed.

Beech stood. "You are not well." He held out a hand to steady her.

"I gave too much of my breath to the fire," she murmured, backing away from the dangerous warmth of that helping hand. She hit a solid edge and fumbled behind her, her fingers encountering the well-worn wood of the...the... "What is the name for this?"

She shifted around, gliding her hands along its smoothness, both the cool slickness beneath her palms and the struggle for the white man's word welcome diversions from the power this man had over her senses.

"Table." His deep voice rumbled closer than he'd been when he'd offered to steady her.

"Table," she repeated, moving away, gripping the back of the thing in which one sat. "And this?"

"Chair."

"Chair," she said, smoothing her hands along its back. "Chair," she repeated as she sidestepped around the table, lightly tapping its surface as she went. "Table," she reminded herself.

With a deep inhale, she steadied her light head before she crossed the room and pointed to the long platform against the wall. She repeated "counter" after him and touched a shorter platform mounted on the wall above it.

He came around the table. "Shelf," he said, pointing to the bottom one. He waved to include all of them. "Shelves."

She nodded, holding up a finger. "Shelf." Next, she held up all her fingers. "Shelves."

A smile broke free across his face, chasing the wariness from his eyes.

Her breath caught at his carefree handsomeness, at the open appeal of such an expression. How many times had he flashed such a look at his mother or his father? And his sister? Did he often give her such glances?

To keep from dwelling on how much she desired more of those looks for herself, she pulled something from the shelf, plunking it onto the counter.

"Plate," he said.

"Plate," she repeated.

And so it went, her eagerness and delight growing as she pulled items from the shelf one by one: "Bowl." "Cup." "Fork." "Knife." "Spoon." Skeletons of words she'd known as a girl broke free from the dormant recesses of her mind, her mouth building their form and her breath giving them life.

The openings that let in light were windows, their wooden wings shutters. Barrels, their tops and bottoms flat, but their middles as round as a well-fed horse, held supplies. There was a trunk, four walls, a floor, and a roof. The mouth that held the fire was a fireplace. The white man slept upon a mattress just as she had during her winters as a young girl.

"Soft," he said as he sat and sank into its depth. He patted the wooden frame. "Hard."

She tapped the packed dirt floor with her foot. "Hard," she said then looked around for something other than the mattress to illustrate her understanding of the contrast with hard. Finding nothing else, she hesitated then sank into the softness beside him.

At her appreciative "soft," his smile widened, revealing strong, even teeth.

She drew a half circle in the air before his mouth with her finger.

"Smile," he said then swiped his tongue across his teeth. "Teeth."

She fingered her lips, her chin, her cheeks, and her ears. Her mouth struggled to keep up with the flight of her fingers.

He laughed, grabbing her fingers as they flitted to her hair. "Slooowwww."

She dipped her chin to her chest and lifted it in the manner his word had described, showing she understood its meaning

He nodded his approval, pressing her fingers to his chest just below his wound.

His heart, beating steady and strong beneath her fingers, attested to how closely Running Bear's arrow had come to ending his life. Loss, deep and poignant, enveloped her. She had not lied when she said she was glad he had lived. With Grey Owl and his people gone from her, Beech was the only one left who knew her as she was now. Soon, she would leave that person behind, for the white man expected Ella Hastings, not Little Brave of the Lakota. She gave words to her fear. "What if I cannot find Ella Hastings?"

"Already she returns with your speaking of the white man's words, but..." He angled his hand so that his fingers slid between hers, linking them. "From what I have seen, Little Brave has much to offer Ella Hastings—spirit, determination, courage. Qualities that anyone would admire. Qualities that will only make Ella Hastings a stronger, better person."

She couldn't help the tightening of her fingers around his as she placed their linked hands over her own heart. "But what if Ella Hastings no longer lives in here?"

"Then Little Brave will have to show her how to live in there."

It was an answer, but it seemed insurmountable without more guidance. She searched his face, hoping to find something more to help her. He must have more answers, for he had already taken this journey. His gaze grew wary again and he stood, slipping his hand free. "There is a bucket outside the door. Go to the creek behind the cabin and fetch water. You will find beans in the barrel over there. Put them over the fire to cook." He moved away, picking up the rifle leaning against the wall next to the door. "I will hunt for meat to go with the beans."

Only the creak of the door sounded as he slipped from the cabin.

She followed a well-worn path behind the cabin to the creek. Various prints in the moist earth told her the four-legged creatures used this path more often than the two-legged ones. Along the way, the scent of wild onion filled the air. She followed it until she found a patch of the fragrant green shoots. Slipping her knife free from her moccasin, she freed several of the tender and tasty roots from their earthy home. Already, her mouth watered at the flavor they would add to the beans.

The creek ran clear and cold with water from the snowmelt. It rushed over gravelly sand and rounded river rocks on its dash down the mountainside. She stepped from stone to stone until the water ran deep enough to fill her bucket. The container filled quickly when she dipped it into the water's thrust. She lifted it free with some effort and curled her moccasin-encased feet more securely around the slippery stone, balancing herself to account for the heavy bucket. It was much trickier than carrying a deerskin pouch.

Suddenly, her scalp prickled, the fine hairs along her neck and arms lifted.

She froze, listening. Only the rush of the mountain stream filled the air. Darting her gaze around, she looked for any sign of movement. Save the water, stillness ruled.

Ella's Choice

The bucket grew heavier, straining her muscles, the rough rope digging into her skin.

Another moment passed and the fine hairs flattened, the prickling eased.

Cautiously, she stepped to the next stone, ears still straining, gaze still darting.

Off in the distance, she heard the crack of a rifle.

After a few more steps, she regained the shore and hurried back to the cabin.

-*-*-

Twilight was falling as Beech approached the meadow home of his youth. The smoke curling from the cabin's chimney with its welcome home scent threw him back in time. Beside him, a blond-haired, blue-eyed father walked, after their long but fruitful day of hunting or trapping, his father's strength and resourcefulness at all times showing him the way of men. The large hand, palming the back of his head, spoke of this man's pride and love. Inside the cabin, a dusky-skinned, dark-eyed mother with gentle and loving ways waited, to feed and fuss over him. With mock irritation, she would complain that it was time to sew yet another buckskin shirt with longer arms, pants with longer legs.

A deep-throated neigh tossed him back into the present. From the corral next to the barn, August nodded his head in welcome. Beech gave an acknowledging wave but his feet drove him to the cabin. The sudden evaporation of his long-ago vision had not left him with such deep pangs of loss as it normally did.

He gained the porch, but the latchstring did not hang through its hole in the door. He would not think the woman inside to be fearful of her surroundings, but he rapped gently. "Little Brave," he called loudly enough to be heard, but softly enough not to startle.

The latch released, the door swung open. No fear was in her face, but that worried pucker was between her brows.

"Why do you have the door latched?" he asked.

"Someone was watching me while I was at the creek."

"Did you see them?"

"No," she answered calmly, "and I did not hear them, but someone was watching me."

Because she'd lived ten winters among the Plains People, he did not doubt what her senses had told her. He laid the rabbit on the counter, but did not lean his rifle against the wall. His stomach growled heartily at the aroma of wild, spring onions and beans. "I will go to the creek to check for signs of who has been there."

"It is almost dark."

"Then I best hurry."

When he returned from his search of the creek, the latch released once more at his rap and the call of her name. He entered to the aroma of roasting rabbit mingling with that of the onions and beans. He pushed the door closed behind him and leaned the rifle against the wall, ignoring the insistent rumbling of his stomach to answer the question in her gaze.

He shook his head, adding, "But I felt someone had been there. Tonight, I will keep watch." He crossed to the fire, stirred the beans and sipped at their broth. "Mmmm." He swiped a finger through the juices dripping off the roasting meat and popped it into his mouth. "Mmmm, we should have biscuits, too."

"Biscuits?" she repeated.

He fetched some dry ingredients from one of the barrels. With Little Brave at his elbow, watching with avid interest, he named the ingredients in English as he put two handfuls of flour into a bowl, added some baking powder and a pinch of salt.

He described the process as he mixed the ingredients with a fork, made a well in its center then poured in enough water to fill it. Beside him, she murmured everything he said. He stirred again until the contents of the bowl formed a sticky dough then he rummaged beneath the counter until he found the heavy Dutch oven. He sliced off some of the roasting meat and scoured the inside of the heavy black pot.

"So, they don't stick," he said, putting his palms together then miming their reluctance to part.

She nodded her understanding, but her concentration kept her gaze on his performance of the final steps of scraping the dough from the bowl into the oven and securing its lid then placing it on the grate beside the beans.

"What now?" she questioned with a show of her palms.

"Now, we fetch more water."

She scurried after him, snatching at the bucket as he picked it up. "I will carry the water," she said with a meaningful glance to his wound.

He laughed quietly, placing his fingers to her lips as he let her take the bucket from him. "Shhh!" He tried not to notice the lush softness of her lips as she nodded at his reminder to be quiet.

He palmed the handle of his knife, assuring himself it still remained sheathed at his waist then reached for his rifle. He eased open the door a crack, letting his eyes adjust to the deepening shadows around the cabin. It could have been an old mountain man or a wandering Indian who had spied on Little Brave by the creek. But his years crisscrossing this land in search of his father told him the watcher could just as easily be someone intending harm.

155

She slipped behind him as he eased out the door and into the shadows along the porch. He settled the yoke for carrying two buckets at the back of her neck. Even in the dimness, he could see her smile at the cleverness of the simple tool as he hooked a bucket at each end.

Silently, they went down the path to the creek, moving from shadow to shadow, the night creatures louder than any sound their footfalls made. Once they reached the creek, Beech unwound a rope from around the yoke, tied it to the handle of the bucket then let the swift current carry it until it filled with water. He hauled it in then did the same with the second bucket. Once again, her smile told him she appreciated his working-saving tricks.

Once they were safely inside the cabin, she asked, "What about the horses?"

"August will let no one but me catch him, and he will fight anyone who tries to steal from him."

"As it should be."

Her agreement affirmed his need to protect her, but the pink glow of exertion tingeing her cheeks and the jeweled sparkle in her eyes at their shared adventure stoked his desire to share more than his protection.

A happy sigh parted her lips, and she reached up to palm his cheek. "Thank you, Beech Richoux, for not leaving me at the fort, for bringing me with you to give me time, for showing me your home."

Her words were chaste and sincere, but her touch and the slight huskiness in her voice had him swallowing hard. His gaze was unable to leave hers and the air between them suddenly thickened in expectation. Her thumb dropped to his mouth, its slow stroke across his bottom lip showing him what she desired while the look in her eyes confirmed it.

His heart beat with the rhythm of *my woman,* but the fire crackled and popped in warning: *white woman.* He coughed to dislodge the hoarseness of desire from his throat, "We should check the biscuits."

Disappointment was in her eyes before she cast them downward. Her hand fell from his cheek, and she moved away to pick up a square of cloth to protect her hand from the heat.

He watched her as she lifted the lid of the Dutch oven. She was as capable as she was beautiful, eager and willing to learn. She didn't blink an eye at a hint of danger and her Lakota ways were as natural to her as they were to him, but she wore the skin of the white man. She was not meant for him.

He sucked in a huge breath of air and kneaded the knotted muscles in the back of his neck for this night would indeed be longer than three nights on the open prairie.

Chapter 11

The sight of the biscuits in the heavy pot revived a long-ago memory of a light, flaky, tasty bread and their aroma set up a yearning to reacquaint her tongue with their taste.

Beech spoke over her shoulder. "They are ready."

She replaced the lid and tugged at the handle. Much heavier than the thin metal pots the white trader brought to Grey Owl's village, it did not budge.

One of his hands closed around the handle next to hers. "I will get it," he said.

"No." She felt guilty that he'd carried it to the grate in the first place. She tightened her fists, sidled closer to the pot, determined to wrestle it to the table on her own.

His arm snaked around her waist, yanking her back against him.

In surprise, she released the handle.

Lifting her and the heavy pot, he whirled. Dropping the Dutch oven on the table, he growled into her ear, "You could have set yourself on fire."

Her face burned at her foolishness. She knew better than to get so close to open flames with her long skirt.

He set her back on her feet but did not release her, his mouth remaining close to her ear.

Did he intend to scold her more? Another wave of heat surged across her face, but she did not struggle against his hold. She waited, her heart thudding at the solidness of his chest against her back, the strength of his arm at her waist, but his heat weakened her muscles from neck to knee and set up a fluttering in her belly.

His hold loosened, but still he did not free her.

Her breath caught as his fingers found the jut of her collarbone.

Anticipation rippled along her spine.

Slowly, he traced the bone from one shoulder to the other. She turned her head until her cheek met his lips. They moved against her skin, trailing fire down her neck. She tilted her head, exposing more of her skin to his hot, hungry mouth.

Muscles flexed in his forearm as she slid a hand along the arm at her waist, intertwining their fingers, holding them securely against her body.

His other hand left her shoulder, traveled down her arm, his fingers gliding around the swell of her breast, cupping it. The fluttering converged into a ribbon of wanton desire coiling tighter as his thumb grazed the tip of her breast. She longed to shuck her dress, to feel the sensation of those calluses on his fingertips upon her sensitive flesh. She dared not, lest her pale skin remind him why he did not want to lay with her.

"Little Brave," Beech whispered, his voice hoarse and raw. "We cannot do this."

But even as he said it his body curved around hers, his chin dipping so that his lips could press into the hollow at the base of her throat. She rubbed her cheek against the smoothness of his hair. "There are no white men here," she whispered.

"But tomorrow, we will be among many white men."

"And Little Brave will begin to disappear," she reminded him.

By the way his hold tightened, she knew he understood. She turned in his arms, her fingers spiking through his dark hair that gleamed blue-black in the firelight and lifted his head to her gaze. "I do not want Little Brave's last memories to be ones of such pain and loss."

The shadows hid his eyes from her, but not the flare of his nostrils.

She touched her lips to his, letting their movement convey her intense need for this experience.

He groaned, crushing her against him, his lips taking possession of the kiss. His passion stole her breath. When his tongue slipped inside her mouth, she returned his fire with even greater fire of her own. Her hands slipped from his hair, exploring the breadth of his shoulders, the strong contours of his back, tunneling beneath the edge of his shirt.

He bunched her skirt until its hem reached mid-thigh. Her wish became truth as those roughened fingertips glided over her bare thighs, sending shiver after shiver of sensation whipping through her.

Her head fell back, her fingers digging into the firm flesh of his waist as his fingers slid through the moisture between her thighs. His thumb pressed at their peak, sending a tremor through her that obliterated all thought and reason.

Existing in fevered desire, her hips thrust against his hand, demanding more. His fingers spread across her bare bottom, dimpling into its softness, awakening a dark sensuality. He lifted her. Her legs wrapped instinctively about him, her insides trembling at the hardened ridge that nestled between her wet, swollen folds. He perched her on the counter, and her hands flew to the ties on his trousers, freeing the part of him that would give her release from this overwhelming need.

He caught her hands before she could do more than stroke his velvety steel once. Her gaze flew to his, dreading to see that somber look on his face—the one that said he had

160

thought better of their coupling. To her relief, all she saw was raw desire etched in his masculine features.

A strained smile lurked at the corner of his mouth. "There will not be much of a memory for you, if you continue to touch me like that."

"Hiyee," she breathed softly, a wave of feminine power sweeping through her at the effect she had on him.

He kissed each palm then settled her hands on his shoulders. His eyes closed as he nudged against the opening between her legs.

She angled her hips to meet his blunt thickness.

His hands gripped her hips, hindering their movement as he eased into her body.

The stretch to accommodate him was exquisite torture—almost more than she could bear and yet, not enough to satisfy.

All at once, he withdrew.

She whimpered, her hips straining against his hold.

His eyes opened, so darkened in desire that they matched the hue of his hair, but there was a harsh line to his mouth she did not understand.

A guttural sound issued from deep within his chest as he plunged back inside.

Her inner muscles quivered around him.

His grip eased.

Her hips thrust to meet his as he withdrew and returned, each time, quicker and harder than before.

She was barely aware of his hand fisting into her hair, his mouth covering hers, swallowing her gasp as the spasms overtook her.

She floated like eagle soars high in the sky.

Free from pain, from loss, from the memories.

Indescribable sensations swept over her, carrying her higher.

But her joy was not complete without him.

She twisted her hands into his hair, her lips demanding he join her, but abruptly, his lips parted from hers. Her gaze sought a reason and found harsh restraint in his face. She mewled her frustration, and tightened her thighs around him. His muscles quivered, she angled her hips to take him deeper. He groaned—a raw, desperate sound—then plunged back into her so hard and so deep she floated again. His release came with his gaze on hers, and she knew she'd found a place in which she could soar forever.

With another thrust, he groaned again—a sated, finished sound—then collapsed against her. He wrapped her into his embrace, their breath laboring as one.

Soaring with him had been glorious, but this oneness she felt with him afterwards was beyond glorious. It was paradise. The way his hand cradled her head to his chest made her feel cherished. The sturdy thump-thump of his heart beneath her ear echoed safety. She realized she could exist here for an eternity, but too soon, his arms dropped away.

His hair fell like a dark shield across his face as he refastened his trousers. He stepped back, pulling her skirt over her legs. Without a word, he turned away.

At the door, he picked up the rifle. "I'll check on things outside then we will eat," he said without looking at her.

Tears pricked her eyes as the door closed behind him. She scrubbed them away as soon as they fell. What had she expected? Affectionate words such as husbands and wives share afterwards? A longing look of a lover as he left? They were neither lovers nor spouses.

Hiyee, he'd given her what she'd asked for, but she'd been a fool. He might desire her but he did not want her. He had given her the memory she had asked for, to soar beyond the pain and loss. And he had given her even more when he had cradled her in security and acceptance afterwards. But, all of it was to be only a memory.

_*_*_

By the time Beech finished the rounds of the homestead, the sharp cut of the mountain's night air had subdued his desire, but not his emotions. He paused before the door of the cabin, palming the rough wood. His heart still battled fiercely with his logic, arguing that the pale-skinned woman with the rich russet hair had been his from the moment he had spoken the words, "my woman," to the Crow scout. Finding his release with her was his right.

His logic fired back. Tomorrow, she would be among the white man once more and the ways of the Lakota held no merit in that world. The speed, at which the white man's words were reawakening within her, told him before long she would fully return to those ways. Then her grandfather—a man with longer and stronger ties than he— would come. And soon, she would not want or need a half-breed scout in her world.

He fisted his hand, knuckles scraping against the splintering wood, as he readied himself to deal with the sight of Little Brave inside the cabin. Her esteem for this as his home, her movement about it as a woman in a home moves had stirred emotions he'd thought he would never feel again, make him long for things he could never have. Regardless, for the sake of her future in the white man's world, their intimate liaison could go no further.

He expelled a ragged breath as he rapped and called to her to lift the latch. He entered, propping his rifle in its usual place next to the door, but he avoided looking at her. Still, he was acutely aware of her movements. She ladled out two bowls of the aromatic beans and set them on the table across from each other. Tin cups and flatware had been laid out, as well as plates. She sliced hunks of meat from the roasted rabbit, placing them onto the plates then lifted the lid on the accursed Dutch oven and plopped steaming pieces of biscuit beside the meat.

His stomach rumbled vigorously.

She gestured to the chair across the table from the one in which she now sat. "Eat before it becomes cold."

Slowly, he crossed the room, keeping his gaze on the succulent meal before him. Still, he noticed she waited for him to sit and lift his spoon before she picked up hers. Was this a recall of manners, or a show of deference? He chanced a glance at her face and the stoicism he'd first encountered in Grey Owl's village was firmly back in place. That pained him. Not only was he the reason for its return, but her guise would also deny him the company of the brave and spirited woman he'd found behind that protective mask.

He swallowed his first bite of beans. They did not go down easy. He dropped the spoon back into the bowl with a sigh. "Little Brave, my heart is heavy because I have caused you pain."

Her chin lifted. "You have done only what I requested."

He nodded. To speak beyond that truth would only open a door that they must not go through.

She said no more and fixed her attention firmly on her food. While his stomach was more than appreciative of the delicious fare after many days of trail rations, he realized his tongue was barely aware of its taste. Still he ate, for tomorrow would bring another long ride. He didn't realize he'd finished his meal until she'd taken his bowl and refilled it. He caught her gaze as she sat. "Thank you."

There was an imperceptible shrug of her shoulders, but something eased in her eyes. She broke off a piece of biscuit. "The biscuit is good," she said in slow English then placed the morsel into her mouth.

He dropped his gaze back to his meal as her tongue swiped away the crumbs on her lips. It would not be wise to feed his hunger for her.

"How far to Cheyenne?" she asked.

"The time it takes for the sun to travel across the sky."

"What is the white man's word for that time?"

"A day."

She nodded, repeating the word to herself then asked, "And one sleep?"

"A night."

After repeating that word, she fell silent. The click of their spoons against the bowls as they ate and the crackling of the fire filled the air. These sounds were his constant companions when people came together as much for conversation as to share the last meal of the day. He'd been content with such solitude, actually preferring it, but suddenly the quietness grated on him. He struggled for something to say, to fill the unusually unnerving silence.

"What if your aunt and uncle do not want me in their home?"

He spoke to soothe the worry he heard in her voice. "They have a big house. All their children, except for Grace, are grown and gone."

She stared with a mutinous look on her face. "That does not mean they will want me there."

He cocked his head, kneading the knotted muscles at the back of his neck. His aunt had accepted Grace without question, for she had been an infant, small and helpless, but with him the story had been different. He stared at Little Brave's fisted hands, the tight line of her lips, the hardness of her eyes. They dared him to tell her otherwise.

What could he tell her?

How many times had he worn such a look? Most of his youth. Overwhelmed by anger and resentment at his

165

father's abandonment, the uncertainty of his future, the frustration of trying to adapt to ways that were foreign and oftentimes senseless to him. His uncle had been busy with a thriving business. His older cousins involved in school and their friends. His aunt preoccupied with managing a household, in addition to her toddler son and baby Grace. They had little time to deal with a sullen, angry, half-breed boy. What if he'd had someone who'd understood? Who had taken the time? Felt he was worth the time?

He engulfed her fists with his hands. "I know your heart is heavy with grief and sadness over all you have lost. I know it burns with anger at the unfairness and it is full of fear that your world will never make sense again. But you came from the white man's world and you have a grandfather who has been looking for you." It was much, much more than he'd had.

Her fists clenched even tighter beneath his hands. "What if my grandfather does not want me?"

"He has searched for you. Why would he not want you?"

"You do not want me. You are not even sure your aunt and uncle will want me. Why would my grandfather want me?"

He saw the fury sweep across her face in a red wave, her eyes as snapping blue flames. If he had not understood her feelings, he might have been worried, but he did understand. Her emotions, like smoke in a tepee, needed a place to escape, or all within would eventually suffocate and die.

"Your heart feels that is how things are now, but once time has passed, you will find your place."

"What if I choose not to be with my grandfather?"

He was not surprised at her challenging tone. Had he not questioned his father, even as he had brought him and Grace to his aunt and uncle's? Had he not defied his aunt and uncle every summer when he left to search for his father?

"If not with your grandfather, then who?"

She looked startled for a moment, her mouth working in silence until her words found her voice. "I will stay here."

"You cannot stay here."

"Why? You do not live here."

"How will you survive?"

"You do not believe I can take care of myself?" She jerked her hands from his, gathering the dirty dishes and stacking them in the washbasin. "I will hunt and fish."

He watched her heave the oven from the table to the counter as if to say there wasn't anything she couldn't do if she was determined enough.

"There is wood for fire and plenty of roots and berries to gather." She poured hot water into the basin from the kettle on the fire, added some cold water then began vigorously washing.

"I know the Plains People have taught you well how to live off the land, but you will be all alone." He left the table to stand behind her, desiring nothing more than to palm those proud shoulders which jerked vehemently as she scrubbed at the crust left by the biscuits in the Dutch oven. He longed to turn her in his arms and cradle her head against his chest, to comfort her, to reassure her, to—he did not trust himself to touch her. He swallowed hard, but the rasp still lived in his voice. "Would you rather be all alone?"

-*-*-

Little Brave scoured the Dutch oven, but it was no distraction against the deep rumbling of his voice caressing her ears, his heat reaching for her as he stepped up behind her, his aura of strength assuring her, his rationality soothing her. No, she did not want to be alone. But loneliness could happen even when surrounded by many faces as she'd been in the village of the Blackfeet, or in a large, well-furnished, well-stocked house with only a cranky, resentful housekeeper for company when she'd lived in her grandfather's house.

She tackled a particularly stubborn patch of crust on the black pot, her breath puffing with her efforts.

"Being alone is better than being among those who do not want me."

Chapter 12

Little Brave awoke to the dimness of her tepee—no, it was not her tepee. The softness beneath her body was the white man's mattress, not buffalo hides on firm ground. She froze, letting her senses attune to her surroundings. She gazed at the cracks of light between the shutters and around the door as she became aware of the itching of her neck from the wool blanket covering her. Behind her, she heard the sound of even breathing.

Slowly, she turned her head, remembering from the first night on the trail how lightly Beech slept. Wrapped in his own blanket, peace inhabited his features. Peace she longed for.

All throughout the night, visions had plagued her. Faces crowded around her—sometimes white, sometimes red. Always talking, but not to her. Always looking, but not at her. The visions had been fraught with an overwhelming sense of loneliness. The loneliness eased as she tracked the even rise and fall of Beech's chest as he slumbered, but it was fleeting. Today, they rode to Cheyenne where he'd leave her at his aunt's and uncle's to await her grandfather.

Finding little solace in that thought, she carefully inched off the bed and slipped out of the cabin. The morning air was crisp and cool, the sun a thin, yellow line above the eastern range. She stretched, trying to loosen the ache the

169

softness of the mattress had put into her back. Sundance whinnied and she went to the corral. All three horses crowded the rail, jockeying for scratches behind their ears, rubs between their eyes.

Simultaneously, they froze, their nostrils quivering, their ears pricked forward. The fine hairs on the back of her neck rose as prickles sped across her scalp. She turned, catching a movement at the edge of the tree line. The sun burst over the mountains, blinding her. She threw up an arm to block it, but whoever had been there was gone.

"Little Brave."

From the cabin, Beech came striding toward her, eyebrows flat and that hard line to his mouth.

"Did you see someone in the trees?" She pointed to where she'd seen the movement.

He grabbed her arm, pushing her before him into the barn. Once inside, he peered through the crack between the doors.

She jerked her arm against his grasp. He hauled her against him. Her breath whooshed from her lungs.

"You should not have been out here alone," he growled.

"You were sleeping so I thought the danger was gone."

"There is always danger. You should know that after ten winters with the Plains People."

She did know that. What she did not know was why he was so angry. She palmed his chest, looking to quell his anger. "I can take care of myself."

Her assurance did not placate him. His fingers spiked into her hair, twining until her head was immobilized. His other arm snaked low around her waist, his fingers digging into her thigh.

She stifled her cry of pain and surprise.

"Take care of yourself now," he challenged.

# Ella's Choice

She had very little leverage with her arms bent at the elbows and crushed between their bodies and her legs trapped by her long skirt. Her strength was no match for his, but if she could get him to loosen his hold...and if she was quick enough...she needed to distract him.

He shifted. A snippet of white bandage flashed beneath his collar.

There!

She jerked her gaze toward the barn door as if she'd caught a glimpse of something.

His attention followed her gaze.

She jammed her fingers where she knew his wound lay under his tunic.

Surprise flitted across his face as he grunted in pain. His teeth clamped shut on anything else he might have said as he released her waist to drag her fingers away from the tender skin.

She twisted away forgetting about the hand in her hair. The sharp sting in her scalp sent her back ten winters. Terror engulfed her.

Copper skin, black hair. The stench of sweaty bodies. The angry cadence of words she didn't understand.

She fought blindly, recklessly.

They had taken her once. She wouldn't let them take her again.

She met an implacable wall of sinewy muscle. Trapped again, she thrashed her head about wildly. Her forehead slammed into bone, her teeth met skin. She clamped down, felt the reverberations of a howl. She bit harder. The corded muscles rolled beneath her teeth.

Suddenly, she was free. She stumbled. Hands gripped her waist. She pulled for breath, clawing at whoever held her then caught the scent of leather, wood smoke and eucalyptus, heard her name being called.

In a rush, the present returned.

While her mind scrambled to reorient itself, she was reeled in and cradled against Beech's warm, solid strength.

"Shhh."

His soft words, rumbled soothingly beneath her ear. Tears stung her eyes. She buried her face into his chest to squelch them. Failure clogged her throat. She'd disintegrated into an unseeing panic, trying to prove she could take care of herself. Shame and disappointment forced the tears from her eyes. Their salt stung her wind-chapped cheeks.

"I was wrong to push you like that," he said.

The leather fringe of his tunic abraded her cheek as she shook her head in disagreement. He was right. She would not be safe by herself. She must go to Cheyenne.

As her mind finally accepted it, she allowed her body to sag deeper into his embrace. His hand moved gently down her back then hitched her closer. She let her arms creep around his waist, drawing comfort from him, however short, however bittersweet.

Soon, she wedged space between them with her hands on his chest, and looked upward. The slice of light from the crack between the barn doors highlighted the proud contour of his nose, the strong line of his jaw, but it also revealed the question in his eyes.

But there was no question, not if she wanted to survive. "I will go to Cheyenne." Not wanting to see the relief in his eyes, she dropped her gaze. It caught on the blood oozing from beneath the bandage. She stared at the wounds on his neck caused by her teeth. "You are bleeding."

He fingered the bite. "It is nothing." He rubbed the blood from fingers with a swipe of his thumb.

He bled beneath his bandages, too. She'd hurt him, trying to prove something that was beyond her capabilities. Guilt consumed her. She tugged him toward the cabin.

-*-*-

Grudgingly, Beech sat while Little Brave stoked the fire and put on water to heat. She was his responsibility, not the other way around.

"Take off your shirt," she said as she rummaged through one of the barrels.

With a grimace of pain, he removed his tunic. If he hadn't goaded her—

She set clean rags and a bar of soap on the table.

If he'd had talked to her rationally—

Steam rose as she poured hot water into a bowl. "Hold still." Carefully, she peeled away the bloody bandage.

Her womanly scent surrounded him, and her curves shifted subtly beneath her dress as she worked.

He fisted his hands to keeping from reaching for her.

She lathered the rag and the clean brace of eucalyptus filled the air.

Dammit! He'd had no choice but to make her understand the dangers of being alone. He flinched as she pressed a hot rag to his open wound.

"I am hurting you." Contrition marred her brow.

He shook his head. "The soap stings."

She cleaned the wound with sure, but gentle, movements then laid aside the rag. "I do not have any healing herbs." She tore a thin cloth into strips and knotted them together. "Perhaps your aunt will have some when we reach Cheyenne."

When we reach Cheyenne.

She wound the strip over his shoulder and beneath his arm several times.

Once they reached Cheyenne, he'd put a safe distance between them.

She tied off the ends neatly.

There would be no more rash actions that only created heartache for both of them. He gritted his teeth as the soap from a freshly lathered rag stung his neck

"I am sorry that I bit you," she said.

He tilted his head to give her better access. "Do not be sorry. You reacted to protect yourself."

Water slopped onto the table as she doused the rag. "But I could not take care of myself." She twisted it with a vengeance, but then gently swiped at his neck.

"My actions were not meant to make you feel weak or unworthy, but to show you that being out here alone is not a good choice."

"I have said I will go to Cheyenne with you."

He locked gazes with her. "And once you are in Cheyenne, you will stay with my aunt and uncle until your grandfather comes for you?"

Her chin notched up. "Once you have left me with your aunt and uncle, it will no longer be your concern."

"You will be my concern until you are safe with your grandfather."

Water sloshed across the table as she tossed the rag into the bowl. "Why? Because of a promise you made to the white military man at the fort?"

"No, because I care about you."

"Care about me? One who cares does not say the words 'my woman' in one breath then takes them back in the next. One who cares is not intimate body and soul then walks away without a word or a look afterwards."

He reached for his shirt as he stood, wondering how to make her understand that in this case one who cared did all those things. "My heart bears much pain and no pride in those actions. One day, you will understand why it is impossible for us to be together."

"I will never understand such a thing. And if this is the way of the white man, then I do not want to be a part of his world." She busied herself gathering the unused rags and putting them back into the barrel.

Wearily, Beech tugged on his shirt. There was nothing more he could say in this moment to help her understand, to cool her anger, to soothe her hurt. The best he could do was to get her to Cheyenne so she could begin finding her place in the white man's world, and forget the pain and sorrow her heart held because of him.

-*-*-

Beech did not look back as they rode from the meadow that held his childhood home, and neither did she. It would only add to the longing and sorrow in her heart, which already held more than enough for two lifetimes. Now more unhappiness awaited her as she rode toward a world that would deny two people their happiness because of her pale skin and the rich copper hue of his.

Regardless of the intensity of her thoughts, she scanned the surroundings as they rode single-file along the trail. She would not let her emotions dull her to danger once again.

The scout led the way with his rifle across his lap, his body moving in perfect unison with Big Black as if he hadn't a care in the world.

But she knew he searched for clues as to who had been watching them.

At the crack of a twig, he brought his rifle to his shoulder.

Stealthily, Little Brave withdrew her blade from her moccasin. Ahead of them, a doe and her fawn crashed out of the underbrush, darted across the narrow trail then disappeared out of sight.

After another minute of waiting and watching, he lowered the rifle to his lap but his finger remained poised at the trigger. He looked back, his gaze traveling to the knife she still held against her thigh. "What do your senses tell you?" he asked, his focus returning to the forest around them.

"I do not feel anyone's presence like I did last night at the creek, or this morning when I was with the horses."

His finger eased off the trigger as he sent Big Black forward again. "Neither do I, but keeping your knife near is wise."

She shifted her grip on the knife, letting it rest across her lap. "Who do you think has been watching us?"

His broad shoulders shrugged. "Someone who knows how to cover their tracks."

"Why do they watch us?"

"I think they were waiting for us to leave the cabin."

"I saw no sign someone had been there before us when I first entered it yesterday."

"Neither did I, but I'm guessing they will help themselves to a few supplies now we have left."

The calm manner in which he spoke of some stranger, taking what belonged to him, was refreshing after Running Bear and the other young warriors in Grey Owl's village. Raiding those who raided against them had been a favored pastime of those warriors. "You will not be angry and seek retribution if someone raids your cabin?"

"If they take only what they need and leave the cabin as they found it, then I will bear no grudge."

"Hiyee," she said admiringly, "you bear the wisdom of an old one, Beech."

"To be compared to Grey Owl is high praise indeed," he said, flashing her one of those rare, open smiles.

She caught her breath at his captivating handsomeness.

He returned his attention to their surroundings and spoke no more until the trees disappeared and the land leveled. Both land and sky opened before them and his smile returned. "Let's ride," he said.

She could not resist his enthusiasm and accepted his proposal by nudging Sundance into the rocking motion that was the most comfortable of all the little mare's gaits. Beside her, the paint mustang tossed his head, joyfully keeping pace. Soon, she heard the heavier beats of Big Black's hooves behind them.

Leaning over Sundance's neck, she let the wind slip over her head and along her back as if she were one with the golden mare. She lost herself in the feeling of flying across the prairie, heady with power and freedom and belonging. If it were possible, she would exist in this moment forever.

A stream appeared in the distance, its surface glittering intensely in the bright rays of the midday sun.

Big Black surged ahead then circled in front of them, slowing them. Walking the final stretch to the water allowed the horses to cool and catch their breath before the grass yielded to a muddy shore that delved into the water.

Little Brave slid from Sundance and moved farther upstream where the bank remained grassy at the water's edge.

Beech squatted next to her, following her lead in drinking his fill then he balanced back on the balls of his feet, his forearms resting on his knee while he scanned their surroundings.

How soon after they arrived in Cheyenne would this man with his keen senses and his quiet steady focus return to his tracking and scouting duties with the Army? In spite of the warmth of the sun on her back, she shivered at the thought of his departure.

He swiveled on the balls of his feet, questions in his eyes, concern in his tone. "What is it?"

She took in his lean strength, the broad, copper-hued features and the dark, gleaming hair that mirrored that of Grey Owl's warriors. As much as he was like the Plains People, he was different, mimicking the white man in those differences. His fluid movement between the two worlds never ceased to amaze her, and invoke her admiration.

Once he left her in Cheyenne, she would be surrounded by people she did not know, a language she barely understood and ways that had not been hers for ten winters. She would be alone, waiting for a grandfather who most likely did not want her. Suddenly, the memory he'd given her last night, the one she'd asked for only held pain and loss.

She stood, straightened her spine and pressed her hands to the beaded buffalo on her belt. She masked her features with the stoicism the Plains People had taught her all too well.

"It is nothing."

Chapter 13

They crested a rise, and the place called Cheyenne filled the view. It stretched from where the sun rose to where it set, crowded the base of the rise, and sprawled in the opposite direction as far as the eye could see.

"How many white men live in Cheyenne?"

"Three thousand," he said.

Three times the number of soldiers on the plains before the fort. Oddly, the soldiers' camp had felt more familiar, less threatening, with its tents and outdoor campfires, its ability to gather itself up and move. This place squirmed and writhed in place. Dust rose from it—like breath from one massive being—and hung in the air above itself. Clogging. Choking. Smothering. Instinctively, she covered her mouth and nose.

"You are ill?"

She blinked at his question, swallowing, tasting nothing it seemed but dust. Her non-answer must have been answer enough for he reached for the canteen and passed it to her. In spite of its warmth and the tinny flavor it had absorbed from the metal, she gulped the water. She handed it back to him. Pressing hard, she swiped the back of her hand across her lips. She tucked the stray strands of shorn hair behind her ears, wanting nothing to hinder her view as she rode into the belly of this being.

Halfway down the rise, she heard a howl not unlike that of wolf on a full-mooned night. The earth rumbled like buffalo moving across the prairie. Sundance jigged beneath her; the paint tossed his head, dancing out to the end of his tether. She forced her body to relax, settled deeper onto the little mare's back to calm her, and reeled in the paint. A trail of dark gray smoke billowed from the glistening black beast. It issued another keening howl. She knew this beast, had ridden in its bowels as a girl. She pointed.

"Train," Beech said.

"Train," she said, awakening the word from its ten-winter slumber in her mind.

Once the train had passed, they crossed its tracks. Deep, mournful bellows filled the air, along with a gagging stench. "Stockyards," he said. "The cattle will be loaded onto the train and shipped back East for their meat."

She shivered and turned her gaze from the creatures, crowded in the pens, mired in mud and filth, their eyes too much like those of the buffalo. The Plains People would never mistreat the bounty from Mother Earth in such a manner.

They left the stockyards behind, but the bellowing and the stench followed them as they approached long, wooden buildings. Wagons passed, rattling in their emptiness, as they pulled alongside raised platforms that ran the length of the 'warehouses'. Men shouted to each other and to no one in particular as they heaved barrels and crates off the 'docks' and onto wagons, which groaned beneath their weight as they lumbered away. The clamor was discordant, each sound vying for dominance in the hustle and bustle.

The warehouses gave way to two-storied buildings similar to the one she'd been in at the fort. Wooden walkways fronted the buildings and men, as well as women, strolled along them while children dashed about. 'Carriages' drawn by one or two glossy, prancing horses joined the

180

wagons lumbering up and down the very wide, very dusty path between the buildings. This path was called 'Main Street'.

Finally, they left behind the unsettling activity at the center of Cheyenne. The air grew quieter, but her thoughts did not. The buildings, farther apart now, oftentimes set well back from the road, were homes, large and well cared for, like her grandfather's home. His home had been full of things which must not be touched, with a housekeeper who did not like the inconvenience of a little girl, a place where children were to be seen, but not heard. She scoffed at herself. She was no longer a little girl; she was a woman of eighteen winters, survivor of the Blackfeet, daughter of Chief Grey Owl of the Lakota. Her spine straightened, her chin lifted.

They turned onto a side street beside a two-storied white house with a porch that curled around it like a snake. The road went past a small barn behind the house then out into the prairie. Had Beech changed his mind about leaving her with his aunt and uncle? Like he'd changed his mind about leaving her at the fort with the military man and his woman? Her heart floated up into her throat, and anticipation shimmered over her skin.

He halted at the barn, gesturing to the house behind them. "This is my aunt and uncle's place."

Her heart dropped, disappointment settling heavy, her shoulders slumping. Slowly, she dismounted, her legs feeling none too sure beneath her. She leaned back against the railing of the corral, clutched her meager, blanket-wrapped belongings to her chest and surveyed her surroundings while he led the horses into the corral.

A garden, leafy and green, filled the space to her right. Beyond it, closer to the house, sheets whiter than freshly fallen snow hung from a line and billowed in the breeze. The back door of the house was propped open but

181

she could not see inside. She turned in place, leaning against the solid railing, breathing easier as her gaze fell upon the wide-open plains beyond the corral. Out there is where she knew how to be herself. Not here, in a house, in a town, in the busy confusion of the white man's world.

The corral shook, startling her, as the gate closed. Beech stood next to her that kind light shining in his eyes, but it was mixed with that sorrow the commander at the fort had worn when he first saw her, the kind of sorrow that people had looked at her with after her mother had left for the next world. She did not want or need this sorrow and she averted her gaze, looking instead at the horses drinking deeply from the water trough at the far end of the corral.

Sundance and the paint were free of their bridles, but Big Black still wore his saddle, a halter over his bridle. It was, as she knew it would be. He would stay no longer than to leave her with his aunt and uncle. She looked once again to the open prairie, inhaled deeply of its fresh air, taking all it had given her into her heart, fueling her strength and her courage.

"I am ready to meet your aunt and uncle," she said, holding her gaze for another moment on the place that had made her who she was today then she turned to him, adding, "And your sister."

A shadow passed over his face, but she did not stop to analyze it as she marched toward the house.

Near the snow-white sheets, he caught her by the elbow. "Wait, there is something I need to tell you."

She shook her head against the hope that he might have changed his mind.

His fingers tightened on her elbow, his gaze burning into hers. "Hear me."

It was an old saying, meaning that what one was about to say was of the gravest importance, that to ignore such importance would not be wise. She returned his stare from behind the mask of her indifference. She did not

182

understand why he would need to tell her such a thing. They barely knew each other. Soon, he would return to the fort, her grandfather would come for her. She most likely would never see Beech again. That thought stung, and her indifference slipped. He must have taken that as a sign for he drew her closer. The sheets billowed around them, enveloping them in a world of stark whiteness, hushing all outside sounds.

"Grace does not know she is my sister."

The bleak look on his face caused her indifference to fall in shreds around her feet. She inched closer, her hands cradling his cheeks. "Why?" She did not want him to spare her the truth.

His eyes closed, his lips tightening, his body quivering from suppressed emotion.

Confusion? Hurt? Anger?

"If anyone knew she was part Indian, she would be shunned, and no respectable man would have her."

She shook her head at the nonsense of it. "But that doesn't mean *she* cannot know."

"I promised my aunt."

"Why would—"

"It is better this way." The roughness in his voice told her it wasn't better this way. Not for him and she told him so. He took a deep breath, his eyes opening, the burning replaced by the hard, clear blue of determination. "It *is* better this way." He gathered her hands, placed them against his heart. "Promise me you will not tell her."

Suddenly, the breeze died, the sheets fell away from them and the hush became filled with the sound of twittering birds. A horse neighed, far away a door slammed. Normal, everyday sounds but this—to be denied the last of your family—was not everyday. And it was not normal. It was heartbreaking. And cruel. Emotions clogged her throat. Had she not been denied the last of her family just days ago?

"How—how can you keep such a promise? Without her, you are alone." That bleak look returned to his face. She fisted her hands into his tunic. "If it were my family, I could never keep such a promise."

"But she is not your family, she is my fam—" His hands closed around hers and pressed them tight against the wild thumping of his heart. "Promise me."

She swallowed against the hard ache in her throat, the churning in her stomach, the emptiness in her heart for him—for herself. Of course, she would not tell. She gave a small shake of her head, trying to clear her head of the pain and the anguish she was feeling so that her mouth could work, so that she could assure him that his secret was safe.

Desperation filled his face at the shake of her head and his hands curled painfully around her upper arms, dragging her up against him, his dark hair falling forward, sealing them within the intensity of his emotions. "Promise me now, or I will take you back to the fort."

Now, his heart pounded furiously beneath her fists. She held his gaze with her own, hoping he saw the truth there, that he heard the sincerity in the fierceness of her tone as she said, "I would never tell a secret that was not mine to tell."

The desperation eased from his face, but not the bleakness.

She shivered.

His hands dropped away from her as he took a step back. "You are right. I am alone."

At this declaration, she shook her head. No, he wasn't alone. Her mouth opened to say the words, but they wouldn't come. She threw herself at him, wound her arms around him and melded her ear to the beat of his heart. He stood there, rigid and quivering in her embrace, his arms hanging loosely at his sides. She held him fiercely, trying to absorb his pain, his anguish and his grief.

184

When still he did not accept the comfort she was offering, she twined her fingers into his hair and tugged.

He resisted.

She stood on her tiptoes so she could bury her face into the crook of his neck. "You are not alone, Beech. You have me." She tasted the salt of him as she murmured against his skin. Or was that the salt of her tears? She couldn't tell because then she was being crushed in his arms, his body curling around her, his face burying in her hair, his body trembling violently in her embrace. The breeze rose, the sheets billowed and cocooned them in their silent, white world.

_-*-*-_

Many, many years had past since Beech had experienced such pain and anger over the loss of his family. He fisted his hands next to his thighs as he stepped into the kitchen. He watched his aunt stir a pot on the stove, wondering where all that emotion was supposed to go. The few moments in Little Brave's arms outside hadn't appeased his feelings; her embrace had merely unleashed the pain.

His aunt turned, her eyes widening, her hand flying to her throat when she saw him standing there.

He froze, not knowing what to say, not really ever knowing what to say to this woman. She was so very different from his mother, the only other female, besides his sister, who he'd spent any considerable time around.

Naturally, she regained her voice before he did. "Beech, you startled me." Her hand moved from her throat to her heart, pressing there as if to keep it from jumping out of her chest. She gave a small humorless laugh. "You always did move more like a cat than a person." She tilted back her head, eyeing him. "A very big cat." Her hands clasped across her stomach in a play of calmness. "What are you doing here? Heaton told me you would be away all summer."

"I had planned to but—" He wasn't sure how to broach the favor he needed.

"Your uncle will be home from the mercantile soon. I'm sure he'll want to hear all about your travels. Mercy me, he certainly does love to hear about them." She fluttered her hands dismissively then turned to the cupboard that held the dishes. "Will you be staying for dinner?"

This was how it was with his aunt. He'd no sooner begin talking, pausing to reach for the right word or gather his thoughts, then she would be chattering, filling the gap of silence, causing him to lose his train of thought. Then she would bustle off, oblivious, or maybe not so oblivious, that she had left him mid-sentence.

He glanced around for Little Brave. She still stood in the doorway behind him, and he motioned her forward. Her gaze warily tracked around the room as she entered the kitchen to stand beside him.

"So that will be four, including you and Grace." His aunt set the plates on the table without looking up then turned to reach for the glasses. "Heaton can't make it in for supper more than once or twice a week, he's got so much to manage out at the ranch with you being gone, but now you're home." She set the glasses on the table, looking up. "You are home, aren't—"

Beech was ready this time. "This is Ella Hastings. She needs a place to stay until her grandfather comes for her."

"Well, I—"

No doubt, his aunt was trying to reconcile the sight of a white woman dressed as an Indian. "She has lived with the Lakota Sioux for the past ten years."

"How—Why—"

For once, she seemed at a loss for words. "Her father was killed by the Blackfeet. She was taken in by the Sioux."

"Mercy me!" His aunt bustled around the table and gathered Little Brave's hands into her own, her face a mixture of grief and sympathy. "Let's get you cleaned up and into some proper clothes."

Little Brave's face held none of the panic when Mrs. Heisenberg had tried to lead her away, but still, she resisted his aunt's efforts. It would be easiest if she went along with his aunt now. He could slip away, return to his life as it had been before he chanced upon this woman who'd managed to upend his world, make him remember things that were better left in the past, make him long for a life much different from the one he was living. But his chance for slipping away evaporated when his sister swept into the kitchen then stopped when she saw them.

Blonde-haired, blue-eyed like his aunt, Grace passed naturally for their aunt's daughter, but there was a slant to her eyes and a height to her cheekbones that reminded him painfully of their mother.

"Oh my goodness," she said, a hand flying to her own golden, upswept hair as she stared at Little Brave's jagged, shoulder-length locks.

For once, Beech was grateful for his aunt's ability to fill the silence as she looped an arm through Grace's and pulled her forward. "Grace, this is Ella Hastings. She will be staying with us for a while."

"Hello, Ella," Grace said slowly, extending her hand even more slowly.

"Ella, this is my daughter, Grace."

"Grace." Little Brave shook hands with his sister.

"Why are you dressed like an Indian?" Grace asked, her nose wrinkling.

Little Brave looked at him, eyebrows rising.

187

He translated, quashing the urge to apologize for his sister's show of distaste.

Grace's eyes widened. "She doesn't speak English?"

"She does but it is rusty. You must give her time."

"I lived with the Lakota," Little Brave said in her halting English.

"Lakota?" Grace said.

"The Indian word for Sioux," Beech said, grimacing at the thought that under different circumstances the word Lakota would have been a part of his sister's everyday vocabulary.

"Oh," Grace said faintly.

Again, silence filled the room but not for long.

"So, that will be five for dinner," said his aunt.

"No, I have to get out to the ranch," said Beech.

"But you must be starving after coming off the trail, and your uncle will be disappointed to miss you."

His aunt was right. His uncle would be disappointed and he was starving, but the tight, hard look on Little Brave's face told him that now was the time to leave.

"You are leaving now." She squared her shoulders.

"Yes," he said, giving no further explanation. It was better this way. Her anger would drive a wedge between them, would allow her to concentrate on seeking something better than an attachment to him. He raised his hand then dropped it, resisting the urge to feel the soft skin of her cheek one last time. "You will find your way, Ella Hastings," he said in English then turned and headed out the door to the corral.

He swung himself into the saddle, but she was there. And he understood the disconcertion his aunt felt when he moved about more like a cat than a person.

"Take me with you," she said, biting her lip.

His gut clenched at the words echoing from his past. "No, your place is here." He reined August away.

She ducked under the gelding's neck, using her body to block the horse. "I know the ways of the prairie, your ways. They are my ways." Her hands fisted around the reins. "And if you take me with you—you will not be alone, and I—" Her knuckles whitened. "And I will not be alone." Quiet desperation entered her voice. "Please."

Her whisper barely registered in the everyday sounds surrounding them, but her plea reverberated in his head, rushed through his veins, pounded in his heart as the past and present collided. A boy, a man by most standards, denied the same request by his father. He jerked at the reins, desperate to get away from the painful repetition of history. No, this wasn't a repetition. Little Brave—Ella—had come from this world. He had not. Leaving her here was right.

"Ella," Grace called from the kitchen doorway, unabashed curiosity on her face, puzzlement ringing in her voice.

Little Brave glanced over her shoulder, distraction loosening her grip.

Beech dug his heel into the gelding's side with unprecedented cruelty. August lunged sideways.

She gasped, her eyes widening in surprise, her grip breaking free.

"It is better this way." He spun August then galloped past the corral. He bent over the gelding's neck, urging him to outdistance the panicked neighs coming from the little mare being left behind, to escape the look of betrayal on Little Brave's face, to block the memory of his father's defeated look as Jean Luc Richoux had ridden away from him and his sister for the last time.

Beech did not slow August until they rounded the ridge that hid his ranch from the main road. The descending darkness cloaked the curve of the road, but they followed it without sight through habit. August traded bugling whinnies with the yearlings, soft, welcoming nickers with the broodmares and their foals. But the peace Beech normally felt upon returning to the small breeding operation he'd built from the ground up eluded him.

Inside the barn, he took his time untacking, striving for that peace as he rubbed handfuls of straw along the gelding's sweaty sides. Still, his thoughts tumbled through his mind, his muscles remaining rigid with tension. He tossed the spent straw over the stall door and dumped a double ration into the gelding's feed bin. August nickered his thanks, but all Beech could hear was Little Brave's whispered pleas as he'd left her behind. He kicked at the matted heap of straw as he slammed the stall door shut behind him.

Little Brave was where she belonged.

And he was where he belonged.

His strides devoured the distance between the barn and the small cabin until the cock of a rifle rent the inky darkness.

"I'd halt it right there, mister, if you want to live a second longer."

Beech paused with one foot on the bottom step, holding his hands aloft, struggling to rein in his raging emotions, to will some matter-of-factness into his tone as he said, "Just me, Heaton."

The rifle uncocked and the door swung wide. "Hell, cousin, you sneak around the place like a thieving In—"

Thieving Indian. His mind finished the slur as easily as it had slipped from his cousin's mouth. He brushed by the younger man, dropping his saddlebags on the table.

"Wasn't expecting you 'til the leaves turned." Heaton leaned the gun next to the door. "Long way to come just to visit."

Beech merely grunted as he dropped into a chair next to the table.

"You hungry?" Heaton asked.

"Starving."

Heaton crossed the room to the fireplace and poked at the banked coals until they roused, threw on a couple of logs then clanked the cast iron skillet onto the grate. "Coffee or something stronger?"

"Something stronger," Beech sighed wearily.

Pork sizzled as it hit the pan. "Now, that's telling."

"Nothing to tell."

"That's where you're wrong, cousin. There's always something to tell." Heaton set a whiskey bottle on the table with a dramatic thunk. "And this is just the thing to help you tell it."

Beech hunched over the table. "On second thought, I'll have coffee."

"Your call," Heaton said as he dunked the coffee pot in the bucket of drinking water then set it on the grate next to the frying pan. "But either way, you're not getting any sleep until you've told me your tale."

Beech stared at the flames, tracking their yellowish-orange tongues flickering around the skillet where the pork sizzled and popped. Short of saddling up and riding back out, there was no way to avoid this leap from the frying pan into the fire. His cousin pestered as only the youngest of four siblings could.

"So, why are you back, cousin?"

"The job petered out."

Heaton snorted. "With three armies marching toward the Powder River Country, I doubt that."

"Where'd you hear that?"

"Soldiers coming into the mercantile from Fort Laramie. They say President Grant's aim is to push all the Indians onto the reservations, once and for all."

That was certainly the truth; Beech had read the order for himself.

"Makes the territory safer for more settlers to come in." Heaton continued, cracking the eggs into the skillet to cook alongside the pork. "Pa says the politicians and businessmen want the population to swell so they can apply for statehood."

Just like he'd told Little Brave when they looked upon General Crook's camp below Fort Fetterman, the change wasn't a matter of if, but when. And now he understood the why. He gulped from the steaming cup of coffee his cousin set before him, focusing on the scald in his throat as he swallowed.

Heaton set a heaping plate of pork and eggs before him then dropped into the chair beside him. "How are you going to get the money for the stud horse now?" he asked, with an ease and carelessness, which came from being the son of a white successful businessman.

Beech stabbed at the food, shoveled it into his mouth, not really tasting it as he chewed, focusing on the scrape against the scald on his throat as the mass awkwardly slid down.

"I can pick up work on the railroad while you stay and mind the ranch," Heaton said.

The younger man's face was shadowed, but Beech knew its cast. He'd been seeing it—mostly from over his shoulder—since Heaton had happily relinquished that doted-upon baby role to Grace and become Beech's shadow—traipsing after him with hopeful eagerness and anticipation whenever possible.

But Beech didn't want a shadow. He wanted—It didn't matter what he wanted. He was destined to be alone. Or he would be, once his cousin was gone. He tossed the coins Commander Heisenberg had given him onto the table. "There's what I owe you."

"What do you mean, that's what you owe me?"

"I mean, I don't need your help anymore."

"In case it slipped your mind, cousin, I wasn't here helping. It was my way into the ranch. Remember that deal?

You work to get the stud while I mind the ranch, then we start to put this place above break even."

"The stud's not happening, therefore neither are we."

"And I said, I'll work the railroad to buy the stud. Hell, you could work the railroad, but I know that goes against some mysterious code to which you're so committed, but won't ever talk about." Heaton shifted back in the chair, his biceps bulging, his forearms flexing as he crossed both arms over his chest.

His cousin had filled out with the ten hours a day of physical labor tending the ranch required.

"So, what really happened with the tracking job?"

And his voice had deepened, too. By all accounts, he was a man. Perhaps, it was time he heard the truth like a man. "Almost every soldier in the detachment I was guiding was killed in an ambush."

"By Indians?"

"Yes."

"How did you survive?"

"I look more like one of them than I do one of you." Beech didn't care what conclusion Heaton drew from that, as long as it sent him packing.

"Hell, cousin. You sacrificed a whole company of soldiers because—because—" Abruptly, Heaton stood, the chair crashing to the floor with the force of his movement. "I don't believe you. You're not like them. You have never been like them."

Beech stood, leveraging the couple of inches he had over the younger man, letting his long, dark hair frame his face. "Like them how, cousin?" he asked, mangling the term of affection into a dark threat. "Like a murdering savage, an uncivilized half-breed, a cheating Injun?" Beech stepped closer, wrapping his fingers around the hilt of his knife for effect. It worked.

Heaton darted his gaze to the knife then he held up his hands, palms out. "Look, cousin, I understand why you're upset. You feel responsible for the death of those soldiers but—"

"I don't feel responsible. They got what they deserved." At least, Captain Baldwin did, but Beech didn't let himself dwell on the *white* lie.

"You can't mean that."

"I mean it."

"Well—uh—" Heaton's throat convulsed as he retreated a step. "The horses will be expecting their feed at the first crow of the cock so I—uh—best be getting to bed." He gestured toward the bed in which he slept.

"Best if you head on back to Cheyenne tonight." Beech slipped the knife free of its sheath then laid it beside his half-eaten plate of food as he sat again. "I'm not feeling too generous toward the white man tonight."

Chapter 14

Little Brave submerged, scrubbing the soap out of her hair, then rose, sluicing the water from her shortened locks. She leaned back against the tub with a sigh, the deliciously warm water cradling her, the scent of eucalyptus filling the air, her skin tingling from the thorough washing she'd given it.

Now, she closed her eyes and rested her head on the rim of the tub, reveling in the sense of leisure she'd associated with hot, sunny days, when work was light enough she could spend time frolicking with other young women and girls of the village in a cold, sparkling stream. They would swim and dive and float until their skin puckered and their lips turned blue then they would lounge in the sun until their bodies warmed again, whereupon they would dress and return to the village.

A sound roused her. Instantly, she was alert. The sound didn't come from the door that led to the rest of the house, but from the door through which Beech had left just before dinner. Her heart leapt. He might be returning, but instinct had her reaching for her knife, on the chair beside the tub. She shifted, crouching in the tub, only her eyes and the top of her head visible above its edge, as a man came through the door. Instantly, she knew by his smaller stature, and the careless way he entered the kitchen he was not Beech.

He dropped a large bundle from his back to the floor and hung his hat on the hook beside the door.

She shifted her grip on the knife as the man turned. Something unknown was always a danger until it proved itself otherwise. Surprise filled his face when he saw her, but amusement took over as he crossed his arms and rocked back on his heels, saying something in a teasing manner, which she did not understand.

The muscles in his arms and legs told her he was no stranger to physical labor, the tan of his face below the white line where his hat rested said he labored out of doors.

He stepped closer to the table.

She did not move a muscle, but tracked his movement with her gaze.

He turned up the flame of the lamp, revealing his resemblance to Beech's uncle who she'd met earlier at dinner. This must be one of the four sons. He asked her a question, a grin lurking at the corners of his mouth.

She recognized the word 'name' but did not feel inclined to answer. "Go," she said, for that was the only English word she recalled at the moment, which conveyed her desire to be alone.

The grin broke free. He was obviously enjoying the disadvantage at which he had her, but he made no move to come closer.

"Heaton," the aunt said as she entered the kitchen.

Heaton. That was the name Little Brave had heard mentioned in the conversation between Beech and his aunt earlier today.

"I didn't expect you back." She shooed the young man toward the door that led from the kitchen into the hallway.

"I didn't expect to be back," he said then issued Beech's name with some disgruntlement as the aunt pushed him through the door.

Had this Heaton encountered Beech as he was returning to the fort to resume his duties? She held her breath as she tried to discern more from the conversation beyond the door. There was anger in the man's voice while the aunt answered in soothing tones, but Little Brave could not understand what they were saying.

The aunt returned, setting a 'towel' on the chair and draping a 'nightgown' and a 'wrapper' over the back then left again.

The peace of the moment lost and the water starting to chill, Little Brave dried off and dressed. After the weight of her doeskin dress, the nightclothes settled against her skin with a sensation of nothingness. She pulled on her moccasins, staring at the water in the tub, considering the amount of prairie dust required to turn it such a dark color. Fabric swirled around her legs and tickled her skin as she scooped up a bucketful of water and lugged it out into the cool night. She poured its contents among the leafy inhabitants of the garden then eyed the sky with its blanketing of stars.

Memories of those who'd denounced and abandoned her but whom her heart still missed overwhelmed her. Where were they now? Were they safe? Did Grey Owl's band—she refused to think of it as Running Bear's—know of the white man's soldiers gathered at the fort? What would happen when they met? She shivered, gathering close the thin fabric, which was no match against the spring chill.

The aunt summoned her from the doorway.

Slowly, Little Brave made her way back to the house whose windows shone with lamplight like owl's eyes gleamed in the moonlight. Unsettled, she entered, heard the word 'sleep' in the jumble of words that fell from the older woman's mouth, and nodded her understanding. She gathered her things, and the blade of her knife reflected the gleam of the lamplight.

The aunt gasped. A hand flew to her throat in the same way it had when she'd first seen Beech earlier today.

Little Brave realized the aunt was afraid. She had spent considerable time dwelling on the possibility the aunt would not want her in her home, but she'd never considered the woman might be afraid...of her.

"No hurt," Little Brave said as she slipped the knife beneath the beaded belt laying over her doeskin dress.

The aunt nodded, but her gaze remained locked onto the bundle Little Brave held in her arms.

***

Like a Lakota village, the household had its morning routine, and after many days, Little Brave found a small niche. Or rather, she'd been allowed a niche. Her offer to make biscuits had been met with careful consideration, for much as a Lakota first wife rules the tepee when her husband takes a second or a third wife, so did the aunt rule her kitchen.

Little Brave remembered well the way that Beech had taught her to make the light, flaky mounds of bread, but his aunt had many refinements to add. Little Brave mastered them under the aunt's watchful eye. However, when she had offered to slice and fry the salt pork, the aunt had turned her down with a quick, "Oh, no, no." Little Brave could not help but wonder if the aunt still might be afraid of her.

Now, when the biscuits were prepared and in the oven, Little Brave would sit quietly at the table, listening to the conversation between the aunt, Henry—as the uncle was called—and Grace. Her reacquaintance with her native language improved by leaps and bounds, but rarely did she lend her tongue to it. The short sentences and small phrases that were sufficient in the beginning now seemed trite and too simple for the mother and daughter's rambling conversations.

The uncle spoke more clearly and deliberately, giving her ample time to respond when he asked her a question. But he was away most of the day, working at the 'mercantile' so rarely did she push herself to practice speaking it. But she listened, particularly when he read from the newspaper.

"Listen to this," he said which meant he found something particularly interesting or significant. He folded the paper in half to focus on what he wanted to share. "Colonel Joseph J. Reynolds, the cavalry officer responsible for locating and burning one hundred and five Cheyenne lodges on the west bank of the Powder River back in March, has been accused of dereliction of duty for failing to properly support the first charge with his whole command, for burning the captured supplies, food, blankets, buffalo robes, and ammunition, instead of keeping them for army use, and most of all, for losing the eight hundred captured ponies."

At the words 'burning' and 'Cheyenne lodges', Little Brave's fork had paused between mouth and plate to concentrate on every word.

The aunt stopped sipping her coffee to ask, "Is that the battle they're referring to as the Battle of Powder River?"

He scanned the article further. "Indeed, that's the one." He flipped over the paper. "The incident that brought all this down on Reynolds' head is that 'in his premature haste to withdraw, he left behind three dead soldiers, as well as a badly wounded private who was subsequently torn limb from limb by vengeful Indians'."

"How can anyone tear someone limb from limb and call themselves a human being? I declare, those Indians are nothing but savages." The aunt gripped her coffee cup, staring venomously at the air above Grace's head.

Indians. Savages. Little Brave's fork clattered to the plate at the hatred in the blanket statement.

"Mama," Grace whispered, glancing furtively at Little Brave.

Little Brave stood, her expressionless Lakota mask slipping into place as she looked directly at the aunt, her brain scrambling for something more than the trite or simple. "Not every Indian is a savage. I—I—" Her mask held, but she felt her face blush at the frustration of trying to eloquently express that she was living proof of that. Instead, she resigned herself to saying, "I am not hungry." She left the table, exiting through the back door and into the bright sunshine.

Sundance nickered as she stumbled across the yard to the corral. Quickly, she bridled the little mare, swung onto her back and headed out across the prairie. She rode until she reached the copse of trees she'd discovered the day after Beech left her. There was not a day that went by that she didn't come here. She slid from the mare's back and sat as she always did, watching the wave of the grass in the breeze, soaking up the heat of the sun as it traveled toward its zenith and beyond, feeling the beat of the prairie, the cadence of her life for more winters now than not.

How much longer did she have here?

Suddenly, her scalp prickled, and the hairs rose on the back of her neck. She pulled her knife from her moccasin and crouched low among the tall blades of grass as a man appeared in the clearing.

He halted, held up his hands in gesture of no harm intended.

Slowly, she rose, keeping the knife hidden within the folds of her skirt and studied the man.

200

Dull, yellow hair, fading to an even duller yellowish-gray around his crown and temples, fell past his shoulders. A thick beard, threaded heavily with the same yellowish-gray color, covered the lower half of his face above which light blue eyes, watery from age and life, studied her. He was dressed in buckskins, well worn, missing the fringe on the left side of his chest. Moccasins, darkened with age and sagging from heavy use, encased his feet.

"What do you want?" she asked, pacing the English words to make them seem as if she was speaking slowly and distinctly, and not struggling to get them in the right order, with the right inflection.

He shook his head slightly then said, "You traveled from the Laramie Mountains with my son."

The unexpected Lakota words overshadowed her questions at how he'd known that, filling her instead with such a sharp ache in her heart that she had to close her eyes and breathe deeply through her nose to keep the emotions at bay. She opened her eyes and answered to the sad and hungry look in the man's eyes. "Your son is Beech Richoux?" The words of her adopted people felt right on her tongue, soothing to her ears.

He nodded slightly then cast his gaze skyward, uttering grateful words in a language she did not understand. He moved closer and gestured for her to sit with him.

She followed him down, sitting with her legs to one side as her skirt dictated while he sat cross-legged before her. There were so many questions on the tip of her tongue. Why had he left his children all those years ago? Why hadn't he returned before now? Why was he here now? But now was not time to ask them.

He eyed the knife she still held. "The Lakota taught you well."

"They were my people for many years."

201

"And now they are not?"

"They cast me out because of my pale skin," she said. Bitterness caused her to speak plainly to Beech's long-absent father. "Have you seen your son?"

A flash of pain crossed his face then his eyes seemed to water even more, but he did not return her bitterness. "I think it would be wise to know more about him, as he is now, before I see him again."

Her bitterness did not ease in the face of his wisdom; it only shifted into Beech's camp. Abandonment, whether through passionate urges or calculated reasoning, left a scar for life. "If you want to know more about him, you will have to ask him yourself."

"Then you must come with me to his ranch when I speak to him."

"Why—" The question of why she should come with him was lost in her confusion. "His ranch?"

"You did not know he had a ranch?"

Little Brave shook her head.

"It is but a short ride toward the place where the sun sets," he said.

"He is there now?"

He nodded.

Little Brave swept to her feet, pacing out to where Sundance was grazing beyond the tree line. Why had Beech not told her he lived close to Cheyenne? That he was not going back to the fort? That he had a ranch? It hurt that he had trusted her with his sister's secret but not this. Envy joined the hurt. Not only had he found his balance between their worlds, but he had a home, a place to call his own, no doubt work to fill his days and give him purpose.

She stared at the backs of her hands as they rested on the little mare's back. Already, they were paling, growing limp with inactivity. Her senses were dulling for lack of purpose. How long would it take her to find her place, her purpose, a home in this world?

"You will come with me?"

The hope on his face urged her to say yes, but the memory of his son as he'd left her, his parting words that it would be better this way stopped her. "I would be of no help to you," she said. She gathered her skirt with one hand and grabbed a handful of mane with the other, her movements jerky from the recall of Beech's rejection as she swung onto the little mare's back.

Beech's father held Sundance's reins as she'd held Big Black's reins that day. "I will be here tomorrow. When the sun is high in the sky as it is now," he said then he released the little mare's reins.

She reined around Sundance. She would not be here. It would do her no good to see Beech again when he had no desire to see her. With a dig of her heels, she headed back toward the white man's town—a place she had no desire to be.

***

Little Brave entered the kitchen, hoping she could pass through without encountering the aunt who would no doubt chide her again for taking to the prairie. At least the aunt, unlike the commander's wife at the fort, was gentle in her chiding, and kind in her talks about what was expected of proper young ladies. The talk of all those forbidden things made her head spin faster than a late summer dust storm, and she did not want to hear about them yet again.

Unfortunately, the aunt and Grace sat at the table, chattering with excitement. They paused when they saw her and regarded her with a happy speculation which did not foreshadow a talk about proper young ladies, but it made her want to avoid them just the same. She sidled sideways, keeping her gaze on the pair as she inched toward the door that led into the hallway, and up the stairs to her room.

They rose in tandem. "Ella, I have such good news," the aunt said.

Little Brave stopped and struggled to switch her thoughts from Lakota to English after the encounter with Beech's father.

The aunt nudged Grace. "Go on upstairs now, Grace."

The girl moved toward the door that had been Little Brave's destination, but paused short of going through it, her head turned in anticipation for the news to come.

"Come, come, sit." The aunt excitedly waved Little Brave to the table.

Little Brave sat, but she doubted the news would excite her as it did the woman now leaning toward her.

"Mr. Chapman has received word that your grandfather will arrive tomorrow."

Little Brave looked down, unsure she could hide the emotions overwhelming her. Her grandfather? So soon? Would he be the same as she remembered him? She was not the same. Would that disappoint him? Did he think as the aunt thought? That all Indians were savages?

"Now, don't you worry about a thing. I've sent Grace upstairs to pull out some of her best dresses. We'll find one that suits you," The aunt patted her arm in a manner that was meant to be reassuring.

But Little Brave did not feel reassured. She fingered the fabric of the dress she wore. It was well-worn and faded, but comfortable, lightweight. It did not have the layers and confinements of the dresses the aunt and Grace wore. She looked up, her mouth taking on an uncompromising line. "I like this dress."

The aunt looked surprised then vexed. "Oh no, no, it won't do at all. Your grandfather is a very important man. He's coming all the way from Washington D.C. You must make him proud when he first sees you after all these years."

Little Brave nodded reluctantly. She wanted her grandfather to be proud.

"You're a very lucky young lady. Imagine living in the hustle and bustle of our nation's capital."

Little Brave did not want to imagine it.

But the aunt prattled on. "Oh, what I wouldn't give to go back to St. Louis. You know I didn't always live here."

"St. Louis," Little Brave echoed blankly, still deciphering the gist of the aunt's remarks.

"Oh, it's not Washington D.C. but it's far more civilized than Cheyenne."

"Cheyenne is not civ-i-lized?" Little Brave rolled the complex word around on her tongue as she contemplated its meaning.

"Yes, of course it is. Certainly compared to what's out on the prairie."

"Where the savages live." She clenched her fists but kept them resting on her lap.

"Oh, Ella, I'm sorry I brought up those horrible memories this morning with my thoughtless comment. Lord knows what you went through living with those, those— Indians. Well, it's all over now." The aunt clucked in a manner meant to soothe.

But Little Brave was not soothed. "I had a home with those...Indians...the Lakota." She stood, giving herself time to gather the English words she needed to express herself. "My father, Grey Owl, was kind and...peaceful. The Lakota love and laugh. Have children. Live and die. The white man comes. He moves them from their home, kills them if they do not go." She held her arms rigidly at her sides. "You tell me now. Who is the savage?"

Chapter 15

Beech faced the thin pink line of dawn as he rode out from the ranch. His mount jigged beneath him, as did the two geldings he held in tow. They tossed their heads, craving to be free of restraints so they could take the wide-open prairie on their own terms. He held them close until they acquiesced and fell into the rhythm he set. He rolled his shoulders to ease the soreness in his muscles. He'd waited too long to get the five-year-olds into town, but with Heaton gone—he gave a snap to one of the lead ropes to resettle one of the geldings—well, he hadn't given enough credit to the younger man for the workload he'd been shouldering.

He entered Cheyenne on the road that passed his aunt and uncle's place. Noting the absence of his uncle's sorrel mare and Heaton's bay gelding, he kept riding. Little Brave's mare whinnied a come-hither greeting, and the geldings arched their necks and floated their tails as they pranced sideways to get closer to the little palomino. He legged his mount back into some semblance of straightness and jerked on the lead ropes to get the other two to fall back into line behind him. When he passed the house, without the appearance of Little Brave to check on her neighing mare, he told himself it was better this way, that the heaviness in his chest was due to his tiredness and the strain of the extra work he'd been carrying.

Once he entered the town's business district, he had to concentrate on keeping the young horses focused and calm. By the time he reached the livery which sat caddy corner from the train station, he felt rivulets of sweat running down his back and along the sides of his face while his muscles ached from the constant load of holding three horses in check.

He halted in front of the barn and its owner greeted him with a lift of his pudgy fingers. Robbed of adult stature by nature, Karl Godfrey possessed stubby legs and an off-kilter balance which left him little talent for sitting a horse, but no one knew horseflesh like Karl.

"Expected you in last week," the livery owner said.

"Been busy." Beech dismounted.

"Yep, losing your right-hand man tends to send things in that direction."

Beech led the horses through the barn to the round corral behind it. He didn't want to talk about Heaton. He steered the conversation back to the geldings who drank greedily from the water trough. "Any interest?"

"Mr. Pierce from the bank."

Beech rubbed down one of the sweaty animals with handfuls of hay. "Mr. Pierce doesn't have the seat to ride one of these geldings."

"It ain't for him but his son."

"His son?"

"Yeah his son, Frank."

Beech's hands went still at the girth. "What's he doing back?"

Karl shrugged. "Don't rightly know, but he's due in on the 2 o'clock from Ogden." The pint-sized man peered from beneath the horse's neck and added, "Same train as Heaton."

207

Ruby Merritt

***

Brakes locked the iron wheels to a screeching halt as a billow of acrid smoke filled the air. As the shrill of the whistle faded, passengers began streaming from the train. Beech stood at the far end of the platform to minimize his chances of encountering Frank Pierce while he waited for Heaton. He held no fear of the banker's eldest son, only fear of what he would do to the bastard if he was ever close enough to lay hands on him again.

The crowd thinned without a glimpse of Frank Pierce or Heaton. Beech turned then saw his cousin walking next to the boxcars strung out far beyond the platform.

When the younger man saw Beech, he changed his walk from a stroll to a saunter, but his eyes held a hint of wariness as he approached

"New rifle?" Beech pointed to the weapon Heaton cradled in the crook of his arm.

The wariness disappeared; Heaton's features became animated as he held out the rifle for Beech to examine. "It's the latest model of repeatin' rifle."

The younger cousin, eager to please and ready to share, had returned. "Better than the '73?" asked Beech.

"Without a doubt, cousin. This one has more power, longer range. No chance of outlaws getting close with this in my hands."

"So, you're killing for a living now?" Beech slipped in the disapproval casually.

The animation faded. "If killing is what's called for when doing my job." A muscle in his jaw jerked. "Same as when you scout for the Army." Heaton looped the rifle's strap across his chest, letting the weapon rest against his back.

The muscles in the back of Beech's neck tightened, warning him again the man his cousin had grown into during his absence was not to be discounted. Heaton, like

208

the young geldings he'd brought into town today, was chomping at the bit to prove himself, to take on the world and make it his own. Unlike the horses, Heaton was free to come and go as he pleased. It wouldn't do for Beech to try to strong arm his cousin into his way of thinking. Silently, he cursed himself for letting his emotions rule his tongue the night he'd told Heaton to leave the ranch.

Suddenly, Heaton's attention shifted beyond Beech. He gave a low whistle of appreciation. "She sure did clean up pretty."

Beech turned. His aunt and Little Brave—actually Ella Hastings seeing as she was dressed from head to toe as a white woman and her skin had paled considerably—stood on the platform. Although he should be thankful for Little Brave's return to the white man's ways, he couldn't help the surge of pride at the proud tilt of her chin and the cautious, measuring manner in which she surveyed her surroundings. She had not abandoned all her Lakota ways.

Beech followed a few steps behind Heaton as the younger man swaggered toward the two women.

His cousin offered his hand to Little Brave once he reached her. "We meet again, Miss Ella Hastings...although under much different circumstances."

Color rose in Little Brave's cheeks and there was the slightest dip of her chin.

What circumstances? Beech stepped up next to his cousin, ready to curb his cousin's teasing if necessary.

His aunt surged around Little Brave and wrapped her youngest son into her arms. "Oh, thank the Lord, you're back safe and sound," she said, leaning back to inspect Heaton from head to toe. "I hope you've given up this nonsense of working for the railroad."

"Protecting the railroad isn't nonsense, Mama."

"No, it isn't, but you weren't intended for such coarse, violent work." She gave her son a shake. "Leave it to those who are more suited to it."

Heaton extracted himself from his mother's hold. "Riding security is an honest living, Mama, and it pays well."

"So does the mercantile. Your father's fit to be tied to have someone in there he can trust when he runs for the territorial legislature."

"Let one of my brothers do it."

"William has his hands full running the store back in St. Louis, Thomas is determined to make a go of the store out in Ogden, and to even suggest your oldest brother is grabbing at straws. He has a thriving law practice in San Francisco."

"But, Mama, just like Henry Jr., I'm not cut out for the mercantile."

"You're certainly not cut out for railroad work, either." At her son's mutinous look, she turned to her nephew. "Beech, talk to him. He's always listened to you."

Reluctantly, Beech shifted his focus from Little Brave's inscrutable features to his aunt's desperate ones. He should jump at the chance to get Heaton back to the ranch, but all he could think about was Little Brave. How was she regarding him through her white woman eyes? He wanted to explain why he'd left her in the manner he did two weeks ago. And to tell her how much he had missed her. No—she was well on her way to finding Ella Hastings again; he couldn't get in the way of that.

He focused on his cousin's defiant features, so reminiscent of childhood days when his aunt would tell Heaton he couldn't traipse after him when Beech went out hunting or riding. What stubbornness Heaton had always exhibited, able to get his own way more often than not.

Now that stubbornness was against Beech. And in a man-sized dose.

Beech took a deep breath. "Heaton, there is more than enough work for two on the ranch."

"You don't have to tell me that, cousin."

"No, you're right, I do not. You shouldered it all when I was away," admitted Beech, nodding.

Heaton crossed his arms over his chest and shifted back onto his heels, his eyes narrowing.

No sign of the younger cousin, who'd always been eager to do his bidding. "I acted rashly when I sent you away. I need you back at the ranch."

Relief flickered in the younger man's face then it firmed with determination. "You said so yourself, cousin. If we're going to make the ranch profitable, we have to have the stallion. I'm working for the railroad until we have enough money." Heaton stood taller, his arms flexing across the chest.

"Oh, goodness gracious," Aunt Claire said, looking pleadingly at Beech. "Your uncle can loan you the money for the stallion, Beech."

"No," said Beech and Heaton in unison.

"Guess who I ran into," announced Grace as she approached with her arm looped through that of the banker's son who was closer to Beech's age than Grace's.

"Why, Frank Pierce, what a delight to see you," Aunt Claire said as she glanced appraisingly from the handsome, well-dressed man to her daughter and back again. "Henry Jr. wrote that he ran into you out in San Francisco. Did you find the city to your liking?"

"Very much so, Mrs. Chapman."

The small talk faded into background noise as the rage flared through Beech at the memories that flooded his mind. The battered face of the young girl, not much older than Grace, her torn bodice, her hiked up skirts as Frank Pierce thrust into the girl, taking his lecherous release.

211

Beech didn't realize Little Brave had moved beside him until he felt her hand on his arm. He looked at her at the same time his aunt called for her to come meet the banker's son. He glanced sharply at the man he'd cold-cocked that night six years ago. The cold grey eyes were regarding Little Brave with a manly appreciation that bordered on lewdness in Beech's mind. His soreness forgotten, every muscle coiled within him, ready to strike if necessary.

Little Brave ignored his aunt for the moment. "What is it?" she asked him.

Frank curled his lips in disgust at Little Brave's Lakota words and his gaze lost its appreciation as her hand tightened on Beech's arm.

Beech was no stranger to reactions like these. "This man has no honor," Beech replied in Lakota to Little Brave, but he kept his gaze trained on Frank. Defiantly. Challengingly. Looking at a white man this way could land him in jail, get him hanged, but *my woman* roared through his veins, pounded in his heart.

His aunt stepped into the space between the two men, reaching for Little Brave and drawing her forward. "Frank, may I present Miss Ella Hastings. We are meeting her grandfather, Captain Colonel Jonathan Russell, today. He's coming all the way from Washington D.C. to fetch her."

The pride with which his aunt announced Little Brave's lineage only prompted the banker's son to hide his disgust behind cold blandness.

If not for the fact that Henry Chapman was one of the leading businessmen in Cheyenne and his wife was making the introductions, Beech doubted the man would have even bothered to tip his hat to Little Brave as politeness dictated.

For her part, Little Brave merely nodded in return.

As for his aunt, she prattled on in her usual manner, ignoring the tense undercurrents.

212

Ella's Choice

Little Brave did not care to meet Frank Pierce. At first, he looked at her as Running Bear often did, with the raw desire of a man to possess a woman. In the next moment, he looked upon her as coyote would upon the lowest member in his pack. If it had not been for Beech's aunt holding her in place, Little Brave would have turned her back upon such a forked-faced man. Why did the aunt yet talk to him? Why did Grace yet cling to his arm? Could they not see he was not an honorable man, as Beech had said?

The man who'd spoken the truth stepped behind her. His heat warmed her back while his scent of honest man, leather and horses surrounded her. She stood a little taller and let her expressionless features speak of the little regard she had for the dishonorable man standing before her.

Frank Pierce slid his gaze from the woman ruling the conversation to Beech standing behind her. They narrowed in slyness then fell upon the young woman at his side, a snake's smile spreading across his face.

Grace caught her breath then her face brightened like Mother Sun bursting over the horizon.

Behind her, Beech shifted, readying himself as cougar would before leaping upon his prey.

With a glint of satisfaction, Frank Pierce patted Grace's hand then gently removed it from his arm. He held Grace's hand a moment longer as he spoke words slicker than the grease which held back his hair tight against his head.

Little Brave did not understand all the words, but she understood the younger woman's sigh and the aunt's encouragement to pay them a visit at home. It wasn't until he strode away that Little Brave returned her attention to the man behind her.

Beech was watching Frank Pierce weave his way through the crowd on the platform like hawk watches mouse scurry from clump to clump of wiry bunch grass. It wasn't until he disappeared inside the station house that Beech's gaze fell upon her.

"Tell me if he comes around my sister," he said.

That he referred to the golden-haired woman who now spoke animatedly with Heaton and the aunt as his sister told her the dishonor of this man was great indeed. The blush upon the younger woman's cheeks told her Beech's sister would welcome another visit from the man called Frank Pierce. With a slight dip of her chin, she agreed to Beech's demand, but in the next moment, her anger rose.

How was she to tell him if she did not know where to find him? And all her other questions fell into line behind that one. Why had he left her the way he had? Why had he not told her of his ranch? That he was not returning to scout for the white man's Army? Why was he here today? It was only the familiarity of his strong features, their likeness to her recently lost people, and the comforting cadence of the Lakota tongue as he asked how she was that quelled her anger to emotionless features and unyielding posture. But behind that wall, her questions still raged.

"My grandfather comes today," she said, trying to ignore her burning questions.

Something flickered in his eyes then it was gone. "That is good."

She did not know whether he meant good for him or for her, but she did not ask. Either answer would only stir her anger and fill her heart with sadness.

Beside them, the train issued its departing wail, then shifted laboriously into motion, drowning out any sounds save its own. There was flurry of activity as the aunt clutched her youngest son to her, then held him at arm's length and shouted something. Again, she clutched him to her before he managed to free himself.

He hugged Grace then turned to her. Amusement danced in his eyes as he lifted his hat, but they sobered when they turned to his cousin.

The strength at which the two men shook hands spoke of more than a simple farewell. Then he hopped onto the steps of one of the railcars as the train labored to pick up speed and waved his final farewell.

Once the caboose cleared the platform, the aunt and Grace fell into conversation with some friends who had arrived to meet the next train.

Little Brave spoke quietly to Beech. "You have missed more than his help at your ranch."

The emotion that had flickered in his eyes when she told him of her grandfather's arrival appeared again. This time, it held.

She caught her breath as she recognized what it was: regret. And sadness. She understood his feelings over Heaton's departure, but had he the same feelings over her departure, as well?

As if he read her thoughts, he said, "Heaton is not the only one I have missed."

She squashed the urge to tell him she had missed him, too, for what use were words when they did not change things.

"I am sorry for the way I left," he said, tendering her silence with the notion that words could change things.

She let the silence marshal its strength and speak for her, but the wind gusted and a flag snapped its salute, shutters banged and the station's hanging sign shrilled a rusty protest. His dark hair lashed across his face, but it did not hide the pain and sorrow she saw there. "Was it better that way?" she asked, recalling the reason he had given her as he'd surged past her onto the prairie that day.

215

"No."

His voice rumbled even in its quietness, and she wrapped her heart around that sound, waiting for him to say more, but he did not. Instead, he looked down the tracks in the direction Heaton's train had departed, the direction in which she would depart. Suddenly, regardless of whether her words would change things, she did not want to spend their final moments together without speaking of what was in her heart. "I am glad you have come."

He returned his gaze to her, the pain and sorrow easing, softening the sharp edges of his face. A smile lifted the corners of his lips. "I brought three of my horses to town." Pleasure lit his blue eyes. "To accustom them to its ways, its noise and activity."

Little Brave nodded in understanding and approval for it was no less than the Lakota did when they readied their own horses to hunt among the thundering herd of buffalo. Or to fight in the violent chaos of battle. Inwardly, she shuddered. She would not miss the warriors returning from their raiding, but from their hunting...she struggled to remember something in the white man's world that compared to that joy. Mother Earth's bounty kept all hands busy for many sleeps, harvesting food, shelter and tools from the huge beasts with much feasting and dancing whenever the sun took her rest.

"The thought of my horses pleases you?" he asked.

She blinked and realized she had been smiling. She let it yet live on her face. "Are they as fine as Big Black?"

"Finer."

"Hiyee. I wish to see them."

"They are over there."

She turned her head in the direction he gestured then pushed at the straw bonnet which frustratingly and perpetually hindered her peripheral vision. It slipped free and hung down her back. "I don't see them." She wondered how she could have missed such fine horses as she scanned those tethered up and down the dusty, bustling main road of the town.

"They are in a corral behind that barn."

Little Brave stared at the wooden building painted an earthy red, labeled with letters of which she recognized 'L' and 'e'. Instinctively, her tongue formed the initial sound.

"Livery," Beech supplied when her tongue struggled to conjure the sounds for the remaining letters.

"Livery," she repeated, drawing out the sound of the one that looked like an inverted tepee, letting it vibrate against her bottom lip before she finished off the word. Hurriedly, she loosened the straps of her bonnet and held it before Beech. She pointed to the purple flowers wreathing its crown. "Violet," she said. Anxious for him to understand the connection she'd made, she held up two fingers in the form of the inverted tepee and repeated the word the aunt had given her this morning for the purple flowers.

He did not disappoint her as he gave words to her discovery. "Violet starts with the letter 'V'." He tapped her parted fingers. "That's a 'V'."

"V. Vi—what is after 'V' in violet?"

"I."

"What shape is 'I'?" He held up one finger and punched the air above it with another.

She nodded in understanding. "Vi-ooo." She formed a circle with a thumb and forefinger. Seeing him nod, she rushed on. "Vi-o-laa. 'L' is next. Vi-o-laa-ehh. 'E' as in Ella. Vi-o-leh-tuh." She made a circling motion with her hand as she reiterated the last sound, willing its letter to emerge from some dormant pocket of her mind. The moment it surfaced, she said, "T" with such triumph that people turned to stare. She crossed two fingers, perpendicularly, to make its shape then shook her head in amazement at her recall. Her short hair swished across her

217

cheeks in a haphazard manner which brought the aunt scurrying over.

"Ella," the older woman chided, taking the bonnet from her. "We must get you presentable before your grandfather arrives."

At the mention of her grandfather, buffalo sat on her chest and sparrow flitted about in her stomach. Little Brave closed her eyes as the older woman slipped the hindering cover back onto her head, tucked stray hairs beneath its confines and tied it firmly beneath her chin. She opened her eyes.

"There." The aunt stepped back to survey her from head to toe, stepped close again to pluck at a sleeve then smooth a wrinkle from her shoulder. "Now, you are ready to meet your grandfather."

Snake joined buffalo and sparrow, coiling about her middle, the pointy knobs of his spine digging into her soft flesh, grating against her ribs, stealing her breath so her words stalled in her throat.

I am not ready to meet my grandfather.

Chapter 16

"That must be him." The aunt pointed to a trim, uniformed man appearing on the platform of the railcar.

He descended the steps with an authoritative bearing, which in an instant Little Brave knew like the back of her hand. But his hair, whiter than winter's first snowfall, was a shock.

The aunt waved to capture his attention.

A backwash of engine smoke swirled around him, blurring his features as he came toward them. He was taller than Grey Owl, but, she thought with odd satisfaction, he was not as tall as Beech.

The sun caught the gleam of medals on his chest as the smoke cleared. Snake vised tighter. She clutched at his coils and encountered only the fabric of the tailored dress and the boning in the corset it demanded she wear. She looked up into her grandfather's face as he halted before her. Skin sagged at his jowls and beneath his chin, creases stacked his brow, and crow had trampled in glee at the corners of his eyes, but beneath his stark white brows, his eyes—a mix of the autumn browns and spring greens of the prairie—were clear and measuring.

"Ella?"

A thousand sleeping memories awoke at the familiarity of his cool tenor, but its tentativeness did not match her remembrances of a man who never doubted his sureness in all things. "I am Ella." She was careful with the white man's tongue, lest he think her a savage.

His hands fisted at his sides as if resisting some undesirable urge then his fingers unfurled as hawk stretches her wings. Slowly, he raised a hand.

Its trembling—like leaves fluttering on the wind—surprised and confused her.

He touched her cheek, his fingers cool against the warmth of her skin. "You still have your mother's eyes." He caressed a stray tendril of hair. "But your hair is darker than hers."

Emotions she couldn't afford to name in this moment crested, threatening to overwhelm her and rob her of the support of her legs. She drew on everything Lakota to remain upright and dignified before the man who had not approved of her coming West with her father, who had pronounced her worthless. A man of great military standing and resources who had not found her in ten winters.

"You're not happy to see me?"

Hearing his question, she realized the teachings of her adopted people had not failed her. "I do not know." Her answer, though simple, was honest.

Beside her, the aunt shifted. "I'm Mrs. Henry Chapman, Colonel Russell," she said. "Welcome to Cheyenne. Ella's English is still rusty. Give her time, and I'm sure she'll be chattering away before you know it."

Regardless of the aunt's talk of time, Little Brave felt the heaviness of expectation in the arm the woman laid across her shoulders, the sense of urgency in the squeeze she gave her.

Her grandfather let his gaze linger for a moment longer, his lips parted in readiness to ask more questions.

Questions she did not know if she could answer.

Finally, they firmed and he shifted his attention to the woman next to her, tapping out conversation.

His words came out in the efficient and direct manner that meshed with her memories of him. Buffalo shifted, snake eased his grip, and Little Brave pulled for air, but the ribs of the corset prevented her from refreshing her lungs. She longed for the simple, cotton dress she usually wore. And for her moccasins. The leather boots, each with ten buttons that required a special tool to fasten them, pinched her toes and chafed her ankles. She made do with a short breath and concentrated on the words flowing between her grandfather and the aunt to keep her mind off her aching feet.

"...at the hotel...find a good horse?"

The aunt was speaking now about the livery.

Little Brave spoke before she thought. "Beech Richoux—" they looked at her as she struggled for the English words, "have—has good horses."

"Oh, Ella, Beech's horses aren't ready yet."

"Who is this Beech Richoux?"

The look on her grandfather's face set her firmly back in a wood-paneled room, a massive desk, the tang of tobacco and leather-bound books, a shaft of sunlight that made her squint, and she but nine winters. No, years. She shook her head, trying to right herself between the past and the present. She was eighteen years—winters.

"I am Beech Richoux."

The deep rolling voice suddenly so close steadied her, pushed the past back to where it belonged.

"This is my nephew, Colonel Russell," said the aunt.

"You are the man who rescued my granddaughter."

A statement, for her grandfather far preferred those over questions.

"I did not *rescue* her."

Beech's meaning was clear to her. Would it be clear to her grandfather? She had not been a captive of the

221

Lakota. She'd had a father, a home, a community. She'd been happy and content with her life among them.

Her grandfather looked down the length of the tall, sinewy man beside her, those sharp eyes noting every detail from the worn moccasins, and buckskin clothing to the straight dark hair that brushed his broad shoulders and framed his proud, stoic features. Finally, the older man nodded and held out a hand. "Thank you for safely bringing her to me. She is the last of *my* family."

Last of my family. The words struck her as they must have struck Beech, for he glanced at his golden-haired sister who stood apart from them, chatting happily with friends who shared her pale skin, but not her heritage. Little Brave's heart seized in sorrow for him, for, unlike her, he could not claim the last of his family.

Nevertheless, he took her grandfather's hand, showing none of the anguish and pain he'd shown her the day he'd revealed the promise he'd made to his aunt.

Her heart hammered, echoing her words to him that day. *You are not alone, Beech. You have me.*

But he could not hear them. And would not heed them, if he could. That had been his choice the day he'd ridden out onto the prairie, leaving her behind. He was only here today because of his horses and his cousin.

"I would like to see your horses, if they are *good* like my granddaughter says," her grandfather said.

The look he gave her was not unlike the one Grey Owl would give her when they were alone at the end of a day, and she moved about their fire preparing dinner or sat working at her beading. *Hiyee!* The sun must be playing tricks on her eyes.

"Little Brave—I mean Ella—wanted to see my horses, too."

Her English name sounded strange on Beech's tongue, nevertheless hearing it from his lips put a blush on her cheeks she knew her pale skin could not hide.

He gestured across the dusty road. "They are at the livery, Colonel Russell."

"The livery is no place for a respectable young woman." The aunt looked to her grandfather for his consensus.

Little Brave squeezed her lips together in determination. Since Beech had left her, she'd learned *respectable* and *proper* meant confinement and constraint. She did not want to be thought of as a savage, yet she was finding the white man's codes not only senseless but dispiriting, too.

"No harm will come to her, if I am escorting her, Mrs. Chapman."

"Yes, of course, I've no doubt of that, Colonel Russell." She turned to Little Brave, taking a moment to fuss with the high collar around her neck then adjusted the ties on her bonnet. "Remember all that I've told about how a proper young lady should act."

Little Brave nodded again, but she was not focusing on proper behavior, but of spending time with Beech and his fine horses.

-*-*-

"He is like a child, but yet, he is not." Little Brave took the stunted hand the livery owner offered, looking him over unabashedly as she shook it.

Rarely being the object of a woman's attention, let alone a beautiful one, Karl's grin took over his face.

"What did she say?" Colonel Russell asked. When Beech translated, a pucker appeared between his bushy eyebrows, uncannily resembling the one, which appeared between Little Brave's more elegantly shaped brows when she was worried or bewildered. "She certainly speaks her mind."

"It is the Lakota way." There was a beat of silence as they watched Karl gesture Little Brave over to meet the horses stalled within his barn.

"She looks so much like Lillian, yet she doesn't act like her," Colonel Russell murmured.

Sensing the Colonel's words were an escape of his thoughts rather than a remark directed at him, Beech did not comment. Besides, to him, Little Brave would always be Little Brave, although he could see more of Ella Hastings emerging. Her English had improved, and she was regaining her reading skills as evidenced by their conversation at the train station.

She certainly looked the part of a white woman, clad in a dress, which revealed little of her skin, but candidly followed her curves. The endless row of tiny buttons jauntily rode the swell of her breasts, dove between the narrow confines of her waist to end suggestively at that most womanly of all places between her thighs. This he did not understand about the white man. They were strict about acceptable interaction between men and women, but their women dressed in a manner which left less to the imagination than the simple dresses his mother's people wore, and yet his mother's people were marked as uncivilized.

But there was nothing uncivilized in Little Brave's interaction with the horses or the unusual livery owner. Her deference and attention to the pint-sized man as he showed off his most prized possessions would rival any proper lady's in white society. Beech couldn't help the surge of pride, knowing that while Little Brave had noted Karl Godfrey's oddness, she did not treat him as an oddity as most proper ladies would.

After stroking and cooing to each of the placid creatures contentedly munching hay in their stalls, Little Brave offered the livery owner her hand and thanked him in her careful English.

Beech didn't think Karl's grin could get any wider as he said, "The pleasure is all mine, Miss Hastings."

The Colonel cleared his throat but it wasn't a sound of impatience for he swiped at his eyes as he emitted the sound. The older man had been struggling with his emotions from the moment he'd faced his long-lost granddaughter. Regardless of how much Little Brave tried to hide them, she was struggling with hers, as well. Beech was confident that in time, they would find their way. The hole in his heart deepened at the thought of Little Brave leaving, but he thrust that aside. "Karl, the Colonel wanted to rent a buggy for the afternoon."

Reluctantly, Karl pulled his gaze from the Colonel's beautiful granddaughter to the older man who'd regained his commanding presence. "Yes, of course. Two seater or four?" the livery owner asked, once again all business.

"Two will do."

"Fine, fine. A lively stepper or something more placid?"

The Colonel looked inquiringly at his granddaughter whose features expressed surprise then lit with pleasure at being consulted.

She took a moment to answer and Beech stood ready to interpret if necessary but finally she said, "Lively."

The grandfather beamed as he said to Karl, "You heard the lady."

"Indeed," Karl said with the grin, which now seemed to be a given whenever Little Brave was involved. "Give me a few minutes and I'll have everything ready to go." He gave the Colonel a businesslike nod then trundled away to fill the request.

Little Brave turned to Beech. "Now, I will see your horses."

"They're in the corral out there." Beech gestured to the open doors, which led to the rear yard of the barn. Little

Brave exited the barn while Beech and her grandfather followed at a slower pace. They paused in the doorway as they watched her approach the corral. All three of the geldings trotted over to the railing, necks arched, hides gleaming. They were full of the confident curiosity his careful handling had instilled. She held out a hand, and they good-naturedly pushed and jostled for their turn to investigate her opened palm. Then they moved on with gusto to the flowers on her bonnet.

Little Brave stroked his handsome homebreds, her face beaming with delight.

"How amazing. Lillian detested horses," the Colonel remarked, awestruck at his granddaughter's ease with the spirited animals.

Little Brave looked back, speaking in Lakota then stopping in midsentence as her gaze fell upon her grandfather. She switched to English, her mouth working deliberately at forming the words, "They are fine horses, Beech."

"You are right, Ella. They are indeed magnificent," boomed Colonel Russell.

There was a moment of puckered brow as she processed what her grandfather had said then she gave him a shy smile and nodded.

The Colonel grew taller, his face assuming a pleased expression if not quite a smile at his granddaughter's acknowledgement.

Just then one of the geldings nipped at the flowers on her bonnet and inadvertently tugged it free from her head. Little Brave laughed, full and true.

It was the most beautiful sound Beech had ever heard and the delighted look on her face at the horse's innocent antics was a picture he would carry for the rest of his life.

She turned back to the horses and the wind caught her short locks, lifting them to dance merrily in the breeze.

"Lord have mercy, what did they do to your hair?" asked Colonel Russell.

Little Brave turned at her grandfather's outraged tone, confusion then fear on her face as he marched toward her.

Beech had not seen that level of fear in her since the soldiers had come to Grey Owl's village. With a few quick strides, Beech planted himself between the two, protectively fanning his arms out behind him. "You are scaring her." Family or not, he would not allow Little Brave to be traumatized more than she already had been.

"What? Nonsense." Colonel Russell gestured dismissively.

Beech did not budge.

The Colonel eyed him with a commanding silence, but when that didn't dislodge him either, the Colonel expanded his chest with the mighty inhale characteristic of military officers. "I am her grandfather. She has no reason to fear me."

Beech jerked his chin toward the medals lining the Colonel's chest. "The soldiers came to her village, killed one of her people, forcibly moved them—"

"Her people! I am her people."

Little Brave stepped around Beech, the sun striking the fiery lights in her hair as it shifted in the breeze. "You did not come."

Her words spoke of the pain and resentment Beech knew had been festering within her for ten years. While he was thankful she was speaking of it to her grandfather, he couldn't ignore the stab of pain at what that meant. She would heal. She would become Ella Hastings fully and wholly once again.

"What do you mean I did not come? I am here," her grandfather countered.

Little Brave's mouth worked, her brow furrowed as she struggled for her explanation in English. She looked to Beech in silent question and he nodded in agreement. He would not deny her the ease of speaking in Lakota at this crucial moment with her grandfather. "You did not find me in the ten winters I lived with the Plains People." She lifted her chin, challenging her grandfather to explain that as Beech translated for her.

Now Colonel Russell's mouth worked in struggle for his defense. "Ella, I searched. Not a year went by that I didn't search for you."

"The books at the fort said you came only two times to search for me."

"Yes, that is true."

If the Colonel was surprised by her knowledge, he didn't show it.

"But my work took me overseas, and when I could not come, I made inquiries of every expedition that went into the Powder River Country."

Even before Beech finished translating her grandfather's words, Little Brave's hands were fisting in the folds of her skirt, stoicism freezing her features, matching the winter in her tone. "You chose your work over finding *the last of your family*."

Her grandfather flinched as Beech translated Little Brave's use of the phrase he'd used earlier. Wrinkles stacked his brow and he seemed at a loss for words. Finally, he spoke. "My dearest child, I can't imagine what unspeakable horrors you lived through...for that I am truly sorry."

Beech did not translate these words, instead he let the quaver in the old man's voice, the tremor in his hand as he reached for her convey more than words ever could.

Little Brave held her rigid pose as the last of her family stroked her hair.

The tiniest bob of her Adam's apple told Beech she was holding onto her emotions with tenuous control just as she had at the train station when her grandfather had greeted her for the first time in ten years.

"I cut it when my father died," she said.

Little Brave's grandfather stilled his stroking. "Your father has been dead for ten years."

"Not my white father. My Lakota father, Grey Owl."

"Your Lakota father," he murmured.

His hand fell to his side as Beech saw his understanding finally dawn. The man's granddaughter was changed in so many ways and had experienced so many things in the ten years ago she'd been lost to him that it was not a simple matter of picking up where they'd left off when she'd traveled West with her father.

The Colonel coughed to clear his throat then backed up a step. "I'll go check on the horse and buggy."

Little Brave's posture did not ease until her grandfather disappeared into the livery then she turned back to the corral.

Beech joined her, bracing his forearms on the railing.

The horses vied for her attention and she stroked their glossy necks each in turn. "It will take time to know my grandfather again."

"Yes, it will. Ten winters cannot be dealt with in one sleep or even one moon, but it will happen if you work at it." She looked at him with an expectation on her face he did not understand.

"If your father returned, would you embrace him as if he had never left?"

Her question surprised him, but he had no trouble in answering it. "That is different. My father left me. You were taken from your father."

"Your heart hurts all the same, does it not?"

He wrapped his fingers around the warped wood, his calluses protecting his skin from the rough surface. "It was wrong for my father to leave."

"Maybe he had reasons you would not have understood then, but you would now."

In his mind, Beech knew what she saying, the parallel she was drawing with his situation to make sense of her own, but the clench in his gut, the hard thump of his heart in his chest prevented him from acknowledging it. "There are no reasons good enough for abandoning your family."

Disappointment flickered in Little Brave's eyes as a buggy pulled around to the back of the livery. "It is as I thought." She turned to join her grandfather in the buggy.

Too late, Beech realized how she could apply his words to her grandfather's efforts to search for her.

Chapter 17

"The Blackfeet told me you were dead," her grandfather said.

He had talked to the warriors who had killed her white father? The ones who had held her captive for two years?

"It was the third summer after you were taken." He focused on steering the buggy between two lumbering wagons, heading in opposite directions of each other.

His focus gave her time to think. By the third summer she'd been traded to the Lakota and adopted by Grey Owl. How did her grandfather know she'd even been with the Blackfeet?

"There was a girl in their village, an Indian girl who wore black leather boots and a cloth dress. The fabric looked similar to one of yours, and I guess—"

"Yes, yes, it was mine." Little Brave patted her chest in emphasis of her point. "I traded—it was too small."

"Then you were there? They hid you from me?"

"No, no." She shook her head vehemently. "I was with Grey Owl."

"Your Lakota father?" he asked.

She nodded.

"But why would they tell me you were dead?"

"Not make enemies of the Lakota." Betrayal to the white man was not taken lightly. But still, she was confused. "Why send people to search when you...you..." She struggled for the right words.

"When I thought you were—" He swallowed hard before he uttered that last word. "Dead?"

She nodded again.

Her grandfather scrubbed at his brow. "I can't explain it. I was devastated at what the Blackfeet told me. I returned to Washington and took a post overseas to distract myself, but I guess somewhere deep down I didn't believe it to be true." He reached for her hands folded in her lap, his eyes full of sorrow and regret. "But, I'm sorry I didn't return to search for you."

Suddenly, the words she'd uttered only moments ago haunted her. *Maybe he had reasons you would not have understood then, but you might now.* She stared down at the hand still holding hers, a hand which she realized appeared completely unfamiliar. How could she understand his reasons, when he himself did not understand them?

He squeezed her hands then released them. "I thought we could depart for Washington the day after tomorrow."

"In two days?" She was barely grasping what he was suggesting.

"Yes, a day to pack."

Pack? She owned nothing but the clothes she'd ridden into town with and two ponies. Would she be able to take Sundance?

"And you can say your farewells tonight at the Chapman's."

Farewells? Say goodbye to Beech Richoux? *Tonight?* Why did it seem too soon?

"I cannot leave in two days."

"I don't understand. What do you have to keep you here?"

232

"I can't explain." She used his earlier words because they were true. She couldn't explain to him why the thought of leaving in two days had her heart howling like lonesome coyote's. She scrambled for a reason. Hadn't Beech said it would take time?

Hiyee, more time!

"I need more time."

***

Little Brave set the stack of dinner plates on the lace-covered table, sighing in deep relief at what her grandfather had promised her. More time. Ten sleeps—days she corrected. That had been part of the trade. For more time, she would work on her English and learn all she could from the aunt about being the mistress of a household. And oh, be fitted for a proper wardrobe. She didn't know how many dresses one needed for a *proper* wardrobe, but from what the aunt said, it was at least ten.

Little Brave moved to the 'sideboard' as the aunt had named it and began lighting the lamps. She would have preferred opening the heavy window coverings and letting the soft evening light fill the room, but she did as the aunt had asked. When she was mistress of her grandfather's home, they would eat by the rosy glow of twilight instead of—a sound caught her attention as she ignited the last lamp. Awareness prickled her skin, telling her who it must be, but she gasped when she looked to the doorway.

She did not know this man.

Dressed in the whitest of shirts, trousers that hugged his long, lean legs and brushed the tops of gleaming black boots, he appeared every inch a white man. Her gaze swept back to his face, the burnished copper of his skin and his blue-black hair—its shine rivaling that of his boots— reassured her it was indeed Beech Richoux. He wore his

233

hair pulled back, revealing every strong contour, every arresting angle of his face. He looked no less confident and in control than when he rode on the plains—only more restrained, as if he had to be more protective of what was exposed.

He walked toward her with the easy grace of cougar, no less breathtaking when dressed as a white man but certainly more pronounced. She was accustomed to how agilely he moved between his two worlds, but now, she added her awe at how effortlessly he mingled the two. The lamplight played with the planes of his face as he approached, softening then sharpening them as he passed through its glow. Deep in her belly, sparrow fluttered as this new version of Beech halted before her. The deep blue of his eyes approached the black of night just before the moon rose, drawing her into the hold he alone had over her. Suddenly, she wanted to show him she too could exist in both worlds. She licked at her dry lips, struggling with the English words to express her surprise, for he had not accepted his aunt's invitation to dinner at the train station.

"You are here," she finally managed to say. Although her words were not complex, at least they were appropriate.

"I am." Paper crinkled as he held out a package.

It was thin and flat, wrapped in shiny, brown paper like the packages that came from his uncle's mercantile. This one was different, however, for it was not bound with string, but a ribbon—a ribbon the color of a cloudless blue sky.

When she did not reach for the package, he shook it, its crisp edge grazing her knuckles. "It is a gift."

A gift? She did not know why he was giving her a gift. Slowly, she took the package and carefully untied the ribbon, fingering its softness, admiring its color. She looked at him. "It is pretty."

"Like you."

234

Her cheeks warmed in self-conscious pleasure at his compliment, but she could not tear her gaze from his. His eyes held her in some kind of spell and her head filled with memories of their times together—the night in his arms after her people had abandoned her, the afternoon by the stream when they'd first come out of the canyons, the evening at his parent's cabin when her flesh had twined with his flesh. And she knew he was remembering those times too by the way his eyes softened, the hard way he swallowed.

Too soon, he coughed and tapped the package she held in her hands. "Open it."

Her gaze dropped, disappointed he'd broken the spell, but curious for what lie hidden beneath the thick paper surrounding the package. Eagerly, she unwrapped it, the paper falling to the floor with a whisper.

She stared at the sketch of the mightiest creature on the Plains, framed by the golden plains and a soaring sky the color of the ribbon she still clutched in her fingers. Little Brave stroked the smooth surface which appeared so lifelike she could see the acceptance of self-sacrifice in the buffalo's eye at providing for the Lakota's every need.

"Wildlife of the Great Plains," he read as he pointed to each word in the title. "Look inside."

Little Brave didn't need anymore urging as she flipped open the book to a handwritten note. The letters were strong and vibrant like the man who must have written them. "You wrote this?"

He nodded and came to stand beside her, his finger tracking beneath the words as he read them. "June, 1876. A reminder of your home upon the Great Plains. Your friend, Beech Richoux."

Beech Richoux was indeed a friend, for this was a fine book. The pages crinkled crisply in the quiet room as she slowly flipped through the black-and-white sketches, her memories supplying the color for the animals she'd seen countless times on the prairie. She grinned when she turned to the drawing of the prairie chicken, puffed up in his mating dance.

Beech grinned too, his teeth flashing white, as he bent closer to get a better look.

"Ella?" Her grandfather stood in the doorway, a questioning frown on his face as he looked from her to Beech then back again.

Little Brave rushed forward, holding out the book. "Grandfather, look." She flipped through the book, pointing to one animal after another, naming each in the Lakota tongue.

He shook his head as he held up a hand. "English, Ella."

She glanced at her grandfather, the commanding man she remembered as a child stared at her. Anxious to please him, to show him she was holding to their agreement, she nodded then fixed her gaze on the caption beneath the drawing. With a finger beneath the letters, she tried to combine the sounds into a word that made sense. Judging by her grandfather's silence, she was not succeeding. She stole a look at Beech, wondering if he too was disappointed in her efforts.

His brows were flattened over his eyes, like they were the morning she been outside the mountain cabin by herself.

He, too, was not happy. The joy she felt in his generous gift vanished, and she closed it with resignation. "The table," she said, gesturing to the stack of plates still waiting to be set. She did not want Beech's aunt to appear with the food and be disappointed in her, as well.

"Of course, I didn't mean to distract you, Ella." Her grandfather gestured for her to tend to her duties.

She approached the table, keeping her gaze on the stack of plates.

Ella's Choice

-*-*-

"Colonel Russell," Beech said as he followed the man into the hallway and hopefully out of earshot of Little Brave. Perhaps Colonel Russell did not realize how a look and a few words could discourage the woman who in many ways still viewed her grandfather through a nine year old's eyes.

The Colonel turned. "Yes?"

"Give Little—Ella time. It is hard to deny ways that have been your ways for so long."

"In my experience, the sooner one stops unfortunate habits, the sooner they'll no longer be habits."

In his experience? Unfortunate habits? Beech flexed and curled his fingers, his fists craving to tell the Colonel exactly what he thought about *his experience,* to show him what *unfortunate habits* he'd struggled to overcome. But he held his fists and curbed his tongue, casting about for some way to make this easier for Little Brave, not about proving himself to a white man who did not know the world as he knew it.

"I can help Ella with her English," he heard himself offer. *What? When?* With Heaton gone, he hadn't a spare moment in his day.

Surprise lit the Colonel's face, followed by doubt. "You've already gone beyond your responsibilities by bringing her here, instead of leaving her at the fort."

"She would not have been happy there."

The Colonel's expression eased. "Yes, I can imagine. My daughter, Ella's mother that is, found fort life to be a drudgery."

Beech knew drudgery would have been only part of the reason for Little Brave's unhappiness, but he did not mention Commander Heisenberg's and his wife's attitude toward Little Brave. Hopefully, she would not be required to see them when they came to Cheyenne.

His uncle appeared, home from his day at the mercantile. "Ah, you must be Ella's grandfather, Colonel Russell," he said, extending his hand. "I'm Henry Chapman."

After the two men had exchanged pleasantries, Uncle Henry said, "I see you've met Beech." His uncle clapped him on the shoulder and squeezed it. There were many years when Beech had been too absorbed in his anger over his father's abandonment to appreciate this sign of affection from his uncle. Now, he welcomed it, particularly in the presence of the man who held Little Brave's future in his hands. It was…reassuring.

"Yes, he showed me and Ella his horses today," the Colonel said.

"You won't find a better breeder or trainer around these parts."

"Quality horseflesh indeed," the Colonel agreed. "But I'm partial to a good pacer myself."

"I'll agree with you there, Colonel. I brought my old Fox Trotter up from Missouri, and Beech bred her to a Morgan stallion, which belongs to a rancher just east of town. The little filly out of those two has gaits smoother than butter and twice the brain. Steadiest little mare, even around the rail yards."

As his uncle continued to extol the virtues of his beloved mount, Beech let his thoughts stray to the rancher who now had that Morgan stud up for sale. The man had acquired a younger stallion, which Beech didn't think was half as solid and talented as the Morgan, but he wasn't about to argue with the rancher. If the man wanted to sell, Beech wanted to buy. If only the scouting job had worked out. "Colonel," Beech said, realizing Colonel Russell was speaking to him.

"You wouldn't have another pacer that I can ride while I'm here? I'd be willing to pay more than the livery rate."

Beech shook his head ruefully. Depending on how long the Colonel was planning on being here, that could have been some money to put toward his purchase of the Morgan.

"I'm sure I'll find something passable at the livery," the Colonel said.

"Karl's horses are more than passable," Beech said. He was happy to send his friend the business, although Karl had no pacers.

"How did Ella like the book you picked out?" Uncle Henry asked.

Had he told his uncle the book was for Little Brave when he'd purchased it at the mercantile along with his weekly supplies? There was a twinkle in his uncle's eyes as Beech stared at him, trying to recall what he had said to his uncle. His uncle winked, reminding him of Heaton. Father and son both had a humorous, playful side that often had Beech smiling, if not laughing aloud occasionally. This time, he did neither.

"You gave my granddaughter that book?" The lines piled up on the Colonel's forehead as he raised his eyebrows.

"I knew she would like the drawings." There was more to it than that, but Beech was not about to speak of it to Little Brave's grandfather for the military man from the well-settled East would not understand.

"She was very excited to show them to me," the Colonel said.

Beech wondered about the speculative look upon his face, but then Aunt Claire came through the kitchen door carrying a platter laden with meat. Grace followed, carrying steaming side dishes.

"Dinner is served," his aunt announced.

As Beech entered the dining room, he tried to catch Little Brave's gaze, but she avoided him and he could understand why. He should have said something to reassure her before he'd left the dining room earlier, but he'd been so angry with her grandfather for the unreasonable demand he'd made on her that all he could think about was confronting him.

Looking at the Colonel who was now chatting easily with Grace, he realized things had turned out much better by keeping a level head with the older man. And if Uncle Henry hadn't interrupted their conversation, the Colonel might have given his approval for him to help Little Brave with her English.

Beech shook his head at the notion of seeking a white man's approval for anything, but casting his gaze about the room until they fell upon Little Brave, he realized how much he'd do to spend time with her before she left Cheyenne. He'd brushed aside the notion early this morning when he'd thrown these clothes in his pack at the last minute—the white man's clothes, which he rarely wore. Rejected the idea even as he'd come upon the book in the mercantile and tossed it onto his pile of supplies. Even as he'd cleaned up in the barn and secured his hair back at his nape, he'd denied his intentions. But as he gazed upon the woman, who even in her stillness made him feel so achingly alive, he could no longer deny how much he wanted to be around her.

His aunt called for everyone to be seated and as Little Brave moved to take a seat to his uncle's left, Beech slipped in beside her. If she would not acknowledge him with her gaze, there were other ways he could gain her attention. While everyone bowed their head for Uncle Henry's blessing, Beech reached for her hand beneath the table and squeezed it. He hoped he was the only one who heard her startled inhale. He stole a glance around the table.

Everyone's eyes were still closed and heads bowed. As his gaze returned to Little Brave, there was the slightest lift of her lips as she peeked at him. Finally, he could breathe again.

***

Dinner was over and hungry horses awaited him at the ranch. He said his goodbyes to his aunt, his uncle and Grace. To Little Brave, he promised he would be back to see her as soon as he could. Her eyes shone, creating another picture of breathtaking beauty to carry in his mind. Uncharacteristically, he crammed his hands into his pockets to keep from reaching for her.

"I believe the Colonel went out for a smoke," Uncle Henry said. "If you see him, tell him to join me in the parlor for a cognac."

Beech nodded and managed to brush Little Brave's hand with his fingers as he turned to leave then he was out the door, heading to the barn.

Once Beech had one of the geldings saddled and the other two in tow, he led the three horses from the barn.

A match flared and illuminated Colonel Russell's features as the man leaned against the railing of the corral. "Thought this would be better place for a talk than around the dinner table," the military man said.

The leisurely manner the Colonel took in extinguishing the match told Beech he wasn't gathering his thoughts for small talk.

The cigarette glowed brightly with the Colonel's deep inhale, but the man didn't seem to be in any hurry to speak his piece.

Beech pulled on a jacket to ward off the chill, which still crept into the spring nights. The five-year-olds snorted

241

and stamped their hooves as the smoke from the burning tobacco hit their nostrils.

The Colonel removed the cigarette from his lips, rolling it between thumb and forefinger. "Wanted to reiterate how obliged I am to you for looking after Ella, and for bringing her back safely." He returned it to his mouth and took another long draw. "It's understandable why she's so attached to you."

But? Beech slapped the reins against the palm of his hand, waiting for it.

"But it's not right for you to encourage her attachment."

The way the Colonel flicked the ashes free told Beech exactly what the older man thought of the *attachment*. As Beech struggled to douse his rising anger at the narrow-minded judgment, he couldn't help but track the ashes as they fell to the ground. One spark so close to a barn full of fodder could create a raging inferno within minutes. Once he was sure the ashes had extinguished, he looked at the Colonel again. "I'm her friend. A friend who understands where she's been and where she's going."

"Where she's been is no longer relevant, and I am in charge of where she's going now."

Beech didn't know which infuriated him more—the way the man discounted everything the Lakota had meant to Little Brave, or the fact he considered her someone to be ordered around. "Ella is an intelligent woman with a mind of her own. Things will go easier with her, if you treat her that way."

"There's no doubt she's intelligent, but she is a woman, Richoux."

Beech grimaced. Unfortunately, women in the white man's world had about as many choices available to them as half-breeds. "If you force her into something she does not want, you will lose her."

242

Chapter 18

Being immersed in learning the ways of polite society had Little Brave's head spinning. She did not know there were so many ways to greet someone, be they strangers—whom ladies never acknowledged until an introduction was made—friends or acquaintances. And then once greetings were exchanged, there were so few topics of conversation allowed to proper young ladies.

Particularly wearisome was the seating of guests at a formal dinner party. The more promising aspect had been the selection of which dishes to serve, but her excitement dimmed when she discovered she would only select the food, not help prepare it. Her grandfather had been adamant about her not working in his kitchen once they returned to Washington D.C. "That is the cook's place," he had said. The aunt had chirped like prairie dog at how fortunate Ella was to be a woman of such leisure.

Leisure?

Following rigid rules about who to talk to, what to talk about, or where to seat people when they ate was not relaxing. Neither was presiding over a fancy dinner until late into the evening or an afternoon tea in an airless parlor. Leisure was sitting on the boundless prairie, beneath the arc of cloudless sky, breathing fresh air and soaking up the warm sunshine as she did now. But even now, it was hollow because her days had not been filled with meaningful, absorbing work as it had been among the Lakota. Oh how she'd enjoyed her peaceful evenings in the company of Grey Owl and Nimble Fingers as she sat around the fire, working on her beading.

"I wondered if you would come back."

Little Brave jerked her head around to see Beech's father settling on the ground next to her. She'd been so lost in her thoughts she'd not heard him approach. Being unaware would have rarely happened when she was among the Lakota. Now, it happened more often because she had little reason to keep her senses sharp. "I could not be here because my grandfather arrived."

"Your people have taken you back?"

"No—yes." Her heart skipped a beat at the thought the Lakota would take her back, even as she shook her head, knowing it would not happen. "I mean my white grandfather has come from the land of the rising sun for me. I have not seen him in ten winters."

She clutched the book Beech had given to her chest, her throat aching at how much she missed her Lakota family, especially Grey Owl and Nimble Fingers.

"Your grandfather is not with you?" Beech's father peered past her.

"No, he has business at Fort Russell today. He will not return until this evening." Her grandfather had agreed to perform some military inspections during his extended stay in Cheyenne.

"And you are happy he has come?"

She considered his question. She was happy to meet her grandfather again after being apart for so long. He was different in many ways, more affectionate than she remembered, willing to give her time to adjust, but in others he was still the same, namely his desire for things to be done his way. "I am hoping we will find our way as grandfather and granddaughter very soon," she said, wondering how unhappy her grandfather would be if she told him she did not want to become a lady of leisure.

"Then I am happy for you."

He smiled, but it did not chase away the sadness in his eyes. Her heart became heavy knowing he was yearning for the chance to find his way with his own son.

"What is that?" He gestured to the book clutched in her arms.

She'd brought it with her, determined to make sense of its words, but she had fallen under the spell of her surroundings and it remained unopened. "It is gift from your son."

"He is a generous man?"

The hunger to know his son showed plainly on his face. "He is a very generous man. And kind."

This time, his eyes crinkled at the corners as he smiled.

Little Brave's heart lifted, knowing how much that little bit of information had fed his hunger. She could feed him more, much more about the man his son was, but it was not her place. That belonged to Beech Richoux himself. Recalling Beech's pain when he had spoken of the promise he'd made his aunt about his sister, Little Brave said, "I will go with you to see your son." Perhaps if he knew his father again, his pain would not be so great over the loss of his sister.

"You are sure?"

His smile had faded, his eyes lined with worry that she did not mean what she said. "I am sure," she said, pushing to her feet and holding out a hand.

He grasped it, his hand dry and leathery with age, but still firm in its grip as he accepted her help.

The other day at the livery, Beech had been resolute he would not reunite with his father, but had she not thought the same about her grandfather? And had Beech not encouraged her to speak of her grievances to him? She had since discovered there were good reasons for her grandfather's behavior, and she believed it must be so with the father of Beech Richoux, too.

-*-*-

The sound of hoof beats alerted Beech to riders approaching his place—two to be exact. They weren't approaching at a hard gallop, but an easy canter like they knew his place, or weren't worried about riding up unannounced. Beech laid aside the halter for the gelding he'd been about to fetch from the pasture and fetched his rifle instead. He peered through a hole in the door of the barn he'd carved specifically for this purpose.

The glint of red gold in the smaller rider's hair identified her immediately to him as Little Brave, and happy anticipation filled him. Had her grandfather relented about them spending time together? His long years around the white man had him thinking otherwise. More likely, they were leaving earlier than anticipated and she was coming to say goodbye. Still, he doubted her grandfather would allow that and wondered at the man riding in with her. At first, his tallness had suggested he might be her grandfather, but this man did not ride like a military man and he wore buckskins.

When they halted several feet from the barn, Beech didn't relinquish the hold on his rifle for he still couldn't identify Little Brave's companion. Keeping his senses on high alert, he stepped into the open doorway and lifted a hand in greeting. "Little Brave, what brings you here?"

She slid from Sundance's back and came to him, peering up into his face. She gave him a look that asked for his understanding as she wrapped her hand around his upper arm.

The thin cotton shirt was no barrier to the heat of her touch, and desire awakened within his veins.

246

"I have brought someone to see you."

Her scent of warm woman and eucalyptus wreaked havoc with his senses, making it hard to give the stranger his full attention. He wondered at the stranger's familiarity as the longhaired, heavily bearded man lifted a hand in greeting. Beech nodded in acknowledgement. Was he another scout from the fort he'd met in passing, or one of the traders who bartered at his uncle's mercantile?

Then the man threw a leg over his horse to dismount, and a memory meshed with that motion. More memories piled one on top of the other, memories known to him since he was a small boy. "Why have you brought him here?" he gritted through clenched teeth to Little Brave. Giving her no chance to answer, he called out to the man who he now knew to be Jean Luc Richoux, "Why are you here?"

Jean Luc, remaining in place next to his mount, called back. "To see you."

"You have seen me, now you can leave." Beech settled his finger firm against the rifle's trigger, ready to motivate, if necessary, the departure of the man who in no way was his father any longer.

"Beech," Little Brave said, clasping his other arm, facing him fully. "You must speak to him."

"I have nothing to say."

"Then listen to what he has to say."

Her face was so mesmerizingly open with her request and her eyes such an unfathomable blue in her sincerity he felt a moment of pause. But then he remembered all the years he'd spent searching for this man, wondering how a father could abandon his children. And all along the way, he'd been fighting to gain peace and a place for himself between the two worlds.

Like hell he'd listen to what Jean Luc Richoux had to say. Using his rifle, Beech gestured for the man to be on

247

his way. "When I come back out, you better be gone, stranger."

Little Brave's fingers dug into his arms, following him as he turned away. "I know your heart is heavy because your father has been absent—"

"My heart holds nothing for that man."

Her hands cupped his face.

He tried to ignore their softness, the emotional husk in her voice as she pleaded. "You are the man who told me to speak to my grandfather. I have done that. Now, I know things were not what they seemed. Perhaps it is that way with your father, too."

A burning rage erupted in his chest. "Do not call him that."

He could not bear the way her gaze searched his face, asking if he really meant what he'd said. As if she knew him. Knew his pain, his rage, and his bitter disappointment. Knew the gaping hole his father—he clenched his fists at the involuntary reference—the gaping hole *that coward* had carved in his heart. He closed his eyes to escape the emotional rawness threatening to consume him, and to escape the one person who knew and understood everything he was feeling.

Her hands fell away from his face.

For a terrifying split second, he thought she meant to leave him.

Instead, she moved closer, wound her arms around his waist and pressed her cheek against his chest.

The pounding of his heart ratcheted up until he thought it would burst free from his body. As her soft curves settled against him, his rawness headed in another direction. Lust hit him hard. With just a few steps, he could back her into the cool dimness of the barn, and push her down in the sweetly scented hay. There he could spend the turmoil eating him from the inside out between the sweet folds of her woman's flesh.

He put his arms around her, cinched her to him. She looked up, her eyes bright with hopeful expectation he'd changed his mind. He knew the second she realized what was burning in his eyes for she gave a small shake of her head in spite of an answering spark of desire in her own eyes.

"We cannot do this. You showed me, that day by the stream, when I was grieving for the loss of Grey Owl and my people, this is not the way to deal with your pain."

"And what of that night at the cabin?"

She fought to close her features.

He knew she was trying to hide how much their intimate time together had touched her, how alive she'd felt in those moments, how she'd been yearning as he'd been yearning to escape in each others' arms once more.

She failed to slip her stoic mask in place. Instead, she snapped her eyes closed and pushed hard against his chest. "The night with you only increased my pain."

At her stinging words, he let her go.

Her eyes flew open as she stumbled back a step.

Instinctively, he reached out to help.

But she regained her balance, sidestepping him as she swiped the tousled hair from her eyes. Once righted, she firmed her features, her chin lifted. "Speaking with your father is the only way to conquer your pain."

Beech stared at her—this alluring mix of Lakota maiden and white woman. She was finding her path between the two worlds and turning it into wisdom for him. He turned to look at Jean Luc Richoux who appeared, even from a distance, much older than his years. There was a stoop in his posture Beech did not recall, like he'd been carrying a heavy load for many years. He felt a pang of— concern? Empathy? But it was only for a moment. The anger had lived within him too long for it to be much more than that. But there was a loosening in his heart knowing his—that someone who shared his name yet lived. Grudgingly, he said, "I am not ready to speak to him yet, but maybe…" He sighed hard. He was at a loss as to when, if ever, he would be ready.

Little Brave's eyes softened and her mouth eased. "Of course, it will take time." She reached for his hand and squeezed it. "But do not let too much time pass."

***

Beech recognized the well-bred bay horse hitched to the two-seater buggy as belonging to the banker, Mr. Pierce. Although, he'd never seen it parked by the grove of trees he passed regularly on his way to and from Cheyenne before now.

He slowed his horse to a walk, listening closely— male laughter, followed by feminine giggles. It sounded like a courting couple, snatching a bit of privacy, but Mr. Pierce was beyond courting years, and—another laugh—this one with a hint of slyness. The answering giggles held a trace of nervousness. He didn't like what his senses were telling him.

Beech dismounted, pulled his rifle from its scabbard and crept through the tall grass. He crouched behind a tree at the edge of the clearing and peered around it. All he could see was the back of a well-dressed man whose arms were around someone. No doubt the woman he'd heard giggling. His gut clenched at his almost certainty the man was Frank Pierce.

The woman gave a startled gasp as the man's head bent forward, his muscles stretching the shoulders of his fancy coat as his arms tightened around her. "Now don't be a tease."

Beech recognized that ugly tone. He stepped into the clearing. "Let her go, Pierce." He'd knocked the man out cold with the butt of his rifle last time. The bastard hadn't even known what or who had laid him flat.

This time, he'd know.

And this time Beech wouldn't be too late.

Pierce cranked his head around, the guilty surprise on his face quickly replaced by a disgusted impatience. "You have no business here, half-breed."

"You have no business forcing your attentions on the lady."

"Lady?" Pierce sneered. He spun, bringing the woman with him.

Instantly, Beech recognized her blond hair and high cheekbones. *Grace!* His vision tunneled to his sister as Pierce corralled her to his side.

Her eyes were wide with fear then they filled with shame as she recognized him. Her chin dropped to her chest.

As far as Beech was concerned, she had nothing to be ashamed of.

Pierce gave her a lewd look. "She's a brazen little thing."

Beech struggled within an inch of his control to keep the red from clouding his vision, and dictating his actions as Pierce grabbed Grace's chin and forced up her head. "Tell him how quickly you hopped into the buggy when I offered you a ride home from town, how easily you agreed when I suggested a quiet drive through the countryside."

The guilt was heavy on her face.

Beech stepped closer. "This isn't your fault, Gracie."

Her eyes filled with tears at his use of her childhood nickname.

Instinctively, Beech reached out a hand to soothe her.

251

Pierce jerked her out of his reach. "You'd like to put your filthy red hands on this lily-white skin wouldn't you, 'breed." His gaze cut possessively to Grace then back to Beech. He released her chin and swept his hand to her breast, squeezing the soft swell harshly. "Only I can do that."

She flinched, biting her lip to keep from crying out, but tears broke free and spilled down her cheeks.

Beech pressed the barrel of his rifle flush with Pierce's forehead, rage fraying his tenuous control. "Let her go."

"You'd hang if you shot me," Pierce said with all the confidence being a white man afforded him.

Beech cocked the rifle, sighting along the barrel for effect. "It'd be worth it." At point-blank range, Pierce's head would be reduced to slivers of flesh and bone if he pulled the trigger.

And the world would be rid of one more worthless piece of human dung.

Sweat beaded on Pierce's forehead. Slowly, he released Grace and raised his hands.

She stumbled away from his grasp.

Beech caught her with his free arm and wrapped her in his embrace. He kept his rifle trained on Pierce as the bastard backed up a step. "If you ever touch her, I will—" He stopped short at describing the humiliating torture he'd inflict on the molesting bastard because Grace had already been traumatized enough so he merely said, "I will kill you."

Beech twisted his lips wickedly and allowed his dark hair to fall forward to frame his face.

Pierce's confidence slipped and he backed up another step.

Beech tracked him with his rifle until the coward was in the buggy and headed back to town at a break-neck speed.

Beech held Grace away from him, looking her over for any signs of injury. "You are not hurt, are you?"

She kept her gaze downcast as she shook her head. A sniffle escaped then a cry.

Beech pulled her back into his arms. "Shhh, shhh, it's all over now."

He stroked her hair and her back as her small frame quaked with sobs. How long had it been since he'd held her like this? Comforted her as a brother? His heart ached at the moments missed because he'd withdrawn his affection even as a cousin. All because of his pride and anger over the promise he'd made his aunt.

"You must be so ashamed of me," she hiccupped between sobs. She took a stuttering breath. "I'll never be able to look you in the eyes again."

With a finger beneath her chin, he lifted her head until her gaze met his. "I am not ashamed of you. You are my sister, and I love you."

"Your sister?"

He nodded as she shook her head, her eyes wide with disbelief.

"Why hasn't anyone ever told me this before?"

Beech struggled with the right way to answer that question. Finally, he said, "It was better this way." He held off attaching Aunt Claire's name to that sentiment. It would do no good to tarnish Grace's view of the only mother she'd ever known.

"I don't think it was better," she said.

Tenderness tugged at his heart not only for her declaration but her calm acceptance of the truth. "Well, now it doesn't matter because you know."

Beech led her in the direction of his horse thankful he'd been on his trusty black gelding instead of one of the spirited five-year-olds. Otherwise, they'd be walking back

253

to Cheyenne. He mounted up, slipped his foot out of the stirrup and held down a hand to Grace.

She looked up, eyes red and puffy, hair mussed and gave him a shy smile. "You're really my brother?"

"I am," he answered with a wide smile of his own. He hoisted her up behind him, and lightness filled him as she slid her arms around his waist and rested her cheek against his back.

What a turn this day had taken. He'd been on his way into town to take Little Brave's advice. Three days on his ranch, not only alone, but lonely, had convinced him it was time to speak with his father—hopefully to understand why he'd left all those years ago. But he'd never expected this—to be reunited with his sister. He patted Grace's arm wrapped around his waist, still in awe over the way she'd taken the news. But his lips tightened at imagining what his aunt would say.

Chapter 19

Little Brave was in the garden, pouring buckets of water on the thirsty plants when they rode in. The blue ribbon he'd given her was tied around her head, holding back her impertinent locks. As she came over to greet him, he noticed its color heightened the blue of her eyes just as he imagined it would when he'd picked it out. Surprise flitted across her face when he eased Grace down from his horse, but she didn't ask why the younger girl was with him.

Grace gave him a fearful look. He knew she was wondering about telling her parents what had happened with Frank Pierce.

"Is my aunt here?" he asked Little Brave.

She nodded and reached for his horse as he dismounted. "I will take care of Big Black."

Reluctantly, he handed over the reins. He would have welcomed the time unsaddling and grooming the gelding before speaking with his aunt, but Grace was wringing her hands as she stared at the house. Like digging out a bullet before cauterizing the wound, putting off this conversation would not make it any easier. He placed his hand at the small of his sister's back and ushered her toward what awaited them inside the house.

His aunt and his father were standing on opposite sides of the kitchen table, conversing heatedly in a language

Beech hadn't used in so many years it took a few moments for his ears to adjust, for his brain to summon the appropriate greeting in French.

"*Ma fille chérie, où avez-vous été?*" his aunt replied, scurrying around the table toward them.

Anxiously plucking at her fingers and on the verge of tears, Grace said, "Mama, I don't understand what you're saying."

"*Pardonne-moi*—I forget you do not know French. Where have you been? Your uncle says you never returned home." She clutched her daughter by the shoulders. "You told me you were coming straight home."

"Mama, I did such an awful thing." Her voice broke.

Aunt Claire swept the sobbing girl into her arms. She looked over Grace's head at Beech.

"What happened, Beech?"

This was the woman from his younger years—the one who had ably raised four sons and taken him in hand occasionally, not the oblivious prattling woman she'd become in more recent years. "She was with Frank Pierce."

"With Frank Pierce? Where? Doing what?" Aunt Claire didn't give him time to answer. She held Grace away from her. "Is this true?"

Grace swallowed a sob, her face full of shame and misery as she nodded mutely.

"He's a grown man, Gracie. What were you thinking?" His aunt's tone changed from reproving to fearful. "Did he hurt you?" The older woman gathered the hands of the younger woman who was her daughter in every way and held them close to her heart. "Tell me, *ma fille chérie.*"

At those tender words, Grace threw herself back into the arms of the only mother she'd ever known and started sobbing anew.

"I'll take her upstairs to calm her down so I can talk with her," his aunt said with a troubled look in her eyes.

Once the two women had left the room, Beech looked at his father who still stood by the kitchen table.

The now clean-shaven man eyed him warily.

Beech didn't blame him after the unfriendly greeting he'd given him at the ranch the other day. Although anger and pain still lit his emotions from time to time when he thought of his father leaving all those years ago, he'd come to terms with them enough to hear Jean Luc Richoux speak his piece now.

Beech sat across from the older man. It was the first time he'd seen his father up close since he'd returned. Age and life had marked him heavily, and there was a worrisome rasp in his breathing. Was he unwell? Near the end of his life? A sadness Beech hadn't expected hit him and he said with more gruffness than he intended, "I am ready to hear your story."

The older man nodded slowly then began speaking in Lakota, rather than his native French or English. "I have always been a wanderer. Then I met your mother, Swaying Willow—" He coughed a couple of times to clear his throat. "She stopped my wandering. She gave me love, a home, a son."

His father's pale blue eyes rested on him with such feeling as he uttered that last word, *son*, Beech inhaled sharply against his own answering emotion. Thankfully, the older man went on.

"But it was well before your sister was born that life as I knew it was changing. There were not so many beaver to trap, fish in the river to catch, or rabbits and deer on the plains to hunt. Wagon trains once bound for lands farther west began aiming for places not so far west. By the time your mother passed, I had taught you all I could teach you, but I knew it would not be enough. So I took you and your sister to my sister who had chosen a different path than I."

"But you did not have to leave us."

Jean Luc shook his head as if it were inevitable that he should leave. "The first time I left was to find work, to help provide for you and Grace because your aunt and uncle had four children of their own."

"And when you returned?" Beech feared asking why his father left the second time.

"When I returned, I saw how much you had changed, how—"

"I had not changed." Anger surged. This was not *his* fault. He would not let this man make this *his* fault.

His father held up a hand.

Beech took a deep breath to quell his anger and withheld further objections.

"You had learned to read and to write."

"How could you know that? You were only here for a day."

Jean Luc shook his head as only a father could toward his son. "You only saw me for one day."

Of course. Jean Luc Richoux was a master at not being seen if he did not want to be seen.

"I watched you read lists and mark payments as you made deliveries around town for your uncle's mercantile."

"I did that in trade for hunting supplies." His explanation was true, but there was more to it than that. He had been fascinated by his cousins' ability to make sense of the jumble of dashes, dots and squiggles in their schoolbooks. As he'd cleaned traps or oiled tack by the evening's lamplight, he would situate himself next to the cousin who was just beginning to learn his letters. It had not taken him long to learn their shapes and sounds, how they came together to form words. Then he had read anything he could get his hands on—his cousins' schoolbooks, his aunt's grocery lists, his uncle's newspapers. He'd learned to write

258

in much the same way, tracing his letters with a stick in the sand as he fished or on scraps of the packaging paper from the mercantile. He'd balked at his aunt's suggestion he attend school with his cousins, because he did not want to be cooped up for the better part of each day.

"Whatever the reason, you were learning a different way of life," his father said.

"That does not explain why you went away the second time."

Jean Luc fixed his gaze on him, *his* son.

But Beech realized Jean Luc did not know *the* son who sat before him now.

"If I had stayed, it would have only made you yearn for the life you once had, one that could not sustain you, much less a family."

"Family?" Beech stood so suddenly his chair tipped over backwards and clattered disruptively in the quiet room. "How can you speak to me of *family*?"

"Beech," his aunt said reprovingly from the doorway.

She could not have understood his Lakota words, but she would have understood his tone.

"Do not speak to your father that way."

Beech switched to English. "How can you call him my father when he abandoned us?"

"Your father only did what he thought was best."

Her gentle words only cut him deeper. How could she defend what his—his *father* had done? How could she—

His father's eyes, full of apology, shifted to Aunt Claire then back to him.

Beech's pain cooled to cold disbelief as understanding dawned. "Is that what you did, Aunt Claire?"

"Did what?" his aunt asked, fluttering her hands.

A gesture Beech had once taken as dismissive now appeared guilt-ridden. "Did what *you* thought was best for your family?"

"I have no qualms about doing what's best for my family." Her hands went to her stomach in a play of calmness.

But Beech was not fooled. She'd had a hand in his father's departure. "You told my father to leave all those years ago."

His aunt gasped, guilt momentarily flashing in her eyes. "No, that's not true."

Beech scoffed at her contrite tone. "You expect me to believe you, Aunt Claire?"

"Son." His father was beside him, a hand on his shoulder. "It was a decision we made together."

"No," Beech said as he shrugged away his father's touch. "You would have never abandoned us if it hadn't been for her."

"*Je vous ai dit qu'il ne comprendrait pas,*" she said to his father.

"You don't want me to understand, Aunt Claire," Beech interrupted, "but I understand completely. You wanted my sister to be your daughter so badly, you sent away our father to make sure that happened."

"That is enough, Beech," Jean Luc said.

Memories trounced through Beech's mind at his father's decisive tone—so many memories from so long ago, when he was just a boy and his father had still been his father. Suddenly, the screen door squeaked, and Beech's mind pounced on the distraction of Little Brave entering the kitchen.

She paused and her gaze traveled from him to his so-called family then back to him.

He couldn't answer the question in her eyes: *What has happened?* Not here. He jerked his head to the door behind her.

She stepped aside and he exited.

-*-*-

"Ella, we have tea with the minister's wife," the aunt said.

Little Brave looked over her shoulder then back to the aunt. "He is upset." Then she turned, left the house and followed Beech into the barn. Its dimness blinded her for a moment after the intense brightness outside, but soon, she could make out his tall form, the muscles rigid in his broad back, his arms flexing as he gripped the stall railing. The tension vibrated the air around him as she approached. She slid her arms around his waist and pressed her cheek to his back, willing him to share his pain.

He clutched one of her hands and pressed it against his pounding heart.

His heat seeped through the cotton shirt he wore and warmed her everywhere their bodies touched. She inhaled his scent of working man, horse and eucalyptus, grateful he was accepting her comfort, taking a measure of comfort in that for herself. After many moments, he turned in her embrace, his brows flattened as low as she'd ever seen them over angst-riddled eyes.

"It was my aunt who kept my father away for all these years."

Little Brave could not fathom someone denying a child his father. "But why?"

"So I would not follow in my father's footsteps. He says there is no future for me there."

"So, your father had reasons for staying away." It was as she hoped—an explanation to help Beech understand his father's actions.

"It does not mean they were good ones." He clutched her shoulders. "I cannot think here."

261

Her heart slowed to the pace of turtle as she said, "Your mind will clear at your ranch."

He nodded in agreement.

She dropped her arms from his waist as she took a step back. He was leaving again. He always left, chased away by his shadows.

His fingers dug into her shoulders, drawing her close again. "I don't—" His eyes darkened then he looked up. A hard swallow worked the ridges in his throat. "I don't want to go alone. I don't want to be alone."

His gaze found hers once more and she nodded. Relief filled his face as he brought one of her hands to his lips and pressed a kiss to her palm.

Her breath caught as sparks erupted beneath her skin. *Hiyee! Beech Richoux needs my comfort, not my desire.*

Beech readied the horses, and Little Brave returned to the house to let his aunt know where they were going.

The aunt looked up from stirring a pot on the stove. "Oh thank goodness, you're back, Ella. We're to be at the minister's house in half an hour."

Little Brave was puzzled. Why did the aunt not ask about her nephew? Was she not worried he was still upset?

"Go change into the blue gingham," the aunt urged as she laid aside the spoon and wiped her hands on a towel. "I'll help you pin up your hair as soon as I get changed."

"I am not going with you today."

"What?" The aunt's golden brows knitted in confusion.

"I am going with Beech. To his ranch."

"Oh no, Ella. Your grandfather expects you to be at this tea." The aunt dropped the towel on the counter and approached Little Brave. "It's important to him that you learn as much as possible about these things before you leave."

Little Brave lifted her chin. "Beech is my friend. He is upset."

"Your grandfather will not be pleased if you go with Beech."

"You care more for my grandfather's feelings than you do for Beech's."

"No, that's not true, Ella." The aunt reached for Little Brave's hands, giving them a gentle squeeze. "It's just that I know Beech. He needs time. That's the way he's always been. He gets upset. He goes off. He comes back and he's fine again."

The way the older woman gentled her tone told Little Brave that she cared about her nephew, but it did not change her mind. She would go with him and be there for him. To s*how* him that someone cared. That she cared. "My grandfather has helped me by staying longer in Cheyenne. He will understand when I go to help Beech." Little Brave squeezed the aunt's hands reassuringly then turned to leave.

But the aunt held on. "He won't like it."

Little Brave turned back, taking in the tightness of the aunt's face as the older woman dropped her hands and stuffed them into the pockets of her apron.

"He does not want you to spend time with Beech."

"Why?" Little Brave shook her head as she uttered the question. Surely, her grandfather was not like the soldiers who had come to Grey Owl's village? Surely, he was not like the commander and his wife at the fort, or that disdainful Frank Pierce who she'd met at the train station? Surely, he was not one of those people whose looks, and actions and words said they had little use or regard for...for...Indians?

"Ella, I'm sorry."

Little Brave backed away from the aunt, continuing to shake her head. "Does Beech know this?" She hit the edge of the table as she saw the aunt nod. "I must go," she whispered then turned and fled the kitchen.

Little Brave calmed her pace and stilled her features as she approached Beech. He was grappling with his own demons without being burdened with hers, even if they did involve him. She mounted Sundance without looking at him.

"Aunt Claire knows you are going with me?"

"Yes." Little Brave turned Sundance and trotted toward the open prairie.

Beech caught up with her on Big Black. "And she did not object?"

"If you thought she would object, why did you insist I tell her?"

He didn't answer, but looked to the horizon, the set of his face grim. "You should go back."

"No."

He steered his gelding across her path, effectively stopping her. "I should not have asked you to come."

"Why?"

"Because you need to be learning your grandfather's ways."

"That is not why." She cleared the hair blowing across her eyes then defiantly lifted her chin. "Tell me why." When he did not answer, she said, "It is because my grandfather told you not to see me."

With a disgruntled sound, he said, "My aunt is full of revelations today, isn't she?"

"It would seem so," she said, noting that his pain had eased, but the haggardness he'd been wearing when he'd arrived with Grace was still there. Had he been working too hard since his cousin left? Did he eat enough? Sleep enough?

There was so much she didn't know about him, but so much she wanted to know. And so little time to discover it.

Ella's Choice

Little Brave legged her mare around until she and Beech were knee to knee. "I want to see your ranch and the rest of your horses. I want to know what your day is like, when you do which task, which one gives you the most joy and which one is the most challenging."

He shifted in his saddle, eyebrows flattening.

The sight told her he was mounting a rebuttal. She reached for his hand, pressing it to her heart as he'd so often done with hers, her tone softening with an emotion she could not afford to name. "I am choosing to do this because I don't want to remember you as the man who brought me back to the white man, but, as my friend, Beech Richoux."

Chapter 20

Little Brave drank in the sight of Beech's ranch in a manner she hadn't when she'd brought his father here. The barn was the largest structure on the property, and the one that drew the eye when they came up the road. But she didn't miss the pastures that fanned out behind it, the sturdy round corral next to it or the small cabin further up a rise to her left. She couldn't decide which part she wanted to explore first until she heard the welcoming whinny from inside the barn, followed by another and another.

"Normally, the mares and their foals are outside during the day, but I leave them in their stalls when I'm away," Beech said.

Little Brave slid off Sundance's back and followed Beech and Big Black into the barn. It didn't take long to settle their horses into stalls, toss hay and fill the water buckets. Meanwhile, the mares became more ferocious in their demanding while the neighing squeals of their babies joined the refrain for freedom.

"We're coming," Beech grumbled good-naturedly. He grabbed the halter for the first mare, entered the doublewide stall and buckled it on with a practiced ease.

Little Brave stared in delight at the curious baby who peered around its mother's back legs. Doe-eyed and spindly-legged, it tottered behind its mother when Beech led her out.

"Here," he said, handing her the lead rope to hold while he fetched the other pair.

She held the lead rope of the second mare, as well while Beech fetched the last mare.

As they led the placid mares from the barn toward one of the paddocks behind it, Little Brave was entranced with the sight of the foals frolicking ahead, their short bushy tails swishing and twirling in the throes of their freedom. "You get to do this every day," she breathed in envy, glancing at the man strolling beside her.

"Twice a day," he said, pride sharpening his handsomeness to the point it vied with the antics of the romping foals for her attention. He unlatched a gate and they led the mares into a large grassy pasture. He gave a rousing whistle to capture the foals' attention, and they cavorted back toward them, uneasy to be too far from their mothers. Beech secured the gate once all the horses were inside then fastened the halters and lead ropes on it. He moved along the fence line, and Little Brave fell into step beside him.

"These are the yearlings." Beech gestured to the two inhabitants of the next enclosure whose still coltish faces and disproportionately long legs marked them as such.

Tucking their hindquarters, the pair playfully charged the gate where she and Beech stood. Just as suddenly they shifted their weight, spun on their heels and dashed away. Little Brave laughed at their feigned spookiness.

"I've only heard you laugh once before," Beech said.

She looked at him in surprise. He had counted her moments of laughter?

"I love it when you laugh," he added.

267

Pleasure swept through her at the sincerity in his words, at the joy he found in something she did. "I find much to laugh about when I am with you."

He crossed his arms over his chest. "I amuse you?"

His voice rumbled deeper than she'd ever heard it and her stomach knotted. Had he misunderstood the intent of her words? "Yes. No. I mean—"

The corners of his eyes crinkled as his lips curved upward.

She caught her breath then let it out in relief. He was teasing her. "Oh," she murmured as heat warmed her cheeks. She returned her focus to the youngsters who were once again approaching the fence, but this time at an easy lope. She held out her hand, coaxing them with soft words. They stopped several feet away and eyed her with an instinctive wariness.

Beech turned, bracing his forearms on the railing. "I don't get to spend much time with these young ones, but this is exactly what they need. Time with a human—haltering, leading, working on their ground manners." He pushed away from the fence with a weary sigh. "But there doesn't seem to be enough hours in a day."

Little Brave followed him as he walked on. She knew about there not being enough time in a day. Scraping hides. Gathering firewood, or buffalo dung if on the high plains. Digging wild roots. Picking berries and herbs. Breaking and setting up camp when Grey Owl's clan followed the buffalo during hunting season. But it was work that made her muscles ache, and let her sleep well at night.

"The two- and three-year-olds," he said of the horses in the next paddock. While they were proportioned more like horses than yearlings, they were still young about the face and slim in the body. Beech pointed to a bay with a darker mane and tail, and a chestnut with three white socks. "We will break those two to the saddle and bridle in the fall."

268

"You and Heaton?"

A muscle worked in his jaw.

She'd asked out of a desire to know more of how his ranch worked, not to remind of the rift with his cousin.

"Yes. If he makes it back alive," Beech said.

"He does not shoot well?" The Lakota started training their warriors from the time the children could hold a bow and arrow. Of course, there were some who were not as capable as others at handling weapons. Perhaps Heaton was one of these.

"He's a crack shot. I taught him myself."

Hiyee! It was as she thought, Beech's concern extended far beyond his cousin's ability to defend himself. "May the *Wakan Tanka* watch over him on this journey," she said. It was as much as any Lakota would say, for they did not utter empty reassurances.

He nodded in agreement, but did not offer anymore on the topic. Instead, he walked on. In the next pasture were four horses, three which she recognized as those he'd brought to town the day her grandfather arrived. They trotted up to the fence when Beech whistled, but the fourth hung back, swishing his tail and shuffling his feet.

"He is unhappy that his herd has left him."

"I acquired him from a heavy-handed cowboy, so he doesn't have much use for people." Beech pointed toward the horse's midsection. "Spur marks are finally healing, though"

She clucked in sorrow at the mistreatment of the horse. She did not understand why the white man did not ride as the Plains People did. As one with their horses. Without spurs or bits. But thanks to Beech Richoux, this one would be granted a second life, one much different than his first. "You have a kind heart," she said, looking up at him.

His lips twisted ruefully. "If I was kind, I would not have driven away my cousin." He turned and stared at the cabin he and his cousin must have shared.

"You are lonely without him," she said, thinking back on what he'd said earlier about not coming back to his ranch alone.

Slowly, he shook his head, his dark hair brushing the tops of his broad shoulders. "I miss him, but it is not his absence that makes me lonely."

The ache in his voice was so raw that it had her touching her fingers to the back of his hand. "I did not mean to—" He surprised her by catching her hand in his. It was a natural fit, but the roughness of his callouses reminded her how hard he worked every day and how very little she worked, how inconsequential her work was when compared to what he did.

He led her in the direction of the cabin. "Now that you have seen the things which give me the most joy, I will show you the most difficult part of my day." They followed a narrow game path up the rise to approach the small dwelling. Sturdily built with a porch across its front, the cabin faced east to catch the first warming rays of the rising sun, but the windows were shuttered to light and breeze, and no smoke wafted from the chimney. It looked eerily uninhabited, and Little Brave shook her head at the notion. Of course, he would secure the windows and bank the fire when he was away.

They mounted the steps to the porch, his boot falls echoing a lonely strain in contrast to the soft tread of her moccasin-clad feet. He pushed open the door, and gestured her to precede him into the shadowy interior. He released her hand and remained on the threshold as she stepped inside.

She tried to discern the contents of the room—a table and some chairs, a fireplace against the north wall. There was not much more she could see without additional light. She turned a slow half-circle back to him, wondering at his silence. While not unusual, his quietness was heavy with some emotion she couldn't name. The shadows masked his expression, giving her no further clues.

"May I open them?" She gestured toward the shuttered windows.

He nodded.

Moving around the room, she threw back the window coverings, allowing encroaching light to name the contents of the room—the table with four chairs dominating the middle of the small space, two narrow beds set against opposite walls and a work counter next to the fireplace. The counter was stacked with dishes and cooking utensils, beneath it kegs of supplies, and there were pegs in the wall next to the door to hang clothes, coats and hats. Not much else.

She lifted the coffee pot from the table and shook it to determine its contents. "Shall I make fresh coffee?" she asked, hoping he would break his unnerving silence to answer her.

But he merely shook his head.

She set down the pot. Still, he had not spoken nor had he abandoned his position in the doorway. He was neither in nor out of the room. "Come in," she said, indicating her preference with a gesture to the chairs around the table.

He didn't move muscle as he said, "You wanted to know the most challenging thing about my day."

It was a statement not a question, but nonetheless she said, "Yes," encouraging him to speak of what was in his heart.

"It is seeing you here."

"But I have never been here before today." She gave a confused shake of her head.

271

He took a step into the room. "You are here every day."

Little Brave swallowed against the ache in her throat.

"I see you moving about as a woman does. Tending to things that make a house a home."

She dared not breathe, lest she break the spell he was weaving with his words.

"I have seen it every night since I first left you in Cheyenne." He took another step.

Everything within her begged for him to come even closer.

"It was something I dared not hope to have in my life until I met you." He stopped an arm's length from her, an intense need burning in his eyes.

She experienced an overwhelming urge to fill it with her own yawning need. "I have seen you, too," she said. "Every day, since you came into Grey Owl's village. You are one who stands behind what he believes is right. You deal kindly with those less fortunate and protect those you care about."

She held out her hands, willing him to take them and merge their visions.

He stood for many moments, staring at her offering, jaw clenched at the battle waging within him.

Finally, he lifted his hands, fingertips touching hers.

She took a step then another, inching her fingers along the long length of his, sliding her palms into his.

He took over, shifting his hands so their fingers intertwined, his larger fingers settling between hers, stretching the skin, filling the grooves with his heat and mingling with her own.

Ella's Choice

The craving was too strong to resist—the craving to realize his visions which had their roots in the first moment he'd laid eyes on her. He pulled her closer, relishing how freely she came to him. When there was but a breath of air between them, he held her there, bringing a hand to her cheek, letting his fingers drift along the line of her jaw. To touch her with his fingers was not enough, so he took her lips with a kiss that left them yearning for more, but he would not squander these moments in a flurry of lips and limbs. He would drink in every nuance of her slowly, with reverence and tenderness. That's what she deserved, not the swift and rough lust he'd given her that night at the cabin.

He trailed his fingers down the soft skin of her neck, lingering at her pulse until the beat of their hearts matched. When his fingers dipped into the hollow at the base of her throat, he watched her gaze shift to his mouth, her lips parting in request, but he gave a small shake of his head.

Not yet.

He released the first button of her simple cotton dress, followed by another then another, his gaze hungrily following the progress of his dark hands against the impossible white of the chemise beneath her dress. When the bodice gaped to her waist, he skimmed his hands just inside it, spreading it open as he went. Her scent of warm, willing woman urged him to push the fabric off her shoulders and relish the sight of her luminous pale skin. What had once warned him away only beckoned him now.

He poised his fingers just above her skin, reluctant to touch that which might yet still be a dream. He followed the delicate jut of her collarbone, over the slope of her shoulders then across to the sweet curve of her breasts which rose above the chemise's lacey edge.

His hands hovered until her breath caught, thrusting the luscious swells upward in silent offering. With a ragged exhale, he accepted, cradling their tantalizing weight in his palms, freely taking their measure, grateful for the absence of the corset white women wore. In spite of the fabric covering those peaks, it only took a stroke of his thumbs across their tips, to bring them to full arousal.

Thin as her undergarment was, he would no longer accept any barrier between them. With a gentle tug, the satiny ribbon holding it together loosened. With the barest touch of his fingertips, he caressed the exposed skin. It was softer than anything he'd ever felt before, and he knew without a doubt she'd taste even sweeter.

He touched his lips to the valley between her breasts, and she responded by shrugging aside her dress and chemise then pushing her fingers into his hair. The scrape of her nails sent shivers of desire through him. At the lap of his tongue, she gave a little cry of pleasure. Already addicted to the sweet, salty taste of her skin and wanting to hear that cry again and again, he licked and kissed his way over one swell and captured the turgid tip, suckling it until her body writhed against him, her cries building into trembling pants, fists anchoring deep into his hair.

The raw need he'd been rigidly holding in check bolted through him, and he swung her up into his arms, closing the distance to the bed in powerful strides. Gently, he set her on her feet, cautiously watching her face for any sign she'd changed her mind about being with him. Her lids hooded heavy over her eyes, and her mouth swollen and wet from his kisses told him her body had made its decision, but her mind—Without hesitation, she reached for the buttons on his shirt, telling him her mind was set in its choice, too.

She rose on her toes as she released the top button, kissing the skin it exposed. And so her lips followed her hands.

His skin burned everywhere she touched whether with fingers, mouth or breath. At the flick of her tongue in his navel, he resisted the urge to fist his hands into her hair and push her head much lower. Instead, he groaned. She glanced up at him, hands stalled at the buttons on his fly, an open desire to please on her face while his fingers greedily flexed at his sides. He groaned again, harder and tighter then reached to bring her upright. He had forever to teach her all the ways there were for men and women to love each other.

Forever. Love.

The words echoed in his mind and settled in his being. The emotions sang in his veins and suffused his heart. The truth and rightness of it. She was his, and he was hers. He tunneled his fingers into her hair and brought her lips to his. First, he would show her then he would tell her.

The last of their clothing, along with moccasins and boots dropped to the floor. With a hand anchoring in her hair and the other clasping the firm swell of her buttocks, he eased her down onto the bed, grateful for a mattress, but cursing its narrowness.

He hitched her closer, her leg wrapped around his hip and their mouths found each other. Hot and hungry they kissed. Swift and sure they caressed each other. When her fingers wrapped around him, he swelled to the point he thought his skin would split.

Her gaze found his. "Teach me to please you this way."

If not for the wonder and innocence infusing the sensuous cast of her features, he would have made good on her request, but this was about her, not him. He slipped his fingers between her legs, and watched her wonder and innocence melt to euphoria.

She issued a cry of need for more as he slipped a finger, then two fingers inside her hot slickness. Instinctively, her body showed him what it desired by arching against him, thrusting those luscious breasts within easy reach of his mouth. He only reconfirmed that she was the sweetest thing he'd every tasted as he took the hardened nub into his mouth, sucking it greedily.

He pleasured one breast, then the other. When her hips caught the motion of his fingers moving deep within her, he nipped her nipple, not hard, just enough to have her nails raking down his back, her thigh tightening around his hip.

She was ready. He was beyond ready. He shifted her onto her back, rocked forward once, twice, eliciting a deep-throated moan, as he slid against her slickness. She wound her legs around him, yanked at the ends of his hair to pull him down to her, wrapping her fists into the strands at his scalp. The pleasure-pain rippling across his scalp hurtled down to his groin and sent him driving into her.

She cried out as her hips rose to meet him. He'd vowed to go slow, to take his time, to pleasure her as he brought her along with him. But like that night in the cabin, their passion had its own course and their bodies found it, regardless of his intentions.

Their two worlds fell away, removing all the confusion, the restraints, and the barriers. They were man and woman, joining their hearts together in a place where only they existed.

Chapter 21

"I belong here with you." Within her arms, she felt Beech's body tense. Instantly, Little Brave worried that now was not the time for her declaration. Then she heard what he must have heard—the beat of hooves, many hooves.

With the agileness of cougar, he leapt from the bed, snatched up his clothes and went to the window that faced the road. He dressed hurriedly as he cautiously peered out. "Soldiers."

The terse word erupting from his chest had her reaching for her clothes with shaking hands. "Why are they here?"

"I do not know, but the sheriff is with them." He hurried back to the table and strapped on his holstered knife. He glanced at her. "Do you still have your knife?" She nodded as she fastened the last button on her dress. He crossed back to the window. "I will go down there before they come up here."

"I am ready to go," she said, straightening from pulling on her moccasins.

He whirled. "No, it will be better if they do not know you are here."

Her stomach roiled against her remembrance of his words that day by the stream. *I could be hanged merely for*

277

touching you. And they had done more than touch. Much, much more. Now, he could lose his life because of it.

He moved to the door.

She hurried after him and clutched at his arms.

He paused with his hand on the latch.

"If we wait, perhaps they will go away," she whispered desperately. She inhaled his scent, which she knew now was as necessary to her as her own breath and tried not to think of what was awaiting him.

Slowly, he turned. "They will not go away. Not until they have searched every building and found whatever, or whoever—" His voice rumbled his frustration.

She shook her head in denial as he cradled her cheeks.

He kissed her softly, tenderly.

Tears filled her eyes.

"Promise me that whatever happens, you will stay here."

A tear slipped free as she nodded her agreement, but already her mind raced for ways to help him.

He cleared the tear with a thumb then kissed her again this time decisively, full of passion and promise.

Or farewell, she realized too late as he exited the cabin and pulled the door closed firmly behind him. She peeked out the window, watching his confident strides gobble the distance to the barn.

Someone called his name, but she did not recognize the voice. It came from the man with the star on his chest—the sheriff. The horses parted as a soldier with many medals came forward. A chill colder than winter's wind swept through her as she recognized the commander from the fort. Commander Heisenberg and his woman had been free with their contempt for her time with the Lakota, and outraged at her desire to remain with Beech, rather than stay at the fort with them. Was he here to punish Beech in some way for her choice?

"His horse is ready."

The voice was one she knew only too well. As the soldier led a saddled Big Black from the barn, the head of white hair marked him as her grandfather. Why was he—*He does not want you to spend time with Beech.* The aunt's words slithered through her mind, as her legs became no firmer than snake's body. She gripped the window frame for support. Further conversation slowed and wavered as if she were underwater.

The sheriff dismounted, came around and bound Beech's wrists. Quicker than she could think what to do, they had him mounted on Big Black and were heading down the road, dust swirling in their wake. Snake tightened his coils, robbing her of breath. How long would it be until they hung him? Hung him for touching her. A white woman. No, no, no! The protest mounting within her propelled her to the door. She flung it open. She could not let this happen. Would not let it happen. She scurried across the porch then stopped and stared.

Her grandfather marched up the rise towards her. The medals, clinking at his chest and glinting boldly in the sun, affirmed his power to have this deed done. "Ella, I was worried about you."

His words and stern tone confirmed his reason for having Beech taken. She swiped at the tears threatening to spill down her cheeks once more as she stalked toward the man who called himself her grandfather. She met him halfway, the rise of the slope putting her almost eye level with him. "Beech has done nothing wrong."

His eyes widened in surprise, his mouth opening.

She was sure he was mounting a rebuttal, but she would not hear it. "I chose to be here with him. My choice." She slapped her hand over her heart in emphasis of her point. "There is no reason to take him away," she added at the confusion puckering the skin between his brows.

"Ella." He inhaled mightily, tugging at the sleeves of his jacket. His gaze darted away then back to hers, settling into a bearing of duty which must be carried out at all cost. "They took him away for the murder of the soldiers in the canyon."

Relief was short-lived as her grandfather's words registered. She reached out an arm for balance; her grandfather caught it and steadied her. "He did not kill any soldiers. He—" She gulped for breath like fish out of water, desperate to say the words that would free him and bring him back to her. "He was wounded soon after the attack began."

Her grandfather wrapped an arm around her and drew her to him. "Murder isn't the only charge."

She pushed away, squaring her shoulders, determined to hear exactly what other wrongs they thought Beech Richoux had committed. "Tell me."

"The other charge is conspiracy—" He simplified his words at her confused expression. "They say he planned with the enemy to attack and kill the soldiers."

She shook her head vehemently. "He did not know Running Bear or any of the other warriors who attacked that day. How can they accuse him of these crimes? I will speak to them of this." She grabbed her grandfather's arm, pulling him toward the barn. "Take me to these men. I will tell them all I know, and they will free him. Hurry."

They were at the barn doors now and he halted her. "Nothing will be decided today. The lawyer cannot see Beech until tomorrow."

"This is the man who will decide the truth?"

"No, that is the judge. The lawyer is the man who will tell Beech's side of the story to the judge."

"Beech does not need someone to speak his truth for him."

Her grandfather rubbed a hand across his brow. "Regardless, we think using a lawyer will be Beech's best chance at proving his innocence."

"We?"

"I spoke with Henry Chapman as soon as I knew for certain they were going to arrest him."

Beech's father emerged from the barn. "I am here to take care of the ranch while Beech is away."

"You told the uncle and Jean Luc, but not Beech? Or me?"

"I would have told you, Ella, if you have been where you were supposed to be."

She blinked.

"At the minister's house having tea."

"A tea was not important when Beech was upset."

"Learning how to become mistress of my home is what you should be doing, not traipsing after Beech Richoux."

Little Brave lifted her chin at the heat in her grandfather's tone. "Because you see no value in an Indian."

"Ella, you are putting words into my mouth."

"Then why did you tell Beech and his aunt he was to stay away from me?"

"You're my granddaughter. I only want what's best for you."

"What is best for me?" She sliced a finger through the air, pointing at him. "Or what is best for you?" The brown and green of her grandfather's eyes swirled into a muddy tangle she could not decipher. She dropped her hand and let the silence hang between them.

From within the barn, Sundance neighed and kicked her stall, no doubt upset over Big Black's departure.

When it seemed her grandfather had no answer, she turned to Jean Luc. "Come, I will tell you about Beech's horses."

281

***

The following morning, Little Brave met the lawyer, who was to defend Beech.

He stood to greet her as she entered the Chapman's parlor. "Lucas Kline," he said, holding out a hand.

She took it with a murmured, "Ella Hastings." While his clothes and the smoothness of his palm marked him as a man who worked at a desk, the tan on his face and hands told her he did not spend all his time there.

"Please sit." He gestured to the sofa behind her.

She perched on its edge, waiting as patiently as she could while he gathered papers from the low table between them then settled himself into the chair opposite her. A lock of hair the color of river sand fell across his forehead, as he regarded her in an easy, open manner. This encouraged her to ask the question that had been tormenting her ever since Beech had been taken away.

"Tell me, how is Beech Richoux?" Belatedly she tacked on the word, please, which the aunt constantly deemed to be one of the most important to include with requests.

"You have not seen him?" Creases stacked his brow, although he appeared no older than the man he was to defend.

"The jail was closed when I returned yesterday." She'd done very little since then but worry about Beech— worry which had prevented much food from staying in her stomach. "And this morning, the—Mrs. Chapman said the jail was not the place for a proper young lady." Not understanding all the white man's ways, she was reluctant to do something which might jeopardize Beech's chances for release.

"I can see her point." The creases smoothed from his forehead.

Her heart sank.

"But..." He rolled a pen between his fingers as he thought for a moment. "It can only help in the court's eyes to see upright, respectable citizens visiting him."

"Upright and respectable?"

His eyebrows lifted, not in a condescending why-would-you-ask sort of way, but in a sincere I-am-curious sort of way.

Encouraged that she would have an understanding audience in the young lawyer, she said, "For many years, I lived among the—" She hesitated to use the English word, Indian, for it only brought to mind the disdainful way the white man tended to utter it. Instead, she took a deep breath and said, "Lakota." A shadow crossed his face, and he muttered something in a language unknown to her ears.

With a heavy sigh, he set the papers on the table. "It is not easy when people choose to dislike you, because you're different from them in some way."

The way he spoke told her he'd encountered these types of people, too. Was it because of the strange language he'd spoken? Other than that, he looked and sounded like any other white man.

He shifted forward in his chair, regarding her intently. "But remember, beneath the color of your skin or the accent on your words and beyond the ways of your people, the blood which pumps through your heart is no less red than the blood which pumps through theirs."

She nodded, at the eloquence and the truth of his words. There were people who would judge Beech for being half Lakota, and there were those who would judge her for living among the Lakota. It did not make her journey in this life any easier, but remembering all that Grey Owl had taught her, she said, "I hold my head high around these people."

He smiled at her then, but there was more sadness than happiness in it. "Sometimes that's all you can do." He patted her hand, before gathering his papers again. "I will escort you to the jail after we are done so you can see Beech."

"Thank you." She interlaced her fingers, willing her hands to lie quietly in her lap. "Ask me your questions now...please."

He settled back in his chair. "Questions come later. First, I want you to tell me about the day the attack took place."

Little Brave took a deep breath, reeling her mind back to that day which now seemed much farther back in time than it was, and began to speak. She only hoped her English words could adequately portray what had happened that day and that they would help Beech.

"So, you did not hear the argument, which took place between Captain Baldwin and Beech before you entered the canyons?" the lawyer asked once she'd finished speaking.

"No. Their faces told me they argued, but I was too far away to hear them." She wished she could say otherwise, but it would be dishonorable to speak something other than what she knew.

"Who else was close to Beech and the captain?"

"Sun Hair—I mean..." She struggled to remember the English name for the soldier, which had been second in command. He had often scouted ahead with Beech and had not the hard, challenging manner of the captain. "Cummings." Her heart leapt like rabbit, joyous over her sudden recall.

The lawyer flipped through his papers, ran his finger down a neatly handwritten list. "Lieutenant Edward Lance Cummings."

She nodded at the familiarity of the man's rank.

"There was no one else who could have been close enough to overhear the argument?"

The earnestness in Lucas Kline's face made her wish she could tell him differently, but she shook her head.

He flipped a few pages, scanned the writing on another page. Glancing up, he asked, "Do you recall a Corporal Neville Argyle?"

She recognized the last name immediately as the captain had bellowed for the soldier quite often. "Many times, he helped the captain." He'd fetched and held the bag when Grey Owl's people had to hand over their weapons. And sourness rose in her throat as she recalled how proudly he'd spoken of shooting Bird Hopper's pony. "He survived?"

"He was found at the bottom of the canyon, unable to climb out due to a broken leg. He was able to survive on what he found in a travois. Where was he when the argument occurred?"

"I do not know."

He sighed.

Did her words help or hurt Beech Richoux? She longed to ask him, but held quiet at the thoughtful look on his face. It was not unlike the one Grey Owl or others who regularly met in the council lodge wore when they were trying to settle serious matters.

The aunt entered at that moment with a tea tray. She set it on the table between them. "I hope I'm not interrupting, but a little refreshment is never out of place."

"Thank you, Mrs. Chapman," the lawyer said.

"Ella will pour for you," the aunt said with a meaningful look.

Little Brave nodded her agreement even as she wondered how quickly she could perform the ritual so she could be on her way to see Beech.

Ruby Merritt

-*-*-

The door separating the jail cells from the sheriff's office opened, and Lucas Kline, the lawyer who'd spoken with him in the morning, entered, followed by Little Brave. Her beauty took his breath away, her composure settled him, but the sight of her next to the handsome and well-dressed white man drove home the truth to him. She did not belong in his world, even though the memories of yesterday afternoon argued she did. *My woman* thumped in his heart and pumped through his veins as he eyed the lawyer's hand at her elbow.

Kline nodded at him. "It was either me or the sheriff," he said apologetically as Little Brave hurried over to the cell.

Beech returned the nod, far preferring Kline as a chaperone to the man who'd put the cuffs on him.

Little Brave halted at the bars, her delicate features mockingly framed by the cold gray iron. "Are you well? Have you slept? Have you eaten?" Nothing sounded as reassuring or welcoming as her voice issuing her concerns in Lakota.

Against his better judgment, he met her at the barrier that kept them separated.

She reached through the bars and stroked his face.

This woman was home for him. Her touch, her scent, her sigh, everything about her gave him a place to exist in peace and belonging.

"I have missed you," she said, wrapping her hand around the back of his head and pulling him in for a kiss.

Her lips were soft and sweet, even sweeter than yesterday if that were possible. He wanted to wrap her in his arms, meld her to him, heart, body and soul.

The door opened then clicked shut, and she broke their kiss to look behind her.

286

He rested his forehead against the unforgiving metal as he regained his breath. How she affected him with merely a kiss.

"Oh, it is only you, Jean Luc." At her sigh of relief, reality clawed its way back into his consciousness. What if it had been the sheriff? Or Commander Heisenberg? Or any number of people who would not look favorably on a white woman associating with a half-breed, much less kissing one?

At the caress of her fingers on his cheek, he blew out a resolving breath. There must be no further contact between them. He stepped back, blanking his features.

Her fingers hung suspended in midair as her eyes silently questioned his disengagement.

"You must go now," he said.

Her hand dropped and anguished, but reluctant understanding clouded her eyes.

"I need to speak with the lawyer," he said, giving in to his need to soften the hurt of his withdrawal.

Hope sparked in her eyes. "I will come back later and bring you dinner."

"They bring me food."

"Then I will—"

"No." He braced himself for the words he had to say, the words that would drive her away, but would protect her and allow her to live a life free from taint and scorn. "Do not come back." His words reverberated cruelly in the sparse room. He steeled himself against the urge to take them back as her eyes widened in disbelief then filled with that all-too-familiar agony of rejection. First, Grey Owl's people and now, him. He curled his fingers into his palms to keep from reaching for her. The tension radiated up his arms, across his shoulders, into his neck and down his back. He focused on the burn in his muscles, instead of the sear in his heart.

Finally, she lifted her chin, striving for a serenity, which said his rejection was of little consequence then turned with a jarring swish of skirts and left the room. Her departure cast the room into silence.

Lucas Kline crossed the room a measuring look in his eyes.

"Do not let her come back," Beech said.

"She's very determined. And loyal."

Beech didn't miss the glint of admiration in the man's eyes. "And I do not want her at the trial, either."

"You can't be serious." Kline ran a hand through his hair. "Without her, we don't have witness to refute Corporal Argyle's claim that you advised the captain to go into the canyon."

"I don't need a witness. They'll have my word that wasn't the case."

"That will be a tough defense to mount, given—"

"Given that I'm part Indian."

"There is that," Kline admitted.

In spite of the dire circumstances, Beech had appreciated the lawyer's nonjudgmental honesty from their first meeting.

"But what I was going to say," Kline continued, "is given we don't have corroborating evidence the captain was in dire need of medical attention. If we had that, it would cast doubt on Argyle's testimony." His tone turned grave. "Without it or her testimony, it comes down solely to your word against Argyle's."

"Little Brave is not to be a witness." His graveness lent a severe finality to his words.

The lawyer shook his head, a grim set to his face, "I'll return in the morning, after you've slept on it."

"Sleep will not change my mind."

Kline gave him a long contemplative look. "No, but perhaps a sleepless night will." Then he turned on his heel and left the room.

Jean Luc approached the cell.

"What do you want, old man?" Beech asked, vexed at the truth in the lawyer's parting comment. There would be no sleep for him tonight.

"I brought you clean clothes for the trial tomorrow," Jean Luc said, thrusting the items through the bars.

Beech took them and tossed them carelessly on the narrow cot behind him. "There. Now you can go, too."

"You will send everyone away?"

"Unlike everyone else, I am not free to go."

"No, you aren't. But you could be if you allowed Little Brave to—"

"No."

"You would cut off your nose to spite your face?"

"If that's what it takes to keep people from looking at her differently, treating her differently, because she lived among the Lakota."

"You do this to protect her."

It was a statement, not a question so Beech did not comment, but the shrewdness in Jean Luc's pale blue eyes didn't settle easily within him.

"This was how it was when I left you all those years ago," Jean Luc said.

"That was not protection. That was abandonment."

"And that's what you will be doing to her, if you are found guilty."

"And if she testifies and still I am found guilty, then what?" Beech gripped the bars, wishing he could take back that day in the canyon. "She has to endure abandonment, as well as scorn."

"You see…" Jean Luc coughed to loosen the worrisome rasp in his throat, his hands trembling before firming around the bars. "It is not an easy decision to make."

But Beech would not give Jean Luc Richoux this. His reasons were sound—protect the woman he loved with everything within his power. "Abandonment is preferable to abandonment and scorn." If he hung, he wanted to know she would be able to find a life without taint in the white man's world.

Chapter 22

The next morning, Beech sat on the edge of the bed, arms propped on his knees. He stared at the scarred wooden floor of his cell, wondering how much longer before they escorted him to the courthouse for his trial. When Kline had stopped by earlier, he said the time would most likely be midmorning as the judge had a cattle rustling charge to hear first. It appeared by the cast of the sun outside the single barred window of his cell to be about that time. The door opened. He straightened expecting to see the sheriff or his deputy, but not *her*.

"I do not need your visit," he called out, quickly dropping his arms back to his knees and his gaze to the floor.

"You're wrong, Beech." Her tone was calm.

The rustle of skirts told him she approached the barrier between them. But the unyielding metal wasn't what separated them; it was the lies. Years of lies. How many more lies had she told him?

"You would like to think you don't need me," she said.

"I do not need you—" He stopped short of calling her Aunt Claire, for she was no longer his aunt, as Jean Luc Richoux was no longer his father. Not after they'd consciously ripped apart his family.

"There's part of me which believes that you don't." There was a catch in her voice as she made her confession. "And a part of me that even resents you for it."

"Resents me?" He launched from the cot, closing the distance between them in a stride. "Why would you resent me? You have everything. A home, a family. My sister as your own child." His glare challenged her to explain her senseless and selfish feelings.

Clenching her hands tightly over her stomach, she cast her gaze downward.

He made a disgusted noise in the back of his throat aiming to turn away, but her whisper stopped him.

"I don't have you."

"Me?" he scoffed. She looked up at him, like a mother missing her child. He watched her warily, trying to ignore the agonizing thump of his heart.

"Yes, you." She came closer.

Her soothing tone had him imagining another mother.

"You were a scared but determined boy when you first came to us. My heart broke all those times you turned inside yourself, instead of letting me comfort you or help you."

"*You* are not my mother."

She gripped the bars of his prison. "No, I'm not. But I can't help wanting to react like a mother when someone needs one."

He shook his head, trying to deny the memories her words were conjuring in his head—kind words, a gentle hand on his shoulder, an encouraging look, urgings to join in, to be a part of her family. No! It wasn't what he had wanted. He had wanted *his* family, at least what had been left of *his* family. "You sent my father away."

"I didn't send your father away. He was free to return anytime he wanted."

"You are saying this is *his* fault?"

"No, that's not what I'm saying." She shook her head. "I am saying he made a choice. Before he left the first time, we talked at length how things would be for you being half Sioux. We decided the more familiar you were with the white man's world, and the more educated you were in its ways, the better chance you would have at finding a place in it."

"I never wanted to be in it." Anger pushed past all the other emotions filling his throat.

Her knuckles whitened around the bars as she struggled with some decision. Finally, she released them and stood a little taller. "I think that is what pushed Jean Luc to stay away."

He gripped the bars above her head, taking perverse pleasure in the fact his height allowed him to glare downward at her. "Now, you are saying this is *my* fault."

"No, I'm not, Beech."

Some of the starch she'd exhibited when getting after his cousins when they were kids crept into her voice. Her eyes, a darker version of his father's, held his, daring him to argue. He dropped his hands and took a step back. What *was* she saying? Suddenly and inexplicably, he wanted to know. Slowly, he lifted a hand, gesturing for her to continue.

"When your father returned all those years ago, he was so pleased with all you'd accomplished, the ways you'd found to cope."

He opened his mouth to protest, but saw that she held up her hand.

"Yes, there were still tough encounters for you, rough edges to smooth out, but they were occurring less and less. However, once you saw your father again, you were ready to toss it all aside, follow him into the wilderness and take up the wandering, hand-to-mouth life he led."

"But if that's what I wanted—"

"There was—*is* no future in it, Beech."

She cast her gaze over him in the way she did over any of her children when she *knew* her years of experience far outweighed theirs. Did she think he would throw all he'd worked for away to follow his father now? "I am not stubborn and foolhardy like I was then." He was perplexed at his urge to reassure her of this fact.

"Aren't you?"

His fists formed of their own accord, his anger skidding towards a dark place. "Do you think being stubborn and foolhardy is what landed me in this jail cell?"

"No, but I think your attitude is what keeps you imprisoned."

"In case you haven't noticed, I don't have the keys to this cell. I can't come and go as I please. I can't make these charges disappear. I don't—"

"I am not talking about this jail cell."

He struggled with the significance of those words as she continued.

"Why do you focus on what you can't do, what you don't have? Why don't you use who you know and what you have to help yourself?" She huffed an irritated breath. "Why does it always have to be you and you alone?"

Him alone. *Why?* He looked at the ceiling, discrediting the hope her tirade had awakened within him. *No, no. It was too little, too late.*

"Ma'am, I need to take the prisoner—um, I mean your nephew—over to the courthouse."

The voice belonged to the sheriff. Beech kept his gaze on the ceiling. Soon, this would be over.

"Oh, yes, of course," she said. "Beech?"

She waited a moment, but he didn't take his gaze from the cracks in the plastered ceiling. He couldn't look away from them because if he did—cracks would appear his world. She must have reached through the bars for her hand slipped into his.

"It is never too late to ask for help." She squeezed his hand. "Never."

-*-*-

Following behind the aunt and Grace, Little Brave approached the crowd of people gathered in front of the building where the trial would take place. Beech's aunt and his sister greeted people they knew, murmuring in subdued tones about their hopes for an innocent verdict while Little Brave focused on holding her head high and keeping her gaze on the door, which unfortunately was still many steps away. She had no desire to discuss Beech or the trial.

Suddenly, the aunt was reaching for her. "Here she is. Ella, you remember Mrs. Heisenberg, the commander's wife?" the aunt asked as she brought Little Brave face to face with the woman from the fort.

Little Brave inclined her head slightly in Mrs. Heisenberg's direction. Unfortunately, she remembered the woman only too well, the cutting tone of her words and her haughty manner.

"Why, the change is astounding," said Mrs. Heisenberg. "I must commend you, Mrs. Chapman, for turning a creature deprived of civilization for ten years into a respectable young woman."

"Thank you, Mrs. Heisenberg. As her grandfather is a man of some rank and importance, I felt it necessary to give the task my utmost attention."

Mrs. Heisenberg leaned closer. "And I trust you've taken care of the unnatural attachment she had for the half-breed." The aunt pursed her lips in contemplation of a reply, but the commander's wife carried on before it could be voiced. "Of course, it is no reflection upon your good character that you have a relation of inferior breeding."

Finally, the aunt found her voice, drew herself taller and, with a lift of her chin that Grey Owl would have been proud of, she said, "Inferiority is not determined by one's breeding, Mrs. *Heisenberg,* but by one's decisions and actions."

Mrs. Heisenberg's ear bobs danced as she recoiled in surprise. Her skin reddened up her neck, all the way to her hairline.

Little Brave didn't completely understand the nuance of the aunt's reprimand, but she knew it had been made in defense of Beech. Once she heard the commander's wife stiffly bid them good day, Little Brave laid her hand on the aunt's arm. "Thank you, Mrs. Chapman," she said, addressing Beech's aunt with the proper term of respect. In Little Brave's eyes, she had earned it

The aunt patted Little Brave's hand where it still rested on her arm, her gaze soft. "You were right, Ella. Beech should not be left to work things out on his own. He needs us."

Mrs. Chapman whisked them forward through the throng of people only to encounter a greater number inside the building. Most were seated, but the ones who still stood blocked Little Brave's view as she searched the interior for Beech. When Mrs. Chapman had fetched them from the mercantile, she had told her and Grace he had been taken to the courthouse. They had been waiting in the store while Mrs. Chapman had left to run an errand. Given the older woman's change in attitude toward Beech, Little Brave wondered if her errand had been to visit Beech.

Finally, the uncle waved, gesturing them to a row of chairs behind a table at which sat the lawyer and Beech.

As she sat, she focused on Beech's broad back, the sheen of his blue-black hair, and his uncanny calmness as he sat in the middle of the busy courtroom. Everything about their afternoon together rushed back, and everything about their conversation through the bars of his cell yesterday threatened to suffocate it. The physical distance between them was little more than an arm's reach, but yet, the emotional distance stretched much, much further.

All around her people were rising and she stood, too.

An aged man in a flowing black robe entered from a door at the front of the room. He banged a mallet as he sat behind a table set upon a platform.

With relief, she sat as did the rest of the courtroom and her stomach rollicked as if otter were in full play inside.

Finally, after the young soldier who spoke falsehoods against Beech had stepped down from the witness chair, Little Brave's stomach threatened to spew its contents. Since she sat on the end of the row, she exited the room quickly and quietly with a guarding hand over her mouth. Outside the building, she collided with two men, and mumbled a frantic apology as she hurried around the building. At a bush, thankfully some distance behind the building, she emptied what little there was in her stomach. She wondered what would happen to her insides if Beech were actually convicted. She knew what would happen to her heart—what had already happened to her heart.

She held a hand to her quivering stomach, wondering if there was to be another round of retching, but finally, it settled. Gingerly, she straightened and managed a bit of spit to cleanse her mouth of the foul taste. A trickle of sweat broke free from her hairline and trailed down her back. Closing her eyes, she pushed the bonnet off her head to let the breeze lift her hair and cool the heat in her face.

Somehow, she had to will her shaking legs to carry her back to the courtroom. Her testimony was to follow Beech's. Knowing he was next to speak his truth before a courtroom of white men must have been too much for her nerves. But even now it seemed as if her legs wouldn't work. The slightest sound, like the whisper of hawk's wings catching the breeze, caught her attention.

"We meet again, Little Brave."

Her head snapped up in recognition of the voice. She threw up a hand to shade her eyes against the glare of the sun. With the sun behind horse and rider, the man's features were not distinct, but the form was well known, even beneath the blanket that shrouded it.

"Running Bear," she said much weaker than she intended, but her mouth was still dry, her throat burning and her legs now quivering as reeds in a strong wind at seeing the ferocious warrior here. What was he doing in the white man's realm? Suddenly, her arm went slack and her hand dropped. In spite of the brightness all around her, darkness narrowed her view, and she knew as her body folded upon itself that she was going to—*faint.*

_-*-*-_

"The defense calls Ella Hastings to the stand."

"I told you Little Brave was not to be a witness," Beech said through clenched teeth to the man who'd just called her to the stand.

Kline leaned in, returning Beech's quiet but strident tone. "*Little Brave* is not a witness."

Beech glared at the lawyer. Trickster Coyote had nothing on this man who deceived him with a play on words.

A murmur went through the crowd. Beech refused to look, refused to see Lit—Ella, traversing the sea of white men to take the stand on his behalf.

"Ella Hastings, please come forward."

When still she did not come forward and the murmurings of all those who'd come to see him hang filled the air, Beech experienced the heat of his anger chill into desolate realization. Regardless of what he told Lucas Kline,

298

regardless that he'd sent her away, somewhere deep inside, he had counted on her to defy him in her determination to fight for his innocence, for him, for them. But, she was not here, which meant—

The door at the back of the room opened and he could not stopper his hope. The murmuring pitched louder and he craned his head trying to catch a glimpse of whoever had entered the courtroom.

"I want to testify," called a male voice from the back of the room. Boots thumped as the man stalked up the aisle.

"Lieutenant Cummings," Commander Heisenberg exclaimed from his seat across the aisle. "You escaped the canyon?"

It was indeed Lieutenant Cummings, the second in command of the ill-fated detachment. His scraggly hair reached his shoulders. A full beard covered the lower half of a blistered and sunburned face. His clothes hung on his now too-thin frame. "I escaped from the Lakota band which attacked our detachment in the canyon."

The crowd now erupted into a rowdy babble.

Kline leaned over, speaking quietly to Beech. "Lieutenant Cummings was there when you had the argument with the captain."

"Yes, he was."

He grimaced. "Do you think he's here to tell the truth?"

"I cannot say," Beech murmured, recalling the man's unassuming nature. *I hope so.* Although Cummings wasn't a hardened soldier like the captain or the commander, he was a member of the white man's army and an officer at that.

The judge banged his gavel. "Quiet in the courtroom, or I'll clear it." The noise ceased instantly for no one wanted to miss what this survivor had to say. "Come take the stand, Lieutenant."

The oath was administered and the lieutenant was seated, then Judge Sinclair asked, "How did you come to be here, Lieutenant Cummings?"

"When I finally made my way back to Fort Fetterman, they told me about the trial and I figured I best have my say."

"Do you recognize the defendant, Beech Richoux?"

Lieutenant pointed at Beech. "Yes, your honor. That's him sitting there."

"Let the record show the witness has correctly identified the defendant." Judge Sinclair glanced to the clerk then back to the lieutenant. "Were you present on the day an argument took place between the defendant and Captain Baldwin?"

"Yes sir, I was." The lieutenant drew his gaunt frame a little taller on the witness stand.

"And what did they argue about?"

"Whether to go through the canyons or to skirt them."

"And what position did the defendant take in the argument?" The judge adjusted the sleeves of his robe then settled back in his chair.

"Richoux wanted to skirt the canyons." The lieutenant glanced at Beech then back to the judge. "He said we would be at a disadvantage defensively if we were attacked."

"And the captain?"

"He wanted to ride through them."

Murmurings swept the courtroom, but the judge ignored them as he continued his questioning. "And did he say *why* he wanted to put the detachment at risk?"

"Objection," the prosecuting lawyer said, his chair scraping along the wood floor as the man popped up. "Leading the witness."

"Objection overruled." The judge reached for his gavel and pointed it at the lawyer, giving him a stern look. "With almost every soldier in the canyon killed that day, I'd say the risk to the detachment is more than established." He settled his gavel after he saw the lawyer take his seat then returned his attention to the witness. "Go on, Lieutenant."

"He said he didn't want to devote any more time to the hostiles but..." Grimacing, the lieutenant glanced to the back of the room.

Before Beech could determine who Cummings had been looking at he heard the judge clear his throat.

"You are under oath, Lieutenant," Judge Sinclair said.

"Your honor, the captain was ill, very ill."

"Objection, your honor, conjecture, at best," said the prosecuting lawyer, although he remained seated this time.

"Overruled. We heard the same testimony from Richoux."

"That doesn't make it fact, your honor," retorted the lawyer.

A thunderous look overtook the judge's face.

A voice echoed from the back of the room. "I can make it fact."

Everyone swiveled to eye another man in military dress.

"And who might you be?" Judge Sinclair leaned forward in his chair and squinted at the man.

"Captain Robert Morehouse, I serve as military physician at Fort Fetterman."

"Well, hell, is my whole fort here?" Commander Heisenberg said to no one in particular.

Twitters erupted, and an outright guffaw sounded, but the crowd quieted as soon as Judge Sinclair said, "I take it you have intimate knowledge of the captain's health."

"Yes, your honor."

"Well then by all means, come on up here." The judge gestured the military doctor forward before returning his attention to the lieutenant. "One last question, Lieutenant. Was there anyone who overheard or could have overheard the conversation in question between the defendant and the captain?"

"Other than myself, there wasn't." The lieutenant sighed as he shook his head. "The captain had ridden out to where Richoux and I were scouting. By the time the captain ordered me back to inform the men of his decision, the procession was closer, but with all those horses and the wind, even I couldn't hear what they were saying once I started riding away."

"You're excused, Lieutenant Cummings." The judge waved forth the court clerk. "Captain Morehouse, come take the oath."

While the oath was being administered to the doctor, Beech leaned over to Lucas Kline. "Can the judge take over the questioning like that?"

"It's his courtroom." The lawyer's face broke out into a grin. "But I'd say he's doing a damn fine job."

Beech longed to share in Kline's glee but held the urge in check. He had too much stacked against him as a half-breed to count on a not-guilty verdict just yet, regardless of the testimony in his favor.

The doctor had settled himself in the witness chair, and then the judge fired his first question. "When did you first become aware of the Captain Baldwin's ill health, Captain Morehouse?"

"The morning the detachment was scheduled to leave the fort. Captain Baldwin came to my office asking for digestion powders for pains in his stomach."

"Did you examine him?"

"Yes, your honor."

"And what was the conclusion of your exam?"

"It was inconclusive, but based on where the pain was—around the navel." The doctor circled his hand over his stomach. "And the fact that it was firm to the touch, I told him it might be something as simple as bloating. But it could also be the start of appendicitis."

"And what was your advice?"

"As his doctor, I ordered him to delay the expedition for at least forty-eight hours to rule out appendicitis." The doctor's tone turned grave as he panned the crowd. "Appendicitis is not only extremely painful, but fatal if not dealt with surgically. But," His gaze stalled on Commander Heisenberg. "As an officer, I could only strongly advise him since we held the same rank."

"Why didn't you inform the fort commander immediately?"

"As soon as the captain left, a soldier was brought in with a serious gunshot wound." The doctor squared his shoulders and looked at the judge. "Then I had to tend several cases of food poisoning."

"When did you find out that the captain had left the fort?"

"Not for another couple of days." Dr. Morehouse shook his head apologetically.

"And once you realized the captain was gone, what did you do?"

"I informed Commander Heisenberg."

"And what was his response?" The judge's eyebrows rose in expectation of the doctor's answer.

"He was angry to say the least." Dr. Morehouse took a bracing breath. "But he told me he'd deal with the insubordination when Captain Baldwin returned."

"I've heard enough, Captain Morehouse, you're excused." Judge Sinclair sent a searing look to the prosecution's star witness as the doctor exited the stand.

Corporal Argyle squirmed in his seat and red crept up his neck and into his face.

Commander Heisenberg gave the corporal a scathing look then leaned across the balustrade to murmur something to the prosecuting attorney.

The lawyer rose and addressed the judge. "Your honor, in light of this new evidence, the United States Army respectfully withdraws its charges against the defendant, Beech Richoux."

"Wise choice, counselor. All charges are dropped, and the defendant is free to go." With a resounding bang of his gavel, the judge sealed his decision.

Free. To. Go. The words catapulted Beech into action. He had to find Little Brave, give her the news and if it wasn't too late he would—

Lucas Kline grabbed his hand, pumping it vigorously. "Congratulations, Richoux."

Beech thanked the beaming lawyer in a haze.

Then Uncle Henry clapped him on the back. "Those witnesses couldn't have arrived any sooner."

Grace threw her arms around him, sobbing, "I would have hated to lose you, brother, so soon after finding you."

Beech held on tightly, an unbelievable joy filling him—not only at the verdict, but also at Grace referring to him as her brother.

After his sister released him, Aunt Claire clasped his upper arms, holding him at arm's length for a moment before she pulled him close, whispering in his ear, "I would have been devastated to lose you, Beech." When she released him there were tears in her eyes.

He swallowed hard against his own rising emotion. "Aunt Claire, where is Little Brave?" he asked, loathing to hear her answer, but needing to confirm the worst news for himself.

Ella's Choice

"Why, she was sitting next to Grace during the trial," his aunt said, looking around the crowded courtroom.

"Are you talking about the white woman who was with the Lakota band?" Lieutenant Cummings held out his hand in congratulations.

Beech shook it, hoping the man could shed some light on her whereabouts. "Yes. Have you seen her?"

"She ran into me and the doctor as we were coming into the courthouse. I thought she looked familiar."

Little Brave had been here? Where had she gone in such a rush? "Did you see which way she went?"

"Around the back of the building. Although I can't say why."

Suddenly, Beech's hopes soared as he headed toward the door.

Little Brave's grandfather fell into step with him. "Was the lieutenant talking about Ella?"

"Yes." Beech pushed his way through the throng of people, not stopping to return their congratulations on the trial's outcome. In some distant place in his head, he mused perversely at the number of people who had come out to see whether or not he would hang.

"Does he know where she went? I haven't been able to find her," said her grandfather.

"Around the back of the building," After two days in a dark, cramped jail cell, Beech welcomed the bright glare and heat of the sun as he stepped outside and hurried around the building. He quickly picked up the outline of her moccasins in the fine dust blown between the buildings from the churn of traffic along the main street.

"She must have been sick," said Jean Luc once they reached a bush with a noxious smell coming from beneath it.

Beech was not surprised to find his father beside him for when had he ever heard the expert tracker coming.

Ruby Merritt

"The tracks end here, but there are hoof prints." Beech knelt, ferreting out every clue the indentations held.

"Unshod." His father knelt beside him, speaking the details aloud. "And another set of moccasin prints."

Dread seized his muscles at the thought of one of the Plains People kidnapping Little Brave. Or had she chosen to leave?

"Did someone take her?" Colonel Russell pushed between the two men as they rose, his gaze darting to the prints then back to Beech.

"It appears that way." Beech licked at his parched lips and pushed away the notion that she might have chosen to return to the Lakota. Had his words in the jail yesterday driven her away, like they'd driven away his cousin?

"Who and why?" asked the Colonel.

"I need my horse and some supplies," Beech said, his mind jumping ahead to how long it might take to catch up with Little Brave.

"Your horse is at the livery. I'll go fetch him and some supplies too."

All three men turned to see Karl Godfrey, the livery owner, behind them.

"Much obliged, Karl."

Karl lifted a hand in acknowledgement. "Just glad to see you not swinging from the end of a rope."

"Narrow miss," Beech scoffed with a tight smile. He couldn't think about the outcome of the trial until he had Little Brave safely back—if she even wanted to come back. He turned to Jean Luc, knowing he needed to make amends, knowing there was so much to repair between them, but—

It is never too late to ask for help. Was it true what his aunt had said? Looking at the man who Beech now realized was still his father in spite of his long absence, he said, "Two pairs of eyes are better than one. Could you..." Still, long years of not asking for help tied his tongue.

306

Jean Luc laid a hand on his shoulder. "Start tracking. I'll go with Karl to get the horses."

Beech looked at the man, this man, who offered to help without question or resolution. Everything else that had transpired between over the past several days, all that had happened in the past, still needed to be sifted through, measured and resolved. That would take time, but in this moment, it was enough to know that this man was still his father. Beech squeezed the hand on his shoulder, letting his father know that he, Beech Richoux, was still his son.

"You two take up the trail. I'll go with Karl and catch up with the horses," the Colonel said.

"It's a clear trail, Colonel, we won't have any trouble tracking it," Beech said, resisting the notion of having a take-charge military officer along.

"There was only one kidnapper," Jean Luc said, rubbing at one of the tracks with his foot, "but there could be more waiting outside of town."

The Colonel nodded. "You'll need reinforcements. Plus…she's my granddaughter."

The Colonel invoked one of the greatest leverages a man could—blood.

But she's my woman. Beech clenched his fists, but kept them close to his sides, quelling his urge to hit the man with more than the just truth. He wanted to watch the conniving bastard writhe in the dirt as he informed him in no uncertain terms of his honorable intentions towards Little Brave, but for her sake, he held them in check. "You can ride along, but what I say goes."

"I'll grant you know the terrain better, Richoux, but I've years of military training and experience."

"I know the ways of the Lakota inside and out."

"There's no doubt about that," Lieutenant Cummings called out as he approached the group. "If

Captain Baldwin had listened to this man, our detachment would probably still be alive."

Implacability was present in the young lieutenant which hadn't been there before. No doubt the result of the massacre in the canyon, but what of his time with Grey Owl's band now that Running Bear was the leader? Had that had a hand in it, as well? Regardless, Beech was grateful for the younger man's support.

"I'll ride with you without question, Richoux," the lieutenant said with a pointed look at the Colonel.

The Colonel grimaced. "We'll do it your way, Richoux. For now." He gestured to the prints before them. "Start tracking. I'll get the horses and catch up."

Beech agreed with a sharp nod. The Colonel turned and headed back toward the main road with the stunted livery owner hop skipping to keep up.

His father spoke in Lakota. "Do not worry, we can lose him if need be."

Beech half-grimaced and half-smiled at his father. Having him by his side once more felt good.

Commander Heisenberg joined them, looking between Beech and Jean Luc. "I thought there was a family resemblance."

Jean Luc returned to English. "I should have left Argyle in that snow bank last winter. He has caused much grief for my son with his lies."

"It would have saved us both a hell of a lot of trouble if you had, but freezing would have been too quick of an end for him. The little weasel always did have a healthy dose of hero worship for Captain Baldwin, but I didn't realize he'd lie to clear the man's name." The commander's features tightened. "I'll throw him in the stockade when we get back to the fort. He can think about what his deceit has cost him while I take my time on arranging his court martial." Commander Heisenberg turned to Beech. "That agreeable to you, Richoux?" He held out his hand.

Beech eyed the soldier's offering, recalling all his slurs against Little Brave, the Lakota, and the French. He couldn't help but ask, "Why do you want to shake my hand now?"

"Because I admire a man who stands up for the truth, even when he knows the odds are stacked against him."

He wasn't sure if the commander was talking about going up against Captain Baldwin in the wastelands or Corporal Argyle in court. Maybe that detail wasn't as important as accepting an offer of peace and understanding over perpetuating further hostility and hatred.

Chapter 23

Little Brave revived to the smell of bear grease, which the Plains People rubbed liberally over their skin to protect it from insects and the sun. It was a scent as familiar to her as sweet grass, cedar or sage, but today, it wreaked havoc with her stomach. She closed her nose to its scent as she forced her body to remain in rhythm with the pony's movement, lest Running Bear become aware she was awake. Her ribs ground indiscriminately against hard sinewy thighs, while her arms and legs tingled in numbness from hanging freely on either side of the pony. With her hair covering her face, it was impossible to see anything but tufted bunch grass interspersed with gravelly sand and small rocks. How long had she been unconscious? Where were they headed? Why had Running Bear taken her?

Running Bear wrapped an arm around her waist, holding her in place as he leaned back and the horse descended a bank. It splashed through a creek then clambered up the other side.

The slightest shift in her captor's body brought the horse to a halt. The absence of heat on her back told her they were in the shade. Hitching a hand under her arm, he slid her off his lap and let her body drop to the ground. Instinctively, she bent her knees to take the impact, holding her arms aloft to balance. Needle-like sensations surged through her muscles but with no small feeling of satisfaction, she ignored them enough to steady herself then stood.

"Good. You are awake." Running Bear gestured behind her, his face giving no clue to his agenda. "I brought you a horse."

She lifted her chin, and matched his impassivity. "Good. Then I will return to Cheyenne well before dark."

"Do not make me bind your hands and feet, Little Brave."

"What do you want from me?"

His eyes glittered as he stared, but he gave her no answer.

She looked around at the trees surrounding them then to the rocky outcroppings looming beyond. "Where are we?"

"Land of the earthborn spirits," he said.

It was a place where the Plains People said spirits dwelt in every facet of nature from the sky to the rocks. A place where young braves often went for their vision quest—the ritualistic comings of manhood.

A sacred place.

She waited for him to say more, but he only gestured to the horse next to her. She untied it and led it to a knee-high boulder. The many layers of petticoats and her long skirt would not allow her to swing onto its back from the ground.

"How quickly you've returned to the white man's ways," Running Bear scoffed as she hiked up the voluminous amount of material then mounted. "What do they call you in the white man's tongue?"

His intent was clear. He meant to reinforce her people's rejection of her by using her English name instead of her Lakota name. She reined the horse around, denying him an answer and headed in the direction from which they'd come.

He caught her reins, pulling her horse alongside his. "The buffalo have eluded my hunters. The women have no tepees and the children's bellies cramp in hunger."

Hiyee! It was as she thought; he was not fit to lead their people. However, she could not muster any smugness at his failure when it came at the price of their misfortune. Instead, sadness seeped past her stoic mask.

"I knew my people had not left your heart." His eyes gleamed in mean satisfaction.

Denying it would only prolong his torture. "You are right. They have not left my heart."

"Being among the white man has made you agreeable." He ran a finger down her cheek.

She fought to control her shiver.

"But I prefer you fighting me." He curled his fingers inside the collar of her dress and yanked.

Buttons littered the ground around them and her dress gaped open to the waist, but she would not give him the satisfaction of her reaction. She lifted her chin, regaining the blankness, which denied him any glimpse of his affect on her.

"Why have you come back for me?" The exposed skin above her chemise and corset pimpled, but she ignored it as she forced herself to stare into his narrowed eyes. The Lakota warriors admired bravery above all else.

He uttered a guttural sound. "You, too, have not left their hearts." His lip curled as he said it.

Inside, her heart fluttered like hummingbird's wings, but outside, her face revealed no more than a stone would have.

He yanked her horse's reins, bringing it around behind his then urged his pony forward.

As hers followed, her mind whirred with what lay ahead. Did he intend to take her back to their people? Even if he was angry at the fact they missed her? Her heart brimmed in happiness with the knowledge they yet held her in their hearts, but just as quickly, it emptied. They were suffering. Perhaps in Running Bear's absence, they had found the buffalo. Would they still want her among them then? Did she want to live with the Lakota again? She shook her head. She wanted to help them, but in the end, her place was with Beech. *Beech!* The trial rushed back with a suddenness that sucked the air from her lungs.

She had been about to speak her truth so Beech would not hang for the deaths of the soldiers in the canyon. How much time had passed? She checked the sun. It was well beyond the halfway point on its journey across the sky. Surely, the trial had been halted once they realized she was missing. She had been adamant with Lucas Kline that she would testify, regardless of what Beech had wanted. She had faith in the dedicated lawyer who appeared to want justice for Beech as much as she did. He would delay the hearing until she could speak on Beech's behalf, she was sure. Now, she only had to devise a way to escape this canny and powerful warrior.

She stared at the muscled back of her captor, his sinewy legs hanging loosely around the belly of his horse. One hand rested on a strong thigh, the other no doubt twined in the pony's mane as hers did now. His repose was a façade, for motion was as instantaneous to him as the leap was to grasshopper. Escaping him would be as nearly impossible as evading him long enough to make it back to Cheyenne. Her only option would be to outwit him, or incapacitate him.

They ascended into the rocky terrain, the stones, stacked like leaning towers of blocks, reaching higher and higher for the sky. Finally, Running Bear turned off the trail, seemingly disappearing into a solid rock face, but as her pony made the turn, she saw the opening. They had to extend their legs along the horse's back and lay low over their neck to fit through it, but then they emerged into a relatively level area with a perimeter of three tepees. Save the opening they'd just passed through, the area was surrounded by the towering blocks—a natural fortress. The twisted boughs of a gnarled pine projected unnaturally long, crooked fingers of shade over the fine layer of dust covering the ground.

"The earthborn spirits gather here and commune," Running Bear said.

He surprised her with his reverence, and she wondered at his connection to the eerie place. The saturated silence within the enclosure and the absence of any mark whatsoever—not even a mouse print—in the powdered dirt, gave her the feeling they were intruding into a place not meant for physical beings. "Why are we here?"

"To break the hold you have on my people." He dismounted, gesturing for her to do the same. When she hesitated, he jerked her down.

She chastised herself for raising his ire and righted herself as quickly as she could.

He marched her toward the lone pine tree and threw her against it.

Its rough bark scraped against the exposed skin of her chest and shoulders. She sucked in her breath against the pain then stiffened her spine, squared her shoulders and turned, forcing a calmness she did not feel. She would not give Running Bear a fight, for that's what he wanted. His advantage lay in the heat of battle, where instinct and bloodlust ruled.

"How will you break my hold over your people?" She hoped her neutrality would entice him to speak of his plan before acting.

"First, you will renounce all the lies you have spoken."

"And once I have done that, I will be free to go?" Although she knew of no lies she had spoken, she hoped to appeal to his honor if she did as he asked.

He widened his stance, crossed his arms over his chest, but he did not answer.

She lifted her chin. "What lies do you think I have spoken?"

"That my mother died trying to rescue me."

The mother who fell to her death when she tried to rescue her wandering son. What she had said was true, but not in the way he thought, not in the way she'd led him to believe. "Your mother did die trying to rescue her wandering son." Working around the women's fires had allowed her to hear many things of which men rarely spoke. "But the son was not you, but your younger brother."

He nodded once.

Whether it was in acknowledgment of what she'd revealed, or for her to continue she did not know.

"You said my father purposely fell upon his spear in grief over losing my mother."

That not a muscle twitched nor an eye blinked as he said these words told her how her words had affected him that day he'd convinced their people to abandon her. Exactly how she'd envisioned it, toppling the foundation on which any child's life rested—on that of beloved and revered parents. But oh, how she knew the pain of losing a father, therefore she couldn't completely harden her heart to his pain, even knowing he had purposely killed her Lakota father, Grey Owl.

"I twisted what I heard about your father's death." Now, she spoke the truth, hoping her admission would appeal to his sense of honor and he would let her go. There was the slightest flare of his nostrils, but otherwise, there was no acknowledgment of what she'd said so she explained further. "Grey Owl said your father recklessly charged into battle after losing your mother. There, he died from the thrust of an enemy's spear."

"You have learned Grey Owl's knack for twisting words to suit one's purpose."

The heat of anger rose in her face at his attempt to tarnish her father's reputation. "Grey Owl was not devious."

His bared teeth indicated her reaction pleased him well, and she forced her anger into the balling of her fists, which were well hidden in the folds of her skirt.

"You were not with us when Grey Owl was a mighty warrior," he said. "His talk of peace came only after those days had passed."

"Wisdom most often comes in later years."

"Weakness comes in later years." His hand sliced through the air in emphasis of his point.

Little Brave replied with all the command she'd learned from her adopted father, "Yet, only an arrow to his heart kept our people from following him." She aimed to pierce his arrogance with her next words. "And now they suffer because they have been denied his wisdom."

"My people do not suffer. They are camped with other clans of Lakota on Greasy Grass Creek after a successful buffalo hunt." The prideful triumph in his face told her this was not a lie. Now, she knew his earlier assertion had been uttered to manipulate her into revealing her true feelings about the people they shared.

"Then I am happy for them," Little Brave said because it was her sincerest desire their people were not suffering.

"The Cheyenne and Arapaho are joining us there as we wait for the three armies of the white man to attack."

"Then you should be there and not here," she said, hoping to hide her surprise the Plains People knew about the white man's plans.

"Do not worry, I will be there leading our warriors when the white man strikes, but first, I must finish what I came here to do."

"I have done what you've asked so that my hold over our—*your*," she amended, hoping to appease him, "people will be broken. Now, I will return to Cheyenne." She made a move to brush past him but he grabbed her arm hauling her close. The stench of sweaty man mixed with bear grease was overwhelming, and his hot breath sent a shiver through her as it skated over her skin.

"That is not how I planned to break your hold over *my* people." He released her arm and circled her.

She felt his gaze looking over her shoulder at the bared skin of her chest, and she resisted the urge to tug her torn dress closed to hide the swell of her breasts thrust high by the corset. He halted in front of her once more, a formidable hulk of bone, sinew and muscle. His eyes were narrowed with evil intent, his body coiled with a power she could never best.

"How are you planning to break my hold over your people?" she forced herself to ask in spite of the fear closing her throat. Keeping him talking would keep him from acting.

"My people will no longer yearn for you, if your spirit leaves this earth in shame."

"Take my life," she dared him. "But like Grey Owl's, it will bear no shame. The shame will be yours for taking a life that does not deserve it."

"Not deserve it?" There was a slight hint of surprise in his eyes then it was replaced by a cold certainty. "Even as we speak the white man seeks to destroy my people any way they can, because they do not bend to his will." Slyness crept across his face, insidiously showing his teeth. "And what the white man does to me, I will do to him."

"So you *will* take my life."

"I *will* not give you the honor of death at the hands of a mighty warrior such as myself." Without warning, he shoved her back against the tree.

Her head hit with a thud that had stars and darkness swimming before her eyes.

When they cleared, his face was hideously close, the cruel cast of his lips murmuring. "You will take your own life."

"I will never take my own life," she said, refusing to drop her gaze before his. In the early days with the Blackfeet, and the day Grey Owl had died and her people had abandoned her, she would have welcomed death, but not now. Her choice was to live, to return to Beech and make a home with him. "If you want me dead, you will have to kill me yourself."

A barbaric gleam appeared in his eyes. She expected him to pull his knife and hold it at her throat like he had the day he had killed Grey Owl. He would slit her throat then claim her death had been by her own hand, but instead, his hand twisted into her hair. Her scalp stung at his vicious hold, and she firmed her lips to keep from crying out.

"The women of our enemies beg for our knives after we have taken them every way we can."

Suddenly, fear turned to panic as his intention became clear. He would defile her until he broke her spirit, stole her soul and robbed her of any desire to exist in this life. Such purposeful evilness filled her with a black rage, and she reached out to claw at his face and eyes.

With a twist of his head, he dodged her sharp nails. She kicked out at him. He yanked at her hair and she stumbled. He released her. She fell to her hands and knees, dusting puffing up between her fingers. The impact reverberated in her bones and rattled her teeth.

She scrambled to her feet, but he was behind her. He grabbed her and forced her back onto her hands and

318

knees. His fetid heat surrounded her. Dark lank hair fell across her cheek as he hovered over her.

"First, I will take you like a dog."

At the vicious anticipation in his voice, she arched backward and swung fists over her shoulder, threw both elbows up and behind her. He merely grunted when one of her strikes managed to connect with his bone and flesh.

He wrestled her down, pinning her with his weight. Her hands were secured behind her.

She pulled for breath, cursing the corset that bound her ribs. Her only satisfaction was the pant, however mild, in his breathing.

"You fight like a she-cat."

A growl erupted from deep in her throat as his words cut across her ear. The need to fight surged within her again.

He grappled with the fabric twisted around her legs.

She writhed and tried to free her hands. The corset's boning ground against her ribs.

With a feral sound and a vicious tug at her petticoats, he ripped the fabric free. Another softer rip, like a sigh of capitulation, and his hard arousal pressed against the bare skin between her legs.

Tears stung her eyes as he fisted a hand into her hair and yanked her up onto her hands and knees. There was a sharp jab to the soft underside of her breast. Reflexively, she plucked at the offending object—an exposed corset stay.

She worked to free it as he jerked her head back to an impossible angle. Hope glimmered as she freed the stay. She rolled her gaze back toward him.

He gripped her hip then reared up to enter her.

She saw his ugly vanquishing look turned to surprised outrage when she reached between their legs and stabbed the sharp tip of the stay into the most vulnerable place for all men.

He roared in pain and loosened his hold.

She scrambled to her feet, snatching her knife from her moccasin. As she expected, she'd barely taken a step before he grabbed her.

He spun her, his vicious grin triumphant. "I knew you would fight me, *Little Brave*."

"Fight you?" she snarled. "I will kill you." Fury propelled her blade deep into the unguarded region beneath his ribs.

He gave an enraged cry then wrapped his fingers around her neck.

She thrust the blade upward, twisting it.

His teeth gritted; his grip tightened.

She gasped, then coughed, clawing one-handed at his fingers. Blackness ringed her vision, crept closer to its center. An unearthly howl echoed in her ear. It pulsated throughout her body, vibrated all the way to the tips of her fingers and toes and slammed against the bones of her head. The pinprick of light disappeared, enveloping her in silent darkness.

Slowly, Little Brave opened her eyes. Her mouth was full of grit, her throat felt as if a fire had been lit within, and there was a mass so heavy it felt like a boulder on her chest.

Where was she?

As she squirmed to free herself, she realized the weight wasn't a rock. Its pliancy identified it as a living being. Had Sundance tripped and now she was trapped beneath her? She shifted, catching a whiff of bear grease, and it all came back in a soul-sucking rush.

Running Bear.

She pushed every which way she could at the body holding her down, flipping it over as she escaped it. Dizzily, she scrambled to her feet, trying to catch her breath. The sight of her knife protruding from the Lakota warrior caused her stomach to spasm, but there was nothing left to expel.

Once her stomach's dry heaving calmed, she stepped close to Running Bear's motionless body. She squatted, holding her hand above his mouth and nose, feeling for breath, watching for the rise and fall of his chest. He was as still as the heavy silence within the stone enclosure. She reached for her knife, the blade freeing with a sickening squelch from a gaping bloody cavity. Like Grey Owl, Running Bear's eyes remained opened in death, staring unseeingly into a world in which he no longer walked.

She stood, rotating her blade in the waning rays of sunlight, only slivers of metal visible through the blood coating it. She'd sent a life from this world to the next. Tremors of disbelief and revulsion started at the tips of her fingers and the soles of her feet. They radiated throughout her until her whole body shook like the final leaf of autumn in winter's first wind.

"Little Brave."

She jerked her head around. The man coming through the opening in the rocks—alive and well and free—must be a dream like the man lying, still and lifeless, on the ground next to her was a nightmare.

"Ella. Good God, what happened here?"

This man held a note of admonishment in his voice. Her childself knew it well. She looked to the bloody blade in her hand then to the dead man on the ground. When she looked back to the white-haired man, her grownup self stated her truth, before her vision darkened and her legs folded.

"Now, I am a savage."

Chapter 24

Beech caught Little Brave as her knees buckled. Her arms fell away from her body as he scooped her into his arms. Immediately, he checked her over for injuries and to make sure the blood she wore was not hers. "She is bruised, but otherwise seems fine," he said to her hovering grandfather.

Her grandfather then marched over to the knife, which had slipped free from her hand and retrieved it. He examined it as if there was something he couldn't quite figure out about the weapon. When he approached the slain warrior, he eyed him in the same manner.

Beech said, "She did what she had to in order to survive."

The Colonel coughed, muttering something beneath his breath as he motioned to the opening in the rocks. "We'd better get my granddaughter back to Cheyenne."

Beech ducked, rolling Little Brave tighter into his embrace as he went through the opening to the main trail where his father and Lieutenant Cummings waited.

"She is alive?" His father slid from his horse to verify for himself, given her torn clothes, and the blood and dirt covering her from head to toe.

"Yes, but she fainted when she saw us." Beech tucked the unconscious woman into the crook of one arm as he freed the blanket at the back of his saddle. He draped it over her then put his foot into the stirrup and his free hand on the saddle horn to hoist himself.

"I'll take her," the Colonel said, emerging onto the trail.

"No—I mean...it's done," Beech said as he swung into the saddle. Now that he had the woman he loved in his arms, there was no way he was letting her go.

The man bound to Little Brave by blood opened his mouth to say something, then closed it without uttering a word and turned to mount his horse.

"Was it Running Bear?" Lieutenant Cummings jerked his chin in the direction from which they'd come.

"Yes," Beech said. "And he is dead," he added in answer to the question he knew would come next.

"He must have followed me when I escaped from their camp on the Little Bighorn River," the lieutenant said.

Beech did not doubt the wiliness of Running Bear, although it did not explain why the Lakota warrior had kidnapped Little Brave.

"What do you want to do with him?" the lieutenant asked.

"Let him rot." Beech reined his horse around. "But two fine mustangs are in there. Take them in exchange for the trouble he has caused you."

***

Beech poured the next-to-the-last bucket of steaming water into the tub, which had been brought into the parlor. His aunt set a large quilt, towels and soap on a chair beside it. He approached the sofa where Little Brave was sleeping. She'd become conscious during the ride back to Cheyenne, but after his reassurances she was safe and Running Bear was dead, she'd quickly succumbed to sleep again, although a troubled one.

"Little Brave, it is Beech." He spoke softly in Lakota as he crouched next to the sofa. "You'll feel better once we get you cleaned up." He touched her cheek, hoping to wake her gently from her twitching and intermittent cries.

"Beech, let me tend to her," his aunt said.

"No, I will take care of her." He clasped one of Little Brave's hands between his, gently chaffing it.

"It isn't appropriate."

He pressed a kiss to Little Brave's hand then held it to his heart, hoping she could feel it beating for her. After a few moments, he settled her hand back on the couch and rose to face his aunt. Now he would finish what he'd started at the fort when he'd declared Little Brave to be his woman.

"There is nothing more appropriate, Aunt Claire, than a husband tending to his wife." Beech put it into terms his aunt could firmly grasp.

"Your wife? When? Where? How?" Her hands fluttered all about her.

"At Fort Fetterman."

"A preacher married you and Ella while you were at the fort?" Admonishment slipped into her tone." Why didn't you tell—"

"No, we were not married by a white man, but we are bound by Lakota tradition." He doubted his aunt would understand or approve of the Lakota way.

"But she was returning to Washington D.C. with her grandfather."

"I thought it would be best for her, that she would be happiest living as a white woman in white society with her grandfather."

"But now she's not?"

"No, she is not." Beech looked at the woman he could have lost today. If not for her courage and determination, he would have. He couldn't imagine life without this beautiful, spirited and sensual woman who completed him in every way.

His aunt took his hand. "You are so much like your father." Tears filled her eyes. "Willing to sacrifice yourself for what you think is best for those that you love."

Beech shook his head. "I do not want to be like my father. We all suffered over what he thought was best." He gave his aunt a pointed look. "And what you thought was best."

A tear slipped free and slid down her cheek. "I'm sorry I insisted we keep Grace's heritage a secret. It is one thing to keep it from the outside world, but I should have trusted you with it."

He let a heavy breath slip free, a burden lifting from his shoulders with her apology and admission. "I'm sorry I broke my promise to you and told her."

"No, no, no, don't be sorry." She released his hand to wipe the tears now spilling from her eyes. "It was time she knew. I'll have to trust she'll be careful with that knowledge." She took a cleansing breath. "Now as for you and Ella...if you have been bound since the fort, does that mean..." His aunt diverted her gaze as her question trailed into silent insinuation.

"Yes, we have." He didn't say when they'd consummated their marriage. That fact wasn't important. What was important was that he was claiming Little Brave as his now and that everyone honored it.

"Well then, if this is what Ella wants, I'll not stand in your way." His aunt's voice grew softer, almost whimsical. "I've seen how she looks at you, how sad she is when you are away, and how alive she is when you are here." She laid a hand on his shoulder.

There was understanding in her touch, but warning, too.

"You must make this right with her grandfather."

Little Brave stirred. "Beech?" Her voice cracked as she tentatively opened her eyes. "Where am I?"

"You're back home with us, Ella, in the parlor," Aunt Claire said.

Beech was grateful for his aunt's answer for suddenly he found speaking difficult. He pressed her hand to his heart, hoping the gesture would say what he wanted to convey.

She squeezed it, her gaze growing soft in response. "You are free," she said in wonder. "How?"

This he could find words for. "Lieutenant Cummings survived the attack in the canyon."

She closed her eyes and sighed, peace settling over her features.

Awe overwhelmed him at her concern for him, in spite of what she'd been through. He clutched her hand tighter to his heart. He'd been stubborn and foolish not to fight for her, for them.

"I know you are tired, but there's a hot bath waiting for you," his aunt said. She reached over his shoulder and touched Little Brave on the cheek. "Once you're cleaned up, then you can sleep all you want."

Her eyes popped open then as she struggled to sit upright.

Beech put an arm around her to help her up.

Stark realization filled her face as she pushed away the blanket covering her to confirm what had transpired by the sight of her torn and bloody dress. She covered her face with her hands. "No, no, no," she said.

Beech shifted to the sofa then swept her into his arms. "Shhh, shhh," he soothed over and over, stroking a hand along her hair and down her back.

"I killed him," she sobbed.

"I'll make her a drink to calm her nerves," Aunt Claire said then left the room.

"What will he think?" Little Brave stuttered between sobs.

"Who?" Beech knew she meant her grandfather, but having her answer his questions would help her process the traumatic events of the day.

She buried her face into his neck, her hands clutching at his shirt. "My grandfather," she wailed, her tears hot against his skin.

"He knows you had no choice." But Beech knew that knowing and accepting were two different things.

"He saw me with the bloody knife. He saw what I did to Running Bear. He saw for himself that I am a savage."

He clutched her face between his hands, staring deeply into her eyes. "You are not a savage. You are Little Brave, daughter of the revered Lakota chief Grey Owl."

"Which means I am an *Indian*, Beech." The way her lip curled as she purposely used the English word for the Plains People touched that cold and lonely place inside him. It slithered in, unfurling, strengthening the darkness—the darkness which beckoned him back.

"Indian is a word that the white man has twisted for his own purposes. It means nothing more and nothing less than any nation of the Plains People: the Lakota, the Cheyenne, the Blackfeet, the Crow—"

She dropped her gaze and shook her head.

He crushed her to his chest, refusing to embrace that debilitating blackness, determined to keep it from poisoning her mind, breaking her heart and stealing her soul.

With a swift solid motion, he stood then carried her to the steaming tub with determined strides. He would wash away all this ugliness and cleanse her of its filth. He set her on her feet and she swayed, a blank look on her face. Not the impassive look, which said she was hiding her emotions, but a look that said there were no emotions. A vacant look.

He clutched her shoulders. "Little Brave." Her gaze fixed on his chest, seeing only what played behind her eyes.

He gave her a small shake. Her head wobbled, but her stare did not clear. Had the darkness already taken her? "Ella," he said, encouraging her to respond any way he could.

Nothing.

He worked at the fastenings of her corset, cursing as his fingers fumbled over them. He considered ripping or cutting off the stiff binding, but he didn't want to push her further into blackness with any sudden or violent motions. Finally, the corset gave way, but snagged in what remained of her dress. Gently, he pushed the tatters of her sleeves off her arms and her garments fell into twisted shreds around her feet. He gathered the fabric of her chemise. "Lift your arms."

Her arms remained hanging loosely at her sides so with gentle fingers he brushed the straps from her shoulders and pushed the undergarment down her torso.

The pristine paleness of her stomach and legs was a jarring contrast to bloody scratches on her chest and shoulders, to the dirt, which had leached beneath her undergarments to streak the slopes of her breasts. Anger curled his fists, but he soothed it with the fact he saw no other wounds or marks upon her body.

He eased her onto the chair to remove her moccasins, assuring himself with a flexing of her feet that she'd suffered no injuries there. With a cradling arm around her back and a careful one beneath her knees, he lowered her into the steaming water. Her gaze remained vacant as he trickled hot water over her wounds to soak the grime caking them. Grabbing the soap, he lathered his hands, releasing a strong medicinal scent.

"This will sting," he said, hoping the pain would engender some response as he gently cleansed the abrasions. Still, she remained almost as lifeless as the man they'd left in the Land of the Earthborn Spirits. But as he scooped water and dribbled its refreshing drops over her chest and shoulders, washing away the darkened suds, he saw her lids flutter then fall heavy over her eyes. His heart stuttered in relief then resumed its heavy pumping once more.

"I need to wash your hair," he murmured, slipping a hand between her back and the tub. He gave her a little nudge. "Lean forward." His breath came easier when she drew up her knees, wrapped her arms around her legs then rested her forehead on her knees. With cups of water, he soaked her hair then soaped the short strands, working his fingers along her scalp, circling and rubbing until she heaved a trembling sigh. He rinsed his hands, lathered them again and smoothed them over the back of her neck. Mindful of her bruises, he worked at the tightness there, moving to her shoulders when the tension eased. When she turned her head to rest her cheek on her knees, he noticed the zigzagging tracks of clean skin appearing through the mire covering her face. "Keep your eyes closed. I will rinse your hair now."

He scooped clean water from a bucket sitting next to the tub. Given the amount of dirt and blood, rinsing her hair with the now gray and slimy bath water would not do. As he poured he worked the water through her locks, rinsing away every last soiled suds. After he scrubbed her arms and hands, he tenderly cleaned her face with a soft rag.

He scooped her out of the tub, bundled her into a quilt, soft and pliable from many washings then worked at drying her hair with a towel. When he draped the towel over the chair, he realized she'd lifted her gaze to him with tears on her lashes and deep shame on her face. Immediately, he cupped her cheeks and kissed her softly on the lips then peppered her eyelids, taking away the salty sting of her tears.

"You would still want me after Running Bear—" Her words caught on an anguished sob.

He tilted up her face to his. "It does not matter what Running Bear did, only that you are alive and well."

329

"He tried to rape me, but I killed him before—"

"Shhh," he said with a finger to her lips. "We do not have to speak of Running Bear in this moment."

She grabbed his hand and slipped it beneath the quilt she held secured to her body with the other hand. The beat of her heart was hurried beneath his fingers. She pressed them against her warm and silky skin. "Yes, we do. For once we leave this room, I want never to speak of him again."

"But, your grandfather—" He regretted his words as soon as he saw the shame scrunching her features just before her chin dropped to her chest. He lifted her face back to his with a finger beneath her chin. "You are Ella Hastings, daughter and granddaughter of fierce military men who respect and admire courage as much as the fierce Lakota warriors of the Powder River Country."

"Do you really think my grandfather will see me that way?"

"After he saw what you took on today and how you survived, how can he not admire you? He will be proud to call you his granddaughter." Or he would have words with the Colonel.

The click of a door alerted them to his aunt's return. "Here's a drink to steady your nerves, Ella, and I brought you clean clothes."

Little Brave took the drink and made a face after the first sip.

"Now, drink it all," his aunt said. "The Colonel has returned from the livery, Beech. He wants to speak with Ella once she's dressed, but he wants to speak with you now."

Beech understood the warning look his aunt gave him. After the way he had refused to relinquish Little Brave once they'd recovered her, he did not doubt her grandfather would be hell bent to question his intentions, but he would not go into the conversation blindsided. "Have you spoken to him about what I told you, Aunt Claire?"

"No, that is your place, Beech," she said rather crisply.

And she was right.

"Talk to him about what, Beech?" Little Brave asked between sips.

"Us."

"I will talk to him about us," Little Brave said.

"Ella, dear, why don't you get dressed while Beech talks to your grandfather." Aunt Claire wrapped an arm around Little Brave's shoulders, trying to shift her attention to the clean clothes draped over the chair.

But *his woman* planted her feet with a mutinous look on her face. He grinned, brushing a wayward curl from her face.

"You are amused," she said of him.

But the look on her face told him she was not. His grin stretched wider. "No, merely thankful you are mine." He dropped a kiss on her lips. The mutiny melted, and he left the room to find her grandfather.

The Colonel was in his uncle's study, keeping vigil at the window behind the massive desk. The older man turned when Beech closed the door. He did not want any interruptions from Little Brave until he had settled things with her grandfather.

True to his military training, the Colonel took control without preamble. "What are your intentions towards my granddaughter, Richoux?"

"Little Brave has agreed to marry me." No sense in awakening the man's outrage by telling him they were already married in every way that mattered to Beech.

"It's customary to ask the father or in this case, grandfather, for the woman's hand in marriage before speaking to her."

Frankly, Beech did not care about the white man's customs in this matter, but the Colonel was the last of his wife's blood and as such deserved this allowance. "I'm aware of the custom, Colonel, and now I am asking for your permission to marry your granddaughter."

"And if I will not grant it?"

Beech had to check himself from scoffing. Short of hanging him, there was no way this man would keep him from being with Little Brave. "Colonel, this is merely a formality I'm honoring. Little Brave's Lakota father freed her to choose her own path before he died."

"That has no bearing here, Richoux. She is Ella Hastings, a white woman and my granddaughter."

"She is both Ella Hastings and Little Brave, a *grown* woman capable of making her own decisions." Beech narrowed his eyes at the Colonel, but then with a lift of his eyebrows he added. "A trait she comes by honestly."

The Colonel's brow scrunched. "That she does." He turned to stare out the window once more. "She's certainly made several of her own decisions in the past few days. None, however, that I would have chosen for her." Tense moments passed before he spoke again. "Her mother, God rest her soul, was determined to make her own choices too, but I—" He glanced back at Beech, a flicker of guilt crossing his face before he resumed his stare out the window. "Well, I forced a marriage between her and Ella's father. Ella was too young to remember, but it was a very unhappy union." He turned with a determined look on his face. "I will not do that to Ella. If this is what she truly wants, if this will make her happy then I will give my permission."

Beech stood eyeing the man, to whom he was now related, for by Lakota custom, saying it made it so. "You will never have to worry about her happiness or her well being." He held out his hand. "Sir," he added.

He had never addressed a white man as 'sir' before, but Little Brave's grandfather deserved it for allowing his granddaughter to follow her chosen path and for placing his trust in him. Colonel Russell could have reached over the desk to take his hand, but instead, he came around it and shook it—man to man.

"Now, I will speak to my granddaughter. I think she has some misconceptions of what I think of her."

"I've no doubt you can reassure her of your high regard, regardless of what happened today or in the past ten years." Beech gave the man a look that said if he did not, he would have to answer to him.

The Colonel nodded his understanding then marched to the door. He paused with his hand on the knob to look back. "How long before you and Ella are to be married?"

"I will fetch the minister now," Beech said, unable to keep a grin from splitting his face.

The Colonel smiled a bit wryly and with a touch of approval. "I wouldn't wait either, Richoux"

-*-*-

Looking into the parlor mirror, Little Brave checked the ribbon Beech had given her, insuring it was properly restraining her impertinent locks. The door opened and she stroked her beaded belt with the two buffaloes for courage then turned to face her grandfather.

Uncharacteristically, he did not start the conversation, but stood there watching her. Surprisingly, he gestured to her waist. "Did you make that?"

"I did," she said with much pride.

"Buffalos." He stepped closer, eyeing her handiwork intently. "They are so lifelike."

"They represent my fathers. This one," she said, caressing the one with the blood and arrows, "is for Thomas James Hastings." Her grandfather nodded in recognition of the name. "And this one," she gave the other an equally loving caress, "is for Grey Owl." There was a long pause, but she knew from the expression on his face that he had something he wanted to say.

"He was a good father to you? Grey Owl, I mean." His tongue stumbled on the Lakota name.

She nodded. "He did not care my skin was white. He did not care my ways were different." She did not have all the English words to express how much Grey Owl and his band had given her, but she hoped it was enough to make her grandfather understand. "The Blackfeet treated me badly because of these things, but Grey Owl loved *me*."

"Ella, I don't understand all you've been through, how that has changed you, but…" His voice cracked then he coughed. "But, I want you to be happy and I want…" He lifted his hands then dropped them helplessly to his sides again. "I want to know you not just as Ella, but as Lit—" Again, his tongue stumbled.

"Little Brave," she prompted.

He repeated it, coming much closer to the Lakota pronunciation this time. She went to him then, wrapping her arms around him.

"Grandfather," she sighed when his arms closed around her.

When Beech entered the parlor much later, Little Brave hopped up from the sofa where she'd been sitting and talking with her grandfather. A serious-looking man wearing a dark suit followed him. The man carried a big black book and looked at her rather expectantly. Beech gestured to the man. "Little Brave, this is—"

Beech's aunt came in at that moment. "Oh my word, Reverend Sims, I'm so relieved you could come on such short notice."

Her grandfather was now shaking the man's hand, expressing his gratitude, as well.

Questioningly, she looked at Beech.

He moved to her side, catching up her hand. "This man is here to marry us," he said in English.

"But we are already married," she replied in Lakota, for in her surprise she could not find all the English words she needed.

"Yes, we are," he said, switching to Lakota. "But this will be a white man's ceremony."

"I do not need a white man's ceremony." She did not understand why Beech needed it. "Is the way of the Lakota not enough for you?"

"It is enough for me, but remember, *Ella,* we are of two worlds now."

Ella. Her English name sounded odd mixed with the Lakota words. But...what had Grey Owl said? *You have already lived two lives. One you were born into, the other you were adopted into. Now, you have a third.*

She glanced to her grandfather who stood authoritatively but patiently waiting for her to settle this for herself. Beech's aunt was waiting with her hands clasped under her chin, joyful anticipation in her face. Beech's uncle and Grace came through the doorway.

"I hear there's to be a wedding," Beech's uncle said with a happy twinkle in his eye.

Grace ran to Beech and threw her arms around him. "I am so happy for you, brother." Then she turned to Little Brave and clasped her hands. "And now I will have a sister," she said, kissing her on the cheek.

Jean Luc came in and clasped Beech to him, holding him for many moments. Then he turned to her, his pale eyes watering more than usual and kissed her on each cheek before clasping her to him for many moments, as well.

Once he released her, Little Brave gazed at the happy faces surrounding her and Beech. *Hiyee!* Her third life stood gathered around her. She turned to Beech and pressed his hand to her heart, which was brimming over with love and admiration for him. He had given her time to find her path between her two worlds. Like him, it was both English and Lakota. What had her white father said? *No one can change the past. All we can do is make the most of today and all the tomorrows to follow.* She had chosen him and he had chosen her, and now she would make the most of her third life with him. But first she wanted to hear him say what the soldiers had interrupted that day on his ranch and what he'd denied during the trial to shield her. She wanted to hear him say what she knew was in their hearts. And she knew their family would be happy to hear it. In English she said, "Tell me what I am to you, Beech Richoux."

At first, there was confusion in his face then it cleared. He knew what she desired because their hearts beat as one now. "You are mine, Ella." He pulled her hand to his heart. "Your courage, determination and beauty already live here within me, and I want you by my side always, Little Brave."

The joy spread throughout, lifting her heart almost out of her body. "And I am yours, Beech Richoux. You live here in my heart, a man kind and strong and wise." She stepped closer. "Now, we will honor *our* family by participating in the white man's ceremony." She squeezed the hand at her heart. "Then you will take me home."

He wrapped her into his arms. "Yes, Little Brave, I will take you to the home we will make together.

A Note From Ruby Merritt

Thank you for reading. If you enjoyed *Ella's Choice* please...

Write a review so others can read and enjoy too.

Find Lena's Courage the next book in the Spirited Hearts Series here: http://www.amazon.com/dp/B015QIMR9W

Join my Spirited Hearts Facebook group at https://www.facebook.com/groups/SpiritedHearts/ to keep up with all things Spirited Hearts.

Contact me! I love to hear from readers.

Website: www.RubyMerrittAuthor.com
Facebook: www.facebook.com/RubyMerrittAuthor
Twitter: www.twitter.com/RubyMerrittAuth
Pinterest: www.pinterest.com/rubymerrittauth

Join the Facebook group Pioneer Hearts at https://www.facebook.com/groups/pioneerhearts to hang out with readers and writers of Western Romances.

Final Historical Note:

The most   prominent battle of The Great Sioux War of 1876-77 was the Battle of Little Bighorn. This military engagement took place on June 25-26, 1876 near the Little Bighorn River, also known to the Plains Indians as Greasy Grass Creek.   Tribes of Lakota, Northern Cheyenne and Arapaho Indians combined to annihilate five of the twelve companies of the 7th Calvary Regiment of the United States Army. It was a severe defeat for the United States and the last victory for the Plains Indians in their bid to retain their way of life on the High Plains.

65044330R00190

Made in the USA
Charleston, SC
12 December 2016